For my niece, Jennifer Lynn Donahue,
with all my love

In many ways doth the full heart reveal
The presence of the love it would conceal.
—SAMUEL TAYLOR COLERIDGE

McKenna's
Bride

Prologue

County Clare, Ireland
Autumn 1846

Caitlin McKenna crumpled the letter in her hands and stared over the edge of the sheer precipice at the storm-tossed Atlantic below. Seabirds wheeled above the cliff, adding their haunting cries to the crashing of waves against jagged rocks. A raw blast of wind ripped Caitlin's linen cap away and tore loose her hairpins so that her auburn tresses tumbled gypsylike around her face and shoulders. Mist swirled around her, enveloping her in a cloak of opalescence. And a single tear trickled down her cheek.

"You're alive."

The rising gale tugged at the stained paper, but Caitlin held it in a death grip. She swallowed to relieve the aching lump in her throat and read Shane's letter again. The message was short, almost abrupt. She had gone over it so many times that she could have recited the words without looking.

Shane was alive.

He wanted her to join him in America.

Caitlin pulled her woolen shawl tighter around her shoulders and tried to picture her husband's face as she had last seen him. His blond hair, twinkling blue-gray eyes, and warm smile formed in her mind's eye. She could even picture his square, dimpled chin and the sensual lips that had captured hers so sweetly. Handsome as a fallen angel was Shane McKenna and put together as well as the good Lord could create an Irishman. And then to add to the package, the Almighty had given him a deep, husky voice that could charm the birds from the trees . . . as he'd charmed her.

"Seven years!" she cried angrily. "Seven long years without so much as a word."

She'd been but seventeen when she'd defied her family and her church to elope with Shane McKenna on the eve of his departure for the American frontier. That was a lifetime ago . . . before the potato crops had withered and turned to blackened slime . . . before her parents had died and her sister's husband Thomas had been bludgeoned to death by a starving mob.

"Damn your black Irish heart, Shane McKenna!"

From the first day she'd laid eyes on him—barefoot and raggedy as a tinker's lad—setting rabbit snares in her father's woods, Shane had stolen her heart. He was her secret friend, her darling, the only man she'd ever wanted.

He'd promised that he'd send for her as soon as he earned her passage money. He'd promised that he'd write to her. And he'd betrayed both vows.

"Lies, lies!" she shouted into the wind.

Shane. Shane. Surely no woman had ever loved as she loved him. And surely, no wife had been as loyal. She'd waited and prayed for a letter, watched for the sight of him strolling up her father's lane whistling a merry tune.

But Shane had abandoned her, left her to face her family's anger and disappointment alone, left her to pretend that she didn't hear the sly whispers of her neighbors.

Now when she'd all but gotten over him, her husband had summoned her. He wanted her. The trouble was, she didn't know if she still wanted him.

Chapter 1

"Caitlin McKenna!"

With an immense feeling of relief, Caitlin turned to look at the man shouting her name in a slurred, American accent. Her heart sank at the sight of the hard-eyed westerner astride a buckskin horse.

"I'm Caitlin McKenna," she answered.

She'd been waiting for Shane at this landing since the steamboat had docked in late afternoon. Now all the passengers had departed and velvety dusk cloaked the river and settled over the town.

The cowboy swung down from his worn saddle in one fluid motion. "Caity?"

Confused, she stared at him. Had he called her Caity? Her heart thudded. Was it possible that this stranger with his face half hidden under a dark beard could be her Shane?

No, she must be mistaken. The man striding toward her was too tall, too wide at the shoulders. He swept off a broad-brimmed hat, and even in the fading twilight Caitlin could see that his hair was dark brown, not the color of wheat ripening in a County Clare meadow. Her

4

Shane was freckle-faced, fair, and smiling. She wanted to ask this man if Shane had sent him, but apprehension and deep uncertainty made her mute.

The cowboy stopped abruptly, frowning as he brushed a thick lock of hair away from his face. Even standing still, he gave the impression that his muscles were coiled, ready to spring into action.

Dangerous . . . He was dangerous. Instinctively, she sensed the potential for violence beneath that tautly stretched deerskin vest and those tight trousers tucked into high black boots.

He tugged off worn leather gloves and jammed them into his belt. Blue-gray, hauntingly familiar eyes reflected the last of the light as they gazed into hers. "Don't you know me, Caity?"

The wind kicked up a swirling cloud of dust. Caitlin stared at him. This rough stranger's eyes were almost Shane's, but the voice—the voice was not right. There was no lilt of Ireland in this man's speech. Something was wrong. He was wrong. All wrong.

The captain of the riverboat had warned her of desperadoes on the Missouri frontier. This ruffian could certainly be one. A scarred rifle butt protruded from a sheath on his saddle, and he wore a huge knife strapped to his beaded Indian belt.

Was it possible that she wouldn't know her own husband?

His eyes were definitely paler than Shane's, and his lean features were as weathered as Connemara limestone. His nose showed the mark of being broken and healed, and the bronze skin and craggy cheekbones made him look more savage native than the sweet lad she'd wed so long ago.

This scoundrel towered over her. Her Shane had

lacked three inches of this man's height, and surely, her
Shane had never possessed such fierce eyes.

Then the cowboy laughed, and there was no doubt in
her mind that this was her husband.

"Mother of God, girl, I know it's been seven years, but
I can't have changed that much!"

He moved toward her, but she stepped back out of his
reach as the earth seemed to sway beneath her feet.
"Eight, if you're counting," she corrected him. "Eight
years now since we've laid eyes on each other." She took
a deep breath and tried to regain her composure. "You . . .
you look bigger."

He chuckled, a warm, husky sound. "I've put on
inches and pounds, it's true."

"Your hair . . ."

"It's darkened. I was but nineteen when we parted."

"Aye. You were. And I was younger." She knew she
should greet him properly—say how glad she was to see
him—but the words lodged in her throat.

"You're as pretty as ever, Caity, but you took your
sweet time in getting here." There was a hint of resentment in his deep voice.

"I came as soon as you sent for me," she reminded him.

His mouth tightened into a thin slash. She noticed a
faded scar that sliced one cheekbone and vanished into
his full beard. "I'm glad you're here," he said in that
slow, almost lazy drawl that sent shivers racing up her
spine. "It's time we set this marriage straight."

She nodded. "So I thought. I want—" She broke off at
the sound of a childish whimper. Quickly, she moved to
her heaped baggage and lifted a black-haired toddler
from her makeshift cradle between the trunks.

"Shhh, Derry, 'tis all right," Caitlin murmured as she

smoothed the little girl's damp curls. "It's your Uncle Shane come to meet us." Derry stared wide-eyed at him, then shyly burrowed her face into Caitlin's neck.

His eyes narrowed. "You didn't come alone."

"No, I didn't." Caitlin tried to ignore the bite of frost in his tone. "This is Maureen's babe, Derry. You remember my sister Maureen? Things at home are so bad . . . so very bad."

His expression hardened. "Your sister's babe," he said disbelievingly.

A wave of indignation swept over her. Hadn't he heard of the thousands wandering the roads of Ireland in search of food? Was he ignorant of the hundreds dying of starvation and the pestilence born of it?

She stiffened. "Derry is family. Maureen asked me to bring her to America, and I couldn't—"

"Your niece or your child?"

Derry began to whimper as she clutched tightly at Caitlin's neck. "Mama . . . Mama."

Caitlin felt her cheeks go hot. By all that was holy! Shane was accusing her of adultery! Disbelief flared into white-hot anger. "Derry is Maureen's firstborn child," she said in short, clipped syllables. "Conceived in marriage and christened at Saint Anne's."

"Damn it, woman!" he swore softly. "Do you take me for a fool? I've been no saint myself, but we'll have not a tinker's damn of a chance to make this marriage work if you can't be honest with me."

"Despite what I just said, you believe that Derry's mine?"

In all the years since Shane had left County Clare, Caitlin had guarded her absent husband's honor by never once being alone with a man other than her own father. She'd ignored the pleas of friends and family to obtain an annulment or to attempt to have Shane declared legally dead. His accusation was so unfair and so insulting that it took every ounce of her will to keep from slapping his face.

"She has the look of a Shaughnessy about her," Shane said.

"And so she should!" Caitlin flung back. "Her father was Thomas Shaughnessy, God rest his soul."

"Thomas, the middle son."

"I am her aunt," Caitlin insisted.

He shrugged. "Out of the mouths of babes . . ."

"Use your head, man. She's not seen her own mother in five months. I keep reminding her that I am Aunty Cait, but she's that set in her ways. She knows no better than to call me Mama."

He scowled. "As I've said, it's not the sinning that I mind, but the lying to cover it. You're flesh and blood as I am."

"I'm no liar." The peril of her situation made her knees weak. She wanted to turn her back on Shane, but she didn't dare, as she hadn't a shilling to her name.

She had sold most of her good jewelry to pay for Derry's passage. The remainder had gone piece by piece for necessities until she had only the earrings she was wearing. If she and Derry were stranded here in the City of Jefferson, she supposed that she could trade her ear bobs for a few meals or a night's lodging. But what would happen to them then?

She wasn't afraid of hard work, but what if there were no jobs here for women? And what if no one would hire her because she was a foreigner? It hadn't taken her long to realize that penniless Irish were unwelcome in America. Alone, without friends or family, she feared that if she didn't stay with her husband she'd not be able to care for Derry.

"You refuse to be honest with me?"

"I am being honest." Tears welled up and she dashed them away with the back of her hand. "Since you cannot trust me, then perhaps this marriage is best ended here and now."

"Stubborn. As mule-stubborn as I remember you." He nodded. "We'll leave it like that, then." Looking back over his shoulder, he shouted, "Justice!"

Gravel sprayed when a spotted pony galloped up, and the rider reined the animal in sharply. Derry screamed and Caitlin leaped back out of the way as the pinto reared, ears flat against his black head and his white-rimmed eyes rolling.

"Justice!" Shane snapped.

The rider, a sullen-faced boy of nine or ten, glared at her as he effortlessly brought the spirited animal under control, then slid down to stand defiantly beside Shane.

"Where are your manners?" Shane admonished, glaring at the boy. He dropped a big hand onto the child's shoulder and looked back at her. "This is Justice McKenna. My son."

Caitlin looked at the lad in astonishment. His black hair hung loose around his shoulders, as shaggy and unkempt as the pony's mane. The boy's skin was olive, his features broad. She could see nothing of Shane in him. "Your son?" she repeated. Unconsciously, she began counting in her head. Surely Shane hadn't been in America long enough to have a child this old.

"My adopted son." Shane gave her a look that dared her to argue with him. "Justice, this is my wife. She'll be your new mother."

"My mother's dead."

Beneath the angry resentment, Caitlin heard an un-spoken loneliness. It was unfair of Shane to doubt her word about Derry and then surprise her with the lad, but it was hardly the child's fault. "I'm pleased to meet you, Justice."

He merely stared at her.

"My own mother died last year, and I know how much I miss her," she said. "No one can take a mother's place, but perhaps we could be friends. I'm a stranger to Missouri. I'll need a friend here."

The boy shrugged. "You ain't stayin' long."

"I'll tolerate no disrespect, boy," Shane said. "Best you keep that in mind."

"You said so to Mary. I heard you say it. You said *she* was blooded stock, too ladylike to make it out here."

"Whether I did or not makes no difference. It's rude to repeat what someone says." He motioned to the pinto. "Get back in the saddle."

Justice threw Caitlin a satisfied look as he obeyed Shane's command. "You said she wouldn't stay," the boy repeated. "I don't know why you wanted her to come over the water. We was doin' fine on our own."

"That's enough," Shane snapped. "Fetch the wagon."

Justice vaulted onto the pony's back and dug his heels into the animal's sides. In seconds, pinto and boy vanished into the night in a cloud of dust.

"He's not as tough as he seems. His mother let him run wild."

"Obviously." Caitlin wasn't sure which of these males annoyed her more. The thought that her husband had told someone that he didn't think she could make it here on the frontier was infuriating. "How old is he?"

"Justice? Ten."

"May I ask who his parents were?"

"His mother was a good friend of mine. When she died, there was no one else to take him."

"You expect me to accept him without question, yet you don't want Derry?"

"I never said that. Her being here isn't the problem."

"Nothing I can say about Derry will convince you, will it?"

Shane shook his head. "Nope. Like I said, I've been no saint. I'd rather you were honest with me, but if you can't, I reckon I can understand why. I took the coward's way myself when I didn't warn you about Justice. I figured there wasn't a chance of a newborn calf in a blizzard of you coming if you knew about him."

"You really think an orphan child would keep me from my husband's side?" Her anger receded, leaving her with a sense of loss. For years she'd held on to a romantic dream about their marriage. In time, that hope had faded, but Shane's letter had made her think they might recover what they'd had. "Don't you know me better than that?"

"Best we put all the cards on the table. Justice is part Indian. No white woman I know would want him in her house. If you take me, you take the mothering of him as well—real mothering—not just cooking and sewing for him."

She exhaled slowly. "So you sent for me because you needed someone to care for Justice?"

"That's part of it."

"The rest?"

A muscle twitched along his hard jawline. "I'm not a religious man, Caity. I haven't made confession in years, but we took our wedding vows in front of a priest. I reckon we're married good and final." His gaze met hers expectantly.

She waited.

"It's a good life out here. Hard, but satisfying. It's time I had a wife again. Maybe more kids. I'm willing to try to make this marriage work if you are."

No words of love. No regrets for leaving her alone so long. Caitlin let the hurt wash through her. There were no tears left. "And . . . and if I don't accept your terms?"

He crushed the brim of his hat in his big hand. "I'd take you to Saint Louis. I've friends there who would make you welcome until you decided—"

"No need."

"No need of what?"

"You're right, Shane. We are husband and wife. It's best we try to make this marriage a real one."

"You understand about the boy? He's got strong Osage blood. He's what folks out here call a half-breed."

"The devil take them!"

"I warn you, Justice is not easy to handle. He's wild as a woods buffalo and mourning his mother fierce. He barely speaks, even to me."

"Poor lad." The thought of having such a troubled boy as part of her family was daunting, but children had ever been her weakness. Hadn't she brought her father to ruin by trying to fill the belly of every wee one that came begging to their gate?

"This isn't Ireland," Shane said. "Indians are feared and hated. A lot of doors will be closed to you and yours if you claim him."

"'Tis not the color of the child's skin that troubles me," she replied. It was he, Shane McKenna, she thought fervently. She supposed him to be a stranger when she first laid eyes on him, and it was true. He was no more the man she had married than she was the Countess of Wexford. Did he think her heart had shriveled so small that she could not love Justice because of his swarthy hue?

"He's had a hard life, and he's rough in his ways."

"And you?" she demanded. "Are you not rough in your ways?"

"I am, but I hold six hundred acres of good Missouri land because of it. The weak don't last out here, Caity. Are you strong enough to survive?"

A hot reply rose to her tongue as she thought of what she'd witnessed in County Clare: of losing the house and Papa and Mama dying, of the endless wailing of starving children and the hopelessness in women's eyes. She wanted to tell him what strong was, but she held her peace. There would be time enough for that. "God willing," she answered softly.

"Then we'd best get your baggage. Which trunk is yours?" he asked, pointing to the heaped portmanteaus and cases.

"All of them."

"Sweet Joseph!" he bellowed. "How am I supposed to carry all this home to Kilronan?"

"I carried them all the way from Ireland." Six hundred acres. So much land. And Shane said it was his, without a mention of his uncle or his cousin George. She wanted to ask him about his farm, but not if he was going to be troublesome about her belongings.

She noticed that Derry had fallen asleep, and she shifted the little girl's weight to her shoulder. The darling was growing heavier every day on rich American food, but Caitlin didn't mind carrying her. The scent of Derry was baby-sweet and precious. She could put up with a lot if it meant that Derry would be safe and cared for. She supposed she could even learn to deal with Shane McKenna and his son.

"I brought a wagon to carry you," Shane grumbled. "I'd have brought a mule train if I'd guessed you'd bring half of Ireland with you."

In Caitlin's experience with men it was easiest to let them have their grouching out before trying to reason with them. She waited until he paused for breath and then asked him the first question that popped into her head. "Your Uncle Jamie and Cousin George. Will they mind having Derry about?"

Shane had crossed the sea to work on his uncle's farm. His uncle and cousin were originally from Cashel, but they'd emigrated when Shane was a child. She'd never met either of them.

"They won't mind the babe," Shane answered gruffly.

"You're certain?"

He jammed his hat back on his. "They drowned in a flash-flood two years back. Kilronan is mine, Caity. Stay with me and be the wife I need, and in time, I'll add your name to the deed."

"When I've proved myself."

"Yes, if you put it like that."

"'Tis hard to find another way to put it, isn't it?"

He lifted the weight of one portmanteau and groaned. "What did you bring, you greedy wench? All the stones of County Clare?"

"And if I did?"

"I can't offer you what your father provided. My house is—"

"I'm not a spoiled child. I don't expect a manor house. I can do my share."

"Can you? Can you skin and gut a deer? Spin flax? Milk a cow? Put up dried fish for the winter?"

"No, but I'm willing to learn."

"Are you? Then why didn't you come before?" he demanded.

"Before? How before? I've not known where you were since the day after our wedding."

Shane bent and swung a trunk up onto his shoulder, a

trunk Caitlin noted that it had taken two sweating deck-hands to carry off the steamboat. "I wrote for you to join me, Caity. Eighteen months to the day after I arrived in America, I sent you every penny I'd earned for the passage."

He turned his head to look at her. It was too dark to see his eyes any longer, but she could feel the resentment flowing out of them. "You betrayed me, Caitlin. You took my money and never answered a single letter."

"You're wrong." She shook her head. "I never heard a word from you before last fall."

"Strange that you never got my money or my letters." His voice was thick with sarcasm as he steadied the weight of the blue wooden trunk. "But the first time I write to Father Joseph, both letter and tickets to Missouri arrive safely."

"I didn't get any correspondence from you," she protested. Was he lying to cover his own shortcomings? He sounded so bitter. "Perhaps the mail was lost?"

"One letter might be lost, even two. I sent five. From you I got silence. I thought you might be dead until I met Hugh O'Connor. Remember Hugh? His father used to keep the pub in Ennis. I ran into Hugh in Fort Independence, where I sell my livestock to the settlers heading west to Oregon Country. Hugh told me he'd seen you on the street in Lisdoonvarna, very much alive."

She stepped close and laid her hand on his arm. His muscles were hard and sinewy. "I would have come if I'd gotten your letters. You have to believe me."

"You ask a lot of believing of a man who has little left," he said harshly. "We'll try, woman, because I think it's the right thing to do. But I doubt you have the stuff in you to stick."

"If you believe that, why did you bother to send for me?"

"Because you're my wife, and I thought it was the right thing to do."

"And you always do what's right?"

"I try." He motioned to her to stay where she was. "Justice will be back with the wagon in a minute. We'll take what we can in this trip and store the rest at Fat Rose's."

"I haven't eaten since noon. Neither has Derry. Perhaps the hotel serves—"

Shane uttered a sound of derision. "Hotel? We'll waste no money on a hotel. We'll eat when we make camp on the trail. I've Indian fry bread, cold meat, and some cheese in the saddlebags."

"How far is your farm?"

"Kilronan is a good day's travel from here. And it's not a farm. I raise stock, not crops."

She ignored the disapproval in his voice. She was bone weary and wanted nothing more than to sink between the sheets of a clean feather bed. "Surely," she suggested, "it would be better to stay in town tonight and—"

"Yes or no, Caitlin. I'm giving you a second chance. Come with me now or stay here. What will it be?"

"We'll come," she answered softly. "But you may be sure that we'll have negotiations on your terms."

Chapter 2

"My terms are not so unreasonable," Shane replied. "No more than any other man would expect. Be honest with me, work hard, and be the woman I thought I married."

Caitlin didn't answer him. Had she told him what tickled the tip of her tongue, she was certain he would leave both her and Derry at the landing.

Justice returned with a farm wagon. Without speaking, he handed the lines to Shane and untied his pony reins from the rear of the vehicle. He mounted and sat stiffly on the pinto. Caitlin couldn't see the boy's expression, but she could feel him watching her with blatant animosity.

Caitlin glanced away and wondered why this reunion was going so terribly wrong. She didn't want to be the enemy. It might be natural for the boy to be apprehensive about having a stepmother, but his obvious disapproval did little to ease her own fears.

"How much of this luggage is absolutely necessary for us to take?" Shane asked.

"All of it." Caitlin counted her trunks and cases to be certain everything was there. She'd already checked them when the steamboat docked and counted them yet again after the deckhands had loaded them onto the landing. These possessions were precious to her. They contained all she had of home, all she would ever have of her family and Ireland. She'd defended her personal effects against petty thieves and smooth-talking flimflam men. She wasn't about to be bullied into giving up any of her property by Shane McKenna.

"You decide or I will." He heaved a trunk into the wagon bed.

"These two." Caitlin shifted Derry to her hip and lifted a portmanteau. "I must have this. It has—"

"Two more."

His impatience infuriated her. She handed him the leather case and went back to tug at a wooden chest. "I need this."

"Too big. Take a smaller one," Shane replied brusquely.

"No, I won't go without the chest. I have seeds and—"

"Suit yourself." He removed a leather trunk and put the wooden chest in its place.

Caitlin tried to lift one end of the trunk, but it was too heavy. She returned to the heaped luggage and chose a smaller box tied with red cord. Shane took the box out of her hands and jammed it into a spot under the seat. She turned back toward the remaining pile, but he stepped in front of her.

"I'll fetch the rest of it when I find time to come to Jeff City again," he promised. "Now, I'd take it kindly if you'd get into the wagon."

Caitlin glanced back at the things on the landing, then nodded and offered him her hand. Instead, his big hands closed on her waist. Effortlessly, he swung her and Derry up onto the wagon seat.

Shane drove back the way he'd come with Justice following on his pony. After a short distance, Shane guided the team onto a side street that led back toward the bank of the Missouri River.

Lights blazed from a three-story house at the end of the block. Strains of music and loud laughter spilled through the open windows. Several horses were tied near the door, and a liveried servant lingered by a phaeton.

"Where are we going?" Caitlin asked.

"Fat Rose's . . . boardinghouse. I told you, she's a friend of mine. I'll ask her to look after your trunks until I can get back this way." Shane reined the horses into a narrow alley. "You wait here." He glanced at Justice. "Both of you."

Caitlin watched as Shane secured the lines to a hitching post and walked away. "Shouldn't I come with you?" she suggested. "If this Rose is a friend, shouldn't I meet her?"

Justice stifled a sound of amusement.

"Nope." Shane kept moving. "Stay put."

Caitlin seethed. She was not used to being given orders. *Do this. Do that.* Who did he think he was?

Shane had never treated her like this in County Clare. He'd been sweet, understanding, patient. Good-humored.

She shifted restlessly. "How well do you know this Rose?" she asked Justice. "Will she take good care of my things, do you think?"

"Reckon so."

The boy's accent was so strong that she had to listen carefully to understand him.

Shouting echoed from the main street. A voice, definitely a female voice, swore a foul oath.

Caitlin's cheeks grew warm.

"I'm going to leave Derry here while I find your father," she said to Justice. "Can I trust you to watch her for a few minutes?" She carefully laid the sleeping child in front of the wagon seat.

"He said to stay put."

"I know what he said. Can I trust you with the baby?"

He nodded.

"I'll take her with me if it's too much trouble," she said.

"I kin watch her."

"She's a baby. If she was to fall under the horses' feet or if they got excited and—"

"I'll keep her safe." The boy dismounted and climbed up on the wagon seat.

Caitlin nodded. Heart pounding, she started down the alley. Rose's boardinghouse indeed! Sheltered she might have been under her father's roof, but Caitlin was not stupid. At the very least, Rose's was a dockside pub. At the worst . . . She didn't want to consider what the worst was.

She reached the street and followed an uneven plank walk toward the brightly lit house. In an upstairs window, she saw the silhouette of two people dancing to the tinny notes of a cheap piano. Another couple lingered at the corner of the house.

Taking a deep breath, Caitlin walked purposefully toward the front door. She would find her husband and leave this place as soon as possible.

"Evenin', sugar."

Caitlin turned and caught a whiff of hard liquor and unwashed man. A bulky figure in a tall beaver hat staggered from the shadows.

"You're new, ain't ya?" The man lurched closer and belched. "Pretty little thing. Where's Fat Rose been hiding you?"

Refusing to dignify the sot with a reply, she continued on up the brick steps. The music was very loud, a jarring, rowdy tune accompanied by stomping feet and off-key singing.

"Don't go 'way," the drunk protested. "Les be friends."

Caitlin quickened her pace. She reached for the doorbell just as his fingers closed on her shoulder.

"I said, don't go 'way, sweet thing." He pulled a handful of crumpled greenbacks from his pocket. "I got money."

She turned to face him, covering her fear with icy courtesy. "Kindly remove your hand."

"How 'bout a kiss for ole Jim?"

A blast of one-hundred-proof breath made her gag. Twisting free of his grasp, she trod hard on his toes with the heel of her leather boot, then ducked under her assailant's arm as he swore and reached out to grab her.

"Leave me alone!" she cried. "I don't—"

The door burst open and a charging fury nearly knocked her over. Suddenly, Caitlin's back was to the wall, and Shane was between her and the drunken lout. Shane seized the man by the collar of his shirt and lifted him off the ground.

"That's my wife!" Shane shook the stranger hard enough to rattle the man's teeth, then tossed him over the porch railing into the shrubbery.

"I didn't know she was your woman, McKenna. I swear! I didn't know."

Shane leaped over the rail and pounced on him. "You damn well owe her an apology."

"What's ado?" The fattest woman Caitlin had ever seen squeezed through the front door and teetered to the edge of the porch. "I'll have no fighting here. Stop that, Shane McKenna. You let him go."

Shane rose to his feet still holding the protesting drunkard by the shirt front. "He insulted my wife."

"I'm sorry, I'm sorry. I didn't know. I thought—"

Several scantily dressed women with rouged faces and elaborately coifed hair spilled onto the porch, and Caitlin was nearly overwhelmed by a wave of cheap perfume.

"It's McKenna," whispered a tall redhead with bad skin.

Another snickered. "Shane McKenna? Which one is he?"

An assortment of men, some roughly dressed, others in

white shirt and tie, followed the women onto the porch. Several clutched bottles of spirits; one held a hand of cards.

"That's him," a burly riverman said loudly to his companion. "McKenna runs horses at Kilronan."

"What's he doing here?" demanded a stout man wearing spectacles. "I didn't come to Fat Rose's looking for trouble."

An elderly gentleman pointed toward Shane with his walking stick. "You'd think he'd have better sense than to show his face in this town again after—"

"Enough!" The fat woman made shooing motions with her hands. "Inside, inside all of you," she ordered in an altissimo voice. "Do you want the law on me?"

The onlookers filed noisily back inside, and the fat woman glanced back at Shane. "Must I throw you both in the river to settle this?"

Shane gave his victim a final shove, then let go. The troublemaker scrambled away into the darkness. Seconds later, Caitlin heard the sound of retching.

"You know I don't want trouble here," the fat woman admonished Shane.

"He insulted my wife."

"Jim's dead drunk. Last time he was this drunk, he propositioned my old sow."

"I know he's drunk," Shane said. "If he wasn't . . ." He left the threat unspoken.

The woman flashed a wide grin at Caitlin, displaying two silver front teeth. "I'm Fat Rose," she said. "Pleased to make your acquaintance, Mrs. McKenna."

"How do you do," Caitlin replied numbly. She tried not to notice the huge quivering breasts visible above a shockingly scant neckline or the artificially yellow hair that hung around Rose's moon face in long corkscrew curls.

"I thought I told you to wait in the wagon, Caity." Shane's voice was low, but he made no effort to hide his anger.

"We'll discuss this later," she flung back.

"No harm done," Rose said, stretching a plump, ringed hand across Caitlin to pat Shane's cheek affectionately. "Jim won't remember a thing tomorrow morning. If he'd of known she was your wife, he never would have had the nerve to speak to her. You ain't hurt none, are ya deary?"

Caitlin shook her head. "No, I'm fine."

"You'll send Moses for the trunks?" Shane reminded Rose.

"Did Fat Rose ever let ya down?" Silver teeth winked in the lantern light. "I'll send Moses lickety-split after your plunder. Don't you worry. I'll take good care of it. Just like it was mine."

"I appreciate it," Shane said.

"Where's that music?" Fat Rose bellowed in the open door. "I pay for piano. I want to hear piano."

The music began again. After two false starts, Caitlin recognized an old Irish tune called "The Banks of Claudy." A man with a deep baritone voice was singing.

As I rode out one evening, all in the month of May,
Down by the flower garden, where I did often stray . . .

Fat Rose hugged Caitlin to her ample breasts. "You've got a good man, honey, no matter what anyone says. You two take care of each other. And kiss that sweet boy for me, Shane. You tell him that Fat Rose misses him."

Caitlin exchanged bitter words with Shane on the way back to the wagon. "How dare you leave my things with such a person?"

"I told you to stay in the wagon. Why the hell can't you do one thing I ask?" he demanded. "What if I hadn't gotten there in time to save you?"

"I came from County Clare without your protection. I'm capable of dealing with one sloppy drunk."

"You looked capable. Another minute and he'd have had you on your back."

"In a pig's eye. Do you think I've not had to deal with men on my own in the past eight years?"

"I'm sure you have."

"That's a rotten thing to say."

"When I tell you something for your own good, you'd best learn to listen."

"I'm your wife, not your maidservant. That's a house of sin. How could you leave half of what I own in the world with that . . . that creature?"

"Fat Rose is an honest woman."

"The very picture of virtue."

"You shouldn't be so quick to judge. She's been a friend, and I've few enough of those."

Caitlin held Derry tightly against her as the horse-drawn wagon rolled through the streets of the City of Jefferson. Shane sat on the hard wooden seat beside her, reins between his gloved hands, back straight, silent as a rain-washed stone. This wasn't how she'd imagined it would be. He was not the man she'd married in the ruined church at Kilshanny. That Shane McKenna would never have doubted her word about Derry, and he would not have attacked a man in such a violent fashion.

And he would never have frequented a house of ill repute or allowed his wife anywhere near one!

Caitlin watched in silence as the houses and stores grew farther and farther apart. For all its grand name, the

City of Jefferson was only a small town, nothing to rival New Orleans, or even Saint Louis.

Circles of pale yellow light spilled from the windows of the private homes. Here and there, a yard was fenced with white pickets, and she caught the scent of roses. As they rounded a corner, Caitlin saw an elderly man and woman bathed in the glow of a copper lantern. They sat close together on a porch swing, their graying heads nearly touching and their quiet laughter mingling in the still night air.

The couple's obvious affection for each other brought a catch to Caitlin's throat. How many times had she watched her parents sit and talk of an evening, sharing memories and private jests? She'd pictured herself and Shane growing old together, weaving the fabric of their lives so closely that a thread could not be pulled from the cloth without destroying the pattern.

I wanted that, she thought fervently. I still want that. . . . And I want flowers. A yard full of bright blooms that would wipe away the memories of black, rotting fields and fresh-dug graves along the country lanes of County Clare.

She hoped that the seeds she'd carried from Ireland would flourish in this Missouri soil so that she could surround her house with sweet-smelling herbs and flowers. A house couldn't really be a home without the colors and scents of a garden.

As they reached the outskirts of the town there were fewer people on the dusty street. A coach pulled by four horses rumbled past, followed by a solitary rider on a swaybacked horse. A small white dog ran from a yard and barked at Shane's wagon. The animal ran after them, snapping at the near wheel.

Shane paid no heed to the passersby or the terrier. He

kept guiding the team along the streets until he reached a narrow lane that looked to Caitlin like all the other lanes they had passed.

"A few more miles along this track and we'll camp for the night," Shane said. He glanced back over his shoulder at the boy. "Mind what I told you, Justice. Keep a loose rein on that pony's mouth. Move with him, not against him."

A few minutes later, Shane reined in the team long enough to light a lantern. He motioned to Justice, and the boy took the lamp and rode ahead of them, illuminating the road.

"He rides well," Caitlin murmured, wanting to make conversation with her husband, normal conversation that didn't end in a fuss. The child did seem to have a good seat. His back was straight, and he showed no fear of his mount.

"He's coming along," Shane replied tersely. "His mother could ride anything with four legs."

Caitlin exhaled softly. She wasn't certain she wanted to hear more about Justice's mother at the moment. When Shane spoke of her, his voice softened in a way that left no doubt as to his affection for the dead woman. A good friend, he had called her. Just how good? Caitlin was wondering. And why would a man living alone be chosen as a guardian for Justice?

Curiosity got the better of her. "What was her name?"

"Who?"

"Justice's mother."

"Cerise. Cerise Larocque."

"She was French?"

"Her father was a Frenchman, so she said. Her mother was a full-blood, I'd expect."

"A full-blood?"

"Indian. Osage. Cerise never talked much about her

red relatives, but she told me that her mother was Osage."

"Are they dangerous? Indians?" Derry burrowed against her and made small baby sounds in her sleep. Caitlin's one arm was cramped, but she didn't want to risk waking the child. Derry had had another long day, and she'd been such a little soldier. She was normally a good-natured child, but if she didn't get her proper sleep she could be a bear.

"Indians?" Shane broke into her thoughts with his reply. "I expect Indians are just like other people. Some are dangerous. Some aren't."

"But . . . If you aren't afraid of the Indians, then why are you carrying a firearm?" She'd noticed that he'd taken his rifle from the case strapped to his saddle and laid it directly behind the seat.

"Lots of things out here to fear worse than Indians," he said. "I don't look for us to see trouble, but if we do . . ."

Shane's words made Caitlin shiver. What could be worse than marauding savages?

The dirt lane was bumpier than the street, and the wagon seat had no springs. By the time they reached this camping spot of Shane's, she would be black-and-blue. To add to Caitlin's discomfort, the horses' hooves kicked up gravel with every step. Her bonnet and apple-green traveling coat would be filthy by the time she reached her new home.

She sighed and looked around her. The road ran through a thick forest; the trees were so large and heavily branched that they nearly shut out the faint sprinkling of stars winking above. Foliage pressed close on both sides of the lane, brushing the sides of the cart and once nearly knocking her bonnet off her head.

It was very dark, but the velvety blackness came in a

hundred shades of night. Rustling noises and the occasional hoot of an owl drifted over her.

The air was rich with the odors of musty leaves, horses, and oiled leather. Intertwined with those earthy smells were hints of wild mint and a good masculine scent that was Shane's alone.

The cart seat was narrow, and they were nearly in each other's laps as they rocked and bounced from side to side. It was impossible not to be acutely aware of her husband's powerful presence.

How strange it felt to be so close to a man after so many years. This was her lawful husband, and yet . . . not really her husband. It was difficult to know how she should feel toward him, but Indians or ferocious beasts, she was certain that he would keep them safe.

Finally, Shane reined in the team in a small clearing beside a stream. "This is where we camp," he said. "Justice. Tend the horses."

He helped her down from the seat. It felt heavenly to stretch her legs after the long, uncomfortable ride.

"We can make a bed in the wagon for the little one if you want," he offered. "We may see rain before daybreak. I'd put my bedroll under the wagon, if I were you."

Justice dismounted and took hold of the off-horse's bridle. Shane heaved the big trunk out of the middle of the cart to make room for her to lay blankets for the child. "It's best you keep her off the ground," he said. "Snakes breed this time of the year. We're close to the stream. Some may be curled up in those rocks yonder. A mite could die from snakebite easy."

"Snakebite?" Caitlin's voice cracked. "You want me to sleep on the ground around poisonous snakes?" The thought of crawly serpents made gooseflesh rise on her arms.

There were no snakes in Ireland. It was said that the

good Saint Patrick banished them all. She'd never seen a snake until she'd reached New Orleans, and that one was dead, stuffed, and part of a show to sell Dr. Jayne's Snake Oil Wonder Cure.

Justice laughed.

"I didn't say they were likely to bite," Shane said scornfully. "I was thinking of the sprout. I'll build a fire." He spread a blanket between Caitlin's pelisses. "That should be enough room. She's not very big."

Caitlin handed him the sleeping child, and he put her in the makeshift bed. Derry sighed and rolled over onto her side and curled up with a tiny thumb in her mouth.

"She has a name," she reminded him. "It's Derry, not sprout or girl." Caitlin removed her coat and covered the child with it.

Shane grunted assent.

Caitlin couldn't stop thinking about the snakes. "Just how big are these snakes?" she asked, trying to sound nonchalant.

"Six, eight feet and bigger," Justice gleefully supplied. "First you hear a little rattle-rattle, like dry beans in a cup, and zap, they sink their fangs into ya. A wrangler in Johnson's Grove got into a nest of rattlers. He turned black and swelled up until his belly burst like a rotten bladder."

"Boy. Get these horses unharnessed and watered." Shane gathered up an armload of fallen branches. "Don't pay him no attention, Caitlin. I don't mean to let you get bit, and if you do, you won't die from it."

"How comforting."

She climbed back up onto the cart seat and sat there until he had a fire going. Justice finished caring for the horses and joined him. Together, they set out the food, and then Shane went down to the stream and filled his canteen with fresh water. When he returned, she was still sitting on the wagon seat.

"You planning on sleeping up there?" he asked. "Best you climb down and have something to eat."

"No, thank you. I'm not hungry just now." What she did need was a proper place to relieve herself. There was nothing around but woods, and she had no intention of marching off to be devoured by a bear or bitten by a poisonous snake.

"You're mad over the hotel room, aren't you?"

"No, I'm not," she lied.

He looked dubious. "Afraid of snakes?"

"No." She compounded her sin with a second lie.

"It's Fat Rose's, then. You're vexed over my leaving your plunder. Rose won't steal it. And heaven help any poor soul who tries to make off with anything under her protection."

It was a long speech for Shane, the most he'd said to her at one time since they left the City of Jefferson. She knew she ought to return the favor. "They seem well acquainted with you."

"I made that clear, didn't I?"

"You have . . . friends there?" Her mouth went dry, but she couldn't hold back. "Women friends? Other than Rose?"

He chuckled. "Nobody since I wrote for you this last time."

"You expect me to believe that?" she dared.

"Believe it or not, as you please." He shrugged. "It doesn't matter."

"But there have been other—"

"I don't think this is something we should talk about in front of the boy, do you?"

"I need to know if there's someone now."

He shook his head. "I told you. Not for more than a

year. I'm clean of disease." Shane tilted his chin, as if he was waiting for her to reply. Silence stretched between them, broken only by the chirp of crickets and the restless movement of the horses.

"Guess we've said all we need to about that," he observed. "We've a long ride tomorrow. You need to eat and see to your personals. If you're fearful, sleep by the fire."

"And you? Where will you sleep?" she asked.

"I'll keep watch."

Justice finished off his bread and cheese and rolled up in his blanket on the far side of the fire. In minutes he was sound asleep. Caitlin remained stubbornly where she was.

"You intend to sit there until morning?" Shane asked.

"Maybe."

"Suit yourself." He spread his blanket and dropped his saddle at the head for a pillow. "Your bed's ready if you want it," he said. Then, taking his rifle, he strolled away from the firelight and paced a circle around the camp.

As he completed his circuit, he glanced into the back of the wagon at Derry, then settled down against a tree. Caitlin climbed down and dashed into the bushes on the far side of the horses. In less than a minute, she hurried back to the fire and crouched beside it.

Shane nodded to her as he balanced his rifle across his knees. "Eat and sleep," he advised. "We have to make tracks tomorrow. I want to be home by dusk, and we have some rough country to get through."

Far off, across the hills, a dog howled at the moon, an eerie, drawn-out sound. One of the horses nickered and twitched his ears. Caitlin shifted uneasily. Was that really a dog? she wondered. "Was that a wolf?" she called to Shane.

"Just a coyote. Nothing to be scared of."

Caitlin pulled the pins from her hair and began to braid it as she stared into the glowing coals. The words she'd overheard on Fat Rose's porch kept returning to haunt her. What did those people think Shane had done that was so awful? He'd kept Justice a secret from her. Was he keeping other things from her as well?

Something rustled in the grass behind her and she shivered. It would be a long night with a long day to follow. Maybe by morning she'd figure out how to start making things right between her and Shane. Or maybe she'd realize just how big a mistake she'd made in coming here, and take the first steamboat back to civilization.

Chapter 3

The following day proved as difficult as Shane had promised. By late afternoon, despite the lovely scenery, Caitlin had had more than enough of riding in an open wagon. Derry fussed and squirmed on her lap as they rolled up yet another wooded hill. Shane had promised over an hour before that they need go just a little farther. His *a little farther* seemed to Caitlin to run on forever. This Missouri was a fair green land, but she was weary of traveling. Both she and Derry were hot, hungry, and tired.

Sparkling streams and sunny meadows swirled in Caitlin's mind, too many to count. Shane had told her that they had crossed the property line onto Kilronan, but still she saw no sign of human habitation.

When they reached the crest of the rise, he reined in the team and pointed. "There," he said.

On the far side of the valley, she saw a sprawling, two-story log house with three stone chimneys. Not far away were several small cabins, what she took to be stables, and a fenced enclosure. Beyond, horses and cattle grazed.

"That's Kilronan? It's beautiful," she said. "Look, Derry. That's our home." In spite of her fatigue and disappointment over Shane's cool behavior toward her, Caitlin's heart leaped. Surely here, in such a magical spot, she could mend her broken marriage.

"House," Derry echoed. "Mama's house."

"Aunty Cait," Caitlin corrected.

Shane glanced sideways at her, giving her a dubious look. He clicked to the horses, and the team started forward at a sharp trot.

Caitlin clung to Derry to keep her from losing her balance and tumbling under the wagon wheels.

The sun was setting beyond the house, bathing the farmyard in a golden glow. Caitlin shaded her eyes with her hand and tried to make out the waving figure near the largest outbuilding.

Justice gave a whoop and pounded past them on the little pinto. Horse and rider plunged down the steep track, then left the lane and cut across a cleared area before jumping a split-rail fence and thundering up to the stable. There, the boy threw himself off his pony and ran to the slender man.

"That's Gabriel, my horse wrangler," Shane said. "He and Justice are good friends. I expect it's because they're both part Osage. Gabriel can ride better than any man I've ever seen. That makes him pretty tall in any boy's eyes."

"I didn't know you had servants," Caitlin replied. "I suppose with all this land, I should have guessed that—"

He chuckled. "I wouldn't let Gabriel hear you call him a servant. He wouldn't take kindly to it. Until a week ago, I had another man working for me, Nate Bone. But Nate couldn't get along with Gabriel, so I had to let him go. Like I warned you, lots of folks out here don't cotton to Indians."

"So you have just Gabriel to help you?" Caitlin asked. Derry stood up, digging her boot toes into Caitlin's ribs. "Sit down, Derry," she admonished. "We're almost there. I vow," Caitlin said to Shane, "she's going to explode if she doesn't get out of this wagon."

"House! House!" Derry cried, clapping her hands. "Me want milk! Me hun-ger-ee!"

"You're going to eat as soon as we get to the house," Caitlin promised.

The toddler planted a wet kiss on Caitlin's cheek. "Berry woves you." As usual, Caitlin's heart melted. She'd been there when Derry had come into the world, and she loved her more than anything.

"Mary Red Jacket cooks for us," Shane offered. "She lives in one of those cabins." He pointed to a tidy cottage with smoke drifting from the white-washed chimney. "She cleans, when she feels like it. But don't expect too much. This has been a bachelor's house these last few years. I've been so busy outside, I've not had the time to worry about fancy furnishings."

"No matter. I can see to the house," Caitlin said. "You say your cook's name is Mary Red Jacket? What an odd name."

"She's Osage, too. A full-blood, I think. Mary doesn't talk much, but she can cook a decent steak and good fry bread."

"Does she speak English?"

"When she wants to." The team reached the bottom of the hill, and Gabriel came to swing open the heavy log gate. Justice trailed after him, no longer talking but following close enough to tread on the wrangler's heels.

"McKenna." Gabriel nodded solemnly to Shane. Caitlin felt the wrangler's gaze sweep over her, and she wondered if she'd passed inspection.

Gabriel was a wiry young man with heavy-lidded black eyes, high cheekbones, and shoulder-length hair held back by a red neckerchief tied in a band around his head. His skin had a copper-red tinge beneath a heavy tan. He wore boots, loose leather trousers, and a blue cotton shirt that hung open down the front. A beaded strap stretched across his chest and over one shoulder, and held a wicked-looking knife. Gabriel wasn't very tall, hardly taller than Caitlin herself, but he moved with an innate grace that suggested strength.

"This is my wife, Caitlin," Shane offered.

Gabriel's eyes narrowed. After a slight hesitation, he nodded.

Caitlin hastened to offer a cordial greeting, but the cowboy didn't smile in return. Instead, he continued to stare at her with a gaze as hostile as Justice's.

So much for that, Caitlin thought, as Shane drove on to the house. It looked as though it would be Derry and her against all the rest.

"Down! Down!" Derry demanded. She kicked out with both feet and wiggled to be free. She stuck out her bottom lip and scowled. "I want down!"

"Let her go," Shane said. "If she stays away from the corrals and out of the creek, there's nothing much to hurt her."

Caitlin lowered the squirming child to the ground. Derry dropped onto her bottom, and the frown became an expression of delight that widened into a grin. "Klicken!" she squealed. Before Caitlin could get down out of the wagon, Derry darted behind it and charged after a large white duck.

"No! Come back!" Caitlin called. The hem of her dress caught on the corner of the wagon seat. She tugged and heard the material rip. Oh! A surge of regret welled up, but she had no time to stop and examine the damage. She ran after the toddler. "Derry, no!"

"Klicken!" Derry shouted. She dove at the duck and seized a handful of tail feathers. The duck squawked and flapped his wings, then pulled free, leaving Derry holding two soiled white feathers.

The duck flew a few feet off the ground, but crashed

back to earth and waddled furiously away with Derry in hot pursuit.

"Derry!" Caitlin admonished. Before she could reach them, both duck and toddler vanished around the corner of the house.

"Klicken!" Derry shrieked, then broke into a wail of distress.

Caitlin rounded the corner after her.

Derry stood stock-still staring up at a stern-faced, nut-brown woman with a corncob pipe between her teeth.

"Who chasey Mary's duck?" demanded the woman, snatching the pipe out of her mouth. She shook a slim finger at the child. "You? Ba-ad. Bad chasey duck."

"I'm sorry." Caitlin captured Derry's hand. "She didn't mean any harm."

The toddler's small chin thrust forward, and she shook a finger back at the woman. "No! No!" she said, still clutching the feathers in a tight fist. "My klicken. Berry not bad. You baad!"

"Derry, that isn't nice." Caitlin bent and lifted the child in her arms. "She wouldn't hurt your duck," Caitlin explained to the woman. "Really. She loves chickens. She thinks it's a—"

"Duck. Mary's duck."

Derry shook her finger at her again. "Mine."

"It isn't yours," Caitlin scolded the child. "And it was bad to pull the duck's tail." She glanced back at the woman and forced an embarrassed smile. "I'm Mrs. McKenna. You must be Mary Red Jacket."

"Hmmpt." Mary looked at the duck. The creature had taken shelter behind a woodpile and hissed as it preened its ruffled feathers. Apparently satisfied that the bird had taken no serious hurt, the Indian woman scowled at Derry. "Fleurblanche, she lay egg. No happy, no egg.

You wantee eat, no be ba-ad girl, pull Fleurblanche's tail."

"Say you're sorry," Caitlin coaxed.

"Ba-ad klicken," Derry pronounced.

Shane appeared at Caitlin's side. "You need to watch the baby close," he warned. "She'll come to no harm chasing a duck in the backyard, but I've got an evil-tempered bull in the far pound." He paused and nodded to the dark-skinned woman. "I see you've met Mary."

"Yes," Caitlin said.

"Mary, this is my wife, Caity," Shane continued. "You can show her the house. Put her in the front corner bedroom."

"Why you not want Missy-Wife in your room, McKenna?"

Shane flushed under his dark tan. "Caity has had a long trip. She needs time to . . ." He looked at Caitlin helplessly.

"Yes," she agreed. "I'm tired from the journey. It would be a good thing if I could share a room with Derry. Just . . . just until we're settled in." A weight slid from her shoulders. She had hoped he wouldn't expect them to resume marital relations immediately. "A temporary arrangement," she stammered.

Shane's expression of gratitude heartened her, and she smiled at him.

"Mary will look after you," he said. "Gabe tells me that I've got a mare in trouble in the west pasture. It's her first colt, and she's been in labor all day. I don't know how long I'll be. Mary will find you something to eat."

"You won't be sharing the evening meal with us?" Caitlin asked.

"This could take half the night. She's a good mare. I'd hate to lose her or her colt."

"Of course, you must see to your horse," she agreed. "I'll see that Justice has his supper and—"

"The boy comes with me."

"But he must be hungry, Shane. Surely, it wouldn't hurt for Justice to—"

"Stock comes first on Kilronan. If you're going to be a stockman's wife, you'd best know that."

"Yes." Caitlin nodded, trying not to lose her temper. "Naturally, you must take care of your animals, but I hardly think your livelihood will rise or fall on whether or not a child has his supper before he—"

"Boy eat, then help with horse," Mary declared. She stuck her pipe back in her mouth and trudged toward the house.

Shane shrugged. "He'd best eat fast, then."

"You told me that you wanted me to care for Justice as though I were his mother," Caitlin reminded him.

Scowling, Shane turned his back and strode around the corner of the house.

"Berry hun-gry," Derry said.

"All right," Caitlin soothed. "Aunty Cait will find you some supper."

Mary left the back door ajar, and Caitlin entered a large kitchen with log beams and a massive stone fireplace. A long wooden trestle table, two benches, and a rocking chair were the only furnishings. The floor was bare planks; the area in front of the hearth, stone. Two windows were tightly shuttered.

Gloomy, Caitlin thought, looking around. Gloomy as a bat's cave and none too clean. She smelled something cooking and glanced at the kettle hanging over the coals. Her stomach gurgled. "Oh, excuse me," she said.

"Missy-Wife eat," Mary ordered. She took two battered tin plates from a wall cupboard and bent over the hearth. The pipe, unlit, remained firmly in Mary's mouth.

"We need to wash," Caitlin said. "Derry's hands are—"

"There." The woman pointed to a stone sink in the corner.

"Thank you." Caitlin led Derry to the sink. To Caitlin's surprise, there was a continuous flow of water from a pipe attached to the wall. "How lovely," she said, using her hands to splash Derry's dusty face. "Where does the water come from?"

"Spring."

"The water runs all the time?" Caitlin washed the child's hands and looked around for a towel. Since there seemed to be no drying cloths, Caitlin ushered Derry to the table.

"Good spring." Mary placed the two plates none too gently on the scarred table. She removed her pipe long enough to say, "Stew hot. Eat."

"But Justice? Shane said that he could—"

"Eat," Mary ordered. "Mary take care of boy."

Derry grabbed a spoon and dipped into the lumpy gray stew.

"Grace first," Caitlin reminded her. Quickly she offered a blessing and then nodded to the child. Derry began to spoon the food into her mouth.

"Good," Mary pronounced as she dropped a flat pancake beside each plate. "Bread. Eat."

Caitlin offered another silent prayer that the swill would be edible and took a taste. To her surprise, it tasted delicious. The bread, however, was hard and flavorless.

Mary stared at them for a few moments, then produced a slab of roast beef and sawed off several generous slices. Taking the meat and a handful of the bread rounds, she left the kitchen by the back door.

Caitlin surveyed the room in dismay. Dusty herbs and a haunch of dried meat hung from the overhead beams. The cracks between the floorboards were filled with dirt.

The only cooking utensils seemed to be the battered stew kettle, a long-handled frying pan, a Dutch oven, and a blackened tin coffeepot.

"What have we come to, baby?" she murmured, absently stroking Derry's dark tousled curls.

Derry smiled up at her. "Mama," she said.

"Aunty Cait," Caitlin corrected gently.

Derry shook her head firmly. "Mama."

Caitlin sighed. "Mama," she agreed. "Why not? Someone might as well be happy in this house."

In the barn, Shane tightened the cinch on his saddle and thrust his boot into the leather stirrup. As he swung up onto his second favorite horse, a leggy roan gelding, he noticed a movement in the shadows. "Justice?"

"*Oui.*"

When he was troubled, Shane noted that the boy used backwoods French that he'd learned from his mama. "You unharness the team like I told you, boy?"

Justice nodded.

The last light of a fading day cast a pool of liquid sunshine through the open doorway. Shane could see that Justice's eyes were red. Justice never cried, not even when they'd watched his mother's body lowered into the ground. "What's wrong, son?"

The boy chewed at his lower lip. Shane dismounted, crossed the distance between him and Justice, and laid a gloved hand on the child's shoulder. Justice flinched, but not as much as he had when he'd first come to live at Kilronan, and he didn't back away.

"I don't want her here." Justice kicked at a heap of straw.

"Caity's a good woman. You'll like her if you give her half a chance."

"She don't like me."

Justice looked up into Shane's eyes, and he read the fear and uncertainty flickering in the boy's gaze. "You don't know that. It never pays for a man to make quick judgments on people."

The boy's dark eyes—his mother's eyes—took on the sheen of wet obsidian. "I hate her. Her and her whining brat." He kicked the dirt again with a scuffed boot. "We was doin' all right by ourselves."

Shane swallowed, trying to dissolve the constriction in his throat. He wanted to pull the kid into his arms and reassure him with a hug, but he knew better than to try. Justice was as wary as a coyote about letting anyone too close.

"This is hard for you," Shane said. "It's hard for me, and for Caity, too. Change is always difficult, but I sent for Caity because I thought it would be good for all of us."

"Still think that?"

Shane cleared his throat. Justice was a kid, but he'd always treated him like a man. He'd never lied to him or tried to pretty up an unpleasant truth, and he didn't want to start now. "I don't know," he answered honestly. "It's too soon for me to tell."

"You shoulda left her over the salt water, her and her fancy clothes and her fancy talk. Kilronan ain't no place fer them. They're trouble."

"If they don't fit in, we'll know soon enough. Until then, trust me to do what's right." He lifted the boy's chin. "And act decent, do you hear? Give her respect—for my sake if not for hers."

Justice sighed and his shoulders slumped. "If she had to have a kid, why not a boy? Girls are useless."

Shane allowed himself the hint of a smile. "You may not think that when you're older." Then he made his voice stern. "I expect you to play a man's part, Justice. A man protects women, whether he approves of them or not."

"Like you an' Cerise?"

Justice had the knack of asking questions that sliced straight to the gut. He struggled with the urge to shake the hell out of the kid. Instead, he swore under his breath and knotted his hands into tight fists.

A hard fist or a kick in the ribs was Shane's own father's way, but it wouldn't work with Justice any more than it had worked with him. He'd never struck the boy and he never would; Justice had suffered enough of that treatment from his mother.

"I failed her, Justice. I couldn't protect her when she needed me," Shane admitted. "But I swear to you, I'm not the one who stabbed her."

Justice met his gaze and held it, his features immobile, his mouth tight.

"You believe me, don't you?" Shane asked him.

"Yes, sir."

The answer was the right one, but Shane wasn't sure it was truthful. He nodded. "Run to the kitchen. Mary will have something for you to eat. When you're finished, you can ride out to the west pasture and give us a hand with the mare. Deal?"

"Deal." Justice grinned.

The boy's words troubled Shane as he rode away from the farmyard. Maybe Justice was right. Maybe bringing Caitlin to Missouri was the biggest mistake of his life. Shane only knew that he was bone weary of being alone.

Other men had a woman to listen to their dreams and walk with in the twilight. Caitlin was his wife, for all that she'd betrayed him and cheated him out of two years' hard-won wages when she hadn't come the first time he'd sent for her.

But she had come this time, and that should be an end

to the hard feelings on his part. She'd hurt him bad, but a man couldn't move on with life if he wasn't willing to put the past behind him.

As he'd told her, they were husband and wife in God's eyes. He wanted to bring legitimate children into the world. He wanted to put down roots for those that would come after him. He wanted the McKenna name to stand for something solid in Missouri.

There were a dozen good reasons why it would have made more sense to find himself an Indian squaw who wouldn't shirk at the hard work and who wouldn't care if their union was common-law. Many white men did it, rough men, those who lived on the fringes of white society.

He guided his horse alongside a gate and slipped the rope tie off the post. He pushed the gate open, rode through, and then backed the roan up to secure the fence. Dusk was falling fast, but he didn't need daylight to find his way around Kilronan.

God but he loved every inch of it, briars, rocks, and gullies. This land demanded sweat and blood if he was ever going to make it into a prime spread. Oh, Kilronan had beauty aplenty, what with her rich soil, abundant water, and lush grass. But there were trees to cut, fences to build, horses and mules to break.

Livestock was his cash crop, and providing prime animals for the Oregon Trail trade wasn't the easiest way for a man to earn a living. He had no spare time or money to make life easy for a gentle-bred woman.

Which was just what he'd spent every cent he had in the world to bring here. Caitlin had never done a hard day's work in her life. She had a fair face and a figure that would turn any man's head. She could sing and play the harp. She could stitch fancy needlework and recite poetry. None of which were worth spit on Kilronan.

And worse, she'd put horns on him with some other man and tried to pass the babe off as her niece. His wife, the woman he'd once loved more than his hope of resurrection, was a cheat and a liar.

He needed a strong honest woman, someone who could tote water, clean game, plant a garden, cook, and sew, and give him healthy sons. He worked from dawn to dusk, seven days a week, and he wanted a partner who was willing to do the same.

Instead, he had Caitlin.

He'd told Justice that a man shouldn't make hasty judgments, but following his own advice was going to be strong medicine.

"Over here," Gabriel shouted.

Ahead, Shane saw the mare lying on her side with Gabe kneeling next to her. Shane stood in the stirrups and waved. "Coming," he called.

Something whined past Shane's ear, and from the wooded hillside he heard the crack of a rifle. "Son of a bitch!" he swore.

Somebody was trying to kill him.

Chapter 4

Instinctively, Shane threw his weight to the far side of his horse, making himself as small a target as possible while still remaining in the saddle. He snatched his own rifle from the holster, braced it against the gelding's neck, and waited.

A tuft of dirt and grass flew up just ahead of his mount's nose as another shot rang out. Shane swore as the roan shied and began to buck wildly. By the time he got the frightened animal under control, he knew it was too dark to return fire.

"Stay down," he shouted to Gabriel.

He could no longer see Gabe or the mare, but he knew Gabe would have hit the dirt when the bullets started flying.

The last vestiges of twilight vanished into starless night. Whoever was shooting at them had probably high-tailed it out of there, Shane decided. And if he hadn't, it was too dark for the polecat to hit anything.

Then Shane heard the sound of a galloping horse, coming fast in the darkness, behind him. He twisted in the saddle and aimed his rifle toward the source of the hoof beats.

"Shane! I heard shots!"

Justice's voice. Relief washed over Shane. He eased

back the hammer and holstered his rifle. "Go back to the house. Now!" he ordered.

The boy reined his pony in close to Shane. "What was that shooting?"

"Do as I tell you, Justice. I'll explain later."

"If there's trouble, I'm not running away."

"Damn it, boy! Listen for once. Somebody shot at me. I need you to go back and protect the women. Tell Mary to lock the doors and close all the shutters. Now, ride!"

"Yes, sir. Yah!"

Shane heard the slap of leather and the thud of the pinto's hoofs against the grass. When he was certain Justice was safely across the pasture, Shane dismounted and led his horse toward Gabe and the laboring mare.

The wrangler didn't speak until Shane laid a hand on the downed horse's neck. "You hurt?" Gabe asked quietly.

"No." Shane fought the waves of white-hot anger that boiled up from the pit of his stomach.

A man who let his temper get the best of him didn't last long out here. Cold reason could make the difference between living and dying, not just for him, but for Gabe and Justice as well.

"In the morning I'll scout out those woods and see if our shooter left any sign," Shane said.

"That's Thompson land."

Gabe had stated what they both knew, something he rarely did.

"There's bad blood between me and the Thompsons," Shane continued, "but Big Earl's no back shooter."

"Rachel neither."

Shane had a feeling that they were both thinking of the same person. "Beau? He's mean enough, but setting an ambush takes more ambition than Beau's shown me."

Big Earl Thompson's only son was a worthless piece

of buffalo dung, and Earl knew it. His daughter Rachel had more sense and twice the balls Beau did. Trouble was, Rachel didn't fit into the old man's picture of what a daughter should be any more than Beau met Earl's expectations as a son.

Gabe nodded. "Could be Beau, certain. I saw him toss a pup into the river and use it for target practice."

"Whoever it was," Shane promised, "when I find him, he won't get any older."

"You take care, friend," Gabe cautioned. "You shoot Big Earl's son without proof, and hellfire will come thunderin' down on Kilronan."

"Big Earl's a bad man to cross," Shane agreed.

"And so are you, friend."

The mare groaned as another birth contraction gripped her. She kicked with her hind legs, and Gabe stroked her neck and whispered into her ear.

"We'd best tend to this horse and let the shooter wait for daylight," Shane said.

"Right, but there's more you need to know. While you were gone, I found another section of fence ripped down. Five of our horses were grazing on Thompson grass. I drove them back and put up the rails."

"Any chance the horses broke out themselves?"

Gabe made a sharp clicking sound with his tongue, an Indian habit Shane had come to understand as wry amusement. "Six rails high," Gabe added. "New fence."

"Shit." Bad luck had plagued Kilronan since his uncle and cousin had drowned in the floods. Calves dying, fences mysteriously broken, and a pasture fire in the midst of a thunderstorm that had nearly enveloped the house.

But bullets were no accident. And as far as he knew, nobody but the Thompsons had a grudge against him . . . nobody alive, that was.

The mare whinnied anxiously, and Shane ran his hands over her swollen belly. "Do you think we can get her to the barn?" Moving the animal was dangerous, but lighting a lantern and trying to deliver her foal here would be stupid. They'd make too good a target if the ambusher was still hiding out in the woods.

Gabe grunted a reluctant approval of the plan, and the two of them set about getting the mare on her feet. They'd walked her halfway back across the pasture when Gabe signaled a halt.

"Someone's comin'," he whispered.

Shane listened, but he couldn't hear anything but crickets and the breathing of the horses. Then the soft hoot of an owl drifted across the field.

Gabe cupped his hands around his mouth and returned the call. "It's Mary," he said to Shane. "Mary's comin'."

"I told Justice to keep the women at the house."

Gabe shrugged.

Shane thought he heard him chuckle. Then he became aware of definite footsteps coming toward them. He eased his rifle out of the saddle holster. He trusted Gabe, but even Gabe could be wrong.

Two figures loomed up out of the night.

"Shane? Are you all right?" Caitlin called. "Justice said—"

"We're fine. What the hell are you two doing here? I gave orders for you to stay in the house."

"Did you?" Caitlin flinched at Shane's harsh language and peered through the darkness. Missouri seemed so big, so empty. At home, before the potatoes died and everything changed, she'd often gone out of the house at night without a light. She'd known every hedge and lane for miles around. But this place was different. Mary had told her to stay with Derry, but she couldn't. If Shane was hurt, he needed her. And now that she saw that he was unharmed, her fear for him turned to anger.

"Who is trying to kill you?" she demanded. "What kind of place is this that people shoot at—"

"I don't know." He cut her off gruffly.

Another question rose in her mind—one she couldn't resist asking. "And what kind of man are you, Shane McKenna, that someone would wish you dead?"

"You've a sharp tongue, Caity. Best you hold it for a better time and place."

"I will that," she promised him. "Be sure of it."

"Boy tell us locky door," Mary said in her odd singsong English. "He say ba-ad man shoot at you. Mary no bringy lantern. Mary come quick. Missy-Wife no stay house." She replaced her unlit pipe in her mouth and nodded firmly.

The mare raised her head and uttered a strangled moan. Instantly Mary ran her hands along the animal's belly and murmured in a strange language.

"I don't know if we can get her to the barn," Gabe said.

Mary nodded again. "Need light. You help or horse die quick, I think."

A coyote howled off to the north, and Caitlin glanced nervously over her shoulder. Anxiously she followed the three back to the largest stable.

Once inside, Mary lit a lantern, and Gabe and Shane let the suffering mare sink down in a pile of clean straw. "I'll need whiskey," Shane said.

"I'd think this would be a time when you'd need a clear head," Caitlin offered.

Mary grinned, exposing perfect white teeth. It was the first time Caitlin had seen her smile. "Mary bring whiskey."

When she turned toward the doorway, Caitlin asked, "Are you going to the house?" She was torn between remaining here and seeing if Derry was safe. In the end, concern for the child won out and she hurried back.

Mary went into the large parlor, and Caitlin returned to the kitchen where she'd left the children. "Is Derry—"

Justice nearly knocked her down running past. "Where's Shane? Did the mare have her colt?" He didn't stop for an answer. Caitlin heard Mary say something to him, but she couldn't understand what the Indian woman said.

Derry was seated in the chair where Caitlin had last seen her, sound asleep, rosebud lips sucking contentedly. In one chubby hand she clutched a handful of duck feathers; in the other, a piece of Mary's fry bread smeared with honey. She was nearly hidden in the man's shirt that someone had draped around her shoulders.

Caitlin heard the front door close. Suddenly, unwilling to miss out on what was happening in the barn, she picked up Derry and carried her out to the stable.

When she reached the circle of lantern light, she saw that Shane had stripped away his shirt. Naked to the waist, he vigorously soaped his muscular arms over a tub of water.

Caitlin laid Derry in a nest of hay and tried not to stare at Shane's exposed chest. Thin white scars crisscrossed his tanned skin. His stomach was flat beneath bands of hard sinew; his biceps bulged below a set of brawny shoulders.

A fair broth of a man, she thought, and her remaining anger at him drained away. Surely Shane had been brusque with her out of concern for her safety. It was only natural that he'd not want her in the field where someone had tried to shoot at him. She'd been too quick to flare up, as usual, and she'd accused him of being to blame. Her behavior was inexcusable, and she resolved to apologize to Shane as soon as they were alone.

She could not take her gaze from him as her pulse

quickened and disturbing thoughts filled her head. She had lain beneath Shane McKenna, felt those powerful arms around her, known the intimate touch of his long fingers. He was her God-given husband . . . but she had never seen him like this.

"Mary," he said.

The housekeeper uncorked the whiskey bottle and poured the amber liquid over Shane's hands. He rubbed them together, then sloshed the potent brew along his arms to the elbow.

"Oh," Caitlin murmured. She hadn't realized that he meant to use the *uisce beathadh* as a disinfectant. "I thought you were going to drink the—"

"Shane doesn't drink," Justice said.

Another thing she didn't know about her husband. Caitlin's cheeks grew warm.

Shane had drunk in Ireland. Not that he was a drunk like his father, but few men didn't drink, if they didn't wear a cleric's collar. Even the priests in County Clare were known to enjoy a drop or two.

"I'm sorry," she murmured. "I . . ." She trailed off when she realized Shane wasn't listening. All his concentration was on the mare and the small hoof that had suddenly appeared in the birth opening.

The horse's brown hair was drenched in sweat so that she looked almost black in the lantern light. Her eyes rolled back until the whites showed and her nostrils flared. She tried to rise, but Mary and Gabe held her halter tightly.

Gently Shane followed the line of the tiny leg with his hand. The mare quivered and cried out in pain. Then Shane tugged and a second hoof thrust through. He nodded to Mary and she let go of the halter.

The bay mare scrambled to her feet and a wiggling foal, encased in a translucent sack, slid onto the straw amid rivulets of blood and birth fluid. Instantly Shane was on his knees, tearing free the dark head and wiping clean the foal's nose.

Caitlin saw a tiny black face with a white star in the center. Small wet ears pressed back against the curve of the head. Mary joined Shane in the straw. She began to rub the little horse's back and belly with a rough cloth.

Caitlin was so transfixed by the sight of new life that she wasn't bothered by the smells and the blood. The foal was so perfectly formed, so precious.

But it hadn't made a sound or taken a breath. Tears welled up in Caitlin's eyes as she realized that the baby was stillborn.

The mare turned and looked at her foal. She nickered softly and flicked her ears.

"Do something," Caitlin pleaded.

Justice shook his head, "It's dead."

Mary rubbed harder against the foal's limp body. "Filly," she said. "Girl."

Shane leaned down and blew into the baby's velvety mouth and nostrils. When the foal still didn't respond, he repeated the action.

"No use," Gabe said. "We lost her. At least the mother's—"

"No, damn it!" Shane swore. "I won't give up on her." Prying open the foal's mouth, he cleaned out still more mucus. "Give me what's left of that whiskey."

Caitlin snatched up the bottle and handed it to him. He poured a small amount down the filly's throat, then stood up and lifted her. He gave her a hard shake, and fluid poured out of her mouth and nose.

Caitlin heard a sputtering choke, and then a feeble squeak.

"Yes!" Shane shouted. "Breathe! Breathe, darlin'." He

lowered the foal onto the straw and blew two more quick breaths into her nose.

The little horse sneezed and gave a kick with her hind leg. Then the bottlebrush tail flipped and long lashes fluttered. The foal's eyes, large and brown and liquid, opened.

"Oh!" Caitlin cried. "Look at her."

The filly sneezed again and shook her head. Her front legs thrashed in the straw, and she struggled to rise. Shane supported her, one hand under her chest, one under her belly. His eyes looked as moist as the foal's.

The filly's legs folded, but she struggled up a second time. Gabe let go of the mare's halter, and she sniffed the baby, then nudged her encouragingly with her nose.

No one spoke as mother and child became acquainted. In minutes the foal was nursing, standing on wobbly legs and twitching her fluffy black tail.

Finally Shane stretched and moved slowly out of the box stall. Gabe closed the gate as Shane washed and then pushed his damp arms back into his shirt.

"What will you name her?" Caitlin asked.

He smiled at her, a slow satisfied grin. "You choose one."

"Star?"

"That's a sissy name," Justice said. "Call her Cougar."

"Star it is," Shane agreed. He nodded toward the boy. "Into bed with you, boy. It's late."

"I'll finish up here." Gabe began to gather up the towels off the floor.

Caitlin glanced back through the rails at the filly and then touched Shane's arm. "I'd like a moment to talk with you."

"Can't it wait until morning?" he asked.

"No, I don't think it can." She was afraid she'd lose her nerve. "Alone, please," she added. She bent to pick up Derry, but Shane motioned for her to let him carry the child.

Together they walked through the warm, still night toward the house. For all Caitlin's weariness, her heart felt light. Seeing Shane with the newborn foal had told her more about her husband than all the words they'd exchanged since she'd arrived in Missouri. He might not be the same man she'd married, but he was a man with compassion and tenderness toward a helpless creature. A man with a good heart was worth fighting for, she reasoned.

Only a few stars peeked through the low-lying clouds, and they had little effect on the darkness. Then suddenly, only a few yards away, something twinkled. As though the single gleam were a signal, another light flashed and then another.

"Ohhh." Caitlin uttered a small cry of wonder. "Are they fairy lights?"

Shane chuckled. "Lightning bugs. Just a bug with wings."

"An insect? No, I don't believe you." She put out her hand, and one of the fireflies lit on her finger, glowing on and off. "It's wonderful," she said. Her laughter rang out as she twirled around. "They must be fairies. I've never seen the like before." She blew gently on the firefly and it flitted away.

"You've lost none of your fey thoughts," Shane said. "What will you see next? Leprechauns?"

"And if I did?" She laughed again. "I'd follow him home and steal his pot of gold. We'd be rich then, or . . . richer."

He pushed open the front door and carried Derry upstairs to the big double bed in the corner room. "Best not undress her," he said. "She may wake if you do."

Caitlin untied the child's shoes and pulled off her

stockings. "A fine auntie I am," she murmured. "Letting a babe sleep in a pile of hay."

"Hay made a crib for our Lord, didn't it?" Shane said. "If it was good enough for God's son, it should be—"

"I'm sorry that I spoke to you so in the pasture. What I said was wrong." She took a deep breath. "I shouldn't have come out there, but I was worried—"

"No, you shouldn't have," he answered. "You could have been hurt. Next time when I tell you something for your own good, I expect you to listen."

"I'll try," she promised. Taking his hand, she pulled him out into the hallway and closed the door behind her. "Why did someone shoot at you?"

"I told you before. I don't know."

"Someone wants to put you under the sod, and you don't have a clue as to who it may be? Are you shamming me, Shane? Or do you think I'm stupid?"

She dropped his hand. It was hard to hold on to him and speak this way. Her heart was hammering, and her knees felt as weak as milk. "Either you want me here as your true wife, or you do not. And if you do, we must be honest with each other. You have to treat me like an adult, a help-mate."

"I thought I was."

"No, Shane, you were not. You all behave as if I was a not-too-bright cousin that you were forced to welcome for a visit."

He scowled. "What nonsense are you talkin', woman? It's late and I—"

"No, Shane. We got off on the wrong foot, you and I. We were so long apart, and so much has happened that we're more strangers than man and wife. Why did you send for me if you didn't want me here?"

He touched her cheek with a hard-callused hand. "I've

wanted you beside me since the first day I set foot in America."

"There's a start," Caitlin murmured. She was trembling from head to toe, but she couldn't back down. "Can we not forget all that's happened in the past two days and begin again?"

"What do you want of me, Caity?" His deep voice wavered on her name, and his eyes glistened with emotion.

"Pretend that this is the dock," she whispered. "I've just caught sight of my husband and he of me."

"I'm no man for play-actin'."

"What wife would not give her man a proper greeting?" she murmured. And, standing on tiptoe, she put her arms around his neck and kissed him full on the lips.

Chapter 5

The instant her mouth pressed against Shane's, Caitlin stepped off a cliff into thin air. Her senses reeled as his scent filled her head and the taste of his mouth brought back a rush of memories.

His arms tightened around her, clasping her to his broad chest. Shamelessly she clung to him, molding the curves of her body to his, tilting her head so that her lips fitted his perfectly.

She had intended the kiss to be a tender greeting, but she hadn't anticipated the intensity of his response . . . or her own.

A flash of heat swept over her as Shane parted her lips with his tongue and thrust deep inside her mouth. She shut her eyes and savored the feel of him, reveling in the sensual joy of the embrace. For long seconds the searing kiss deepened, as her blood pounded in her ears and her thoughts tumbled, giddy with wild, sweet sensations. And when at last he pushed her away, she was stunned and gasping for breath.

Shane had wooed and courted her. He'd wed her with book and ring, and they'd consummated their union on a bed of wild heather in a wooded glade. Shane McKenna had taken her maidenhood. He'd made her a woman, but he'd never before kissed her like this.

Shane shook his head and stepped away from her. "I missed you more than I thought, Caity," he murmured hoarsely.

Without his strength to support her, she swayed, nearly losing her balance. She felt drunken, dazed. She blinked and tried to think of something to say that would hide her confusion. But the words wouldn't come. Instead, she moistened her lips with the tip of her tongue and looked into his eyes.

"Caity . . ." Shane's mouth—the mouth that she had known so intimately only seconds ago—tightened.

Kiss me like that again! she wanted to cry.

"I want you, Caity."

Trembling, she waited.

"I want you bad. But this is happening too soon between us. It will only complicate things if I bed you now."

Shane's gut wrenched as he watched a deep flush creep up Caitlin's throat and lightly freckled face. Her eyes dilated, and her lower lip quivered.

An oath rolled off his tongue as he realized just how badly he'd hurt her. And himself . . . It took every ounce of his will to keep from crushing her against him and devouring her trembling, honeyed mouth.

His hands ached to stroke the lush curves of her body. He wanted to strip away her layers of silk, undo the ribbons and lace, peel the stockings from her long, shapely legs, and bury his face in her firm breasts.

He remembered Caitlin's nipples, ripe buds of rosy pink against her white breasts. He'd seen her nipples only once, in the misty dawn after their wedding night, but they were not a sight a hot-blooded man was likely to forget. He'd been told that some women's breasts changed after they'd given birth to a child; he wondered if her nipples had darkened in color.

She turned her face away from him, and in that second, he would have given a year of his life to undo those words.

Why had he rejected her? She'd come willingly into his arms, as hot for him as he was for her. He ached, his sex pressed tightly against his trousers. She was his lawful wife, and he was a fool to turn away what was so clearly offered—what was his by right.

"I only meant a kiss," she stammered. "No more than that. A kiss between husband and wife."

Lies. Lies came easily to a woman's lips. Still, he'd shamed her, and he could hardly blame Caity for trying to salvage her pride.

A few soft words and he might still have her. But he knew the price might be more than he was willing to pay. He'd let one woman lead him by his jack, and it had nearly earned him a noose around his neck. He'd not make the same mistake with Caity.

"Best we wait," he said. "Don't think I'm not tempted, but if we sleep in the same bed, you might quicken with child. You see that, don't you?"

"No need to apologize." Her voice was thick with shame. "As you say, it would only complicate things between us." She raised her stubborn chin and stared him squarely in the eye, and he pretended not to see the tears glistening there.

"It was a fine greeting, though," he said lightly. "As fine a one as I've ever had."

She shook her head. "My mistake. It won't happen again."

"I don't want to hurt you, girl—"

"I'm not a girl," she protested. "If you can't see that, then there's no chance for us at all."

Her light brown eyes had always made him think of

ginger. Ginger eyes and ginger spirit. He'd thought that the first time he'd seen her . . . a lifetime ago, when they'd both been hardly more than children.

She had a temper, but she didn't spit and screech like so many females. Caity's anger scorched with a blue flame as her whiskey voice deepened and took on the familiar cadence of County Clare.

"What am I, Shane? Your wife or your guest?"

"You know the answer."

"Very well. If I am your wife, then I expect to have responsibilities. You told me that I was not to meddle in things I know nothing of. Where am I to meddle? Am I to be in charge of the children? The house?"

He frowned, covering his own awkwardness with disinterest. "Do what you like inside these walls, so long as you don't interfere with Justice's chores. You'll not make a dandy of him."

"Fair chance of that." Her eyes narrowed. "And what of Mary Red Jacket? She plainly dislikes me." Caity's hands rested on her hips in a gesture of defiance he remembered all too well.

"Mary's rough, but she works hard. She's alone in the world without kin or home."

"Do I look like the sort to throw a poor woman onto the road?" She took a slow breath, and he could see her trembling with anger. "Am I to have the say of the house?" she demanded. "You give your word to uphold my authority?"

"Within reason."

"None of your shilly-shallying, Shane McKenna. If you'll not set the example and give me the respect due mistress of this house, I'm lost before I start."

"Have it your way, woman. But give me peace in my own home. And you must do with what we have. Don't think I can hand out silver as though it grows on trees."

"Fair chance of that, is there? A tightfisted man you've become. And you with enough land to keep the town of Crusheen from hard times."

"Aye," he agreed. "I'm a tightfisted man, and a hard one. Keep that in mind, and we'll get on." He stalked past her to the head of the stairs. "Good night to you, Madame."

"You didn't tell me who you suspect was shooting at you," she called after him.

He ignored her last remark.

His rifle leaned against the wall at the bottom of the steps. He knew Caity's little girl hadn't the strength to cock the hammer or to fire the weapon, but he'd have to drive pegs over the door to hang it high out of her reach. And Derry would have to learn the rules of living on the frontier. There'd never been a young child at Kilronan, and he supposed a lot of habits would need changing to keep the wee colleen from harm.

Picking up the gun, he inspected it closely, then carried it with him into the kitchen.

Mary crouched by the hearth, pipe in her mouth, banking the fire for the night. Gabe stood by the table, a mug of coffee cradled between his hands.

"Where's Justice?" Shane asked.

Mary motioned to a pallet in the far corner. The boy, still fully dressed and feigning sleep, lay sprawled among the covers. His eyes were tightly squeezed together.

"I know you're awake," Shane said. "Upstairs, in your own bed."

The child's dark eyes snapped open. "I was gonna stand guard, Shane. The shooter might come back and steal our horses."

"I'll do what watchin' needs done tonight," Shane replied.

Gabe met his gaze. "Want my help?"

Shane shook his head. "You get some sleep. I need you clearheaded for tomorrow."

Mary handed Shane a cup of coffee, black as home-made sin and steaming hot. He tucked the rifle into the crook of his arm and carried the coffee with him out to the barn.

Coffee was the one luxury he allowed them, and Mary's tin chest was nearly bare. He'd been ashamed to tell Caity how broke he was. Some men traded at the store at Kane's Crossroads on tick, but not him. He'd seen his own father lose what little they had to debt, and Uncle Jamie had left Kilronan buried in due notes to the bank and supply houses.

By sweat and luck he'd cleared most of what was owed, but he'd have no ready coin until he sold more stock. He would have met Caity at the steamboat landing on time if he hadn't been delayed at Hendrick's farm. He and Justice had stopped to deliver a mule and spent most of the afternoon helping Matt Hendrick pull a cow out of a section of quicksand in the river.

Shane had received no ready money from that trans-action, but he had paid off what was still due from one of his uncle's old gambling wagers. By the time he bought gunpowder, flour, and lamp oil, there wasn't two bits left of his ready cash.

Caity had called him a tightfisted man. He supposed that was true enough, but if he'd been softer, Kilronan would have been lost before this. It wasn't in him to make excuses to a woman. Caity had come from quality, and she'd never understand how much the price of a hotel room meant to a stockman.

He didn't take a lantern to the barn. He knew every inch of the way by heart. Murmuring softly to the horses to settle them, Shane climbed up into the loft. There he swung open a door and sat back against a pile of hay with his rifle across his lap.

He sipped slowly at the coffee, trying not to remember how Caity felt in his arms. He could still smell the faint heather in her hair. Fat Rose's girls bathed in scent. He reckoned you could catch wind of Rose's house a mile downriver. Caity didn't smell like that; she was wholesome and clean, and soft as a new-hatched duckling.

"So why did you come here?" he murmured aloud. "Why this time and not before?" Was it the shame of bearing a child out of wedlock? Or was it possible that she still cared for him?

He could care for her a hell of a lot, if he let himself. His feelings for Caity ran deep and wide. He'd shut them off and built a dam of icy bitterness in his head to stop the hurting. It wouldn't take much to melt that ice and bring the dam crashing down.

"I could love you again, Caity, girl," he whispered. "I could take you and another man's babe as my own, if only I could trust you."

"Ouch! Let go! You're killin' me!" Justice kicked and squirmed, but Caitlin held him firmly by the back of the neck and scrubbed his face until it shone.

"You're to wash your face and hands before coming to the table," she insisted. "And brush your teeth and comb your hair."

"Comb your teeth!" Derry echoed, then burst into a merry giggle.

It was quarter after seven by the watch Caitlin had hung around her neck. She'd been up since five, and she'd attacked the kitchen dirt between patting up round loafs of soda bread and preparing a pot of tea and a large duck-egg omelet.

Caitlin had pushed the leg-of-mutton sleeves of her russet morning gown above her elbows and tied an apron around her waist to protect the delicate cotton percale. She'd braided her hair and coiled the heavy mass into a bun, crowning it with a tiny lace cap, once as white as sea foam but now faded to old ivory. Shane had ridiculed her stylish clothing, but this was the plainest dress she owned. It had been more than five years since she'd ordered a new gown, and her fashions—though made of good cloth and lace—were sadly out of date.

Caitlin released her hold on Justice, and he slid sullenly onto the back bench on the far side of the trestle table. She'd set it with a linen table cover, her mother's blue and white delftware plates, and silver spoons and forks. She'd been unable to find her knives. Either they were in her other trunks back in town or someone had stolen them.

She went back to the hearth and slid the hot loaves of bread onto a plate. She'd found no butter or jam in the kitchen larder, only a tin of syrup. Quickly she sliced the bread and served the children generous sections of omelet. "Will you have tea with your breakfast, Justice?" she asked him.

He jabbed at the eggs with a fork and didn't answer.

"Milk!" Derry proclaimed, grinning until two dimples popped out on her rosy cheeks. Caitlin had dressed her in a light wool dress of red tartan with red lace-trimmed pantalettes. Derry's black hair was neatly braided and tied with tartan bows to match the dress. "I want milk!" she clamored, scratching at her button nose. "Milk!"

"No milky," Mary said. She sat, arms folded over her chest, in the rocking chair. Her coppery face wrinkled in disapproval as she chewed at the stem of the unlit pipe. "Justice like coffee. Tea blaah. Tea for sick boy."

"This is very good tea, Mary. I brought it with me from Ireland."

"McKenna no drinky tea. Drink coffee. No likey eggs mix up like pudding."

"Berry drinky tea," the toddler exclaimed. "Good." She pursed her rosebud mouth and nodded firmly.

"Only a small cup, precious," Caitlin said, kissing the crown of Derry's head. She did indulge the child with tea, laced liberally with milk. At home, she'd seen Maureen give the babe tea to dull her hunger. Here in America, with food abundant, tea would be a much rationed treat for Derry and not an everyday drink.

"I don't like this stuff," Justice said, dropping a forkful of egg on his plate. "This bread tastes funny."

"Wait for grace to be said, Justice," Caitlin admonished gently. "Didn't Shane . . . your father . . . teach you to—"

"I haven't taught myself much in the way of prayers," Shane said.

Caitlin turned to see him filling the doorway, and her heartbeat quickened. "Shane. I was just going to call you for breakfast."

"Coffee?" Mary asked.

"Sure." He splashed water on his face.

"I've made a pot of tea," Caitlin said. "I thought you—"

"Coffee." Mary pushed a dented tin cup into his hand. "Coffee good," she said. "Tea ba-ad."

"Not ba-ad," Derry said. "Good tea!"

Caitlin took her seat at the end of the table. "When you're ready, Shane. Mary, will you join us?"

The Indian woman shook her head. "No eat egg pudding. Fried egg. Coffee."

"Is Gabriel coming in for breakfast?" Caitlin asked. She'd wanted this first morning together to be special. She even wished she'd had the time to pick wildflowers for the table.

Shane sat down, and Caitlin murmured a simple blessing. Derry began to eat heartily. Justice played with his slice of bread while Shane sipped at his coffee.

"Did you see anyone in the night?" Caitlin asked. "Are you going to report yesterday's shooting to the local constable?"

"No to both questions," Shane answered. He took a slice of her soda bread and carefully spread syrup on it. She waited while he took a bite.

"Did I put in too much salt?" she asked anxiously.

"No, it's good," he replied. "Very good. Brings back a lot of memories."

She smiled. "Thank you."

"You brought all this stuff with you?" He indicated the table settings and the linen.

"Yes, I did."

"No wonder your trunks were so heavy."

Justice glanced at her and flashed a taunting hint of a smile. Standing up, he pushed back from the table. His hand caught the edge of the barely tasted plate of breakfast and knocked it to the floor.

"Oh!" Caitlin flinched at the sound of breaking delftware.

"Sorry," the boy called as he fled toward the door. Mary shoved a piece of cold fry bread into his hand, and he vanished outside.

Barely containing her anger, Caitlin knelt to pick up the broken sections of the plate. The original set, made in Dublin as part of her grandmother's wedding dowry, had consisted of twelve place settings. The beautiful delftware had survived two generations without harm and come to Caitlin on her mother's death. Since then, two of the precious plates had been cracked on the journey from Ireland, and the deliberate breaking of this one meant that there were only nine left.

"It was an accident, Caity," Shane said. "He didn't mean it."

"He meant to do it, all right," she replied.

"You should have kept it packed away for good use only. A farm kitchen's no place for such—"

"It's our kitchen, Shane!" she cried passionately. "Our kitchen. Why shouldn't the children eat off nice plates? They shouldn't be brought up like ignorant wild things."

"You think I bring my son up like an animal?"

Caitlin's throat constricted. "You're not being fair."

"Me? Or is it you, to cast blame on a boy for breaking a dish?" He pushed back his own plate. He'd taken no more than a few bites of the omelet.

"I'm trying, Shane," she said. "Can't you see that I'm trying?"

"Try a little harder." He raised his cup and Mary refilled it with coffee.

Caitlin stared down at her own breakfast. She'd been ravenous, but now she couldn't eat a bite. They were fighting again, and that was the last thing she wanted. "I'm sorry," she said, "but this delft was my grandmother's. The set means so much to—"

"You put too much store in things," he said tersely. "Go easy with your changes. We're used to doing things our way here on Kilronan."

"I'm sure you are." But would there ever be a place there for her?

Shane took another sip of his coffee.

Caitlin glanced at the spot where Derry had been sitting, but it was empty. "Derry?" Caitlin looked under the table to see if the child was hiding there. "Where did she get to?" she asked Shane.

Mary pointed toward the open door. "She follow boy."

Caitlin went to the step. "Derry? Where are you?"

Shane came to the door. "Look in the backyard," he said. "She's probably after that duck again."

"Fleurblanche," Mary put in. "Mary's duck. You no let baby chase duck."

Caitlin walked around behind the house and called the little girl's name again.

"Still haven't found her?" Shane asked. He put his hat on his head and pulled it down to shade his eyes. "I'll check the barnyard. Justice!" he shouted. "Have you seen Derry anywhere?"

Caitlin walked faster. How could the child have vanished into thin air? "Derry?" Caitlin rounded the corner of the house. Near the smaller stable, two hens scratched in the dirt. A horse stood with its head resting on the top rail of a fence. Nothing else moved but the clouds overhead. "Derry!"

Shane appeared at the entrance to the barn. He shook his head. "Not in here. Neither of them."

Mary came out the front door and hurried toward the far pound. "Fleurblanche have nest in Goliath's pen," she said.

Caitlin followed her. "I don't see why the duck—" Suddenly Derry wailed, and instantly her cry of fear was muffled by the bellow of an angry bull.

"Derry!" Caitlin cried. Fear washed through her as she broke into a run.

Shane caught hold of her arm at the edge of the six-foot-high stockade fence, but she threw herself against the wall and peered through the space between two logs. On the far side of the enclosed compound Caitlin saw a lean-to stable open on one side. The only gate to the enclosure was a stout wooden door with a foot-high gap beneath it, adjoining the shed.

In the left corner of the log structure, half hidden in the straw, a tearful Derry crouched clutching at the white duck. Between the child and the fence stood a massive roan-and-white bull with huge curving horns.

Caitlin stared in terror as the beast shook himself from snout to tail and pawed the earth with one black-tipped hoof. The bull's hindquarters were turned toward them, his bulging, black eyes focused on the tiny girl in red.

Caitlin dug her nails into the rough logs until two snapped off at the quick. But she didn't feel the pain, and she didn't need Shane's urgent "Shhh!" to be still. Instinct told her that any sudden sound might spook the bull to gore Derry with those terrible horns or to trample her to death.

How tiny Derry looked. How helpless. Caitlin wanted to close her eyes and shut out the horror, but she couldn't tear her gaze away.

An odd buzzing filled her brain and seconds lengthened to eternity as she watched Shane curl lean fingers around the top of an upright post. His frame tensed, and Caitlin realized that he meant to scale the fence rather than take the precious time to run around to the gate.

"No!" Mary's warning came from a few yards away. "Look!" She pointed to the bull.

Goliath snorted. His white-rimmed eyes rolled in his

great head, and the shiny black skin on his nose wrinkled. Slowly he swung his heavy head to look away from Derry.

The duck squawked and gave one flap of his wings as he broke free of the toddler's arms and half flew, half ran across the high-walled pound.

The bull ignored the duck. He pawed the ground again, sending up puffs of dust, and made a short feint toward the shed.

"Wait!" Mary commanded.

Wait for what? Caitlin screamed silently. Wait for the baby to be killed before our eyes?

Derry wept hysterically, deep sobs that racked her small body, and shook a minute fist at the bull. "No!" she cried. "No!" Thrashing in the tangled straw, the child finally managed to rise to her feet. Caitlin's heart broke as Derry tried to run, fell again, and cried out for her. "Ma-ma!"

Caitlin felt the hot Missouri sun on her face and smelled the acrid scent of urine. The red of the bull's hide and the dusty gray of the earth blurred before her eyes. Her mouth tasted of metal and dust. "Derry," she whispered. "No, don't run. For the love of God, don't move."

"I'm going after her," Shane said. He jammed the toe of his boot in a crack in the fence, but in the split second before he leaped, a stone struck the bull's nose.

"Hey! Hey!" Justice shouted. "Bull turd! Weeny pizzle!" Another rock flew through the air.

Goliath threw up his head and bellowed in rage. Behind him, between the animal and the open shed, Caitlin saw Justice leaping up and down and heaving stones for all he was worth.

"Justice!" Shane yelled. "Get the hell out of there!"

"Na-na-na-na-na!" the boy taunted, and hurled another stone.

Shane launched himself over the fence as the bull wheeled and charged toward Justice.

Chapter 6

Shane landed on his feet on the far side of the fence and raced, bare-handed, toward the bull. "Goliath! Here!" he shouted. "Here!"

Seemingly unaware of the man's presence, the bull pounded after the boy. Sweeping the broad head low, he tried to impale Justice on the gleaming ivory tips of his horns. The boy dodged and ran back toward the wall as Shane leaped onto the bull's back and tried to grip his horns.

Caitlin caught only a glimpse of Justice as the bull tossed Shane to the ground and charged the boy a second time. Shane rolled and scrambled to his feet, instantly going after the animal again.

Goliath ground to a sliding halt amid a cloud of dust and eyed the boy. White-faced and trembling, Justice backed up until his escape was blocked by the wall of upright posts.

Caitlin could hear Mary yelling for Gabriel to bring a gun, but Caitlin knew that there would be no time. Whatever happened in the next few seconds would mean life or death for Shane and the children, and it would be over before anyone could help. Snorting angrily, the animal lowered his head and raised his hindquarters, tensing his muscles to charge again. His front hooves dug the ground, and foam dripped from his gaping mouth.

Derry's screams shrilled above the thunder of Goliath's bellow, but Caitlin could only watch in stunned silence.

Unbelievably, Shane seized the bull's horns. Goliath bucked wildly, but Shane clung on and slid under the animal's neck. Through the rising dust, Caitlin saw Shane brace his boot heels against the ground. He twisted the bull's head up and back. And then one horn slipped free and Goliath began to run, dragging Shane along with him.

As bull and man fought their way across the compound, Justice dashed into the shed. The boy snatched Derry around the middle and made a run for the gate.

Caitlin ran around the outside of the pound to the door, but before she could lift the heavy bar, the bull smashed against the gate. She cried out and jumped back, too frightened to breathe. When she pressed her face to a crack in the fence, she saw Shane sprawled in the center of the corral and the bull stamping into the open stable. One of Derry's hair ribbons lay trampled in the dirt, but she couldn't locate either child.

"Derry! Justice!" she screamed.

The bull slammed into something solid, and Caitlin heard wood splinter. Derry had stopped crying. "Don't be dead," Caitlin whispered hoarsely. "Please, don't be dead, baby." Crazed beyond fear, she raised the bar and swung the gate wide. Ripping off her apron, she waved it across the entrance and screamed at the bull.

Goliath turned and stared at the flapping apron. He was panting heavily, and blood trickled from one ear. The animal took a quick, running hop toward the gate, and Caitlin balled up the white cloth and threw it outside of the paddock on the grass. The bull took another step and peered suspiciously at the object. When he began to trot toward the open gate, Caitlin ducked into the space behind the door and held her breath.

Her blood pounded in her ears. She knew that her skirts and shoes and stockings showed under the door, but there was no place else to hide. Seconds passed without a sound from the children. "Please," Caitlin whispered again. "Please."

The gate hinges groaned as the bull lumbered through the opening, brushing against the door with his shoulder. Caitlin smelled the heavy stench of the animal and saw one white hind leg and his dung-caked tail as he broke into a gallop and thundered through the barnyard.

Caitlin ran into the pound and her knees went weak. Shane still hadn't moved. "Not you," she murmured. "I can't lose you."

She ached to run to him, to cradle his head in her lap and kiss his bearded face, but she wouldn't let herself. Instead, Caitlin straightened her back and walked into the shed. She prepared herself for the worst.

"Mama." Derry's dirty face peered from the space beneath a soapstone water trough.

"Derry? You're all right?" Caitlin dropped to her knees and pulled the squirming child out of her hiding spot hugging her tightly to her breast.

Justice wiggled out right behind Derry. His shirt was shredded from shoulder to waist, and both knees in his trousers were split. A purple bruise bulged over one dark eye. "Whew! I thought he had us," the boy said.

"You're not hurt?" Caitlin demanded.

Justice shook his head. "I tease that ole bull all the time, but he never done that before." The child's eyes were still dilated with fright, but he tried to cover his fear with a forced smile.

"You saved Derry's life." Caitlin didn't want to let go

of the little girl. The children were both safe. She was free to go to Shane, but it was hard to summon the courage. What if she'd lost him before they even knew each other again? What if she'd come all this way to have him die in front of her?

Steeling herself, Caitlin released Derry and turned back toward the dusty enclosure where her husband lay so still. "Keep Derry here," she said. "Shane's hurt." She couldn't say that Shane might be dead.

On weak knees, she crossed to Shane's sprawled body, shivering despite the late morning heat.

"Son of a bitch," Justice swore, and ran past Caitlin.

"No!" she cried. "Don't—"

Just as the boy reached him, Shane groaned and rolled over. Caitlin dropped to her knees in the dirt beside him.

Justice looked as though he was about to burst into tears. "That ole bull stomped you, huh?"

"Shane . . ." Caitlin whispered. "Oh, Shane . . ."

He coughed and raised a hand to his bruised forehead. Just above his temple, a lump the size of a pigeon's egg rose beneath his damp hair. And blood oozed from a jagged cut on his left cheek, soaking his beard and trickling down his neck.

"Lie still," Caitlin warned. "Your head—"

"Feels like I've been trampled by twelve hundred pounds of bull." Shane closed his eyes, then snapped them open. "Your girl? Derry? Is she—"

"Derry's fine, thanks to you . . . and Justice." Caitlin took hold of his hand and turned it over. Shane's callused palms were raw, dirt and gravel ground into his flesh. In places the skin hung in shreds.

Tears clouded Caitlin's vision. "That was the bravest thing I've ever seen. You both saved Derry's life."

"Bravest? Or the most foolhardy." Shane tried to sit

up, but he seemed to lack the strength. He let his eyes drift shut, then snapped them open again. "Where's . . . where's the bull?" he slurred.

"Derry shouldn't have been in the bull pen," Justice said.

"It's all right," Caitlin soothed as she put her hands on Shane's shoulders and pressed him back. "Don't move."

Shane groaned and took in a ragged breath.

"Stay still," Caitlin ordered. "You could be hurt worse than you realize. Let me get a wet cloth for—"

"Shit, that ain't nothin'," Justice said. "He won't let a little bump like that slow him down."

"I'm fine," Shane mumbled. "Watch your mouth, boy. There are ladies—"

"Mind what you say or I'll wash your mouth out with soap," Caitlin threatened.

Justice glared at her.

Shane groaned and rolled over onto his hands and knees. "You heard . . . what your mother said."

"She ain't my mother."

"Let me up, woman." Shane pushed her hands away and rose unsteadily to his feet. He swayed drunkenly and looked around. "Where's Goliath?"

"She turned him loose," Justice answered. "Just opened the gate and let him run."

"Smart." Shane took another deep breath. "Shoulda thought of that . . . myself." He put both hands over his face and struggled to remain upright. "Dizzy," he muttered.

"What can you be thinking of?" Caitlin put an arm around Shane to steady him. "You must get into bed. That cut needs a physician's attention. Someone must go for—"

"A long ride he'd have," Gabriel said. He and Mary

had come up behind Caitlin so quietly that she hadn't heard them. Handing a rifle to Mary, the wrangler took Shane's other arm and supported his weight. "The nearest doctor is at Johnson's Ferry."

"I wouldn't let Doc Phebe put a hand . . . on my dead dog—if I had a dog," Shane said. "And I can walk, damn it. I don't need . . . the two of you to carry me."

"We see how good you walk." Mary took her pipe from her mouth and spit in the dirt. "Missy-Wife right. You belong bed."

Caitlin looked up into Shane's face as they led him toward the gate. His eyes were dilated and glazed, and that frightened her. "Surely the physician could—" she began.

"I said I'll not have him," Shane argued.

"Why not?" Caitlin asked.

Shane sucked in a ragged breath, and she could see by his breathing that his ribs were probably injured as well. "Don't trust him."

"What's wrong with him?" Caitlin demanded.

"Stupid," Justice said. "Dumb as cow pies."

"The boy's right," Shane said. "Mary can sew me up." He clenched his teeth, and his face took on the color of tallow.

Caitlin winced as she felt the grating of bone under his skin. "You've a broken rib."

"More than one I'd guess." Shane looked at Gabriel. "Where's my two-hundred-dollar bull now?"

"Hightailin' it across the west pasture. He busted down three rails and jumped the bottom one. I thought I might have to shoot him, until he caught the scent of those heifers."

"That should hold him." Shane nodded.

Caitlin glanced back at Justice. "Bring Derry for me, please."

Derry ran to Mary and clasped her hand. "Ba-ad moo cow," the little girl said. "Chasey my duck."

"Mary's duck," Mary corrected sternly.

Derry went on chattering. "I chasey ba-ad moo-cow," she said. "I firstey."

"Mary find you something to drink," Mary answered. Then she said something too low for Caitlin to hear, and Derry giggled.

The distance from the pound to the house seemed vast to Caitlin as they half led, half carried a semiconscious Shane inside and up to his bedchamber. Even with their assistance, he could barely manage the stairs. Once they had Shane on his bed, Caitlin instructed Gabriel to fetch soap and warm water.

The cowboy scowled, and for a moment Caitlin thought he was going to refuse to obey her orders, but then Shane opened his eyes and gestured toward the door.

"Best you do as she says," he grated hoarsely. "She'll give us no peace if you don't."

She waited until Gabe left the room, then tugged off one of Shane's boots. Her hands were still trembling from shock, but if she kept moving, she could hold off the terror of what might have been. She couldn't close her eyes for fear of seeing the bull, and she wouldn't allow herself to think that she could easily have been washing Shane for his burial.

Caitlin wished that she had time to go off alone for a good cry, but there was none. For all Shane's protests of being all right, he worried her. He was in more pain than he admitted, and his head wound might be serious. She couldn't understand why he was unwilling to send for the doctor. Any physician would know more about an injury to the head than she did.

"Stop fussin' over me," Shane growled. "I don't need fussing over."

Ignoring his grumbling, she pulled off his other boot and both clean, crudely patched stockings. Shane's high-arched feet were clean as well, his toenails trimmed neatly. Praise God, Caitlin thought, for she doubted if she could live with a pigsty of a husband.

"I don't need you undressin' me," he said. "Mary can do what needs doin'."

"I'm your wife, Shane. It's my place to—"

"I've got a bump on my head. I'm no invalid." He raised his head, grimaced, and sank back. "Can't you make this room stop buckin'?" he said, trying to make light of his dizziness.

"Shhh. Don't try to talk." Caitlin pressed him back against the folded saddle blanket that substituted for a pillow. He closed his eyes and gritted his teeth.

"You need to lie still, before you bleed all over your bed."

His breathing came shallow but steady. She laid a palm on his forehead. His skin felt cool, but she didn't know if that was a good sign or a bad one. His head was still bleeding, but it seemed to her as though the cut was clotting.

"Where is that Gabriel with the water?" she murmured nervously. "I need to wash the dirt out of this before it becomes infected."

Shane muttered something unintelligible, and he seemed to drift off again.

A small sound of concern passed Caitlin's lips as she glanced around the room. Shane's bedchamber was as spartan as a monk's cell, containing little more than a bed, a few articles of clothing hung on hand-whittled oak pegs, another pair of boots, and a single straight-backed chair fashioned of peeled branches. A saddle slung over a trunk, and a pair of deer antlers with a silver crucifix dangling from it were the only other items of note in the room.

Well, Caitlin mused wryly, you've brought no sporting woman to this room. Of that much I can be certain.

She looked back at Shane and was relieved to see that his color seemed to be returning. He had a concussion, she reasoned, and a few cracked ribs. God willing, that was all.

Shyly she reached out to touch a curling lock of his dark hair. It was as soft as she remembered it. "Ah, Shane," she whispered too low for him to hear. In some ways he was the same under that rough exterior. She wondered how his fair hair had turned so dark in the years since they'd last laid eyes on each other.

Shane seemed asleep, and the idea that she could gaze at him and even touch him without his knowledge made her bold. She skimmed her fingertips lightly over his cheek, marveling at the scratchy texture of his beard. His whiskers had tickled her when they'd kissed. It hadn't been an unpleasant sensation, but different.

Not that beards were uncommon among men. To the contrary, most males old enough to lift a glass of spirits grew them. Her own father had worn a beard, and since she'd come to America, she'd seen few white men clean shaven. Still, the Shane she'd married had worn neither beard nor mustache.

Thoughtfully she studied the bloody gouge on Shane's face. Cleaning that wound would be easier without whiskers in the way, and doubtless it would heal faster.

Her reverie was interrupted by the squeak of the door hinges. Caitlin gave a little start and turned to see Mary staring at her.

"Mary bring needle. Sew head." The Indian woman carried an empty basin, a cloth that had known better times, and a needle large enough to sew canvas. Curled in a loop over her thumb was a length of sticky yellow string.

"What is that?" Caitlin demanded suspiciously.

Gabriel followed Mary into the room. "That's sinew, for stitching McKenna up." He placed a pail of steaming water on the floor and beat a hasty retreat from the sickroom.

Caitlin glanced at Shane and then back at Mary. "No, I don't think so," she pronounced firmly. "If you will please look after the children, I'll see to my husband's injuries."

Mary frowned with disapproval. "Mary do," she insisted.

"No, Mary will not do." Caitlin stepped between Shane and the housekeeper. "That needle is . . ." She trailed off and shook her head. "I assure you, I'm quite capable. I cared for both of my parents in their final illnesses."

Mary grunted and shifted her pipe from one corner of her mouth to the other. "Mary good medicine woman. Much heal."

"I'm sure you are. But I can do this."

Mary shrugged and with a final sniff of contempt, she deposited her basin and rag beside Gabriel's bucket and shuffled out of the room.

Caitlin's feeling of triumph was short-lived. She knew she had her own sewing basket with silk thread and tiny needles, but where would she find a man's razor? And what was she supposed to use for disinfectant and bandages?

She would need help. Her own stubborn pride couldn't stand in the way of what was best for Shane. Doubts piled one upon the other in her mind, and she shivered. What if Mary did know more than she did?

"Mary said you needed me," Justice said, appearing without warning in the open doorway. "Is he gonna be all right?"

"He's going to be fine," Caitlin replied with more confidence than she felt. "Can you get me a razor and some soap? No, forget the soap; I have some in my luggage. I'll need more of that whiskey from the barn and—"

"Ain't no more firewater."

"Isn't any more," she corrected.

"'S what I said. Ain't no more."

"Never mind." She had a little cherry brandy in a flask. It was probably six years old at least, but it would have to do. She'd tear up one of her cotton chemises for bandages and . . .

Caitlin glanced back at the boy. Despite his feigned disdain, she could read concern in his eyes. Justice might have a rude tongue, but he was intelligent, and he had nerve. He'd risked his life for Derry, hadn't he?

"Hurry," she said. "If you want to help me do what's best for Shane, follow my instructions. Otherwise, you'll just be in the way."

The boy walked to Shane's side and touched his arm. "He ain't gonna die, is he?" he asked. "I seen a man die one time from a knock on the head. Course his skull was cracked wide open."

"Well, Shane's skull may be a little shaken, but it's not cracked. And he's not going to die."

"That's what he said about my mother," the boy murmured softly. 'You're not dyin' on me,' McKenna said. But she did. Bled to death in his arms." He looked up at Caitlin with eyes too old for a child. "Grown-ups lie to kids."

"Not this time," she promised.

"Swear?"

"Yes," she answered with a catch in her throat. "I swear I won't let Shane die."

Chapter 7

"You're not dying on me."

Shane heard the words from far off. They lodged in his mind and kept tumbling like dry brush balls on the open prairie: *not dyin' on me . . . not dying . . .* He'd said them. He remembered saying them to someone he loved.

His head ached, and he had to fight to hold his breakfast down, but he knew he wasn't going to die from a glancing blow to the head. He'd had worse done to him and survived . . . far worse.

Shane knew where he was. He knew his own name and what day it was. He even knew who was in the room with him. He could feel the mattress under him and hear what Caity and Justice were saying to each other. He was certain he could get up off the bed if he really wanted to. He could . . . It was just simpler to lie there in the warm blackness until this spell of weariness passed.

Caity's hand felt good on his skin. It had been a long time since anyone had fussed over him. He didn't want to worry her, but opening his eyes would take more effort than he wanted to give.

Just a little longer, he told himself. I'll just rest a little longer.

The darkness enveloped him, and his surroundings faded, all but the words that kept coming back to haunt him. "You're not dying on me." His words, but not his voice. Whose voice? *Not dyin'. . .*

Cerise felt so warm in his arms. She couldn't be dying, not Cerise. Instantly sober, he cradled her against him while her blood ran over his hands and soaked her green satin dancing dress.

He couldn't stop the bleeding. He pressed his palm hard against the wound under her breast, but blood just kept seeping through his fingers, and she kept begging him not to let her die.

"I'm scared, Shane. Hold me. Please . . . hold me. If I die . . . If I die, I'm going straight to hell. I don't want to burn in hell. I'm afraid of fire."

"You're not goin' to die, damn it!" he swore. "I won't let you."

"I'm cold, Irishman. I'm cold. It can't be hell if I'm cold, can it?"

"No. No, sweet, it's not hell."

"Hold me. . . . Hold me."

Light flared from a lamp as the door crashed open. A whore screamed, and the hall echoed with angry shouting.

"Oh, my God!"

"It's Cerise!"

"McKenna stabbed her!"

"Somebody get Fat Rose, quick!"

Cerise sighed in his arms. Her dark, liquid eyes opened wide, and she gazed up into his face. "Justice. Take my boy, Shane. Promise me you'll—"

"Promise?" Justice demanded.

The loud voices retreated into memory. Shane was suddenly conscious of how much his head throbbed and his body ached.

"Cerise?" Her name formed on his lips, and saying it aloud opened a cavern in his chest he'd blocked up a long time ago. For an instant, Cerise's image—as she was that first night in Jefferson—rose in his mind's eye.

Amid the smoke and clamor of Fat Rose's whorehouse, a vision of fire and passion moved to the haunting throb of a Spanish guitar. A man couldn't call what she was doing dancing, at least not dancing as he had ever seen it.

All fire and passion ... flying night-black hair and come-hither eyes ... Salome of the seven veils and all the wantons of Sodom and Gomorrah wrapped into one lush, copper-skinned body.

He broke into a sweat just watching her.

Around him, men clapped their hands and howled, but he didn't hear them. Every fiber of his being concentrated on the woman in the green striped satin dancing dress as she whirled and thrust, stamped her bare feet, and parted her moist, red lips. Advancing, retreating, teasing, tantalizing ... she made promises with heavy-lidded, almond-shaped eyes ... and dared him with lush, heaving breasts and long, curvaceous legs.

Her pure sensuality stunned him as swiftly as the strike of a bolt of lightning, stealing his breath and scrambling his brain. He wanted her. God, how he wanted her!

He forgot he was a married man ... forgot what she was, and knew only that he had to have her no matter the cost.

"Cerise ..."

"Shane?"

The swirl of the music grew fainter, and the blackness threatened him again. Shane felt himself falling, and instinctively he tightened his arms around Cerise's body.

And to his shock, he embraced thin air.

"Lie still."

Not Cerise's whiskey voice with its faintly French accent ... and not Cerise's scent. She favored a heavy rose, and this woman smelled of heather. He wondered how— "Ouch! Damn it! Are you trying to murder me?" Shane's eyes flew open as he became aware of a sharp, burning ache along the side of his jaw.

Caitlin leaned over him, a bloodstained cloth in her hands. "Welcome back." Her tone was lamb gentle, but her ginger eyes radiated frost. "Congratulations. I won't need to stitch your face."

Dumbly he raised his fingers to his cheek and brushed a shallow cut. "My beard? What have you done to—"

"I had to shave around the injury to tend it," she replied icily. He'd called out another woman's name in his incoherent mumbling. *Cerise.* Justice's mother.

A thin needle of pain pierced through Caitlin's chest and into the pit of her belly. Such a small thing shouldn't hurt. She knew it shouldn't hurt, but it did. She turned away and rinsed the cloth in the basin to keep him from seeing the tears in her eyes.

Damn you to hell, Shane McKenna, she thought. Damn your black, cheating soul to everlasting flames.

Fool. She was the fool to expect otherwise when they'd been apart so long. Hadn't he tried to tell her the truth? Said that he was no saint?

Ruthlessly she wrung out the washcloth she'd ripped from a worn cotton petticoat. How she wished that she had her sister Maureen or a woman friend here in Missouri she could confide in, who could give her advice. She was alone with no one to trust—least of all her husband.

She'd tried to ignore her suspicions about Shane and Justice's mother, but her worst fears were probably true. She was sure that Shane had been intimate with Cerise, maybe even in love with her. Shane's affection for another woman seemed worse to her than his committing adultery.

Caitlin wondered how many times Shane had made

love to Cerise. Pricks of jealousy made her want to jab him with the needle out of pure malice.

She and Shane had known each other in the biblical sense only once. No, twice, she supposed, if she counted the hasty coming together just before he'd left her at daybreak on the morning after their wedding. She'd been frightened, and Shane had been awkward. She'd liked him holding her, and she'd loved the feeling of his bare skin against hers. But the actual sex had been . . . well . . . uncomfortable.

She'd often wondered if her innocence had been to blame. She wanted desperately to be a good wife to Shane, and she'd supposed that whatever had gone wrong with their wedding night could be corrected in time.

Still, the intensity of her resentment over Shane's involvement with this woman Cerise shocked her. Caitlin thought that she was practical and not given to spitefulness, but it was a slap in the face to find that her husband expected her to raise his lover's son as her own.

He'd asked a lot of her, damn it. Maybe more than she could give.

Shane sat up and swung his legs over the side of the bed. "Why the hell did you shave half of my face?"

Justice snickered and backed out of the room. "Told you not to do it."

The wound on Shane's head began to bleed again, and Caitlin sighed impatiently as a crimson drop rolled down his forehead and soaked into his eyebrow. "Now see what you've done. Lie down and let me see to that wound on your head."

"What? And let you shave me bald?"

"If you can be difficult, you're going to live," Caitlin answered, fighting to keep her anger hidden. Berating Shane for what he'd done with a dead woman would only harm her chances of making the marriage work. And she desperately wanted it to succeed. She'd have to swallow the hurt and go on as if she didn't suspect Shane's relationship with Justice's mother.

"My head doesn't need sewing," Shane said. "And it sure as hell doesn't need shaving."

"If you're afraid of the needle—"

He glared at her but sat in the chair and let her wash and examine his head gash. "Do your worst."

To Caitlin's relief, the injury was not as severe as it had seemed. She poured a little of her father's cherry brandy into the wound to prevent infection and tied the edges together using strands of Shane's hair.

"This wouldn't have happened if you'd kept Derry away from the bull," he admonished.

"No, I suppose not," she admitted reluctantly. "But it's as clear as the nose on your face that you've had little experience with children." Shane was right, and she knew it. Derry could have been killed, and it would have been her fault.

"I've done all right with Justice."

"He's hardly a normal child. And you've allowed him to use language that would shame a tinker."

Shane nodded. "He's like a wild bronc that's never known a bridle. But the foul talk he picked up in his mother's care. I'm trying to curb it. And maybe I should be harder on him, but it's not easy."

"Neither is being a mother." She gave the last knot a hard tug and Shane winced.

"Why do I get the feeling you're enjoyin' this, woman?"

She tucked the silver flask of brandy back into her petticoat pocket and set about cleaning up. "I meant what I said earlier. You're a brave man, Shane. A braver one I've never seen."

He flushed a little under his tan and rubbed at his eyes.

"My head feels like Goliath's still in there and tryin' to kick his way out."

Caitlin turned her attention to Shane's lacerated hands. He made no protest as she gently soaped first one and then the other. Next she opened a tin box and smeared his torn palms with a paste of comfrey root and goose grease that she'd brought from home.

"I suppose you think that no child has ever come to harm under the hooves of a bull in County Clare?" Caitlin demanded. "Derry was so frightened, I vow she'll not go under any fence again."

Shane's eyes shadowed. "I was wrong to blame you. If one of the kids had been killed or crippled, the fault would have been mine. I knew the danger. You didn't. Maybe I should have left you home with your father."

"Small chance that," Caitlin answered tightly. "My father's dead."

"Dead?" Shane's shocked gaze met hers. "You mentioned the loss of your mother, but you didn't tell me about him."

"And you didn't ask. We've talked of you and Kilronan and what you want, Shane McKenna. But you never asked me about those at home."

"I'm sorry."

She blinked away the stinging irritation in her eyes. "Sorry's just a word. You and Papa were like fire and gunpowder. Don't pretend what you don't feel."

That brought him to his feet. He enveloped her in his arms and pulled her against him. "Caity," he murmured into her hair. "Your father hated the sight of me and with good reason."

"He didn't hate you," she protested. "You were Catholic and poor and—"

"And the son of a penniless drunk who beat his wife

and kids senseless whenever he got a belly full of whiskey."

"It was unfair of Papa to—"

He raised her chin and looked down into her face. "It doesn't matter anymore, Caity," he said gently. "You loved him, and he was a good father to you. How did he die?"

"My mother caught a bad fever and the running flux from a cottar's wife. We buried her on Christmas Eve, two years past. Papa lived until the following spring, but his heart was never strong, and he pined without her."

Caitlin pushed free of Shane's embrace and hurried to tell the rest before she lost her nerve and dissolved into a puddle of tears. "Only Maureen is left besides Derry, Maureen and the new babe she was to bear in April. I've not heard if they survived or not. Her husband was killed in the food riots last summer."

"Food riots?"

Caitlin shrugged. "Lives go cheap in Ireland. Thomas was hired to protect the wheat shipment, but the soldiers shot him in the confusion."

Shane reached out his hand, but she stepped back. She didn't want him to pity her or her family. She only wanted fair treatment and a chance. "We lost the house and land. Papa was only tenant manager to Lord Carlston. The estate hasn't belonged to our family in over a hundred years."

"But your father was well liked by both the English and the Irish. He was a wealthy man in his own right."

"Not wealthy, never wealthy, Shane."

He scoffed. "My father kept his pigs in the single room of our cabin, before he sold them all to buy whiskey. You come from money, Caity, Protestant quality. You've never known what it was to go to bed with your backbone grinding against your empty belly."

"It's more of that old argument," she flung back. "I am the lady of the manor and you're naught but a poor laborer."

He flashed a hint of a wolfish grin. "You forgot unlettered papist. I can write my own name, Caity, nothin' more. And I can't even read the words on my own land deed."

"Horsefeathers. If you're ignorant of learning, then it's up to you to set that right. You'll get no pity from me. How many acres did you boast of owning? Six hundred? You may have come from a dirt-floored cottage, but you're a great landowner now. You are the rich one, Shane, while I have nothing but the clothes on my back and the contents of my trunks."

"You're a lady, and that's not something that can be learned or bought with a few acres of Missouri land."

"What do you want of me, Shane McKenna?"

"What's right for us and the children."

"What's right is our living like true husband and wife."

"Maybe," he said. "I'd like to think that."

"You loved me once." The words came softly, drifting up from a secret place where she'd treasured and protected them.

"That I did, but that was a long time ago. I'd like to think I could feel that way again, but I can't lie to you. I just don't know."

Her chest felt so tight that she could hardly draw breath, hardly speak. "Since you've said it, so shall I. I'm as confused as you, but did we not agree to try to make this work?"

His features hardened. "I sent for you, didn't I?"

"Is that all you can say?"

He shrugged. "I've no pretty words. We can try, but the odds are against us."

"If I'd thought about that before I left home, I'd have

stayed in County Clare. Sometimes a man or a woman has to take risks."

Shane seemed to mull that over for a while. Then he nodded. "All right. I'm no stranger to risks. Finish what you started. Shave off the rest of this beard."

Caitlin couldn't contain a sound of amusement. "You sound like a convicted felon going to his hanging. Do you think I'll cut your throat?"

"You might," he grumbled.

"I used to shave Papa. He found it relaxing."

"Don't push your luck. Just shave the damned whiskers."

She reached for the straight razor. "My pleasure, sir. When you ask so sweetly, how can I refuse?"

He turned his face so that she could soap his other cheek. "I'd do it myself, but my hand's none too steady."

Neither was hers. For all her bravado, she was nervous. Shaving Shane was nothing like performing the service for her father; this was strangely intimate. She kept remembering the feeling of his arms around her and how safe she had felt.

Shane was infuriating, insulting, and she was certain that he'd betrayed her with Cerise. Yet something drew her to him. In spite of everything, she wanted him to hold her again.

"Hold still." Her fingers were trembling slightly, and she didn't want to cut him.

"What are you doin'?"

She jerked back. "Stop yelling at me. You told me to shave—"

"Use the scissors first, woman. Cut the whiskers off close to my skin, then shave them."

"All right." He was impossible. What had made her think she could ever make her peace with such a demanding, egotistical man? She dropped the razor into the bowl and looked around for the scissors.

Soapsuds dripped down Shane's neck onto his shirt, or rather what was left of his shirt.

"Could you take that off?" she asked, pointing to his ruined garment.

Groaning, he stripped the torn shirt off. She winced as she saw the purple bruising along his ribs.

"Satisfied?"

Taking a deep breath, she tried to ignore the wide expanse of heavily muscled male chest and began to clip away his chin whiskers. She worked cautiously, trying not to jump every time Shane complained.

"Aren't you done yet?"

"If you'd sit still, maybe I could finish." Caitlin gritted her teeth and rinsed off the razor. She finished the last of the shaving just as the sound of hoofbeats drifted through the open window. Caitlin went to look out with Shane not a step behind her.

"Look." She counted no less than five men riding toward the house. "We've visitors." She laid the scissors on the windowsill.

"Visitors, hell! That's Earl Thompson, our nearest neighbor." He started for the door. "Keep the colleen inside. There may be trouble."

"But, Shane, you're hurt. You shouldn't—"

"Damn it! For once, Caity, do as I say!"

"Gentlemen, welcome to Kilronan." Caitlin stepped out the front door and smiled at the men on horseback. She'd miscounted from the window. There were six strangers, all carrying weapons strapped to their saddles, and all scowling like Satan's imps at Shane and Gabriel and Justice.

Her men stood shoulder to shoulder; Shane cradled his rifle casually in the crook of his arm.

"I am Caitlin McKenna, Shane's wife," she said graciously. "I'm happy to meet you, Mr. Thompson."

She didn't need Shane to point out which man was Earl Thompson. He was the stocky, no-neck figure on the tall gray horse. Thompson's hair was white, and his face weathered by wind and sun, but he was still in his prime. Caitlin decided that he was a force to be reckoned with.

"Mrs. McKenna." Thompson touched two gnarled fingers to his broad-brimmed hat. "I thought McKenna's wife was in Ireland."

"So she was, sir," Caitlin answered, "but now she is here."

"What happened to you, McKenna?" Earl Thompson asked. "You look like you've been trampled by a herd of buffalo."

"I had a difference of opinion with my bull," Shane said.

A slighter figure chuckled, and Caitlin glanced at him. The young man was clean shaven and wore a hat that obscured most of his face. His hands were small and dirty, and he wore a leather vest over a baggy shirt.

"McKenna's wife, are you? More's the pity." He reined his bay closer to Thompson, and Caitlin noticed a leather whip coiled over his saddle horn. "You'll not last long out here."

Caitlin flushed as she realized the person wasn't a young man, but a female wearing men's trousers. She seemed a few years younger than Caitlin, but it was hard to tell with her dusty face partially hidden and her hair jammed under the worn felt hat.

Caitlin refused to let this bold upstart get the better of her. "Welcome to you, too, Miss . . ." She glanced at Earl Thompson and sensed his amusement. "Miss Thompson, is it? Or is it Mrs. Thompson?"

The woman spat a wad of chewed tobacco on the ground near Caitlin's feet. "Rachel's good enough. Rachel Thompson." She tilted her chin toward the older man. "Big Earl's daughter." She shifted in the saddle and pointed to a sullen-faced man with small eyes and a sparse mustache. "This here's my brother, Beau."

"Enough socializin'." Earl Thompson turned his attention to Shane. "Heard you had a mare foal last night."

"What if we did?" Shane replied.

"Mind if we take a look at it?"

Shane's eyes narrowed. "Make your point, Earl."

"If it's black with a white star, we aim to claim it," Rachel Thompson said.

Justice balled his fists and stepped forward. "The hell you will."

Gabriel laid a hand on the boy's shoulder.

"My mare, my filly," Shane said quietly. "You got a problem, I'd take it kindly if we'd settle it man to man."

"What?" Rachel demanded. "You don't want her to know that you bred your mare to our stud without paying the stud fee?"

"Shut up, girl," Earl Thompson snapped. "This is between McKenna and me."

"Don't want your woman to know you're a thief as well as a murderer?" Beau taunted Shane.

"Not my woman, my wife." Shane glanced at Caitlin. "Go inside, Caity. Now."

Gooseflesh rose on her arms. Twice before she'd heard that soft tone, once just before Shane had attacked the drunk in the City of Jefferson and again before he leaped a six-foot fence and confronted Goliath. She suspected that it wouldn't take much for Shane to lose his temper and drag Beau Thompson off his horse and pound him into the dirt.

Shane was in no condition to fight. She didn't know how he was staying on his feet.

Caitlin could see that Thompson and his minions carried rifles. Maybe they were the ones who'd shot at Shane, and now they'd come here to finish him off.

"In the house, Caity," Shane repeated quietly.

"She don't look much like a wife to me," Beau crowed. "Sure she ain't another fancy woman like—"

Shane slammed his rifle into Justice's hands and lunged at Beau.

Chapter 8

"No!" Caitlin tried to grab Shane's arm, but he was too fast for her.

At the same instant Shane charged Beau, Earl snatched the bull whip off Rachel's saddle and spurred his big gray horse between the two men. Earl slammed the coiled whip against the side of Beau's head, and the younger Thompson toppled off his horse onto the ground.

"Haven't I taught you better manners, boy?" Earl roared amid the stamping and snorting of the spooked horses. "Are you too damned stupid to tell a lady from a whore?"

One of Thompson's cowboys swore as his horse reared. Another yanked his mount's head up hard and reined the animal back away from Beau's gelding. Rachel sat straight-backed in her saddle and stared stone-faced at Gabriel.

Caitlin bit her lower lip and tried to keep from saying words that no lady should ever think—let alone speak. *They were all mad as May butter, the lot of them!*

Why had she ever come to this wild place where honest men were shot at in ambush and women dressed like common cowhands?

Too angry to be frightened, Caitlin slipped her arm

under Shane's. "There's no need for violence. My husband is no thief, Mr. Thompson. If you believe otherwise, you're greatly mistaken."

Shane shook off her hand and glared up at Earl. "I don't need your help to defend my wife's honor."

Shane's voice was low and deliberate, but Caitlin felt the air around them vibrate with imminent danger.

"Don't tell me how to raise my son," Earl answered gruffly. "But your wife has my apologies. It ain't the Thompson way to insult ladies." Earl's eyes were hard as river stones in his grizzled face as he touched the brim of his hat and nodded to Caitlin. "Ma'am."

"I accept," Caitlin answered.

The older man's harsh gaze flicked back to Shane. "If Beau forgets his manners to your missus again, that'll be the last filth out of his mouth. You have my word on it."

Beau picked himself up off the ground and climbed groggily back into the saddle. Blood trickled from the corner of his mouth, and a purple welt rose from the outer corner of his left eye to his chin.

Rachel's lips curved in a faint smile of mockery as she watched her brother wipe the blood off his face with his shirtsleeve. Her father tossed her back the whip, and she wrapped it around the saddle horn again.

Caitlin fought to retain her composure. "I am Mr. McKenna's lawful wife," she said to Earl in a strained voice. "What your son thinks or says to me is irrelevant. I have never concerned myself with the opinions of the ignorant."

Earl nodded solemnly. "I never doubted you were who you claimed to be, ma'am, a lady and a wife."

Beau hunched down in the saddle and scowled at his father as the other cowhands edged their horses away from him. Only one man, a sour-faced cowboy with an unshaven face and a drooping eyelid, remained at Beau's side.

"Since you're here," Shane said, "you've saved me a trip. Somebody tried to kill me the other night. The shot came from Thompson land."

"You accusin' me?" Big Earl demanded.

"My fences are bein' pulled down, calves slaughtered. Whoever's behind it comes from your direction."

"It ain't me," Earl answered.

"Glad to know it," Shane said. "Because when I catch them, I mean to put a bullet through them."

Big Earl nodded. "Same as I would do. But I can tell you, we've been hit, too. A blooded brood mare is missin'. And we've lost near a hundred head of cattle since Christmas."

"Did we come here to argue over a few stray cows?" Beau asked. "Or did we come to fetch home our rightful property?"

"I'd like to take a look at that foal," Big Earl said.

"My foal," Shane warned. "Try to take it off Kilronan and that makes you a horse thief. The man who touches my horseflesh won't live long enough to hang."

A cold chill raised the hair on the back of Caitlin's neck. What kind of man had Shane become, that he could threaten to kill another over a foal?

"Does that go for me?" Rachel pushed up the brim of her sweat-stained hat. "I don't think you'll shoot me, McKenna. I don't think you've got the sand to try."

"Nobody's stealin' our filly!" Justice shouted.

Caitlin turned to see the boy level Shane's rifle at Earl Thompson. "Get your crew off Kilronan before I blow you to hell."

"Put that gun down!" Shane ordered.

Gabriel snatched the rifle away from Justice.

"That was a fool's trick," Shane admonished. Then he looked back at Earl. "It seems both our sons lack common sense."

"Son, hell. That ain't your son," the rancher replied. "That's nothin' but a snot-nosed Indian bastard. Your uncle would be turnin' over in his grave if he knew that you were pinnin' the McKenna name on a half-breed."

Caitlin saw the muscles tense along Shane's jawline. "Now it is you who are forgetting your manners, Mr. Thompson," she said frostily. "Justice is our son, as legally a McKenna as I am."

"That don't settle our problem over the filly," Rachel said. "Our prize stallion, Natchez, marks ever one of his foals. Black hide, white star. If your filly fits that description, it's ours by right."

"Come on, boys," Earl said. "We'll just take a look in McKenna's barn."

"Your stallion may well have fathered that foal," Shane said. "But I didn't tear down the fence between our land. And I doubt if a rustler would take the trouble."

"You do think we're behind the shootin'," Rachel answered.

Shane shrugged. "Maybe."

"Bull—" Earl's wrinkled face flushed puce. "Manure," he finished lamely with a quick glance at Caitlin. "Your uncle knew me for twenty years, McKenna. Have you ever heard of me backshootin' a man?"

Shane shrugged. "I don't think it's you personal."

"You think Big Earl ordered it done?" Rachel asked. Her voice was rough like a man's, and Caitlin wondered again what kind of woman she was. "Nobody shoots anything on Thompson land without his say-so."

"I guess we both have a pretty good idea what we think of each other," Earl growled. Then he motioned to his daughter. "Take a look at that new filly. If it's got a white star, we're takin' it home with us."

"You lay a hand on my animal and—" Shane broke off with an oath as the cowboy with the drooping eyelid pulled a pistol from his belt and aimed it at Shane's chest. "Damn you, Nate Bone, I warned you to stay off Kilronan."

The man grinned, exposing a broken picket fence of blackened teeth. "I work for Big Earl, not you, McKenna. You or Gabe move so much as a finger, and I'll blow a hole in you that yer missus kin drive an ox through."

Rachel turned her horse toward the stable. Not knowing what else to do, Caitlin followed.

"Wait," Caitlin said as the woman dismounted.

"Your man ain't stole no breedin', you ain't got nothin' to worry about."

"Please, if you'd just listen to me," Caitlin insisted. "Surely neighbors don't need to fight over—"

Rachel yanked open the barn door, and Caitlin's mouth went dry. Would Shane try to fight all these armed men when Rachel saw the white star on the new foal's head?

She had only her husband's word that he wasn't responsible for breeding the mare to Thompson's stallion. Could the accusation be true? Once she would have insisted that Shane would never be dishonest, but now she was no longer certain of anything about him.

It was dim inside the stable after the bright sunlight, but Caitlin didn't need to see clearly. Star's white patch would show up like a lit candle thrown down a well.

"Someone could be killed," Caitlin insisted as Rachel

strode from stall to stall, inspecting the animals. "Don't you care?"

The Missouri woman spun to face her. "Look, fancy city gal, you'd best learn how things work out here. Nobody steals nothin' from Thompson land. Not water, not stock, and not Natchez's seed. If McKenna's stooped to thieving, he deserves what he gets."

"Surely there must be laws? Why must this be settled with angry words and guns?"

"What the hell do you know about anything?" Rachel demanded. "You and your puffy little sleeves and dainty shoes too good to get cow crap on! My mother and two of my brothers died for our land. We've fought Indians, wolves, and renegades to hold it, and we're not about to start backin' down now."

Caitlin retreated a step, scorched by the venom in Rachel's voice. Then something moved, and both she and Rachel caught sight of a figure in the shadows.

"Mary?" Caitlin asked. She'd left the Indian woman in the kitchen with Derry earlier. How had she gotten into the barn without being seen?

Mary grunted and stepped out into the center passageway. "Mary give new mother vinegar. Good for mare. Make milk for baby."

"That baby's what I want to see." Rachel leaned against the box stall railing.

Caitlin held her breath.

"I'll be damned," Rachel swore. "Talk about black Irish luck."

Caitlin ran to the gate. The foal lay curled in the straw beside her mother, ears up, bright eyes alert. The tiny filly's black face was damp; milk dripped from the corner of her mouth, and her bottlebrush tail flicked back and forth.

Her white star was gone.

Caitlin blinked. The foal was as black as Satan's chimney, without the slightest hint of white on her face.

"I'll bet you ten silver dollars that horse has Natchez's blood," Rachel said as she began to chuckle. "Damned Irish luck, that's what it is. Every filly and colt Natchez sires is the spitting image of him but this one." She slapped her palm against the top rail of the gate. "Guess Big Earl owes your man another apology."

Still chuckling, Rachel Thompson walked out of the barn and swung up on her horse. "We were wrong," she called to her father. "Nothin' here belongs to us."

Caitlin stood in the barn doorway. "I don't understand why there are bad feelings between your family and ours," she said. "Now that I'm here, perhaps we can change that."

Rachel threw her a scornful look. "Can't decide if you're for real, fancy woman, but you're sure good for a laugh." Digging her heels into her mount's sides, Rachel slapped the end of the reins against the gelding's neck and rode back to join her father.

Earl Thompson nodded to Shane and led his riders away at a hard trot. Rachel fell in behind them, and as she guided her horse out of the yard, she glanced back at Shane and Gabriel one final time.

"Caity," Shane called. "What just happened here?"

She shook her head. "I don't know." When he started toward her, she went back into the barn. She knew Shane would chastise her for not remaining in the house. But right now, it was more important for her to find out how the filly had lost her white star and why the Thompsons were their enemies.

Mary was still in the stable. Caitlin walked past

her and looked at the foal again. She could have sworn this was the same filly she'd seen Shane deliver the night before. "Mary?" Caitlin asked. "What did you do?"

The older woman shifted her pipe from one side of her mouth to the other and shrugged.

"This foal had a white star," Caitlin insisted.

Mary stood, silent, unsmiling.

"You didn't have time to put another foal in her place."

Shane entered the barn and came to stare at the mare and filly. He didn't speak to Caitlin, but she could feel his barely concealed anger.

"You should be in bed," Caitlin murmured.

Shane glanced at Mary. She uttered a single word, then walked away without looking back.

"What did she say?" Caitlin asked. "Is that Indian she's speaking?"

"Osage."

"And you understand it? What did she say?"

Shane nodded. "I speak it some." He leaned on the top rail of the stall gate and looked at the foal again. "Lampblack," he said.

"What?"

"She dyed the filly's white patch with lampblack." He opened the gate and reached down to touch the foal's head. When he pulled his hand away, his fingers were smeared with black.

"But how did Mary—"

"She's an Indian, Caity. You live around them long enough, you'll find out that they can do a lot of things that don't seem possible. But that's not what's worryin' me now."

Caitlin brushed her hand against his fingers and stared at the stain. "What do you mean?"

"Rachel Thompson isn't stupid. If I figured this out, she should have."

"But she didn't," Caitlin insisted. "She told her father—"

"Never mind what she told Big Earl. It never pays to make quick decisions about people or situations, Caity. There's more to Rachel than what you see."

"Why do they dislike you so much?"

"Big Earl? He hates me. Beau hates everybody."

"And Rachel? Does she hate you, too?"

Shane's eyes narrowed. "Not as much as she'd like her father to think. I've known her since I first joined Uncle Jamie in Kentucky. Rachel was just a skinny kid in pigtails then."

"Thompson knew your uncle?"

"They were friends and neighbors. Uncle Jamie and Earl scouted out this Missouri country together. They found Kilronan and bought it off a Spanish grandee."

"You mean they were partners?" Caitlin asked.

"No. They divided the land right from the start. Half to Big Earl, half to Uncle Jamie. He won the toss of a coin and got first pick."

"The families moved to Missouri together?"

Shane nodded. "Big Earl wanted to raise cattle and oxen. Uncle Jamie thought Kilronan was better for horses and mules."

Caitlin clasped Shane's hand gently, taking care not to put pressure on the lacerated palm. "I'd feel better if you'd come back in the house," she said. "Your head and ribs . . . You shouldn't be on your feet."

He grimaced. "It doesn't feel any better layin' on my back," he said before continuing. "The first two years here were rough—drunken trappers, army deserters, tornadoes. You name it. Earl's wife and oldest son, Al, were murdered by an Indian war party. A younger boy was shot by rustlers. Big Earl took it hard, but for Rach it was harder. She was startin' to fill out into a woman's shape, and she had nobody to teach her how she was supposed to act. She would have turned out better if her mother had lived."

Caitlin liked the feel of Shane's hand in hers. For all his hard manner, he made her feel safe.

"Are you listenin' to me, Caity?"

"Yes, Shane. I am."

"Earl hadn't been around women much, so he didn't know how to raise a girl. He just treated Rach like a boy. Her brother Beau was always a rotten apple, and Rachel got in the habit of followin' me around." Shane met Caitlin's eyes. "Rachel was a kid. There was nothin' between us but friendship."

"Did she think different?"

"There weren't many eligible men around, and none that Big Earl would let near her. And Rachel took a notion that I . . ." He picked up a handful of straw and began to scrub at the lampblack on his hands.

Caitlin waited.

"She kissed me, and I didn't handle it too well. I teased her and told her that she was too young to fool around with a married man. She told Big Earl that I'd tried to take advantage of her."

Shane was telling the truth. He had to be, Caitlin told herself. Her husband would never try to seduce his neighbor's innocent daughter. "There's more, isn't there?"

He nodded. "Aye, more. Big Earl lost his temper and rode over threatenin' to horsewhip me. Uncle Jamie threw him off Kilronan. To my knowledge, the two of them never spoke to each other again."

"And he blames you for that?"

"Earl blames me for Uncle Jamie's and George's deaths."

"But why? It was an accident. You told me that they drowned in a flood."

Shane's mouth thinned. "They died, and I didn't. And Kilronan came to me, lock, stock, and barrel. It seemed too much of a coincidence to Big Earl."

"You loved your uncle. You would never have done anything to harm him or George. I remember you used to talk about them to me, years ago, before you came to America. You told me how you wished your Uncle Jamie was your father."

"Aye, I did. Still do," Shane admitted. "My father was a worthless drunk. He had a bad temper, and when he drank, it got worse. I never wanted to be like him."

"You're not." She leaned her cheek against his upper arm. "You never were."

Shane brushed the crown of her head lightly. "I'd like to think that, but I got his temper. Sometimes . . ." He drew in a slow, deep breath. "I'm tellin' the truth about Rachel, Caity, and about what happened to my uncle. I wouldn't lie to you."

"But you tried to make me think something about Justice's mother that wasn't true," she reminded him. "You loved her—didn't you?" Hurt shimmered in waves through Caitlin, but she braced herself for what she knew was coming.

"Maybe I did," he said huskily. "Honestly, I don't know if it was love or something else. But I care for Justice. Mostly, I think, I wanted to protect him. That's why I didn't tell you everything about Cerise."

"She's still here, isn't she?"

"No, she's dead." Shane stiffened. "Dead and buried."

"I wish she wasn't," Caitlin answered softly. "I wish she was still alive!"

"Why?"

"If she was alive, I'd have something to fight. How do I battle a dead woman's ghost?"

Chapter 9

An hour later Caitlin thrust a spade into the hard, dry soil beside the front porch railing. Derry, eyes wide with anticipation, hopped and wiggled around her.

"Berry help! Berry help!" the child insisted.

For once Caitlin was glad for Derry's constant chatter. The day had started badly and gotten worse. Justice's deliberate breaking of grandmother's plate, Derry's episode with the bull, Shane's injuries, and finally the frightening visit from the Thompsons had all been the stuff of nightmares. The child's familiar enthusiasm was comforting, and it helped to calm Caitlin's nerves.

"Berry dig!"

"Derry cannot dig," Caitlin explained, driving the shovel into the earth again. She attempted to stamp on the top of the blade to tamp the spade deeper, but her boot slid off, and the corner of the metal sliced a hole in her stocking.

"Sweet—" She bit back an exclamation and tried to remain patient. "The ground is too hard," she said to Derry. "You can help water the rose when it's planted." If it's ever planted, she thought fervently.

"Yes, water! I help." Derry drove both hands to the bottom of the bucket and splashed merrily, wetting the front of her smock and soaking her dimity pantalettes.

Caitlin had just bathed her and changed her out of the

outfit she nearly ruined in the bull pen. It was plain that Derry's things were too fine for farm clothing, but she had nothing else to put on the growing child and no cloth to sew sturdier garments. Everything Derry owned, Caitlin had made out of her mother's old gowns and shifts.

An uneasy prickling sensation on the back of her neck caused Caitlin to look up and see an obviously disapproving Mary watching them from the open doorway.

How did she manage to creep around without making a sound? Caitlin wondered as she forced a polite smile. It was positively spooky!

"I'm planting the rose," Caitlin mumbled. Immediately she felt foolish. Of course Mary must know what she was doing.

The Osage woman had been spying on her upstairs in her bedchamber when she'd lifted the dormant plant out of her big wooden trunk and carefully unwrapped it.

Mary had scowled and wrinkled her nose. "Dead," she'd observed.

"The rose is not dead," Caitlin had replied with more enthusiasm than she felt.

She hoped it wasn't dead. The rose had been out of the soil a long time. Her mother's garden at home had been a wonderland of white and pink and red blooms; maiden's blush, musk, damask, and white Lady Banks roses had filled the air with sweet scents of beauty.

Now another woman walked in the garden and cut flowers for the house; at least, Caitlin hoped someone did. Some of the roses had been planted by Caitlin's grandmother, others by her mother. Caitlin had been no older than Derry when she'd stood beside them and watched as they rooted cuttings to give to friends.

Caitlin had never thought of herself as a thief, but the roses belonged to her family. When Father lost the house, she and Maureen had quietly dug several smaller roses and tucked them in among the household belongings to be loaded in carts.

And the night she'd decided to come to America to join Shane, she'd done worse. She'd stolen into her mother's garden and secretly taken cuttings of the apothecary rose—the red rose of Lancaster, the alba—the white rose of York, and her grandmother's favorite, old blush.

The rose she was planting this afternoon was the white Lady Banks, a thornless climber. She didn't know if she'd be at Kilronan long enough to see it bloom in the spring, but a small voice inside her demanded that she set down roots in this rocky soil. In any case, the white flowers would look beautiful against the weathered log house. If she left Missouri, the roses would give Shane something to remember her by.

"Water! Water!" Derry insisted.

Mary shrugged. "Water not make dead grow."

"It isn't dead," Caitlin insisted. "And we can't water it yet, sweet," she said to Derry. "First we have to plant the rose."

The soil resisted the shovel. She could dig only a small amount of earth and stones at a time. Ignoring Mary's scowl, she whispered to the dormant rose. "Sink your roots deep."

"McKenna say you plantee flower?"

Teeth gritted, Caitlin glanced up at Mary again. "Mr. McKenna is resting. I don't need his permission. I'm his wife, and mistress here at Kilronan. Mr. McKenna said that the house was my domain. I can do what I like." *Except get rid of you.*

"Diggee hole in yard."

"The rose will climb against the porch," Caitlin replied with more patience than she felt. "That makes it part of the household."

The Indian woman grunted.

Justice came out on the porch and hunkered down on the top step. "Won't grow," he said. "Looks dead to me."

"Not!" Derry declared. Splashing her hands in the bucket again, she sprinkled Justice with water.

Both children giggled.

Then Derry looked at Mary and defiantly put both hands on her hips. "Bad cow," she said. "Chasey my duck."

"Mary's duck." Mary tapped her unlit pipe against the open door.

Caitlin tried to avoid a confrontation by changing the subject. "Justice saved Derry's life this morning. If he hadn't thrown those stones . . ."

"Save-ed wife," Derry echoed.

Caitlin corrected her unconsciously. "Life, not wife, sweety. He saved your life."

The child nodded vigorously. "I wove *her*."

Justice folded his arms over his chest. "I guess you could say I'm a hero." Then he frowned. "He," the boy corrected. "I'm a man. You don't say *her* for a man. You're s'posed to say *him*."

Derry beamed and nodded. "I wove her."

Justice's face reddened under the copper tan. "She's a baby. She don't know no better." He grinned at Derry, who promptly threw herself into his arms.

The two wrestled playfully across the porch, and Caitlin tried to hide her surprise. She'd never seen Justice behave like a child before.

But Mary, too, had seen what was happening, and it seemed to Caitlin that she was displeased.

"Justice," Mary ordered. "Need kindling for cookee supper." She turned and stalked into the house.

Justice untangled himself from the toddler's embrace and ran off without grumbling.

"Berry help."

"No," Caitlin said. "I need you right here." She wasn't taking the chance of letting Derry out of sight again after what had happened this morning.

Derry stuck out her lip and shuffled her feet. The toe of one leather shoe was badly scuffed, and the other shoe was untied.

"I really need you," Caitlin said. Her throat constricted with emotion as she realized how much she meant what she'd said. In spite of Shane's reaction to Derry, in spite of all the mischief the child had caused on the journey from Ireland, Caitlin loved her with all her heart and soul. "I do need you," she whispered.

Slowly the child came back and looked down into the hole. "Water?" she asked. Her left pigtail had lost its ribbon, and Derry's cheek was smeared with mud, but her eyes sparkled with excitement.

My child, she thought. In a strange way, Shane was right; Derry was her daughter, and she couldn't love her more if she'd given birth to her.

"Come here, you." Caitlin hugged her tightly. "Yes, it's time for water now. Let's put the rose in first."

Caitlin spread the roots, and together she and Derry crumbled dirt around the plant and tamped it down. Then Caitlin let Derry pour water carefully around the rose.

Her small brow wrinkled with concentration as she slowly completed the task. When the last drop fell, Derry beamed with self-importance. "Berry do—good. Berry no baby. Berry big!" She threw her muddy arms wide.

"Yes, Derry is a good, big girl. Now close your eyes and whisper a prayer," Caitlin said. "My mama, your grandmother, always said a prayer when she planted a rose. It's the secret for making it grow."

Derry's eyes widened even further, and she wiggled from head to toe. "Grow, rose!"

"Please, God," Caitlin murmured under her breath, but she knew her prayer was for more than the white Lady Banks.

"More!" Derry cried. "Plant more."

"Not today," Caitlin said. "Tomorrow." She had the cuttings, but she'd have to decide where would be the safest places to plant them. She'd made a start; she'd put down roots. Only the good Lord could know if they would thrive.

Shane woke to the sounds of Mary beating on the iron triangle she used for a dinner bell. His head was still aching, and the clanging added to his misery. Every bone in his body felt as though it were broken. With effort he managed to pull on his boots, find a relatively clean shirt, and run a comb through his hair.

He started for the door, then stopped and ran a hand over his chin. A quick glance into a cracked hand mirror showed him that he needed to finish Caity's poor shaving job. Muttering under his breath, he propped up the mirror and looked around for his straight razor.

Mary struck the bar again, but Shane ignored her. Before Caity and the little colleen had come to Kilronan, he wouldn't have given much thought to his appearance at the table. He'd never been a man who went without bathing regularly, and he tried to keep Justice decent. But it was natural for a bachelor house to be a little wild and woolly. After all the fancy dishes and manners at breakfast, he knew that the time of easy ways was over.

"I must have been temporarily insane to send to Ireland again for her," he muttered.

Again.

Caitlin's betrayals galled him like old saddle sores. Caity was headstrong and determined, traits she shared with Cerise. Looks and Cerise's occupation aside, the two women were probably more alike than not.

Cerise had lied to him and suckered him out of every penny he could scrape together. She'd hooked him with barbs of steel and played him like a fish on a line. And in spite of what she was and how much her death had cost him, he still cared for her. And even stranger, he was certain that Cerise had loved him in her own way.

He'd been hot for Cerise. He'd wanted her so badly that he could overlook her being a whore, and her taste for strong liquor and loud music. And maybe having Cerise was striking back at Caity for the hurt she'd done him, he mused.

"McKenna!" Mary's call echoed from the bottom of the steps.

"Comin'!" he shouted back.

He wondered what kind of war he'd walk into downstairs. Would the table be set with fancy china or tin plates? Which woman had cooked the dinner, and which would stick her nose up at the other's meal?

Damn, but Mary and Caitlin hated the sight of each other. He knew Mary hadn't given Caity much of a chance. And with Mary being Osage, there was no way that he could expect the two to see eye to eye. Facing down Big Earl and his guns had been easier than sitting in his own kitchen for breakfast.

Giving his cheek a last scrape, he put down the razor and dabbed at the bloody spots with his shirttail. There was still a patch of uneven beard around the scrape on his face, but that would have to wait.

Shane took the steps gingerly, one hand on the wall, and tried to put his boots down lightly, as though he were walking on eggs. His ribs were killing him, and he was damned glad that Big Earl had saved him from tanglin' with Beau.

He wondered if Earl was telling the truth about losing cattle. If he was, then they'd both have to look elsewhere for whoever was doing the raiding.

Shane smelled Mary's rabbit stew before he rounded the corner; strong coffee, stew, and Indian fry bread were Mary's staples. He hoped that she hadn't scorched the bottom of the kettle again. Her last rabbit stew had been so bad that even Justice wouldn't eat it.

"Shane." Caitlin smiled at him. "We've been waiting grace for you."

He slid onto the bench beside Gabriel. The table was set with fancy stuff, Caity's silver forks and spoons alongside his nicked and bent eating knives with the bone handles.

He noticed two things out of place. Mary's greasy fry bread spilled out of a blue-and-white bowl onto the white linen tablecloth, and Justice's seat was empty.

"Where's the boy?" he asked.

Caity caught her lower lip between her teeth. It was an old habit, something he remembered her doing whenever she was uncertain. "I asked him to wash his face and hands for supper," she replied. "He said he wasn't hungry."

"Grace!" Derry cried. "I do!"

"Just a minute," Shane said. He went to the kitchen door that led outside and shouted for Justice. On the second try, the boy appeared.

"Wash up for supper," Shane ordered.

"Ain't hungry."

"Didn't ask if you wanted to eat. Put some water and soap to those hands or I'll do it for you."

Caity flashed him a look of real gratitude when he and Justice joined them at the table. Derry lisped her prayer, and they all began to eat, all but the boy, who stared at his empty plate in sullen silence.

"I plant rose," the child boasted.

"Did you, now?" Shane grinned at her.

"A white Lady Banks," Caity said. "You remember, the ones that grew on the west garden wall at home."

Shane reached for the fry bread. "I knew your mother had a lot of roses. But if you recall, I wasn't too welcome in your mother's garden." He grimaced. "Or anywhere on the estate, as I remember."

"Only because the gamekeeper suspected you of poaching," Caity replied.

"Potato!" Derry cried, clapping her hands. " 'Kenna a potato!"

"Not potato, darling," Caity corrected. "Poacher."

Shane's mouth was full of stew, so he didn't attempt a defense. In fact, he had been poaching hares. Once he'd even killed a deer. That meat had kept his family fed for weeks, but it could have gotten them all hanged or transported if they'd gotten caught.

The stew was too oniony and it needed seasoning, but he added salt and pepper without complaining. Mary Red Jacket had her own ways of dealing with criticisms of her cooking.

Caity took another small bite, chewed slowly, and swallowed. If she thought the rabbit stew was tasteless, she was good at hiding her opinion, Shane decided.

"I've brought more cuttings," she said.

He looked up. "What?"

"Cuttings. Rose cuttings. I'd like to start a small garden behind the house."

Mary grunted. "Got garden. Onions. Turnips. Squash. Rabbits."

"I saw your vegetable garden," Caity answered diplomatically. "It's very nice, but I'd like a flower garden." She looked at Shane expectantly.

"Sure," he said. "Whatever you want." He noticed that

she'd changed her dress for something blue, sort of robin's-egg blue, with ribbons down the front and a lacy thing around her neck. The color reminded him of the sky over Rocky Ridge on a clear winter day. It suited her, but it looked kind of out of place for a horse spread.

He broke off a hunk of fry bread and started to mop up his stew with it. Then Shane noticed Derry staring at him, tiny mouth wide in surprise. Hastily he dropped the bread onto his plate and finished the remainder of his rabbit gravy with his fork.

Mary got up, went to the hearth, returned with the coffeepot, and set it down heavily on the table. Justice eyed the fry bread. Only Gabe seemed to be at ease eating off the elegant dishes with a sterling fork.

Shane took a sip of the hot brew. "Caity, I asked you to stay inside today when Thompson showed up at our doorstep."

Justice's eyes widened with delight. Mary looked down at the piece of bread she was spreading honey on. Gabe continued ladling another helping of stew onto his plate.

Caity's gaze met his. "You told me to."

Shane covered Caity's hand with his own. It was warm and soft, and touching her gave him a good feeling in the pit of his stomach. "I told you to stay inside because I knew there might be trouble."

She nodded. "You can't protect me from everything, Shane. If I'm going to live at Kilronan, I have to decide what's dangerous and what's not."

She was right, and he knew she was right. He wanted her to be tough enough and smart enough to survive. He wanted their marriage to work, and he wanted to find what they'd lost somewhere between Kilronan and Ireland.

But Caity was an innocent greenhorn out here. She hadn't lived through Indian attacks or floods or cholera.

And if she wouldn't listen to him . . . he could lose her like he'd lost Justice's mother.

"Damn it, woman," he said softly. "You've got nerve, but you've got to do what I say when I say it."

"Because you are my husband?"

Shane felt an uneasy heat creep up his throat. He glanced at Gabe to see if the Indian was amused by this. He hadn't meant to get into a discussion in front of them all, but now that he'd stepped in trouble, he reckoned he'd have to scrape it off as best he could.

He tried reason. "Because I'm the boss on Kilronan. And I'm the head of this family."

"Oh." Caity smiled as though he'd given her a compliment instead of a talking-to.

Clearing his throat, he pushed back from the table and fixed Caitlin with a stern look. "That's the way it has to be."

She smiled at him again, a smile that would melt ice. "There's an old saying in County Clare. Do you remember? The husband is the head of the house, but the wife is the heart."

He stood up. This wasn't going the way he'd thought it would. She seemed to be agreeing with him, but she really wasn't.

Shane switched barrels and tried praise. "What you said to Big Earl was smart. You kept him from startin' a fight. You were right, and I was wrong."

"Yes," she said. "I was, wasn't I?"

Gabe made a sound that might have been a chuckle.

Shane's patience ran out. "It could as easily have turned out the other way, Caity. There might have been shootin', and you would have been in the middle of it."

"Justice was beside you, Shane. He's ten years old. Why is it all right for a child to stand in the middle of a fight and not a grown woman?"

"Justice is a man. At least, he will be a man." Shane could barely contain his temper. He shot the boy a look and was rewarded by a fleeting grin.

"Berry a man, too!" Derry chimed in.

"You are not," Caitlin corrected. "You are a young lady. And one who's up past her bedtime."

Swiftly Caitlin rose and lifted Derry out of her seat. "If you will excuse us, I—"

"I'm not done," Shane said sharply.

"No, I suppose you're not, but do feel free to finish your supper."

Shane followed her from the room. "You know I wasn't talkin' about the food."

"Oh, you weren't?"

"I'll carry her upstairs for you," he said. "We'll put her to bed together, and then we can finish our *talk*."

Caity surrendered the child.

Derry threw her arms around his neck and planted a damp kiss on his cheek. "I wove you," she proclaimed.

Upstairs, he waited as Caity washed the child's hands and face and put her into nightclothes.

"Story! Story!" Derry urged.

"We always have a story," Caity answered. "A story and prayers."

"Not Mama. 'Kenna. 'Kenna read a story."

"Your . . . your aunt will read to you," Shane said.

"It's all right. I've given up," Caity put in. "She can call me Mama if she wants to."

" 'Kenna read!" Derry insisted.

"McKenna can't read the d—" He caught himself. "I can't read, child. Never learned how. She'll give you your story." Shamed, he retreated into the hall.

When the routine was complete and Derry was tucked into bed, Shane led Caitlin downstairs and out onto the front porch. He was very much aware of the scent of heather in her hair and the graceful way she moved, but he wasn't about to let her win this contest. She needed to know how things had to be on Kilronan.

Not that he wanted to argue with her. He'd have much rather pulled her into his arms and held her against him, just to feel a woman's softness again. But if he didn't have his say, he knew he'd regret it.

"You were wrong to disobey me and go out to meet the Thompsons," he said. "But I was wrong to bring it up at supper in front of Gabe and Mary."

Caity leaned against the railing and looked up at the night sky. "There must be a million stars up there. They seem so close . . . so bright. Is it possible that they're the same stars we watched at home?"

"This is home for me," he reminded her. "But I didn't bring you out here to talk about the stars."

She turned to face him, sending a wave of heather fragrance wafting over him. Desire flared in his loins.

"Maybe you should have."

She was close . . . so close. He knew that if he reached for her, she wouldn't pull away. But he also knew his own weaknesses, and he was determined not to let her rule him because of it.

"What you did today was dangerous," he said.

"But it turned out all right." Her voice softened. "How's your head? Your ribs?"

"I'll live."

"I hope so."

Her voice was a breath of Ireland. Listening to it made him want to smile. Lord in heaven! How many nights had he gone to sleep with a hollow feeling in his chest from missing her?

Now she was finally here. She was in reach, and he didn't know if he could keep her beside him . . . or if he even wanted to.

For the space of a heartbeat, he wished he could turn the clock back. When he'd taken her for his wife, he'd felt like the richest man in the world. And for a few short hours, they'd been together as man and woman.

But that was in Ireland, where he was nothing—worse than nothing. Not fit to take Caity's hand to help her into a carriage, let alone think of marrying her.

If he shoved time back, he'd be that clumsy boy with the thin-soled shoes and the thick accent again. He'd be at the beck and call of any man with a coin in his pocket, and he'd be a husband without a hope of owning an acre of land or of making a decent living for his wife and family.

Here, in Missouri, he'd proved himself. He had Kilronan, and he knew he was the equal of a man like Earl Thompson or any other.

"I don't give you orders because I want to control you, Caity," he said. "It's my duty to keep you safe."

"You would have fought Thompson today, wouldn't you?"

"If I had to," he admitted. "You don't go up against a man like Big Earl halfway. But I couldn't let him take what was mine."

"Wouldn't it have been better to pay him the fee for his stallion?"

"And admit I was a cheat when I wasn't?"

"What will you do with the filly now? You can't keep her star dyed with lampblack forever."

That had been worrying him, too. "I'll think of something."

"Maybe it would be better to try to find a way to make peace with your neighbor than to keep up an old feud."

"His feud, not mine."

She sighed. "Earl Thompson seems a hard man, but I don't think he's the type to commit murder."

"He's not sneaky. He'd shoot me if he thought he had to, but not in the back."

"Then maybe if the two of you worked together, you could find the—"

"Damn it, Caity. Stop tryin' to change things you know nothin' about. Can't you just accept me and Kilronan the way we are? Accept Justice and Mary?"

"Why should she?" Justice demanded.

Shane turned to see the boy standing in the shadows. He's good, Shane thought, as good as Gabe. He'd never heard a sound.

"You've no business here listening to private conversations," he said to Justice. "And I told you before, you're to show respect to your new mother."

"She's not my mother!"

"No," Caitlin agreed. "Not your mother, but someone who wants to be your friend."

"Why should you?"

"Justice," Shane admonished. "I think you've said enough."

"Be my friend?" the boy taunted. "Be nice to the dirty little Indian half-breed? The whore's son?"

"Damn it, Justice!" Shane said. "Shut your—"

"Don't say such things about your mother, child," Caitlin cried. "You don't mean—"

The boy swore a foul oath. "Don't mean it? Course I mean it. Ask anybody. They'll tell you. My mother was nothin' but a cheap, whiskey-drinkin' whore."

"Is it true, Shane?" Caitlin whispered huskily. "Was she . . ."

"McKenna's whore?" Justice mocked her. "Sure she was. The most expensive gal at Fat Rose's. And if she weren't dead, he'd still be with her. Not you! Not ever you."

"Caity," Shane said, reaching for her.

But she dodged past him and ran back into the house, and the sound of her weeping cut him deeper than the dull ache of his broken ribs.

Chapter 10

In the days that followed Justice's angry revelation, Caitlin maintained an uneasy truce with Shane. Her pride was shattered, and she was in no mood to listen to any more of her husband's explanations or excuses.

Shane had broken his marriage vows to become deeply involved with a common bawd who sold her favors to the highest bidder. He'd accused Caitlin of being unfaithful and giving birth to an illegitimate child, while he'd been the one who'd cheated and lied.

Now he expected her to overlook what he had done with Justice's mother and go on as if nothing had happened. And as much as Caitlin wanted to save her marriage, she didn't know if that was possible.

She loved the man he used to be. But maybe love wasn't enough—maybe she should take Derry and leave Kilronan.

Mary and Justice would be happier if she went away. If Shane was steely polite, the Indian woman and Shane's adopted son were anything but. Battles raged on every front. Mary had her own way of running the house, and she was not prepared to share her responsibilities or to change her habits.

And Caitlin was just as determined not to back down. So long as she was mistress at Kilronan, she'd manage the household her way. That meant spotless floors, scrubbed walls, and clean children at meals and bedtime.

Caitlin rose at first light every morning and kept busy until the last of the dishes were done, the kitchen floor swept, and dough set to rise for the next morning's bread.

Since Mary was so deeply entrenched in the kitchen, Caitlin made the front parlor her first project. She found a hammer and painstakingly pried out the nails that held the connecting door between the kitchen and parlor shut.

"Why would anyone build a doorway and then board it up?" she demanded of Shane over supper.

He shrugged.

"Too many door," Mary grumbled. "One, two, three. Three door in kitchen, too many. Not need waste wood to heat empty room."

"Well, we don't need to heat the room now, do we?" Caitlin replied with a forced smile.

"Winter come," Mary said. "Winter always come. Waste wood, heat, 'nother room. Eat in kitchen. All time, eat in kitchen." She spread her worn hands expressively. "Good room. Good food. Good heat."

"It's not winter now, and we will be taking supper in the parlor room as soon as I finish it," Caitlin said firmly. "It will be our dining room."

The following day she inspected the house from top to bottom. Upstairs, in the attic under the eaves, she found a cache of old furniture covered with dusty trade blankets: a dismantled four-poster bed, seven straight-backed chairs, an Irish hunt board, and an old-fashioned dining table crafted of solid walnut.

The front parlor was smaller than the kitchen, but the room boasted a lovely stone hearth, deep window seats, and whitewashed plaster walls. Sunshine streamed through the glass windowpanes onto the pine floor, giving the chamber a warm glow. A second doorway led to the entrance hall.

While Shane ignored her and busied himself with the unending task of caring for his animals and crops, Caitlin attacked the parlor. She coated the walls with fresh whitewash, scrubbed and polished the floorboards, and shined the windows. Then she dragged the dismantled table piece by piece, and the hunt board down two flights of stairs and into the room. These, too, she carefully cleaned and waxed.

The room took longer than Caitlin had thought it would, nearly a week of hard work. But when she pushed the last chair under the table and hung a portrait of her great-grandmother over the hunt board, she was satisfied. Her back ached and she had blisters on both hands, but she didn't care.

"All done?" Derry asked.

"Not yet," she murmured. "Almost, but soon."

A midday thunderstorm had kept both children in the house, and Caitlin had heard them giggling in the kitchen and running up and down the stairs. Then Caitlin heard Justice say something about going to the barn.

"Stay inside, Derry," Caitlin warned.

The kitchen door slammed shut.

"Justice gone," Derry said dejectedly.

"He's a big boy," Caitlin soothed. "He has chores to do."

"Berry do chores."

"Yes, when you're bigger."

Derry trailed after Caitlin as she hurried upstairs to her bedroom. The rain was coming down in sheets, hitting the windows in waves.

Caitlin thought of Shane and Gabriel mending fences, and wondered if they'd taken shelter somewhere.

"Justice catched a f'nake," Derry said as Caitlin picked her up and set her on a chair.

"A real snake or a make-believe snake?" Caitlin asked absently. One leg of Derry's pantalettes was hiked up above her knee, the other drooped over her shoe. Her face was smeared with honey, and her hands were black and sooty.

"No. Don't touch your dress. I'll wash you as soon as I find something."

Derry shook her head so hard that her pigtails whirled in the air. "A blue f'nake."

"Blue? All right." Caitlin smiled. "Sit still. I'll be done in a minute." She was certain that she'd packed four linen swags in the bottom of her big trunk. Once the delicate drapes had adorned her mother's bedchamber; now they would do nicely for the dining room.

At home in County Clare, she'd taken the beautiful furniture, family portraits, and silver for granted. They hadn't been rich, no matter what Shane said, but her parents had lived graciously. Her father had loved books; her mother, music and painting. Maureen had learned to play the piano, and Caitlin the small harp. Caitlin could remember dinner parties and dances and poetry readings that went on until late at night.

Here in the Missouri wilderness there was only endless sky and grass, ancient forests, and rushing streams. Caitlin appreciated the breathtaking beauty of this new land around her, but she also longed for the intellectual richness of her old life.

"It's a good thing I brought my favorite books with me," she said to Derry. "I've seen nothing in this house but a single tattered Bible."

"Like f'nakes. You like f'nakes, Mama?"

"Not especially." Caitlin opened the big trunk and dug

to the bottom without finding the linen swags. "Now, where can they be? I was certain I saw them last week."

"Justice like green f'nakes."

"Umm-hm," Caitlin agreed. "Maybe in the other . . ." Nibbling at her lower lip, she flipped up the lid on the smaller wooden case. "I think I saw—"

Something slithered over Caitlin's hand. She screamed and leaped back.

Derry clapped her hands and shrieked with excitement. "F'nake, Mama! Green f'nake!"

Heart pounding, Caitlin peered into the open trunk. A small garden snake reared up and thrust out its tongue. Two beady black eyes stared into hers.

Derry crowed with laughter.

"Very amusing." Caitlin pushed the lid shut with the toe of her shoe.

Justice's funnies were becoming a bad habit. Yesterday Caitlin had sweetened her tea with a spoon of salt from the sugar bowl, and the night before that, at bedtime, she'd slid between clean sheets and discovered a pound of wet sand.

Justice's stifled giggles came from the hallway.

Caitlin put a finger to her lips for silence and crept to the open door. Then she lunged around the corner and seized him by the ear.

"Let me go!" Justice squirmed and kicked out at her, but she held fast.

"Not yet, young man."

"You're hurtin' me."

"I believe you left something in my trunk," Caitlin said. "Get it out!"

Justice's black eyes narrowed. "I didn't! If Derry said I did, she's a lyin' telltale."

"Get the snake, Justice," Caitlin ordered.

"You're hurtin' my ear."

"I'll hurt you worse than that if you don't get that snake out of my room."

Later, after Justice had disposed of the garden snake, Caitlin bathed Derry and tucked her in for her nap. She located the missing curtains in a third trunk and went back downstairs to the dining room.

Caitlin was standing on the window seat, tacking up the last corner of linen swag when she heard the door to the kitchen open behind her.

She turned around, prepared to defend herself against another of Mary's discouraging remarks. Instead, she saw her husband standing in the doorway, wearing a rain-soaked slicker. In one hand he held his dripping hat; in the other he clasped a bunch of wet daisies.

She didn't know whether to scold him or laugh. "Shane?"

A faint flush washed over his tanned features. Black Irish, she thought . . . silver-gray eyes and Lucifer's own pride. But he'd not get around her with a few soggy wildflowers.

Her grandmother had always said that the devil would never come creeping around with cloven hooves and a forked tail. "More like a fallen angel, he'll look," the old lady had confided. "Clothed in the body of a brawny young man with silver eyes and a tongue to match."

Caitlin felt a sudden flash of heat, but whether it was anger or lust she could not tell. She folded her arms across her chest. "You're dripping water all over the floor."

"Sorry. I didn't know you were in here."

"I am," she replied, steadying herself against the windowpane. "Would it have been all right to drip on the floor if I wasn't here?"

She glanced at her scissors lying on the table. What

would he say if she took them and cut his flowers to pieces? It was no more than he deserved—trying to bribe her with daisies after what he'd done.

"Thought you might want these." Shane dropped the flowers on the table and helped her down from the window seat. "We got caught in the rain."

"I can see that."

Shane shrugged off his slicker. The shirt underneath was wet through, clinging to his shoulders and chest like a second skin.

"Shouldn't you hang that up somewhere to dry?" She pointed to his slicker.

"I thought . . . you planting those roses . . . I . . ." He seemed at a loss for words, and it pleased her to see him uneasy.

He stepped back into the doorway and tossed the slicker onto the kitchen bench. "Gabe and me were mendin' fence on the southern pasture when the storm rolled in," he explained as he turned back to her. "There was a whole meadow of these flowers."

"Thank you." Her words dropped between them like frozen sleet.

He flashed her a faint smile and ran his fingers through the section of wet hair that threatened to cover his eyes. For an instant she saw a flash of the old Shane, but she hardened her will against his charms.

"You need a haircut," she murmured woodenly. "I—"

"Maybe you could cut it for me. Cerise used to—" He realized his mistake and bit off his words.

"McKenna want coffee?" Mary shouted. Poking her head through the kitchen doorway, she looked around. Her hair, always neatly braided into a severe bun at the back of her neck, was nearly as wet as Shane's. But except for a few water spots on the blanket around her shoulders, Mary's clothing was dry.

Gabriel, obviously in the process of removing his shirt, appeared at Mary's side. "Pretty fancy, them cloth things over the windows."

Shane turned and swatted at Gabe with his hat. "Can't a man have any privacy around here?"

The wrangler's inscrutable face belied the twinkle in his dark eyes. "Never known you to pick flowers, boss. You get struck by lightning today?"

"I said out! Both of you!" Shane gave Gabriel a shove and slammed the door in their faces.

Caitlin looked down at the daisies. Did Shane believe she could be bribed with a few flowers after what he'd done with that woman?

"I'm sorry," he said.

For what? Caitlin wondered. For abandoning her in Ireland, for shaming her with Cerise, or for his cold manner toward her since she'd come to Missouri? How could he expect her to forgive and forget so easily when he'd just reminded her again of his illicit relationship with Justice's mother?

I want you to feel ashamed, she thought. I want you to hurt as much as you've hurt me. But I don't want to drive you away.

"They are pretty," she said grudgingly. And they were, even wet. The white daisies with yellow centers were so lovely that it was hard to believe they grew wild.

She swallowed, trying to ease the constriction in her throat. Bringing flowers was the oldest trick a straying man had in his pocket. She'd be a fool to allow herself to be swayed so easily.

"You should change your clothes before you take a chill and catch the ague," she said.

"I s'pose."

She looked back at him. Damn Cerise to hell, she thought. All those nights that she spent crying into her pillow, missing him . . . To think that *she* was cutting Shane's hair, putting her hands on his face, sleeping beside him on cold, rainy nights.

"It's good," he said brusquely.

"What's good?"

"What you've done in here. The whitewash and this stuff." He motioned toward the hunt board. "I should have brought it down for you, but I forgot about it bein' there. Uncle Jamie's wife . . . it belonged to her. She died before I came to America, but I guess he couldn't bring himself to get rid of her things."

Caitlin moved to the table and fingered the daisies. For all their beauty, they gave off a pungent odor that was not altogether pleasant.

"Oxeye," Shane said.

Puzzled, she met his gaze.

He waved at the bouquet with his hat, sending a shower of drops onto the tabletop she'd waxed so lovingly. "The flowers. They're called oxeye daisies."

"Oh," she murmured. "I didn't know." She wanted to wipe away the water, but her feet felt rooted to the floor.

Somehow Shane always looked bigger to her indoors. His pants and boots were as wet as the rest of him. He'd taken the trouble to shave this morning, and she saw that the cut along his cheek had healed nicely. With his hair slicked back and clean shaven, he looked younger, more approachable.

"I could take you there . . . if you like," he offered.

"Where?"

He exhaled softly and shifted his weight. "To the meadow. Where the daisies grow. Maybe you'd like to take a ride out there."

"In the rain?" She knew she should refuse, but then he grinned, and a knot loosened in Caitlin's chest.

"Tomorrow, maybe. We finished the fence work and—"

"I'd like that," she blurted out. "But why, Shane? Why offer to take me to see a field of flowers? That's strange behavior for a man who's made no secret of the fact that he wants to be rid of his wife."

He shook his head. "If I wanted to be rid of you, you'd have been on the next steamboat for Saint Louis."

"Would I? I suppose that's true." She took a step toward him. Wind rattled the glass panes. Lightning flashed outside, and the air seemed equally charged inside. She found herself concentrating on the faint pulse at the hollow of his tanned throat.

"Hell, you don't make it easy on a man."

"Or you on me," she whispered.

"You've a stare colder than a blue norther," he said huskily. "I should have told you about Cerise, but I figured you'd take it hard."

She nodded. "No decent woman wants to think she can be replaced by that kind." Her anger was fast dissolving, leaving a dull, bottomless ache. "It cheapens our marriage . . . and it cheapens me."

"It shouldn't."

Why can't you just hold me? she thought. All I want from you is your love . . . and your trust.

Shane's features took on the hard lines Caitlin had seen so often since she'd come to Missouri.

"Cerise was like most of us," he said. "Some good parts, and some bad. She had a taste for whiskey, and when she drank, it made her mean. But when she was cold sober, there was a lot to admire in her."

"I'm sure." She tried to turn away from him, but he wouldn't let her. His fingers closed around her upper arms, holding her firmly.

"Don't go all stiff and proper on me. It took me half a day to come up with the nerve to say this, so you've got to listen. Like a festerin' sore, this has to be cut out and allowed to heal—if you want us to come to terms."

She nodded, trying desperately to keep from disgracing herself by dissolving in tears.

"You can't blame me for wantin' to keep that part of my past in the past," he continued. "But Cerise was more than just a warm body I could buy for the night. And Justice deserves more than bein' known as a whore's son."

Caitlin's vision clouded as she looked into his eyes. "I'm trying," she whispered.

Then, without knowing if it was his doing or hers, she found herself sobbing against his chest. Shane's arms held her, and he was patting her back and whispering soothing words.

"I never wanted to hurt you," he murmured. "I was lonely, and I thought you'd forgotten me."

"Oh, Shane," she managed.

"Don't. It'll be all right. We'll find a way to make it all right."

Then she heard the door hinges squeak and Gabe's voice, low and dangerous. "What's goin' on, McKenna? Did you hit her?"

"No, I didn't hit her!" Shane yelled. "Now get the hell out of here and leave me talk to my wife."

"Don't sound like talkin' to me. Miss McKenna, you—"

"I'm all right, Gabriel. Really," Caitlin assured him.

Gabe muttered something in Osage and closed the door.

"I . . . I feel like such a fool," Caitlin stammered. She pulled away and met his penetrating gaze. "Oh, Shane," she whispered.

The sour smell of the daisies wafted around her, and the humor of her situation made her smile through her tears.

What was wrong with her? She wanted him to apologize.

She wanted him to come to her and try to make things right. And when he did, all she could do was . . .

"Caity? Are you listenin' to me?" he asked.

She nodded.

"I said, with Mary and Gabe and the kids here, we're never alone in this house."

They would be if they were sharing a feather bed, she thought, but didn't have nerve enough to say it.

"We've been apart so long." He stared down at his felt hat and slowly creased the folds as he searched for the right words. "We're different people, Caity. We won't know if we're suited . . . if we were ever suited."

"We can't be if we never talk to each other," she said.

"We'd have more of a chance if people weren't always interruptin'." He looked meaningfully toward the kitchen door. "I know Mary's been givin' you a hard time since you got here."

"I can understand that it would be difficult for her." Caitlin wiped her eyes and tried to get control of her emotions. They were having a conversation like husband and wife, and she didn't want it to stop. "I told her this morning that I intended to paint a mural on this wall, and she said my head was on backwards."

"A mural?"

She nodded. Why had she burst into tears? Now he'd think her weak and soft when she wanted him to see how strong she was.

"You want to paint a picture on the wall?"

"A flowering tree. Maybe a grapevine. We had a mural of a Venetian harbor in the library at home." Sweet Jerusalem, she was chattering on like Derry.

Shane took a step toward the door.

"Guess I'd best change."

"I will cut your hair . . . if you want," she offered.

"Later." The hurt was still there, deep inside her, but her tears had washed away some of the tension between them. For the first time in days, she felt as though she had somewhere to begin.

Chapter 11

The thunder showers had passed in early evening. Now crickets chirped and fireflies blinked outside Shane's bedroom windows. It was cooler tonight than it had been in weeks, and he should have been able to sleep. He'd been in the saddle at daybreak, and he ached from the mauling the bull had given him. Instead, he lay awake staring into the darkness.

Throwing one arm over his head, Shane rolled onto his side and clamped his eyes shut. His body was tired enough—it was his head that gave him trouble.

He couldn't stop thinking about Caity and how he'd made a dunce of himself by bringing her a handful of wet flowers. And then, if that wasn't stupid enough, he'd tried to apologize and ended up telling her how much he'd cared for Cerise.

Nothing had happened like he'd thought it would when he met Caity at the steamboat landing. All cards were shuffled and it was a whole new game, one where he wasn't sure of the rules or the stakes.

Unable to lie still, Shane rose and padded barefoot to the window. He raised the jamb a few inches and listened. A few frogs croaked from the creek, and off on the hillside an owl hooted.

Mist hung close to the ground. On nights like this the

smallest sound carried a long way. Shane listened until he was certain that nothing was amiss outside; then he closed the window softly so as not to alarm Caity sleeping in the next room.

The absurdity of that reality struck him; his wife was sleeping alone and so was he. It wasn't what either of them wanted, and he had only himself to blame.

He wanted her so bad that he couldn't get her out of his mind long enough to get through an ordinary day's chores. He watched her when she walked across the kitchen and when she tended her roses. He followed her with his gaze when she bent to wipe honey off Derry's chin or swept the front porch. And when she was out of sight, it drove him crazy until he set eyes on her again.

He wanted her, but had he done the right thing in bringing her here?

He'd told Caity the truth when he'd said they were two different people. When he'd wed her, she'd been a lovely girl; now she was a woman.

"With a woman's lying tongue and a woman's deceits." His father's bitter words haunted him.

It was no secret that Patrick McKenna had wed his sweetheart Aingeal O'More unaware that she was four month's gone with another man's child. And it was even less of a secret that he'd made her life hell because of it.

The grave and sixteen years weren't deep enough to silence Patrick McKenna's drunken rages. Damn him to a pitiless hell! Shane had heard his father shout those curses a hundred times at his wife, Shane's mother.

Despite what his mother had done, Shane had hated the old man then, and he hated him still. But Patrick McKenna had planted the seeds of distrust deep in his children.

He loved Caity. But could he ever forgive what she'd done? Was there too much of his father in him to forget that Caity had betrayed him as much as Cerise?

Every day of their marriage, he'd have to look into sweet little Derry's face—the living proof of Caity's adultery. As his father had done with Shane's brother Kevin.

Could he trust himself not to throw it in Caity's face or to find solace in a bottle as Patrick McKenna had done?

He'd never wanted to be like his father—to let temper or drink cloud his reason. Shane had sworn he'd never loose the black McKenna fury on any woman, and he never had but that once. Patrick's ghost had raged the night Cerise died. And if it happened once, could it happen again with Caity?

Was he putting her life in danger by letting her stay?

The damp, twisted sheet under him dug into his flesh, and he tore it off the bed and hurled it onto the floor. Why torment himself because his wife was human? Why couldn't he accept Caity taking comfort with a lover the same way he'd done himself?

Derry was a beautiful child. Even a man with a heart of stone would be enchanted by her. So what if she was fathered by another man? He could be her real father if he wanted to.

He reminded himself that Caity had carried the baby and given it life in spite of her shame. Not like Cerise, demanding money to do away with the child she'd sworn he'd fathered on her.

So why was it so hard for Caity to be honest with him?

Even if he could overlook Derry's birth and Caity not coming when he'd sent money the first time, reason should tell him to be cautious.

He should wait and see how long she lasted out here

before he handed her his heart on a china plate. Even a thick-headed Irish laborer should have sense enough to do that.

Wanting her in bed wasn't enough. This time when he made a commitment it would be forever. He knew he couldn't make another mistake with his heart and survive.

Shane threw a clean blanket over the mattress and stretched out on the bed again. It was his way to sleep naked, and tonight was no different. The cool air felt good on his bare skin, but it did nothing to ease his troubled mood.

"At this rate, I'll be awake when the sun comes up," he grumbled.

Again, in spite of himself, Caity's image rose in his mind's eye, and he remembered the first time he'd laid eyes on her.

Patrick McKenna had gone off on another two-week drunk, and Shane's mother was left without a copper penny to buy food for her children.

Ragged as a gypsy's brat and barefoot in the winter's cold, he'd sneaked onto Caity's father's land with a gnawing hunger in his belly and enough twine to make a rabbit snare.

Caity had caught him red-handed. She could have called the gamekeeper and had him arrested; instead, she'd befriended him. He'd gone home to his mother with two loaves of bread, a round of cheese, and a slab of bacon as well as the fat rabbit.

Caity had invited him to trap rabbits whenever he wanted. She'd even helped him to evade her father's foresters.

And in less time than he could have believed, she became his reason for living.

Shane's breathing slowed as he let his mind drift back to the days when they were both children . . . when his greatest joys were smelling meat browning on a spit and hearing Caity's bright laughter.

Gradually the tenseness drained from his muscles, and he drifted off into a dreamless sleep.

Caitlin thought that what was left of Shane's crushed and soggy bouquet made a cheerful addition to the next morning's breakfast table, even if they were eating in the kitchen.

The day had dawned clear, and the few clouds that remained from the previous night's storm were swiftly dissolving in the bright sunlight. For once, Caitlin had risen before Shane. She had already rolled her biscuit dough when he came into the kitchen.

She could tell by the way he walked that he was still in pain. "How do you feel?"

He scowled. "Don't ask." He started to take his customary place on the bench and then noticed the oversize armchair that Caitlin had dragged down from the attic. "What's this?"

She smiled at him. "It's only proper. After all, Mister McKenna, you are the head of the family."

He stared at the old-fashioned walnut chair with the elaborately carved arms and legs and the lion's-claw feet. Then he slowly rubbed his fingertips over one of the star-shaped brass nail heads that adorned the high back. "I'd all but forgotten this," he said. "It must have belonged to that Spanish grandee we bought Kilronan from."

Long ago someone had replaced the original back and seat coverings with red-and-white-spotted steerhide. The leather was worn and the scarred wood so dark that it looked almost black. "It does look Spanish," she agreed, "but it suits you, and it suits this kitchen."

"This and a little table with the same claw feet were in the cabin Mary lives in now when we bought Kilronan," he said as he eased himself into the chair. "There's an ironbound chest, too. Lots of fancy carving on it. Gabe's been using it to store horse liniment and blankets."

"Where is it?" Caitlin asked.

"In the barn. I think the table's out there, too. You can have them if you want."

"Not if they belong to Gabriel or Mary." She did want the pieces. She had always loved old things, and if the furniture was sound, it would help to fill the empty rooms in this house.

He shrugged. "Mary wouldn't have the stuff in her cabin. She's afraid of the lion feet, says the furniture has a fierce spirit, or some craziness. Besides, they all belong to Kilronan. Anything here you can have—except my best horse."

"I don't want your horse." She poured him a strong cup of tea and carried it to the table. "But I would like to see more of your land. I want to see every foot of it."

Expressionless, he blew on the tea and took a sip.

Caitlin returned to her biscuit making, and tried not to let him see how anxious she was. She'd done a lot of thinking in the night. Shane's bringing her the flowers and apologizing to her were a big step. She didn't intend to let that advantage slip away, even though he seemed as remote as ever this morning. If this marriage failed, it wouldn't be for her lack of trying.

"Please, take me with you today," she finally pleaded.

"If you're serious about seeing Kilronan, you'll have to ride. I can't drive the wagon over rough country without riskin' an axle."

"I can ride."

"Astride." His gray eyes took on a steely glint. "I don't own a sidesaddle."

"I can learn," she promised.

"Derry stays here. Mary will look after her."

Caitlin nodded. "If you're sure she'll be safe."

"The child will come to no harm. Mary's odd, but she has a good heart."

Caitlin slipped onto the bench across from him. His face was still swollen and bruised, and she remembered how terrified she'd been when he went into the pen with the bull. She suddenly wanted to put her arms around him and hold him. "Do you think that whoever tried to kill you is gone?"

He shook his head. "Nope, but I think the shooter is after me personal. I'll leave Gabe here to keep an eye on Mary and the kids."

"If you think it's safe."

"I wouldn't ride out if I didn't believe it was."

Caitlin was surprised when neither Mary nor Derry protested the arrangement. "We'll be several hours," Caitlin said. "I don't know when—"

"Mary do," the Indian woman assured her before leaning down and whispering something in Derry's ear.

Derry laughed and clapped her hands. "Secret!" she cried. "I'm gonna feed Blank-flour!"

"Feed Mary's duck," Mary clarified as she started for the door.

"My klicken!" Derry corrected, dashing after her. "Mine!"

"Be a good girl," Caitlin said.

Derry didn't wait long enough to reply.

Caitlin hurried upstairs to change. She was a little nervous about attempting a man's saddle, but she chose her plainest riding habit, a sensible russet wool with a very full skirt that had once been her mother's. She had always worn pantaloons under her riding clothes, following French fashion. Today she picked out a sturdy linen pair to wear under her shift and petticoats.

The matching russet hat to the riding habit was long gone, but Mama's Italian leather boots were nearly as lovely as they had been when Caitlin was a child. They were long enough, but a trifle narrow on Caitlin's feet.

"Caity!" Shane called from below in the yard. "Comin' or not?"

"Coming." Caitlin pulled on a black felt hat adorned with a pheasant feather, pinned the tricorn securely in place, and tied her stock as she hurried down the steps. She tugged on her gloves as she stepped out onto the porch.

Shane sat astride the buckskin he'd ridden when he'd met her in Jefferson. He was, she decided instantly, a bold sight, this Missouri husband of hers. His fringed leather vest stretched across a brawny chest; his long, muscular legs were thrust into high boots, and his hat was pulled low over his tanned face. A sheathed knife hung from a beaded Indian belt around his lean waist, and a shot bag and powder horn were slung carelessly over one shoulder.

Wouldn't he set the ladies aflutter in the streets of Dublin, she thought. . . . At least he would have before the bad times came, before the hunger started.

She sighed and smiled up at him, suddenly very proud that he was hers in spite of her doubts.

Shane held the reins of a second mount in one hand. The animal was tall and thin with a backbone sharp enough to cut peat. Her hair was short and shiny black, except for one hind leg that was spotted white. Her tail was rope thin and the mane cropped short. And worst of all were the ridiculously long ears, above two bulging white-rimmed eyes.

"A mule?" she cried. "You expect me to ride a mule?"

The hint of a smile flashed across his face before his mood became serious again. "Guess you are pretty gussied up to be ridin' ole Bessie here."

Caitlin looked from Shane to the mule. Was this his idea of a joke? The animal was absurd. The idea that she could ride such a creature was even more ridiculous.

As if prompted, Bessie laid back her ears, showed long, yellow teeth, and brayed.

"No," Caitlin declared. "Absolutely not." Behind her, she heard Justice giggling. "Why do you want to make me look the fool?" she asked.

"It appears to me you need no help. That getup might do for Dublin's park, but here? You'll die of heat, woman. You'd be better garbed in a pair of Gabriel's britches and a linen shirt."

Caitlin felt her cheeks grow hot. "There's nothing wrong with my attire, Shane McKenna. 'Tis proper for a lady. It's you and your stupid mule that make a jest."

"You don't like Bessie?"

"Are you addlepated? I'm not a gypsy to ride an abomination such as this."

"She's the safest animal on—"

"If you fancy Bessie so, you ride her!"

"Must everything be a battle with you?"

Caitlin's heart pounded, but she stood her ground. If she was wed to a monster, as the Thompsons had insinuated, it was better to learn it now. "Shane," she warned him. "Don't—"

"Get on the damned mule, Caity."

"I won't." She backed up a step as the first shiver of doubt seized her. "I won't be bullied by you or any other man," she began. "I—" Her words died in her throat as Shane swung down out of the saddle and started toward her with the devil's own look in his eye.

Chapter 12

Caity held her breath as Shane's long legs covered the distance between them, but she didn't budge. She stood there, hands on her hips, heart pounding, silently daring him to put her on that mule.

"Suit yourself, woman," Shane said as he dropped to one knee and whipped out his scalping knife.

"You wouldn't dare!" Her anger turned to shock as he slashed off the trailing train of her riding skirt.

"Stand still," he ordered as he gathered a section of her habit in one hand. The razor-sharp blade parted the soft cloth and the petticoats beneath it. Stunned, she watched as Shane sliced the material from midthigh to the hem, both back and front.

"You . . . you pratie-digging blackard!" she cried. "You've ruined my mother's riding habit."

"I've ruined nothin'. I've made it useful." He turned to Justice. "Saddle Ladybug for her."

"You've destroyed my skirt. Do you even know the cost of such material?"

Shane shook his head. "Make up your mind. If you're too high and mighty to ride Bessie, you can ride the bay mare. I'll not have it said that I bully my wife." He slid the knife back into its sheath. "And I'm not going to let you ride a spirited horse with your legs all tangled in twenty yards of skirt."

"My legs are my affair," she retorted.

"Some would say otherwise, darlin', seein' as how I am your lawful husband."

"Are you? You seem to forget that more than I do," she flung back at him. She was so mad that she wanted to punch him. She'd never been a violent person, but it was all she could do to pin her clenched hands at her sides.

"I never forget that, Caity," he said. "Your safety is my concern, as your husband and as the ramrod of this spread." He went to the mule and began to untie the cinch. "Ladybug's got more fire than Bessie, so you'd best hold on tight if you don't want to be tossed on your ass."

Caitlin glared at him. She'd looked forward to this time alone with him. She'd wanted to try to mend the breach between them. Instead, they'd somehow vaulted into another full blown confrontation over a mule.

She forced herself to control her temper. "Shane McKenna, you would try the patience of Job."

"Maybe so."

He didn't sound in the least repentant, even though he was at fault, not her. "If I'm going to be so much trouble, maybe I shouldn't go at all."

"You know what you need?" he asked as he whipped the saddle off Bessie and slung it over the hitching rail.

"What do I need?" If he laid one finger on her, their marriage was over, she vowed. Shane might look like his father, but the day he started acting like him, she would—

"This." He slipped an arm around her waist and pulled her close, then lowered his head and kissed her.

Caitlin's first thought was to resist, but the warmth of his mouth on hers was delightfully intriguing. Her anger ebbed, and she found herself in a struggle with her own will.

She parted her lips to voice a half-hearted protest when the tip of Shane's tongue darted to touch hers, sending shimmers of sweet sensations swirling through her body.

Somehow she found herself leaning against him, returning the kiss, fitting her mouth to his, and savoring the feel of his broad hand on her back, losing herself in the earthy scent of him.

And then, just when the kiss was deepening, he released her and stepped back, leaving her giddy and confused. Unsatisfied. "Shane . . . don't."

"Don't what? Don't kiss you?"

Shane's husky brogue fed the weakness inside her. "Don't stop," she whispered.

"Ah, Caity mine." He chuckled softly and brought his mouth down to sear hers.

The second kiss was even better than the first. Heat flowed from his lips to hers and swept over her until her last doubts were utterly lost.

Yes, she thought, yes. This is what I want . . . what I've always wanted.

Shane's magical kiss went on and on until she was forced to wrap her arms around him to keep her feet on the ground. She might have lost her wits altogether if she hadn't heard a boyish giggle behind her.

"Oh!" She gasped. "The children . . ." she stammered when she could speak again. Her lips tingled, and she could still feel the shape and texture of his mouth against hers. She could still taste him.

"You want me to put the mule's saddle on Ladybug?" Justice asked in an innocent voice.

Shane was still looking at her, and the intensity of his stare made her stomach feel as though she'd swallowed a handful of butterflies. She wanted to laugh and cry at the same time; she wanted all the world to vanish so they could go on kissing and touching, so that he could keep holding her so tightly that she could feel the beat of his heart.

Shane grinned, and for a moment Caitlin glimpsed the boy she'd once pledged her life to.

He lightly traced her bottom lip with a fingertip, and a wall of ice crumbled inside her.

"Seems to me," Shane said, "that it's better that Justice sees us kissin' than fightin'." The steady gaze from his silver-gray eyes caressed her.

Caitlin nodded and looked away, too full of emotion to answer. She moistened her lips with the tip of her tongue and tried to ignore the throb of blood pulsing through her veins.

"Caity?"

"Yes," she managed, finding her voice. "You're right, husband."

"McKenna?" Justice held tight to the mare's halter as she tossed her head and whinnied frantically to her foal in the barn. "Do you want me—"

"No, thank you," Caitlin said. "I've changed my mind. I'm going to ride Bessie."

"You're certain?" Shane rubbed his fingers along the faint scar on his cheek.

Caitlin nodded. "You know your own animals best, and it was foolish of me to argue with you over so small a thing."

"Do you want this horse or not?" Justice demanded of Shane. "If she's not goin' with you, I will."

"You heard her, boy. Put the mare away. And you're to stay here at the house and keep an eye on things." Still looking pleased with himself, Shane began to resaddle the mule.

"Gabe don't need my help," Justice said. "I heard you tell him to stand guard. I want to come with you."

"Not today."

Justice kicked the dirt with the toe of his boot. "But I want—"

"Do as you're told," Shane ordered. "If you want to be treated like a man, then you'll have to accept a man's responsibilities."

Sullen-faced, Justice led the mare away.

Caitlin watched Shane saddle the mule, then allowed him to help her mount. "I guess Bessie's not the only mule-headed creature here," she said. He adjusted first one side of the saddle and then the other, before tucking her feet solidly into the leather stirrups. "Justice seems disappointed. Maybe we should take him with us," she ventured.

"Nope. I mean to have you all to myself." He patted Bessie's neck. "Keep her head up. Her gait's not the smoothest, but Bessie won't spook on you the first time a leaf blows across her path."

"Neither will I." Caitlin was glad that Shane wanted to be alone with her, and that Justice was staying behind. She just hoped she wouldn't come home to find horse feed in her flour canister.

Shane swung up on his buckskin and looked at her questioningly. "Neither will you *what*?"

"Spook at the first sign of trouble," she answered confidently. "I'm used to taking care of myself."

"Me, too," he said. "It seems the both of us will take some practice in this husband and wife stuff."

"I suppose so," she agreed. "There's one thing in particular that I know I need instruction on."

"And that is?"

"The kissing. It's been so long since I've kissed a man, that I fear I've forgotten how."

He smiled. "Aye, Caity. On that point we agree."

Her eyes widened in surprise. "What's wrong with my kissing?"

"Nothing practice won't cure, wife," he teased. "And I'll consider it my husbandly duty to teach you everything I know."

"What do you think?" Shane lifted Caitlin from the saddle and set her feet lightly on the ground. "Is Kilronan the closest thing you've ever seen to paradise?"

She nodded and took a few tentative steps away from the mule. They'd been riding for more than an hour, and she'd seen old forests and sunny meadows that seemed to stretch to the horizon. Everywhere she looked the land was green and full of life. Deer moved among the big trees, geese and ducks flew overhead, and horses and cattle grazed in the open pastures.

"It's so big," she said.

He tied the mule's reins to a sapling and came to stand beside her. Almost shyly, he took her hand in his. She liked the feeling.

"Do you think you could be happy here?"

She nodded. "I do, but . . ." She sighed and pulled away. She wondered if Shane intended to kiss her again and if she should let him. Sweet Lord. When Shane touched her, she couldn't think straight.

It seemed strange to be wary of her own husband, especially since his kisses were so wonderful. But things were complicated enough between Shane and her without adding more to the stew. Suppose she let nature take its course? She and her husband would be bedded by nightfall. The thought was delicious and frightening.

"But?" Shane's question broke into her reverie.

"I . . ."

"You miss the life you had before you came to America," he supplied.

"Oh, that." She swallowed, trying to ease the constriction in her throat. *The life she had?* Didn't he realize what Ireland was like now? And how could she make him understand? "Not the way it's been the last few years," she hedged. "It's nothing like you remember. But I do miss having women friends and church and parties. It can be lonely, your Missouri."

How could she tell him that there was nothing left of County Clare to go back to? That everyone and everything that had been dear to her had been lost in the stench of rotting potatoes and pestilence?

"The potatoes rotted," she said. "Like they did the year before you left home. But not just a few fields, all of them. One day County Clare was green as heaven, and the next blackened as the gates of hell."

Bile rose in her throat as she remembered the smell, not just of putrid potatoes but of death.

"I didn't know it was so bad," Shane said.

"The blight spread," she continued. "I don't know where it started, but whole counties lost their crops. And for the working families, there was nothing to eat. Nothing."

"We've heard rumors, but—" His voice rasped with emotion.

"The English don't want the rest of the world to know the truth," she said bitterly. "English lords still send boatloads of wheat and beef out of Ireland, but the poor people starve. Thousands wander the roads begging. Desperate men and women will do anything to feed their hungry children."

Caitlin took a deep breath and looked out over the green hillside. Remembering the bad times ripped open the half-healed wounds inside her, but the telling had to be done.

If she bore witness to what she had seen, maybe the nightmares would stop haunting her. Maybe she'd stop waking in the night with the taste of disease in her mouth and the sound of wailing in her ears.

"Good Squire Lawton of Lawton Hill was murdered for his driving pony, Beauty. She was black, with a white mane and tail, and she carried her head high. Oh, Shane, she was the sweetest pony you've ever laid eyes on. But they butchered her and ate her half raw. They boiled her hide to make a soup and even smashed her bones to get at the marrow."

Shane swore softly. He reached for her, but she shook her head. If she went into his arms, she would break down, and her tears would keep her from telling him what he had to hear.

"We tried to help. Lots of good people did. You can feed a dozen guests who show up uninvited for dinner. But what do you do when twenty come the next day, and thirty the day after that? My parents lost everything, Shane. What do you say to the hollow-eyed children who come too late for a crust of bread or a saucer of cabbage?"

"Why didn't you tell me all this before?"

"You didn't ask. And . . . and I didn't think you'd believe me. Who would if they hadn't seen it with their own eyes? My parents tried to help. They gave everything they had . . . even their lives, and it didn't help. It didn't matter at all."

"Maybe it did," he said. "Maybe some of those people survived because of their sacrifice."

"Do you think so, Shane?"

He nodded. "A few, maybe dozens. It matters."

"I'd like to think that."

"That's why you came to America, because you couldn't stay in County Clare."

"Yes. That's why I came." She looked into his eyes and saw the pain flickering there. "But I would have come before, if I'd gotten word from you. I never stopped watching for your letters . . . hoping."

"I want to believe that, Caity. I swear I do, but it's hard."

"Marriage is supposed to be about trust," she said.

"Aye, it is, but I'm a man with little to give."

"Why, Shane? What made you change? You weren't like this when I married you."

"I was younger then. Softer maybe."

"No," she replied. "Sweet maybe, but never soft."

He laughed wryly. "Sweet? Me? You're the first to say it. When Da died, and my mother remarried five weeks after the funeral, it was me my mother packed off to the hiring fair. My brother Kevin was older, but she kept him with her. She said I was fierce with too much of my father's temper to keep peace with her new husband."

"I remember when you left. I cried. You were gone from the village for two years and three months."

"My first master was Dan Duffy. He fed his pigs better than his hired hands. I served him for two years before being laid off and going to work for a dairy farmer nearly as harsh."

"You never told me that."

"There was no need, was there? I was sixteen by the time I returned, old enough to hold my own against a grown man. And wiser. Duffy was a bare-knuckle boxer. He knocked the hell out of me, but I learned a little of his craft."

Caitlin sighed. "When your mother moved away with her family, I was afraid that I'd never see you again. I expected you to settle near your family."

"You were my family, Caity. You were the only one I thought of. If my mother didn't want me near her, why should I follow her to another county?"

"But your brothers and sisters . . . Surely, you—"

"I went to see them once. My sister Molly had married a sailor and moved to London. Kevin and I always rubbed each other the wrong way, and I was a stranger to the little ones. My mother made it plain that I was welcome for supper, but she had no room for me to stay the night."

"You think she turned her back on you?"

"Aye."

"First her, and then me."

"Maybe."

She went to him and touched his arm, feeling the heat of taut muscles beneath his skin. "Whether you believe it or not, Shane, I've always been honest with you."

"If you say so."

"I do." Stubborn, he was stubborn. And no matter what he said, she knew he still didn't believe her about his letters or about Derry.

She squeezed his arm. "Tell me about Cerise."

"You don't want me to talk about her."

"I asked, didn't I?"

He looked away toward a wooded hill. "She said she loved me, but when she quickened with my child, she wanted to get rid of it."

A child! Caitlin hadn't thought that he could say anything about Cerise that would hurt her more than she'd already been hurt, but knowing they'd conceived a child together did.

"I cannot imagine," she said thickly. "I don't under-stand a woman who wouldn't want her own child."

"We fought over the baby the night she died. More than just words, Caity."

The tone of his voice sent a chill down her spine. She shuddered as a question rose in her mind, a question so terrible that the answer could destroy her future. She didn't want to ask it, but she had to know. "Did you kill her? Did the thought of Cerise killing your babe make you do something to her?"

"I was drunk, Caity, but not that drunk. Somebody put a knife into her, but it wasn't me."

Relief made her knees weak. Her husband was mortal, with all the failings of flesh and blood, but he was no monster.

Caitlin tried to keep her voice steady as she asked, "Who did murder Cerise?"

He shook his head. "I don't know, nobody does. I saw the shadow of a man as he escaped out her bedroom window."

"And you were blamed?"

"By some people. Earl Thompson for sure. Not by Fat Rose, and not by the law."

"What about Justice?" she asked. "Does he have any idea what happened?"

"I don't know. He was asleep in the attic. Cerise never liked him in her room. He doesn't talk about the night his mother died. Not a word."

"He worships you, Shane. He'd not do that if he thought you killed his mother."

"Maybe, maybe not. Justice had a strange relationship with Cerise. They weren't like any mother and son you've ever known. Maybe she wasn't capable of being a good mother."

"Well, he has a good father now," Caitlin said.

"I try, Caity. Trouble is, I never had a decent one myself. It's like the first time I got on an unbroken horse. Eventually I learned to ride him, but I took a lot of spills along the way." Shane shuffled his boot heel along the ground, much as Caitlin had seen Justice do when the child was frustrated. "I want to do right by him. I promised his mother I would."

Caitlin, moved by his concern for the boy, touched Shane's arm lightly. "Maybe bringing me here was wrong for Justice. He hates me."

"He'll come around."

"I've tried everything I can think of. What if he never accepts me? Can we be a family if he doesn't? Or will there come a time when you start to resent me as much as he does?"

"He's a good kid, Caity. But he's got strange ways. I didn't see much of him when his mother was alive. She sent him off to live with his Indian relatives a lot. After he came to Kilronan, he went nearly two months without speakin' a word to me. Gabe he took to, right off. And when Mary came, the two of them were easy with each other. And then, inch by inch, like gentlin' a wild colt, I got closer to him. Somebody treated him hard, and gettin' past that takes a lot of patience."

"But if he had an Indian family, why didn't they take him?"

"Cerise wanted me to do it."

"Have you talked to them? Let him visit—"

"I don't want anything to do with them. Cerise had something against her kin. I don't know them, and I don't want to."

"And?" She held his gaze without wavering. "There's more, isn't there?"

"I want him to forget his mother. I want to forget her. Any relative of hers would just make it harder to do that."

For a few minutes they stood there side by side, and then Shane motioned to the animals. "We'd best get back in the saddle, Caity. There's more I want you to see."

As they rode on, Caitlin tried not to dwell on what Shane had told her about Cerise and the child they had made together. That was in the past, and nothing could change what had happened. What mattered now, she told herself, was what she and Shane could build together.

Shane's joy in his land was evident, and his enthusiasm was hard to resist. He seemed more open than he had been since she'd arrived, and they were able to share easy conversation about simple things that had happened in the past week.

"Derry wants a cat," Caitlin said. "Did you know that? The captain of the riverboat had an orange calico, and Derry was fascinated by it. I thought I'd have to carry her off the boat in a trunk to keep her from stealing that cat."

"A cat, is it?" Shane arched a dark brow and chuckled. "I mind the tomcat your father kept, the black one. It hissed at me whenever I came anywhere near it."

"Noah? He wouldn't hurt a flea. He was terrified of mice." She smiled at Shane. "Derry's got a name all picked out. She wants to call her cat McKenna."

"That little colleen is one of a kind."

"She calls you Papa; did you know that?"

"Does she?" A faint smile tugged at the corner of his mouth as he reined his buckskin close to Caitlin's mule. "I'd give her my name. You've only to say the word."

Caitlin tried to ignore the tightness in her chest. "And if I did, Shane, would that mean I'm admitting she's a child of my body? Must we fight this battle—"

"No. I could lie to you and tell you that I believe your damned story about Derry, but I won't. My own mother lied to my father about Kevin their whole life."

"Isn't it possible that—"

"Show me a five-month's babe born alive with hair and fingernails, and I'll show you a piece of the true cross."

"So I'm to be condemned for your mother's folly?"

"Nope. I'll not condemn you, Caity. I just won't swallow what can't go down."

She blinked back fresh tears. "You make it difficult for me—"

"Watch Bessie's head. Pull up on the reins," Shane ordered. They were approaching a fast-running creek with a steep bank on the far side. "Pay attention, Caity. The creek is low. In a flood it can spill over these banks and take out hundred-year-old trees, but now it's barely up to your mule's knees."

Caitlin gritted her teeth as he guided his horse into the water ahead of her. How could they ever settle their differences so long as Shane believed her a cheat and a liar? It was all useless. Shane was impossible.

He twisted in the saddle and shouted back. "Let Bessie pick her own way over the rocks. She's surefooted."

Caitlin held tight to the front of the saddle as the mule shifted her hip and slid into a hole in the creek bottom. Caitlin gasped as water splashed up over her boot tops and wet her skirt, but just when she thought Bessie's legs would crumble under her, the animal struggled up into the shallows. Shane's horse was already out of the stream and climbing the rocky incline on the far side.

Caitlin leaned forward on the mule's withers as Bessie leaped forward and charged up the creek bank. A section of soil slid away under Bessie's front feet, but the mule plunged ahead. They'd nearly caught up with Shane when Caitlin heard an odd noise.

The sound wasn't loud, just a dull rattle that could have been loose seeds in a dried gourd. But in the split second before Bessie exploded under her, Caitlin's mouth parched with fear. Shane's horse reared up, and Caitlin's scream was drowned in Bessie's bray of fright.

The mule sprang straight in the air, ears laid back, head jerked up at an impossible angle. Her forelegs slammed into the earth, jarring Caitlin's teeth and making her see stars.

Caitlin fell forward onto the mule's withers and hung on as the animal jumped sideways, kicked again, and broke into a dead run.

Terrified, Caitlin clung to the reins and concentrated on keeping her seat. Rocks and trees sped by at an alarming rate. Bessie's hooves threw up so much dust that Caitlin could barely keep her eyes open. At any second she expected to be thrown to the ground or smashed against a tree. One foot came out of the stirrup, but she locked her fingers into Bessie's close-cropped mane and wouldn't let go.

Gradually the mule's breathing became labored, and she slowed her breakneck pace to a ragged gallop and finally a spine-crunching trot. When she tapered off into a walk, Caitlin got up the courage to pull on the only rein she had left.

Bessie plodded obediently in a circle.

"Whoa," Caitlin pleaded. "Whoa, girl."

The mule stopped short and hung her head.

Caitlin cautiously slid out of the saddle. Her boots touched the grass, but her legs refused to hold her. She kept sliding until she was sitting on the ground, nearly under the mule.

Bessie didn't move. Her dark hide was soaked with sweat, and foam dribbled from her open mouth. Her white-rimmed eyes were bloodshot, and her long ears drooped forward limply.

"Poor old girl," Caitlin murmured. Adrenaline still raced through her body. She knew she should be afraid, but she wasn't—not for herself. All she could think of was Shane. Had he been thrown? Had the snake bitten him? It must have been a rattlesnake, she decided. What else could have panicked the animals so? What if the snake—

A horse's high-pitched whinny caught her attention. "Shane!" she called. She scrambled up and looked around. Shane's horse trotted toward her through a grove of trees, but the saddle was empty. "Shane?" His name came out in a croak.

Keeping one hand on Bessie's reins, Caitlin reached out to catch Shane's gelding. The horse didn't seem to be hurt, other than a pair of skinned knees. His chest was wet and his eyes wild, but if the snake had bitten him, it didn't show.

"Where's Shane?" she demanded irrationally of the animal. If he was hurt or dead . . . An awful numbness spilled through her.

She had to find him, but she didn't even know which way to go. Dragging both animals by the reins, she started back toward the trees where she'd first seen Shane's buckskin.

She'd reached the stand of oaks when she heard him call her name. "Caity?"

Her fear turned to joy as she saw him. "Shane! Here! I'm here!" she shouted back. Tears blurred her eyes. Instinct demanded she run to him, but her knees were too weak to carry her.

"Caity! Are you all right?"

No man who could run like that was badly injured, she decided in the last seconds before he swept her off her feet.

"Caity."

She wanted to tell him that she was fine. She wanted to ask him if he'd fallen off his horse. But suddenly all that mattered was that she was in his arms, and that he was kissing her as she'd never been kissed before.

Chapter 13

"I couldn't stand it if I lost you," Shane said when he stopped kissing her long enough to take a breath.

She snuggled closer, savoring the sweet music of those words. "I feel the same," she answered softly. "I was afraid that the snake had killed you."

"That rattler was probably halfway to Oregon country by the time I hit the ground. Poor old diamondback, just sunnin' hisself on a rock, mindin' his own business when he looks up and sees Cherokee's hooves coming toward his head."

"Who?"

"Cherokee. My buckskin. My best horse—the one I told you that you couldn't have." He tilted her chin up and kissed the tip of her nose. "You've a fine nose, Mrs. McKenna," he teased. "Has anyone ever told you that?"

"You never told me your horse had a name." Shane trailed a ribbon of light kisses up to her eyelids, and she uttered a small sigh of delight. "That tickles."

"You never asked me if he had a name." He planted a caress against the left corner of her mouth and then gently nibbled her lower lip. "There are . . . lots of questions . . . you've never . . . asked me."

Thrilled, she pressed closer to him. She wanted to pinch herself to see if this was really happening, or if she'd conjured it up out of a dream. And now that she was wrapped in Shane's strong arms, she couldn't resist teasing him. "Such as . . . how did your horse throw you?"

"You're a cruel woman," he pronounced. "And I wasn't thrown. I bailed out when Cherokee switched ends and started fallin' backwards on top of me." He groaned. "It didn't do a damn thing for my sore ribs. They must be just cracked. If they were broken and I'd hit the ground that hard, I'd be pushin' up clover."

"Oh, you poor thing." She reached up to stroke his face, running her fingers over his high cheekbones and tracing the curve of his brows. He had shaved that morning, but already a tiny stubble of gold had sprung up on his face; she liked the feel of it against her skin.

"Never ask a horseman how he was tossed off." Shane caressed the nape of her neck, sending shivers of anticipation through her. Then he kissed her again, so thoroughly that she forgot her fear of the snake and Shane's tumble off his horse. All she could think of was the way he was touching her and that she didn't want this embrace to end.

"Caity." His breathing deepened, as though he'd run a long way, and he fumbled with the linen stock at her throat. "Caity . . . let me love you."

"Yes . . . yes." She strained against him. She wanted more, wanted to be so close to him that she wouldn't know where she stopped and Shane began.

His kisses became demanding, urgent, feeding the flames of the heat inside her. "Caity, girl." He groaned. "I want—"

The sound of a gunshot cut through his words.

"Son of a bitch!" He stiffened and pushed her reluctantly away. "Talk about bad timin'." Instantly alert, he looked around and ran to his buckskin to yank his rifle from the saddle scabbard.

"No . . ." She was stunned, aching for more. "What's wrong?"

"That was gunfire."

Her heart was still racing, and she felt weak inside, but whether it was from fright or disappointment, she couldn't say.

All traces of desire and tenderness had vanished from Shane's hard features. "Stay where you are!" he warned as he mounted his horse, wheeled Cherokee around, and drove his boot heels into the gelding's sides.

"Shane, wait!" she protested. "What if something's happened to Derry? I want to come with you!"

But he was already too far away to hear her.

"Shane!" she shouted again. "You can't . . ."

She exhaled sharply. "He can't keep doing that to me. If he thinks I'm going to spend the rest of our married life waiting while he tends to trouble, he's got another thought coming."

Shane hadn't been with her in County Clare when she'd had to arrange her father's funeral, and he hadn't been there when she'd faced down a dozen starving beggars intent on ransacking her house.

She hadn't survived by waiting for a man to come to her rescue. And she wouldn't last long in the wilderness if she played the Dublin miss.

The question was, could she get on this abominable creature without assistance? With a shrug, she decided that there was only one way to find out.

"Easy, Bessie," Caitlin coaxed as she approached the mule. "Nice beast. Pretty girl," she lied.

Bessie flicked her ears, and her bulging eyes took on a malicious gleam.

"Good mule," Caitlin soothed as she seized the reins. Bessie pawed the grass with one hoof. "Stand still."

The mule backed up a few paces, nearly yanking the leather reins from Caitlin's hands.

"I said, stand still!" She snapped the bridle sharply, and Bessie rolled her eyes. "You behave, or I'll have Mary slit your gullet and roast you over an open fire," Caitlin threatened in a cold whisper.

The mule froze.

Muttering a prayer under her breath, Caitlin thrust the toe of her boot into the stirrup and flung herself up and over the saddle. Bessie started forward. "Whoa!"

The mule kept walking as Caitlin struggled to untangle her leg. Bessie broke into a trot, and Caitlin pulled hard on the reins.

The animal stopped short.

"Yes!" Caitlin cried. "That's it." She jammed her toe into the stirrup, hauled the mule's head around, and slapped the leather across Bessie's neck. "Get up!"

The mule broke wind, shuddered from neck to rump, gave a halfhearted kick, and began to trot in the direction Shane had ridden.

"Faster!" Caitlin shouted, and urged Bessie into a bone-pounding canter.

To Caitlin's relief, nothing seemed amiss as she rode into the barnyard. She could see Mary and Derry standing on the front porch while Shane, Gabriel, and Justice talked to Rachel Thompson near the paddock.

Shane was still mounted on Cherokee, and Justice had climbed the corral fence and was hanging off the top rail by one arm, obviously listening to the conversation.

Derry looked up and saw her, waved, and then went back to playing with the corn-husk doll Mary had given her at breakfast. Mary nodded but didn't speak. Her face was stern as usual, yet her attention seemed focused on Shane and the others.

Bessie needed no urging to join Shane's buckskin and Rachel Thompson's horse. The mule brayed and trotted over to nuzzle Cherokee's rump.

Shane looked up. "I see you got here under your own power." He gestured toward Rachel. "She says that someone slaughtered one of their cows last night."

"But we just heard a shot—"

"Gabe fired off a round to bring me in," Shane explained.

"Nice mount." Rachel grinned at Caitlin.

"I like her," Caitlin replied dryly. "She has such a comfortable trot."

"I'll bet." Rachel whipped off her Spanish vaquero's hat and slapped it against her leg. She still wore men's clothing, and her face was dusty, but her hair was clean and pulled back severely in a single braid.

She had a pleasant face when she smiled, Caitlin realized. "You say your father lost a cow?"

"Didn't lose it," Rachel answered as she put her hat back on. "Somebody carved off the back quarter."

"Cow stealing is serious out here, isn't it?"

"About as serious as you can get. Your man, here, hung a rustler last winter." Rachel glanced at Gabe for confirmation. "Didn't he?"

Gabriel nodded.

A hollow feeling filled Caitlin's belly, but she refused to give Rachel the satisfaction of letting her see how the thought of Shane's taking a human life tore her up. She bit back her swelling questions and waited in silence.

"Don't fill Caity's head with such stuff," Shane said, dismounting and reaching up to help her down from the mule's back. "I executed a rustler. But he was worse than a cow thief. He and another lump of buffalo dung raped and murdered an Indian woman. I came on him too late to stop it, and too late to catch his partner. I had to bury the woman, so I thought it best to send him to his heavenly reward as well."

"Why didn't you take him to the magistrate?" Caitlin demanded. "Surely there are laws against murder—even in Missouri."

"Not when a white man kills an Indian," Gabe said. "If McKenna got the bastard to the nearest settlement without getting backshot by the other rustler, it would be his word against the killer's. And if the law did convict, it wouldn't be for murder."

"Last white man arrested for shootin' a Shawnee boy was Jeb Hammer, over to Kane's Crossroads. As I remember, Jeb got thirty days in jail and a fine," Shane said. He motioned to Justice. "Take these animals, son."

Justice leaped off the fence into Cherokee's saddle, and Shane handed the boy Bessie's reins. The child guided both horse and mule around Rachel's bay, and rode over to the stable door.

"You know what the fine for killin' an Indian is around here?" Shane asked Caitlin.

She shook her head.

"Two dollars," he replied.

Caitlin stared at him in disbelief. "That's outrageous."

Rachel nodded. "That's what the jury thought. But hell, the judge needed to pay his liquor tab at the bar, so somebody had to ante up some silver."

Rachel's horse watched the other animals until they were out of sight in the barn; then she shook her head and danced nervously.

Gabe ran a hand gently over the animal's neck and whispered softly to the mare. The bay quieted and rubbed her nose against him. Obligingly he scratched under her chin.

"Is that Indian you're speaking?" Caitlin asked.

Gabe nodded. "Osage." He flashed a rare smile. "Love words."

"You've a rare hand with horses," Rachel said.

"I like them."

"It shows." Rachel glanced back at Shane. "I'd best get riding. Big Earl will beat the shit out of me if he finds out I rode over here to warn you about the rustler."

"I'm surprised he doesn't blame me," Shane replied wryly.

"Naw, Beau thought of it first. Anything my brother comes up with, Big Earl pisses on," Rachel said. "Big Earl thinks you're lower than an Ozark hellbender, McKenna, but not low enough to shoot one of our cows for the meat."

"Your father's gettin' soft in his old age, isn't he?" Shane asked. "Takin' my part against Beau's?"

Rachel laughed. "He'd take Satan's part afore Beau's, and that's a fact." She shrugged. "Can you blame him? Have you ever seen a more worthless pup than Beau Thompson? It's a damn shame them renegade Indians kilt my big brother Al and left Beau alive." She looked at Caitlin. "If you see Beau, steer clear of him. He's meaner than a prairie tornado and as stupid as hog turds."

She pulled her hat down tighter and retied the cord under her chin. "Only one has anything to do with Beau is that half-wit you shoved on us, Nate Bone. More trouble I never saw than him. No patience with horses and shoots like a blind man."

"I didn't send Nate to Big Earl," Shane said. "I ran him off Kilronan because he's an Indian hater. He couldn't stomach workin' with Gabe. Your father didn't need to hire him on."

"Sure he did," Rachel answered. "Thought it would get your goat. No end to the mess Big Earl will get his-self in if he thinks it will hurt you. Even hirin' on prairie trash to ride herd on his stock."

"You watch Nate Bone. Watch him close. He could be responsible for the trouble on both places. I catch him at it, there'll be another hangin'—if he lives long enough for me to string him up."

Rachel shook her head. "I doubt it's Nate. He's a sly, whiskey-suckin' snake, but one man couldn't cause such mischief alone. Big Earl thinks it's renegade Indians, and I'm inclined to believe he's right. I hear tell there's been cows slaughtered over to John Mahee's spread near Twin Forks."

"Well, Big Earl might be right," Shane replied, "but one way or another, it's got to be stopped. I appreciate you comin' over, Rachel."

She grinned. "Keep your powder dry." Her smile faded and she grew serious. "I have to warn you to stay clear of Thompson land. Big Earl's given orders to shoot trespassers on sight."

"We'll keep that in mind," Shane said.

Gabe climbed the rail fence and dropped a lariat over a horse's neck. "I'll ride back with you to the line," he said. "McKenna will want our animals driven in tonight, anyway."

Shane nodded. "I'll get the mules and the cattle out of the east pasture. You bring in the rest."

"No need to put yourself out on my account, Gabriel," Rachel said. "I don't need no watchin'. I sure ain't no Irish gentlefolk."

Caitlin noticed that Rachel's eyes softened as she watched Gabe saddle a pinto gelding. And it didn't escape her notice that Rachel waited for the Indian wrangler, or that they rode out side by side, not talking, but obviously easy together, as if they were old friends.

"How did you get on Bessie?" Shane's hand closed on the top of her shoulder.

"What?" Caitlin turned to look directly into his eyes.

He grinned and tipped her chin up with the pad of his thumb. "I asked you how you got back in the saddle by yourself?" Then he leaned close and brushed her lips with his.

Instantly she felt a flash of heat shimmer through her. "Easy," she said breathlessly. "All you have to be is meaner than the mule."

Supper that night was Mary's infamous rabbit stuffed with wild onions and sage, some sort of baked root that tasted like potatoes, and raw wild greens drizzled with bacon fat. Naturally Mary provided a large wooden bowl of Indian fry bread to accompany the meal.

Out of deference to her, Caitlin thought, Mary had served her feast in the newly furnished dining parlor. Caitlin wondered what her mother and grandmother would think of their precious delftware being used by a pipe-smoking Indian woman, a cowboy, and Shane McKenna. Somehow she thought that her mother would be most distressed by the last.

When the meal was finished, it was customary for the men to leave the table while she and Mary cleared away the dishes. Tonight Caitlin had come to supper with another idea in mind. She watched until Justice was nearly done eating, and then she brought a book from under her apron and propped it against the table.

"I promised Derry that I'd read to her tonight," Caitlin said. "I hope you don't mind if I do it here where the light is good." Without waiting for an answer from any of them, she opened the green, leather-bound cover of *A Thousand and One Nights*, translated from the Persian by Edward W. Lane.

Derry climbed up into Caitlin's lap as she began to

read quietly. After a few pages, Caitlin glanced up and peeked through her lashes to see Gabe listening intently to the story. Justice made a great show of wanting more fry bread, but she noticed that he didn't eat it; he merely crumbled it on his plate.

By the time Caitlin reached the part where the beautiful queen held the sultan mesmerized with her tale, Caitlin's audience was hooked. Even Shane leaned forward to hear what would happen next.

Derry's head nodded, and Caitlin felt the child's breathing slow.

"Sleepy, darling?" Caitlin murmured. Derry didn't answer.

"Why stop story?" Mary demanded as she poured her coffee into one of Caitlin's delft saucers. "Good story like Osage stories. Sky People stories." She reached across the table and touched the book. "Is more?"

"Much more," Caitlin assured her. "Treasure and magic and wicked genies. But it's time for Derry to be in bed."

Mary nodded. "So. Maybe you read more tomorrow night."

"Maybe," Caitlin agreed. "If Derry wants to hear this book." She flashed the Indian woman an innocent smile. "She might want another one."

"No," Justice chimed in. "She'll want to hear the rest of this one. Derry likes genies."

"I'll carry the little colleen upstairs for you," Shane offered.

As the three of them left the room, Caitlin heard Gabe ask Justice, "What exactly is a genie?"

"It's an animal. They have them in Ireland," the boy supplied quickly. "A genie is something like a weasel, only bigger."

Upstairs, Shane stood silently and watched as Caitlin

removed Derry's dress, petticoats, pantaloons, and shift, and tugged a white linen nightgown over her head. Derry slept soundly through the process, only sighing and snuggling down when Caitlin tucked her into her bed.

"I feel awful putting her in without giving her a bath," Caitlin whispered to Shane.

"What she really needs is her own room," Shane said, slipping an arm around Caitlin's waist.

She stepped into the hall and closed the bedroom door. "I don't know how she'd take to that. She's slept with me since we left Ireland."

He moved to pin Caitlin playfully against the wall. "I think it's time we did something about all our sleeping arrangements." He leaned close and kissed her on the mouth. "I want you, Caity—as a husband wants his wife."

Heart thumping, she turned her face away. Her lips tingled from the heat of his kiss, and desire fluttered in the pit of her stomach.

Her throat constricted so that her proper words flowed like warm butter. "The arrangement between us made sense," she murmured. "After being parted for so long . . ."

Was it normal to feel this way? she wondered. Did a decent woman long for her husband's touch the way a wilting rose yearned for rain?

"Too long, Caity." He kissed her forehead. "I want to be with you. I need you."

Caitlin shivered. "Not now, Shane—not while the children are awake." She wanted him to sweep her up in his arms and make love to her, but uncertainty still lurked in the back of her mind. There was so much about Shane that frightened her. . . .

He nodded. "Aye. As much as I'd like to, I can't stay with you now. Gabe's going to stand guard from midnight to dawn, but I need to take the first watch so he can get a few hours of sleep. I'll knock on your door when I come in."

"I can't promise," she answered, moving out of the circle of his arms. "I want things to be right between us, but I'm not certain that this is the time. What if you get me with child?"

"If I do, then that will settle our question, won't it? Wait for my knock, Caity." He gave her a long look before turning away and descending the stairs.

Her heart was fluttering, and she struggled for breath. Thoughts—brazen thoughts that she didn't know she possessed—taunted her. "Come soon," she whispered, too low for him to hear.

But if you do come, will I have nerve enough to open the door?

It was past nine when Mary finished the last of the kitchen chores and retired to her own cabin. For the better part of an hour, Caitlin sat at the dining parlor table stitching the sleeve of a dress she was mending for Derry. Finally, when she was sure that Justice was asleep in his bed, she went to the kitchen and poured hot water into a basin to wash.

There were no sounds in the house but the sighing of the fire and the slight creak of settling timbers. Moonlight poured in the kitchen window, illuminating the room with a pale golden glow.

Using a bit of French soap that she'd brought with her from home, Caitlin carefully bathed herself from head to foot and dried herself with a clean towel. She had washed her hair the day before, but she took great pains to brush it and pin it up in a soft knot.

The room was warm, but gooseflesh still rose on her arms and shoulders. She felt as nervous as a bride on her wedding night.

She was a bride. Not only had she not been with any man in eight years, she and Shane had been together only a few hours before he went away to America.

"If only I was a virgin," she murmured. "Better we had never consummated the marriage." Then, at least, Shane would have known that she'd been faithful during their separation.

A log snapped in the fire, and she jumped.

"I'm not afraid," she lied to herself.

Trembling, her mouth dry, she tiptoed up the stairs and into Shane's bedchamber. She'd brought no candle, but she needed none. She made her way to the bed and slipped under the blanket. And then she waited.

Chapter 14

The moonlight shimmered silver against the surface of the black water as Shane waded into the rocky creek near the house. He gasped as the icy current closed over his knees and then rose to cover his hips and groin. A few yards down, he'd cleared away the stones to form a pool deep enough to swim in. Taking a breath, he closed his eyes and dove under.

From the stream bottom, Shane scooped a handful of sand and gravel. When he came up, he scrubbed his chest and arms until his skin tingled.

The cold water numbed his flesh and shriveled his sex, but he wasn't worried. He was in no danger of losing his virility. The way he'd been thinking the past few days, it was a wonder he hadn't heated the creek to the boiling point.

Tonight he would take Caity as his wife or know the reason why. She was ready and willing—he'd read that in her ginger-brown eyes. He'd nearly thrown her down and made love to her on the edge of the meadow this morning. Whatever they had to settle yet between them would be easier to manage once he was back in her bed where he belonged.

Strange how a man's mind worked. When he'd first come to America, he'd thought of nothing but Caity. He'd turned down a lot of women he could have had—

some without paying a dime. But Caity had been his first, and he'd wanted no other.

Then, when he'd sent the money and waited futilely for months, a callus grew inside him. He'd drunk too much one night and laid down silver to bed with a blonde at a filthy tavern on the Mississippi River. And after that there had been a widow he met at a dance, and a handful of women whose faces he couldn't remember. None of them had been Caity, and once his physical need was satisfied, he'd been ashamed of himself.

As the years passed he'd thrown himself into the work of helping his uncle build Kilronan, having as little to do with females as possible—until he met Cerise. It was Cerise who'd taught him how to please a woman. He supposed he should be grateful for that. He'd been as green as grass the night he and Caity had consummated their marriage vows.

"Draw, fumble, fire," Cerise had said after they bedded the first time. "You've all the right equipment, but none of the know-how." Her words had wounded his pride sore, cutting as deep as a Shawnee scalping knife. But once he'd had a taste of her—pepper and all—he'd come back for more, until even she was satisfied with his performance.

"It's time I let you go," he whispered into the night. He took a deep breath and sent one final thought Cerise's way. *Fare thee well, wherever you've landed.* Then he dived under the water again and didn't surface until his lungs were screaming for air.

Shivering, teeth chattering, Shane splashed to the creek bank and scrubbed his legs and feet. Aching cold seeped through to his bones, but he didn't care. The clear, rushing water had eased the aching in his ribs and made him feel clean inside as well as out. He'd not felt this cleansed since he'd sought out a priest after Cerise's death, made confession for his sins, and received his first holy communion in many years.

He regretted the sins he'd committed in the eight years he and Caity had been apart. He'd kept his penance, and he hoped Father Gregory's absolution would count with the Lord.

He wanted the chance to be a husband to Caity again, and he wanted the past to stay buried. He prayed it was possible.

Cherokee nickered from the paddock, and Shane reached for the rifle he'd left propped beside his clothing and boots. Then he caught sight of Gabe beyond the pasture gate and heard the wrangler's pinto whinny a response.

He was jumping at shadows. If a hungry Indian had slaughtered Thompson's cow, he'd be a long way from here by now. He sighed. Trouble was, it didn't sound to him like any Indian he'd ever known. Most were not given to waste a rabbit hide, let alone three-quarters of a beef.

He and Gabriel had driven all his stock close to the house, and Gabe was riding guard. He'd have to trust Gabe's good sense, he decided. After all, what rustler worth his salt would try to drive off animals on a night as bright as this one?

With one last glance around, Shane picked up his rifle, boots, and clothing, and started back toward the house and Caity.

She'd promised herself that she wouldn't fall asleep in Shane's bed, but as the hours passed, her morning in the saddle and the day's work took their toll. Caitlin drifted off and didn't wake until she heard the squeak of the bedroom door.

"Oh." Her eyes snapped open, and she stared at Shane

in astonishment as she remembered where she was and why. And all the while he stood not two feet from the bed with his boots in one hand and a shirt over his arm. "Shane?"

"And who else were you expectin', darlin'?" he answered.

Heat radiated under the surface of her skin as she realized that he was as naked as the day he'd been born. The moonlight danced over his broad shoulders and muscular chest. It gleamed like gold dust off his flat belly and narrow hips, and accentuated his tumescent shaft springing from the curly mat of dark hair below.

Caitlin's breath caught in her throat. She wondered if she should pinch herself to find out if she was dreaming or awake.

The air in the room seemed charged with energy, as if Shane had brought the outdoors with him. She caught the sweet odor of basswood flowers and the faint scent of new mown grass. No, Shane was not a dream; he was as real as life.

But the feeling of being caught up in a dream remained. Surely even a married woman should feel shame at looking at her husband this way, she thought. But she could not tear her gaze from him, and she could not prevent the lustful thoughts rising in her mind. Moistening her lips with the tip of her tongue, she struggled to regain her composure.

"I thought I'd have to track you down," Shane said in a husky voice. "And here you are, exactly where you belong."

Unconsciously she jerked the corner of the sheet up to cover her breasts and sucked in a deep, ragged breath. The hair prickled on the back of her neck, and goose bumps rose on her skin. "You must think me . . . a brazen hussy," she said. "I didn't want to wake Derry, so I came in. . . ."

"Ah, Caity girl, you needn't make excuses for comin' to your husband's bed."

She trembled as he took hold of the sheet and pulled it back. "You're a fair sight, Caitlin Mary."

She slid to the far side of the bed and scooted up on her knees. Her white linen gown covered her from ankle to throat, but the fabric had been washed so many times that it was as thin as morning dew. She could feel the cloth clinging to her breasts and thighs, rubbing against her sensitive nipples and stretching tightly over her buttocks.

Feeling foolish, she crossed her arms over her chest and watched wide-eyed as he slid onto the mattress beside her.

"Don't be afraid of me, darlin'," Shane murmured.

His words spilled over her like warm, sweet-scented honey. "I'm not afraid," she protested.

Lies, she thought. How could she not be afraid—frightened that he'd be disappointed in her, that she would not be a match for his Cerise?

"You know I'd never hurt you, Caity."

Did she? She was trembling from head to foot, and the air seemed too thin to breathe. "I want you, too, Shane," she whispered. "I do."

He reached over and touched her hair. His big hand that had seized the horn of a monstrous bull was so gentle that he might have been handling a newly hatched chick. "Let it down," he said. "I want to see your ginger-red hair fallin' over your shoulders."

His searching fingers closed on a hairpin, and he pulled it free. Then he drew out a second and a third. Her knotted tresses tumbled gypsylike down her back. "Better. I always thought you had the most beautiful hair I'd ever seen."

Her tongue felt stuck to the bottom of her mouth. She wanted to say something in turn, but she was too full of emotion to speak. She felt so strange, as though her body belonged to someone else. Just having Shane so close to her was enough to make her giddy.

How many nights had she lain awake thinking of him and wanting him beside her? How many nights had she prayed that they'd have another chance to be together?

"Say something," he coaxed. "Else I'll think I'm here alone and just dreamin' you're beside me."

"Your hair is nice, too," she stammered woodenly. "Even brown."

He laughed, then leaned close and kissed her lips tenderly. She closed her eyes and savored the caress, not giving and not retreating, just feeling with every fiber of her being.

"Stay right where you are," he said.

To her surprise, he sprang off the bed and went to the far side of the room. She heard the scrape of something hard against the floor; then Shane heaved up the heavy trunk and carried it to the door, blocking the entrance. "There," he said. "That should keep the rascals out."

"Which rascals?"

"All of them. Big and small." He turned back to her. "I've waited so long to have you here. I'm not about to let us be disturbed by man or beast tonight."

She chuckled softly. "It would more likely be a child—yours or mine." And then she sighed with contentment. "I thought perhaps you were barring the door to keep me in."

The mattress rustled as he climbed into the bed. His scent reached her first, male and a little unnerving. "You'll not want to get away, darlin', I promise you. Of course, if you did need to escape, there's always the window."

He covered her hand with his and brought it to his lips, turning it gently so that he could kiss the length of each finger in turn, then her palm, and finally the sensitive skin over the pulse at her wrist.

Caitlin gave a small sigh of pleasure as a rainbow of sensation spread up her arm and warmed her body. Then Shane trailed slow, teasing caresses up to the underside of her elbow. She could feel his breath through the thin linen sleeve of her nightgown. "That tickles," she whispered, trying to keep the mood light.

But his kisses didn't really tickle; instead, they stirred her in a way that she could not fathom. They made her weak and vulnerable.

He slid closer and pulled her other arm away from her breast. "Don't hide from me," he murmured. "I want to see you, Caity, all of you." Again he started at her fingertips and kissed her hand and arm until she cupped his cheek in her hand and lifted his head so that she could kiss him full on the mouth.

Then, somehow, without thinking or knowing how it happened, her arms were around his neck and he was holding her so close that his long, naked legs pressed against hers.

"Shane . . ." What kind of woman was she that she could feel so undone at a man's touch? The heat between her thighs had become a throb; her bones were so heavy that she had no strength to move.

"Yes, darlin'?"

She sighed again. "I like this."

"You'll like what's to come even more," he promised.

A shiver of anticipation ran down her spine. "We should have done this on the first night I came to Missouri," she dared.

He chuckled. "You're right, and the fault was all mine. But now we have all that time to make up for."

He ran an exploring finger over her lower lip, and it seemed the most natural thing in the world for her to open her mouth and gently suck the callused tip. "Caity," he groaned. "You'll unman me."

They kissed again, and this time it was the tip of his heated tongue that she drew in and toyed with. She liked the taste and unfamiliar sensations that made her want to deepen the caress until they joined in a swirl of pleasure and forbidden thoughts.

"Wife . . ." Shane kissed the corner of her mouth and her cheek, and then the hollow beneath her ear. His tongue brushed her lobe and she moaned softly. He continued on, planting warm, moist kisses down her neck to the top ribbon tie of her nightgown.

And all the while he kissed her, her hands were busy, touching his face, tangling in his hair, and rubbing the hard taut muscles on his neck and shoulders. Not only were their legs entwined, but she could feel a rising heat against her belly.

"Ah, darlin'," he whispered.

She felt a slight tug as the first tie came undone and then the pressure of his warm mouth against her skin. She could see the curve of his naked shoulder and the corded muscles along his back.

He cupped her breast in his hand, and her nipples tightened into hard, aching buds. "Do you want me to stop?" he rasped.

"No." It came out more as a breath than a sound. She couldn't say what she felt. She couldn't describe the pressure building in the pit of her stomach, the heat that spiraled tighter and tighter.

How could this be? She was no virgin. She and Shane had consummated their marriage eight years ago, but she had never experienced these sensations then or since. She had not known that they were possible.

Another tie came loose.

Caitlin squeezed her hands into tight knots and squirmed closer to him. Shane was teasing her nipple with the pad of his thumb; his skin was rough against the thin cloth, and she felt the catch and release of individual threads of linen.

How hard Shane's shoulders were, how soft the curling hair that sprang from his broad chest. Her searching fingers brushed a male nipple and he gasped. "Two can play this game," she said.

The third tie loosened, and Shane kissed the hollow between her breasts. She arched against him, reveling in the touch of his lips and fingers, wanting to be closer.

Then he reached down to tug at the hem of her gown, and she made no protest as he pulled it over her head, leaving her as bare as he was in the pale yellow moonlight.

"I want to kiss your breasts," he said.

The thought made her bold, and she lifted one for his caress. No man had ever done that before. And no one had told her that the feel of his lips and tongue on her nipple would shatter her body with tremors of delight.

He kissed first one swollen bud and then the other, making her breath come in quick, deep shudders and her fingernails scrape the surface of his skin. He drew her nipple between his lips and suckled gently until the fire in her belly flared into a whipping flame.

"Darlin'," he crooned as he moved one hand lower to trace the line of her hip with slow, warm fingertips and brush the nest of curls below her belly. Shamelessly she let him go on laving her nipples with his tongue, suckling and teasing, let him touch her in the secret places that churned with a white-hot passion she had not known she possessed.

"Shane . . ."

He pushed her back upon the pillows and rose on one knee to stare into her eyes. "Trust me, sweet. Trust me."

She closed her eyes, cradling his head against her breast as he pressed lower with gentle, exploring fingers, rubbing slow, sensual circles on her skin.

Caitlin urged him on with small, quick gasps and the rhythmic motion of her body. "Please," she whispered. "Please."

"What do you want, woman? Do you want me to touch you here?" He cupped the mound between her thighs, and she moaned with desire as an unfamiliar moistness spilled onto his hand.

"Yes . . . yes."

"You're ready for me now, aren't you?"

"Oh, yes . . ." She waited for him to shift his weight on top of her, waited to feel the heat of his enlarged shaft drive into her woman's sheath. To her shock, he lowered his head and brushed her nether lips with his tongue.

"Shane!"

"Sweet, sweet woman," he whispered.

Brazenly she opened to him as his hard, hot tongue delved ever deeper into her damp folds.

It was wicked. It was wild. It was . . . wonderful. The spiral tightened, sending shock waves through her veins, turning her need to a raw hunger. Then, when she thought she would die from the sheer ecstasy, she cried aloud as her world exploded in multicolored, shimmering stars.

Clutching him, she rode the wave of utter release for seconds or minutes; she couldn't tell. Finally, shaken, her body sheened with a film of perspiration, she drifted down to find herself cradled safely in Shane's strong, protecting arms.

"Oh, Shane," she murmured. "I . . . I . . . You didn't . . ."

He kissed her mouth. "Not yet, I haven't, darlin'. But we've time, plenty of time. The night's young."

"But I didn't . . ." she began, not knowing what she meant to say.

"I think you did," he teased, gently closing his lips over her lower lip and nibbling at it.

"I didn't know," she confessed. "I never felt like that before. Not the first time—" She broke off, suddenly shy with him. "Our wedding night," she finished lamely.

"You were an innocent then, and in many ways you're still an innocent now," he whispered. "I wanted to give you pleasure tonight. Did I?"

"Oh, yes." She sighed and snuggled close. "Yes."

"Good." He kissed the tip of her nose and her chin; then he wound a lock of her hair around his finger and brushed it against his lips. "I know it's not been easy for you here, but I promise to try to make things better."

"And I will, too, Shane."

"You will?"

"Of course, anything."

"Well," he murmured. "That little thing you did."

"What thing?"

"When you touched me here." He brought her hand to his chest and pressed her fingertips against his nipple. "That felt good."

"I wanted it to," she answered softly. In a way she felt as if she were still floating above the earth, still seeing pinwheels of color in the sky. She didn't want to talk, not really. She just wanted to lie there, safe and contented, savoring the magic.

Shane cupped her breast, idly circling the nipple with a fingertip. And to her surprise, she felt a renewed stab of desire deep inside. "A husband likes to be touched as well," Shane said. "Here." He moved her hand lower. "And here."

"Oh."

She had never held a man before. His skin was smooth, the swollen flesh hard beneath her fingertips.

Curious, she brushed her fingers down the length of him and was rewarded by a moan of pleasure.

"Is that good?" she teased.

"It's a start."

Then he kissed her again, and one touch led to another. Caitlin's inhibitions fell away as Shane lured her farther and farther into a sensual world of taste and smell and sensation. His hands moved over her, painting her skin with sweet fire, and the need for fulfillment grew and grew in her until the moment that she cried aloud for him to ease her exquisite agony.

Shane parted her legs and knelt between them. "Are you ready for me?"

She could not speak, but her whimper of longing was enough. She felt the touch of his shaft on her wet folds, and she arched her hips to meet his thrust.

Shane entered with her name on his lips, and this time there was no pain for her, only a sense of glorious completion as he plunged deep inside her slick, tight passage.

"Yes!" she cried. "Oh, yes."

Shane groaned between quick, hard breaths. "Caity," he gasped.

"Ohhh."

"Darlin' . . ." He pulled back slowly and then drove again, filling her until she moaned with pleasure at the glorious sensation. Shane clung to her, sweeping her into the timeless rhythm of his movement, and she quickly matched his ardor with her own.

She'd thought that what she'd felt earlier was a miracle, but no words could describe this passionate coming together.

Together they rode the whirlwind to the top of the mountain and leaped headlong into space beyond. And when Caitlin felt the rush of his hot seed fill her, she had no regrets. She felt only a bright rainbow of joy that for this one night they were not two separate souls, but one.

Chapter 15

Late the following morning, Caitlin opened her eyes and stared sleepily at the unfamiliar surroundings. The spacious room smelled of saddle soap and fresh-mown hay. Shane's room. She was alone in his bed, she realized. And she was as naked as an egg.

All that had happened the night before between her and her husband came rushing back, and she uttered a sleepy sigh of contentment and stretched. The sunshine was pleasantly warm on her face, and a fresh breeze drifted in through the open window. She had never felt more alive.

"Shane . . ." she whispered. Then she yawned.

In truth, neither of them had gotten much sleep . . . or had wanted any. Warm shivers of delight rose in her breast as she remembered the intense feelings and emotions induced by Shane's glorious lovemaking.

She'd never imagined that sexual union could be so wonderful between a man and woman, or that she could be so devilishly wanton in her husband's arms.

Caitlin pulled Shane's pillow into her arms and curled around it. If every night were like the last one, how would she ever get any work done? She rubbed her eyes and wondered just how late it was.

Her hair was all a tangle, and her nightgown . . .

Where had she left her nightgown? She couldn't wander into the hall wrapped in a sheet; Justice or Mary might see her. Surely Derry was awake by now. She'd be—

The echo of footsteps on the stairs broke through her reverie. Shane pushed open the bedroom door.

Caitlin's heart leaped at the sight of him, so tall and brawny. He wore a faded blue shirt she'd not seen before and brown pants that clung to his hips and legs like a second skin. He'd shaved and he'd slicked back his hair with water, but stray curls were already springing free around his face.

Last night she'd threaded her fingers through his silken hair. She moistened her lips as she remembered.

"Mary sent this up to you." He smiled as he brandished a steaming tin mug.

She suddenly realized how much of her was exposed and snatched the sheet up to cover herself. "Good morning, Mr. McKenna."

"No need to hide from me. I saw more than that last night, and I like you in the altogether." He came to the bed and sat down beside her. "The least you could do is kiss me."

"The least?"

"After last night. You wore me out, girl. Look at me. The sun standing at half past nine, and I'm not even out of the house."

"Half past nine?" She sat up, holding the sheet and blanket over her breasts. "What about Derry? Is she—"

"Had her breakfast. Dressed and braided so tight, her eyes are beginning to look like Mary's. The two of them are inspecting the papaw tree and digging wild ginger, or maybe it's digging ground nuts. Mary's English can be vague when she wants it to be."

"Are you sure Derry will be safe?"

"As safe as she'd be with you. Mary's taken a likin' to your little colleen, in spite of herself." He leaned over and kissed her. "Good mornin', Mrs. McKenna."

"Mmm," Caitlin murmured. "Will you promise to wake me up every morning like this, husband? And tell me that's tea I smell." He handed her the cup, and she felt a rush of excitement as her fingers brushed his.

"Not likely to the first question, and I can't say to the second," Shane replied lazily in the quaint Missouri drawl that Caitlin found endearing. "Mary steeped the brew herself with some of your tea leaves and some of her own. She may be turnin' you into a prairie skink for all I know."

"A skink?"

"Sort of a lizard."

"Great." Caitlin flashed him a mischievous smile and took a sip from the cup. "Ummm, whatever it is, it's good. Flavored with honey." She held the mug out to him. "Taste."

Shane shook his head. "I'm gun-shy. Mary made me a potion to break a fever once, and it tasted worse than polecat stew. I stick to coffee when I can get it, and chicory when I can't."

"I've seen you enjoy a cup of tea."

"Aye, proper Irish tea, not Mary's Indian roots and sumac lemonade." He took the mug from her and held it out of harm's way while he kissed her again.

Caitlin closed her eyes and savored the touch and scent of him. For an instant she thought that Shane was going to make love to her again. But when he retreated and skimmed a callused thumb across her lower lip, she opened her eyes and stared at him.

His expression was pensive. "You are a rare woman," he said as he fumbled in his shirt pocket and produced a thin, silver Celtic cross on a chain. "I've never given you a wedding ring," he continued almost brusquely. "I don't have one now to give you, but this cross was my great-great-grandmother's. Her name was Regan O'Driscoll, and 'twas told in our family that she risked death from the English to wear it. My own grandmother, Ciannait McKenna, gave it to me when she was on her deathbed, and I took a beatin' from my da for hidin' it and not tellin' him where it was. I know you're not a Catholic, and I'll not hold it against you if—"

"You want me to wear it?" Shane's being Catholic when her family was Church of England had been one of the things her father held most against him, but it had never been a big obstacle to her.

Shane's lips tightened and he nodded.

"I'd be honored to wear your grandmother's cross, Shane."

"You would?" A smile began at the corner of his mouth and then spread like sunshine over his rugged features.

"It's the most precious gift anyone's ever given me," she replied. "Thank you." She leaned forward so that he could fasten the chain around her neck.

"My fingers aren't made for this," he grumbled as he pushed the hair at the back of her head aside. Then he lowered his head and kissed the nape of her neck.

A tremor of joy flashed through her. "Thank you," she repeated.

After a few tries he managed to hook the tiny silver clasp. "There," he said as he stood back and admired the cross hanging between her breasts.

"It has a good feel."

Shane nodded. "My grandmother said it had special powers to protect the wearer."

"I'll cherish the cross always."

"Now I want you to get dressed, have some breakfast, and come outside. I'm goin' to teach you to shoot a gun."

"But I don't want to learn," she protested. "I hate guns. I'm afraid of them, and—"

"I asked you to wear the cross, but I'm tellin' you this. It's an order, Caity girl. I want you to—"

"I said *no*." The room had suddenly become cold. "I've seen enough of death and dying. I'll not argue with your ways, but I'll thank you to respect mine."

His jaw hardened, and a stubborn gleam flashed in the depths of his stony gray eyes. "Roses, you may have, woman. You can paint my walls and line the tables with teapots, but your safety is my concern. Earl Thompson's wife might be alive today if she'd had a rifle to fight off her attackers. This is not County Clare. There are bad men out here, and I'll not lose you to them if I can help it."

She sighed impatiently. "You don't understand. I don't want to—"

"An hour, Caity. Meet me near the creek in an hour. And wear something beside silk and lace." With that, he turned and left the room.

She stared after him, annoyed and puzzled. What had happened to the tender words and the sweet feel of his mouth against hers? An order, he'd said. She didn't know if she was ready to take orders from a man, even if that man was her husband. But short of throwing a temper tantrum or outright rebellion, she didn't know what to do.

"I won't," she muttered. "I'll not give in about his guns." But her argument sounded weak in her own ears. This was something Shane seemed to want badly. Was it worth antagonizing him over? She fingered the silver cross thoughtfully.

"Pick your battles," her grandmother had always said. "Fight when you must, Caitlin, but use your head first."

She wondered if this was one of those times when discretion was better than insisting on having her own way.

"You never make things easy, do you, Shane McKenna?" she declared into the empty room. She set her teacup aside without finishing it, and slid out of Shane's bed.

"Men," she grumbled aloud. "Naught but trouble from start to finish."

As she reluctantly came from the house an hour later, Caitlin heard Derry's laughter. She looked around and saw that Derry and Shane were together at the base of a large chestnut tree that grew near Mary's cabin. Shane was pushing Derry on a swing—a swing that had not been there the day before.

Caitlin hurried toward them. Derry saw her and waved. "Hold on!" Caitlin warned. "You'll fall."

Derry squealed as Shane pushed her again.

As Caitlin drew near, she saw Mary sitting on a stool beside the open cabin door and Justice stretched full length on the ground. The boy appeared to be investigating a small mound of dirt.

"It's about time you came out." Shane's twinkling eyes drew the smart from his brusque words.

"Be careful with her," Caitlin warned. "She's just a baby."

"Not a baby!" Derry proclaimed. "Big."

"Not very big," Caitlin answered. It was true that she was growing like wild heather. Next week would be her third birthday, and dresses that had fit the child well when they'd arrived in Missouri seemed suddenly too tight and too short.

"Big," Mary put in. "Big girl help Mary find good plants. Listen. Watch. Remember. Good eyes."

Caitlin smiled at this unexpected praise for Derry. Not knowing what to say that would not destroy Mary's mood, Caitlin glanced at Justice. "What are you doing?"

"Boy lazy," Mary said. "Watch ants work. Learn."

Caitlin wasn't sure that this wasn't a joke on her. "Watching ants," she repeated. She looked at Shane, but he only grinned and kept pushing the swing.

Caitlin shook her head. "I don't understand."

"Gabriel teach boy break horse," Mary explained. "Easy jump on horse, spur, ride to earth. More work, talk soft, move slow, learn to think like horse."

"Gabe breaks colts the Indian way," Shane said. "He gentles them. He's been working Star's mother for you. Justice is training a gray to the saddle, but he was too impatient to suit Gabe or Mary. I think watching the ants all day is a punishment of sorts."

Mary shifted her unlit pipe from one side of her mouth to the other and paused in sewing beads on a leather vest. "Not punish," she corrected. "Osage not punish child. Teach. Ants good teacher."

"Push me!" Derry reminded Shane. He did as she ordered, and the child giggled and kicked her feet.

"Careful," Caitlin cautioned.

"Let girl be," Mary said. "She fall, next time remember hold on tight."

"I don't want her to fall," Caitlin said. "She might hurt herself."

"Better teach girl swing high, hold on," Mary observed.

Caitlin bit back a sharp retort and sighed. "Did you make the swing for her?" she asked Shane.

He nodded. "She was swinging on the kitchen door and the barn doors. She told me she needed a swing."

"Big swing," Derry said.

"You'll have to swing yourself now," Shane told her. "I'm going to teach your mama to shoot a rifle. You stay here with Mary and Justice. I don't want you anywhere near us. Do you understand?"

Derry nodded solemnly.

Shane's gaze met Caitlin's. "Ready?"

She shrugged. "As ready as I'll ever be, I suppose. I still think this is a terrible idea."

"This rifle is light, accurate, and dependable. I could teach Bessie to shoot it," he replied.

She trudged beside him as he rounded the house and started toward the creek bank. "Wonderful. I'm certain your mule would enjoy it more than I will." She hated guns, despised the noise and smoke, and was terrified of the damage they could do.

"You'll have to trust my judgment on this."

Caitlin didn't answer. She could hear Derry's high laughter behind them, and the rush of the stream just ahead. The sunshine was warm on her face and the sky as blue as a robin's egg. A few lacy clouds floated along the western horizon, but the day was lovely by any standard.

She was happy, Caitlin realized. Just being there with Shane and Derry, knowing there would be food on the table and a roof over their heads. Missouri might be lonely, but it was beginning to feel like home.

"That story you read the other night . . ." Shane said.

"The book? After supper, you mean?"

"Aye. It was a good story. Justice and Gabe were talkin' about it. Maybe you could read some more tonight."

"Maybe." She averted her eyes so that he wouldn't see her amusement. "It's a long story."

"That's all right." They reached the edge of the creek, and Shane took her hand. A line of rocks formed a stepping bridge over the fast-flowing water. "Watch your step," he warned. "The rocks can be slippery."

His hand tightened around hers, and she liked the sensation.

"I could teach Justice his letters," she suggested. "He must learn to read, Shane."

He nodded. "You're right. And if he's to learn, it will have to be you that teaches him."

"Because there's no school nearby?"

"None yet, but if there was, he still couldn't go. Most folks wouldn't stand for a kid with Indian blood sittin' beside their children."

"That's the most ridiculous thing I've ever heard of!" she exclaimed.

"Might be, but it's truth. I told you: the color of a man's skin counts out here."

"Justice isn't a man; he's just a little boy."

"Folks figure that if he goes to school with their kids, he might expect to court one of their daughters. And that's just not gonna happen. It's a pity, but there's no changin' it. Take Gabe, now. A more decent man never walked the face of the earth. He's smart, and he's honest. He'd like to walk out with Rachel Thompson, but Big Earl would see him hangin' from a rope first. People like Big Earl put Indians somewhere below mules."

"It's wrong," Caitlin said. "It's not Christian. The good Lord made Gabriel as he made Mr. Thompson."

"Maybe so, but Gabe can't set foot on Thompson land so long as Big Earl or Beau live, not if he wants to keep breathin'."

"That's ignorant."

Shane shrugged. "Life's not always fair. I can't help what other folks do or think." He stopped and pointed to a tin can sitting in front of a large oak tree. "That's your target, Caity."

"That little thing?"

"By the time we're done, you'll be hitting the center of that can every time."

"You can teach me to do that today?"

Shane chuckled. "Not unless you're a better shot than I think you are. It will take a while, but I'm a patient man."

"I doubt that," she grumbled. But she gave him her undivided attention as he began to show her how to properly load the rifle.

Shane wasn't satisfied with her marksmanship in days, or even in a month. But as the weeks passed and summer turned to autumn, Caitlin began to lose her fear of the weapon. Every afternoon in good weather, Shane took time to take her out beyond the creek for target practice. And three times a week, he had her mount Bessie and ride around and around the paddock under his watchful eye until her back ached and her thighs were chafed by the mule's rough gait.

And evenings, after supper, Caitlin read to Derry, Shane, Gabe, and Mary. In time, she finished the *A Thousand and One Nights* and began another book, *Robinson Crusoe*. Persuading Justice that he had to learn his ABCs was easier than she'd thought it would be. For once, Mary, Gabriel, and Shane agreed that the boy needed to learn to read. Faced with such an array of formidable foes, Justice gave in with good grace and applied himself so enthusiastically that he memorized the entire alphabet in three days.

"I want to read books," he insisted. "I don't need to write letters."

"You will when you're a man," Shane insisted. To

Caitlin's surprise, he joined the two of them in the dining room for lessons every night after Derry was tucked into bed.

"You don't," Justice replied.

"No," Shane admitted. "I don't read or write, and many's the time I've regretted my lack of schoolin'."

"I could teach you," Caitlin offered.

Shane grimaced. "Not likely." But she noticed that he paid close attention to everything she told Justice.

Caitlin's days were full. Her roses flourished, and she had hopes of seeing them blossom in the spring. Her riding improved, and Shane began to take her out with him to ride fence lines or check on the livestock.

When the day was finished and the house was still and locked, she and Shane made love and then slept wrapped in each other's arms. They had moved Derry into Shane's room, and Shane had joined Caitlin in the larger, corner bedchamber.

Why can't I be satisfied with what I have? she mused one night when the only sounds she could hear were the chirp of crickets outside and the steady murmur of Shane's regular breathing as he slept beside her.

But she wasn't satisfied.

In the shadowy recesses of her mind, Caitlin knew that Shane still questioned her honesty and her ability to survive on the frontier. She had seen again this morning the brooding look on his face when he talked with Gabriel, and she wondered how many concerns her husband kept from her . . . and how many secrets.

He made glorious love to her, but he'd never told her that he loved her. They could have no chance at a lasting marriage so long as each continued to doubt the other. And until she knew that she was staying on Kilronan, she feared becoming pregnant.

"And I want to be certain of you," she whispered as she stroked Shane's tousled hair. "I want it with all my heart and soul."

Chapter 16

Nate Bone bellied down in the tall grass, steadied his rifle against a rock, and sighted down the barrel at McKenna's wife. The red-haired woman on the back of that mule made an easy target silhouetted against the blue sky. The half-breed brat, astride a pinto, rode just ahead of her.

Nate paid him no mind. "Bang. Yer dead," he said, pretending to pull the trigger. And then he laughed.

Beau Thompson wiggled back until he reached the shelter of a tree before climbing to his feet. "Hellfire, Nate, that ain't funny. Shootin' McKenna's one thing. The bastard deserves it for futterin' my sister. But killin' a white woman—Big Earl would shoot lightnin' bolts out his ass over that."

"Shit on Big Earl." Nate pushed up on his elbows and spat a wad of tobacco juice at a beetle trudging through the grass. "I didn't shoot her, did I? Can't you take a joke?"

"McKenna's the one what wronged us. I ain't gonna see you shoot no white woman, Nate. You listenin'? I ain't part of murderin' no decent females."

"Not like McKenna, are ya? He sure sliced that Cerise Larocque. Blood so deep on that whorehouse floor, they said, you had to wade through it."

Beau stiffened. "Reckon he did carve her up, but a half-breed whore don't hardly count."

"Shit, Beau. I didn't shoot McKenna's wife, did I? Had her dead in my sights, but did I pull the trigger?"

"No," Beau admitted, "but—"

"You're soft as a lil' girl," Nate scoffed. "How do you expect to best a hard case like McKenna without having some iron in your bowels? No wonder your old man beats the shit out of you. He ain't got one girl; he's got two."

A purple vein throbbed along Beau's temple. "I ain't no girl, Nate. Don't be callin' me no girl."

"If you had balls, you woulda got settled with McKenna by now," he taunted as he shoved his rifle in the saddle holster. "Rachel's got bigger stones than you do."

"Shut up about Rachel," Beau warned. "I caused McKenna plenty of trouble before you came to work for Big Earl, didn't I? I been pullin' down his fences and shooting his calves ever since he murdered his uncle and his cousin."

"Shit! Pullin' down a few fences? You think that's scarin' him? That's pissant stuff. Why, your sister Rachel—"

"Why you keep bringin' up Rachel? You best not be gettin' ideas about her."

"You think I got a taste for her? She ain't what I look fer in a woman." He coughed and spat again. "Now, McKenna's woman, that's something else. I wouldn't mind havin' a taste of that."

Mollified, Beau nodded. "Me, too. She's a fine handful of woman."

"You ever had a lady?"

"Reckon I have. Had me a French whore in Saint Louis claimed to be a countess."

"What did I say before?" Nate exclaimed. "Whores don't count. Real ladies is bred tight as a rattler's skin and hot as gunpowder."

"That Frenchy girl, she was like that."

"I'd like to give McKenna's woman a ride she'd remember."

Beau reached down under his belt and adjusted his genitals. "I saw that, first time I lit eyes on her."

Nate grinned as he gathered his reins and mounted up. Baiting Beau and then making him forget he'd been insulted was as easy as shooting snapping turtles in a barrel. But anybody as stupid as Beau Thompson deserved what he got.

He glanced over at the younger man. "Remember, your ole man ain't gonna live forever. I'm your amigo, ain't I?"

"Yeah."

"So I'm lookin' out for what's best for you. When Big Earl's dead, who does his spread belong to?"

"Me and Rachel." Beau reined his bay close to Nate's horse.

"And if McKenna was dead, who does Kilronan go to?"

"That Injun boy. Him or McKenna's woman."

"Not if you deal the cards right," Nate said. "The boy's a half-breed. McKenna murdered his uncle to get the place, so why would the law hand all that prime land over to a redskin bastard or a foreign woman?"

"I never thought of that."

Nate took the lead, urging his mount down the steep hillside away from McKenna's property line. Keeping Beau Thompson worked up against McKenna was gettin' to be a full-time job. If his own aim had been a little better when he'd gotten a shot off at him this summer,

McKenna would be rotting in his grave, but the darkness had made it a tricky shot.

Nate spat out his wad and stuffed a fresh pinch of tobacco in his cheek. Maybe it was for the best that he hadn't killed McKenna outright. Nate was a patient man, made more so by two years' captivity among the Comanche when he was only half grown. Them filthy savages had murdered his father and treated him worse than an animal. Yep, he reasoned, the Injuns had taught him how to hate deep and wide, and how to take his time in getting revenge.

Thoughts of the Comanche made his bowels clench. Nate tried to put those bad years behind him in the daytime. The devil knew he couldn't at night. He wished he had a silver dollar for every time he woke from a sound sleep with bile rising in his throat, the screams of his own pappy ringing in his ears, and the stench of his father's burning flesh in his nostrils.

His brother Frank had taken him in once he'd escaped the Comanche. Frank had seen him through the months when he didn't care if he lived or died. Frank was all he had in the way of kin.

Nate owed Shane McKenna plenty, first for running him off Kilronan, and second for hanging Frank. Some men would have been satisfied to backshoot McKenna and call things even, but not Nate. Once a man tasted the finer points of Comanche revenge, he wouldn't settle for shortcuts. He'd sworn on Frank's memory to see McKenna gutshot, castrated, and begging for a bullet through his head before he was done.

Besides, he was getting a little old and stiff in the joints to ride out and start over someplace else. Beau Thompson would be the ticket to a warm bed and a hot meal.

Who knows? he thought. In time, he might even be

able to stomach that shrew-tongued sister of his. A desperate man will poke most anything in the dark on a cold Missouri night.

Nate chuckled and sucked a chunk of tobacco out of his hollow tooth. Beau Thompson weren't none too bright, he mused, and that was God's truth. Once Big Earl's son got control of both places and had title to all that land, almost anything could happen to him. He could get throwed off his horse or accidentally shoot himself whilst he was cleanin' his rifle. And if he did die, sudden-like, Rachel's man would inherit everything.

Bad luck for Beau, Nate thought, but good luck for whatever smart man was left holding the stakes.

Caitlin drew her mount alongside Justice's pinto. The two of them were riding Kilronan's fence line, a task that Shane insisted the boy do several times a week. Checking for downed fences was easy work, and it freed Shane and Gabe to concentrate on haying and other chores that had to be done before the first snowfall.

Caitlin enjoyed being outdoors, and she welcomed the chance to befriend Shane's adopted son. But when she'd mentioned accompanying Justice, Shane had flatly refused to let her.

"It's not safe. You don't know enough about this country yet," Shane had said.

"But Justice does," she'd argued.

"I'll not put the responsibility of protectin' you on a boy's shoulders. Stay close to the house, Caity. I'll try to find more time for you to ride with me."

Caitlin had been disappointed, and as the days passed, Shane's decision had seemed more and more unfair. This morning, she'd just asked Justice to saddle the mule for her. Shane's infuriating habit of controlling her had to stop somewhere, and the sooner he learned to respect her independence, the better.

Since she'd begun to teach Justice to read, he'd stopped bedeviling her with mischievous pranks, but he still remained aloof. He never initiated conversations with her, and he usually responded with terse answers. But if Justice suspected that Shane had forbidden her to ride fenceline with him, he said nothing about it.

She was determined to break down the barriers between them, and being alone with Justice seemed the best way to start. She'd seen how patient he was with Derry, and she knew he had a good heart beneath the tough exterior.

"Justice." She broke the silence between them and urged her mule closer to his mount.

His black eyes, always alert, widened. He turned his attention to her, but he didn't speak.

He was a handsome youth, fast losing the gawkishness of childhood. His thick black hair, high cheekbones, and bronzed skin made him a stunner. No doubt Justice would break hearts, Caitlin thought, if he ever learned to smile.

"When is your birthday?" she asked.

"Got none."

"But you must have—"

He pointed to the outcropping of willow trees ahead. "I saw Goliath in there last week. We'll ride around. He's too bad tempered to mess with."

Caitlin nodded agreement. Shane had told her that the bull was still running loose on the property, but that the animal was no danger to anyone on horseback. She hadn't seen Goliath since the rampage in the corral, and she didn't want to.

They reined their animals away from the fence and through a low spot in the meadow. The day was cool; the trees had begun to take on a rainbow of autumn colors, but the grass was still lush.

"Everyone has a birthday," Caitlin insisted. "When were you born?"

He shrugged. "Don't know."

"But surely your mother must have given you birthday gifts."

Justice stared at her as if she'd suddenly sprouted a second head. "I had food from Cerise when she was sober, an' the back of her hand when she was drunk. Nothin' more."

Caitlin winced. "You have no birth records?"

He made a sound of derision.

"You're a Catholic. You must have been baptized."

Justice nodded. "Mary did it." Then he said a word that Caitlin couldn't understand.

"What did you just say?"

He shrugged again. "It's just Indian talk; don't mean nothin' much."

"I've heard it before," she pressed. "You use it when you talk to Mary. Is it a term of respect?"

He clicked to the pinto, and the animal leaped forward into a trot. Caitlin urged Bessie to keep up.

"It's nothing to be ashamed of. I'd be proud to know another language."

He seemed to ignore her, but a few minutes later, as his pony reached down to snatch a mouthful of grass, Justice glanced back at Caitlin. "It means *grandmother*. Osage people respect elders. Mary's not her real name, just her white name."

"Do you know her real name?"

He nodded and quickly said an impossibly complicated phrase that Caitlin couldn't begin to repeat. "It means Winter Swan," he explained.

"Do you have an Indian name?"

Justice shook his head. "Just a baby name. I'll get a real one sometime. Gabe said he'd tell me when I'm old enough. I have to go off alone without food or water and wait for a spirit to appear to me. The Osage don't just give you a name; you have to earn it."

Suddenly he pulled his pony up short and stared at the hillside on the far side of the property line.

"What is it?" Caitlin asked, seeing his unease.

"Somebody's watchin' us."

Caitlin looked, but she didn't see anything but trees and rocks. The hillside rose sharply beyond the split-rail fence that divided Kilronan from Thompson land.

Two crows rose in the air, cawing loudly. "Come on," Justice said. "Let's get out of here." He slapped his reins across the pinto's neck.

Caitlin's mule rocketed forward into a rough canter, and Caitlin held on for dear life as Justice's pony led them on a zigzag course over a stretch of rugged ground. A tiny creek loomed ahead of them, but Justice did not slow his steed's pace. The pinto leaped over the water and kept going. Bessie followed.

For an instant, when the mule's forefeet struck the far bank, Caitlin thought she might lose her balance, but she leaned forward on Bessie's neck and stayed in the saddle. They galloped through a grove of chestnut trees and then another open field.

As the two approached the outlying barn, Caitlin felt a shiver of relief as she saw Gabe standing in the bed of a wagon, forking hay up into an open loft window. Shane was nowhere in sight.

"Mama! Justice!" Derry called, running from the poultry house. Mary, a clutch of eggs cradled in her apron, followed the child.

Justice reached Gabe first. Caitlin was too far away to hear what the boy was telling the wrangler, but she hoped

Gabe wouldn't think they'd both been foolish. After all, she and Justice had ridden home at breakneck speed without actually seeing or hearing anything amiss.

Justice slid down off his pony and called out to Mary. The Indian woman hurried toward the boy speaking rapidly in her own tongue.

He answered her in the same language, and Caitlin heard the word that Justice had told her meant *grandmother*. Mary's reply in Osage was quick and heated.

"He's not hurt," Gabe said. "Likely there was nothin' in the brush but a deer."

Clearly unsatisfied with Gabe's remark, Mary scowled and squeezed the boy's leg.

Why is she so upset? Caitlin wondered. It's not like Mary to become alarmed without reason. Then an odd notion rose into Caitlin's mind. Was it possible that Mary was the child's real grandmother?

If she was, it would explain why Justice allowed Mary so much control over him, and why the two seemed so comfortable together. And if Mary feared Shane's Irish wife would want to be rid of the half-Indian boy, that would help explain the Osage woman's antagonism toward her.

Gabe took hold of the mule's bridle and helped Caitlin to dismount. He didn't speak to her, but one glance into those accusing dark eyes told Caitlin that Gabe knew Shane had forbidden her to check the fences with Justice.

"I'll ride out and see if I can find any tracks," Gabe volunteered.

Justice nodded. "I'll come with you."

"No, you stay here. McKenna's huntin' for strays. He should be back directly. He'll want to hear what happened."

"Nothing happened," Caitlin said. "Nothing at all."

Gabe shrugged and handed the mule's reins to Justice.

"Put the animals away. Tell McKenna I'll be back by midnight. If I go onto Thompson land, I want to do it after dark."

Mary looked at Caitlin as if expecting an explanation.

"I doubt there's reason for worry," Caitlin said.

Mary sniffed. "Missy-Wife have worry," she said. "When McKenna find out, you have big worry."

"I told you I didn't want you ridin' without me!" Shane said as he stormed into the kitchen where Caitlin was rolling biscuits for supper. "Are you thickheaded or just obstinate that you can't obey a single order I give? When am I goin' to be able to trust you?"

Biting back an angry retort, Caitlin glanced at Derry. "Find Mary. Ask her to tell you a story."

Derry looked from Caitlin to Shane, then beat a fast retreat out the kitchen door.

"Don't speak to me like that in front of Derry," Caitlin said when the door closed behind the child. She wanted to scream at him, to tell him how much it hurt her that he didn't have faith in her, but she didn't. Instead, she said calmly, "You're overreacting."

Shane swore a foul oath, and Caitlin flinched.

"You have no need for such language in this house."

"You drive me to it, woman." He stood over her, glowering.

She dusted flour over her dough and kneaded it into a ball. "I was nearly eight years the judge of my own behavior," she replied tersely. "I may be your wife, Shane McKenna, but I'm not your hired hand. I'll not be told when and where I may go."

"Damn it, Caity. You could have been shot."

"Or fallen off the mule and broken my neck?"

"That, too."

She slammed the wooden rolling pin on the table and

glared at him. "I'm making biscuits, Shane. Maybe my apron will catch fire, or I might quicken with your babe and die in childbirth. There are no guarantees in life."

"It's my duty to keep you safe."

She picked up the wooden rolling pin again and began to flatten the dough. "There was no danger. No one shot at me. Nobody was there. And I'll not be kept a prisoner in this house."

"You'll heed me, Caity, or you'll not stay at Kilronan."

"Maybe I won't, then. Maybe it was a mistake to come here in the first place. Maybe I should get back on a steamboat and take Derry east, where people don't kill each other over stray cows."

"Do what you need to do. If you stay here, you've got to listen to what I say." He turned toward the door. "Don't wait supper. I'm ridin' out to find Gabe and check for signs myself."

"Good. If you stayed here, I'd likely put poison in your stew anyway."

The back door slammed.

She kept rolling the dough until she realized that it was thin enough for flat dumplings. Then, dashing tears from her eyes with the back of her hand, she scraped the dough together and flung it back into the bowl.

Why did they do this to each other? she agonized. Why did they have the same fights over and over?

She wasn't ready to give up on him yet, though. Surely they'd patch up this argument in bed, as they always did.

Why in God's name was her husband one man between the sheets and another the rest of the time? There was a dangerous side to Shane. That aspect of his personality frightened her and sometimes made her wonder if there wasn't some truth to what people said about him.

Maybe Shane was right, she thought with a shiver.

Maybe she was thickheaded, too stupid to know whether she shared a roof with a cold-blooded killer or not.

But late that night, when Shane did come home, her fears and anger faded in the face of his apology.

"You were right," he said as he set the kerosene lamp carefully on the table. "I shouldn't have yelled at you like that in front of Derry."

Caitlin sat up in bed. "You said you can't trust me," she accused.

"How can I? You get something in your head and go chargin' off on your own. You don't listen to me or Mary." Shane tossed his hat on a peg and began to unbutton his shirt. "Damn it, woman, you're green. You don't know what this country can do to innocents."

"I suppose you mean well," she conceded, "but—"

"What if you'd been shot?" Shane draped his shirt over the back of a chair.

Caitlin threw her pillow at him. "What about Justice? You send a boy out to—"

Shane caught the pillow and flung it back. "He's not a boy. Least not what you think of as a boy. He does a man's part on Kilronan, and he has to take his chances like Gabe and I do."

"It makes no sense to me," she admitted.

"I don't want to argue with you, Caity." He sat down and began to pull off his boots.

"I don't want to fight with you either," she said. "And I was wrong to tell you I was leaving. I don't want to go, Shane. I want to stay here with you."

"I want you to." He shed his pants and slid under the covers beside her. "It's drives me crazy to think of you being hurt."

She knew she shouldn't let him get around her with a

few sweet words, but it was hard to resist him when he lay naked beside her. "Did you find anything?"

"Tracks of two horses and two men. It doesn't prove anything." He pulled her into his arms. "I care about you, Caity."

The thrill of his touch made her giddy. "I know you do." He kissed her tenderly.

"If you start that, neither of us will get any sleep tonight."

"I know."

"You're bad," she teased.

"Wicked," he murmured lazily. "That's what I want. Can you be wicked for me, darlin'?"

His long, powerful fingers kneaded out the sore spots of her shoulders and upper back. It felt so good that Caitlin sighed with pleasure and curled her legs around his. They'd have to have it out once and for all about his bossy ways, but this wasn't the time. "Don't stop," she whispered. "That blasted mule gets rougher every time I ride her."

"Be patient, sweetheart. Gabe's working the mare for you. When she's ready, her gait will be like sittin' in a rockin' chair." He nuzzled her throat and then kissed her full on the mouth.

Caitlin's fingers strayed to Shane's bare chest; he brushed the curve of her breast, and she made a contented sound deep in her throat.

She lifted her face to meet his kiss. Strange how they fitted so perfectly, how it seemed the most natural thing in the world to savor the taste and smell of him, to caress with her tongue and teeth . . . to feel such joy in his embrace.

Shane pulled her on top of him as desire shot through him with the intensity of a lightning bolt. His swollen shaft throbbed with readiness. "Caity, Caity," he murmured. He couldn't keep his hands off her. Her skin was soft and sweet; her scent drove him wild.

No woman had ever been so eager, so willing to give of herself. He could hardly get through the days for thinking of her. Each night was a new wonder, and no matter how many times they made love, he only wanted her more.

The thought that she'd once lain in another man's arms like this taunted him, and he pushed it away. Past was past; she was all his now.

She moved against him, brushing her body against him, letting her unbound hair trail over his face and chest. He buried his face in her warm, silken breasts and drew the hard nipples between his lips, then suckled until she whimpered and rubbed against his rock-hard phallus with her moist cleft.

He could stand it no more. With a cry of eagerness, he seized her hips and lifted her high so that he slid into her depths.

Having Caity on top and in control was a new sensation. And when he finally felt her reach a climax, his excitement was at such a pitch that his own release came hard and fast.

And later he held her in the crook of his arm and kissed her a dozen times and then a second dozen, and whispered sweet words into her ears until she fell asleep.

It was nearly dusk, and a light rain was falling. The sky was an ugly gray, and mist seeped up from the hollows to paint the landscape in ghostly hues.

Shane could hear Caity, Justice, and the baby ahead of him, but he couldn't see them. Derry's voice pealed out, a rainbow of tingling laughter amid the somber, muffled thud of his horse's hooves and the dull creak of saddle leather.

"Wait up!" Shane shouted. "Caity, wait! I'm coming!" He dug his heels into his mount's sides, but instead of quickening his stride, the animal slowed his pace and flung up his head.

"Cherokee? What's wrong with you?" he demanded. But when he looked down, it wasn't Cherokee under him. He was riding Big Earl Thompson's stallion, Natchez.

And then he remembered. He'd insisted that Caity ride his buckskin.

Caity's and the children's voices had nearly faded in the pearly haze. Shane felt a stark uneasiness settle over him. His breathing quickened, and he began to sweat despite the cool, damp air.

"Caity!" he called again.

No answer.

He listened but heard no sound except the steady tread of Natchez's feet and the drip of water off the overhanging tree branches.

Suddenly, without warning, the air rumbled. Not the far-off crack of thunder, but a grinding din that seemed to rise out of the earth beneath him.

Shane cried out and slashed Natchez with the ends of the leather reins. The stallion bolted forward out of the mist and into a clearing beside a nearly dry gully.

Ahead, halfway across the ancient creek bed, Shane saw Caitlin on Cherokee. Derry rode in front of her, and Justice walked beside them leading his pinto pony. "Hey!" Shane called. "Come back!"

Caity twisted in the saddle and waved. She was smiling, but she made no effort to halt the horse.

Then the ground quivered again. As Shane watched in horror, a flood of water surged down the dry riverbed, churning tree trunks, mud, and the swollen carcasses of cattle into a wall of destruction twenty feet high.

"Caity!" he screamed.

His warning came too late. First they were there, standing in the dust of an old arroyo course, and then there was only a sea of brown, tumbling water.

Shane spurred his horse into the flood, but Natchez's forelegs folded under him. The animal pitched headlong into the maelstrom, thrashed wildly, and went under. The black's head thrust up, his eyes rolled white, and he whinnied frantically. Water streamed from the stallion's nostrils as he tried to reach the safety of the bank. But before he could find his footing, an uprooted tree smashed into his head. He gave up the struggle and was washed away with the others.

Shane ran down the edge of the sluice calling Caitlin's name. Amid the swirl and crash of the deluge, he spied a flash of color. Caity's dress? Heedless of his own safety, he plunged into the torrent and tried to swim to the spot where he thought she might be, but the tide of mud and water was too strong. It bore him up, tossing him like a seed pod in the March wind and flinging him up on the far bank.

Wet, exhausted, and cold, he searched the creek bank for them, running, staggering, and finally crawling on numbed hands and knees. And at last he saw a still form sprawled at the water's edge.

"Caity?" he said. "Darlin'." But when he turned the lifeless body over, he stared into Cerise's accusing eyes.

"You killed me!" she rasped. "You killed me, and you'll be the death of her as well. . . ."

"No," Shane protested. "Cerise, I—"

"What did you say?" Caitlin murmured.

Shane jerked away, feeling the give of the mattress under him and the warmth of Caity's breath on his cheek. "Nothin'," he grated.

"Cerise, you said Cerise." Caity pushed herself up on one elbow. "I heard you say her name."

His heart was hammering; his sweat-soaked skin was cold and clammy. "A dream. Just a dream."

"You're dreaming about her?" she accused.

"I can't help what I dream about."

"No, maybe you can't." She stiffened and turned her back on him.

He laid a hand on her shoulder. "Don't—"

"Leave me alone. Go back to sleep. Maybe you'll dream about her again."

Shane flopped down on his back, but he couldn't shut his eyes without seeing the wall of water crashing down on her and the children, or without picturing Cerise's dead eyes. For more than an hour he lay awake, then slowly eased from their bed.

Old demons rose to haunt him as he pulled on his trousers and his boots. Grabbing a shirt and his rifle, he slipped from the room and went downstairs and out of the house.

He tried to tell himself that it was just a dream. Only Indians and the superstitious believed in such things.

His uncle and cousin had died in a spring flood, and he had nearly drowned with them. It wasn't his fault, and the dream didn't mean that something bad was going to happen to Caity and his family.

Shane didn't need to think twice to know what Mary would say about it. She would believe it was a sign of coming danger—maybe even death.

Shane had always believed in what he could see and hear and touch, but he wasn't a fool. He had faith in Justice's instincts. If the boy said someone had been watching him and Caity, then it was probably true.

He hadn't told Caity that the horses who'd left the tracks he and Gabe had found were shod. That meant that they weren't Indian horses. In spite of what Rachel said about Thompson losses, suspicion pointed to someone on their spread. And that meant Beau or Nate, maybe both.

He had to find out who was raiding Kilronan and put an end to it. And if he had to kill Big Earl's son in the process, it would mean a shooting war with the Thompsons.

He should send Caity and the child away, before it was too late. Shane didn't mind risking his own life. But in spite of what they'd done to each other, and regardless of whether they could live together as man and wife, he would always love Caity. And her life would be too high a price to pay for Kilronan.

Chapter 17

December wind tore at the barn door and sent dust devils spinning across the stable floor as Shane led his horse inside and closed it tightly behind him. Several stablemates nickered a greeting to the buckskin, and Cherokee blew softly through his lips in reply.

Shane yanked off his hat and smacked it sharply against his thigh to knock the snow off before it melted and ran down his back. He was cold and his bad knee was stiff. Damn if a man didn't start feeling his age early on a cold December morning, he thought.

He'd been up before dawn after a relatively decent night's sleep. The weather had been so foul the night before that neither he nor Gabe had bothered to stand guard. It was going to be a rotten winter. He could smell it the same way he could smell the storm rolling down out of the north country.

"Too nasty for outlaws," he murmured to his horse. Damn straight too foul out for Beau Thompson to be up to mischief. There had been no trouble for weeks, and Shane had begun to hope that whoever had targeted Kilronan had moved on.

Snow had been falling since midnight—not serious snow, just large, hard dry flakes accompanied by a sudden drop in temperature. November had been warmer than normal, except for a bitter spell in the middle of the month, but a bear Gabe had shot was fatter than normal, and his fur was thick and shaggy.

"Bad winter," Mary had predicted when she'd seen and felt the pelt. "Raccoon and beaver have heavy coat, too. Bad winter. Best you hunt meat quick."

Not one to argue with Mary unnecessarily, Shane had hunted. He and Gabe had brought in deer and ducks and geese. He'd traded a young oxen for three pigs, and he'd slaughtered the hogs as well. The women had been busy for days, curing and salting hams, making sausage and scrapple, and straining and boiling down lard.

Preserving the meat for winter was heavy, tiring work, and Shane was surprised to see that his wife did her share without complaint. If Caity was inexperienced at such tasks, Mary was an old hand. The Osage woman was so valuable that he'd made no protest when she'd insisted that they needed another girl to help with the chores.

Actually, Caity and Mary had taken Urika in while he was away trading for the hogs. He'd come home to find a strange Indian girl standing over a pot of boiling water in the yard, plucking feathers from a wild goose. When he'd asked who she was, the startled wench had dropped the bird, let out a shriek, and run into the kitchen to hide behind Mary.

"Urika good worker," Mary had informed him. "Osage woman strong."

Urika didn't look as if she were strong or a woman to Shane. Urika's rail-thin face was scarred with pock-marks, and her undeveloped girl-child body seemed too frail to pull her own weight.

"I can't afford to hire more help," he'd said firmly. "Feed her for a day or two, and send her on her way back to her family."

Mary had smiled and shifted her pipe from one corner

of her mouth to the other. "No pay," she clarified. "Urika work for food."

The Indian lass had stared at him with huge, frightened eyes, and Caitlin had looked anxious.

"Please, Shane," she'd said. "The girl is an orphan and half starved. Someone has treated her badly, and she has no place to go. Mary says that Urika walked for three days to get here. Surely we can manage another plate at the table. It wouldn't be right to turn her away. Not when there's so much to be done."

"Mary told you," he'd grumbled.

God knew the girl looked needy enough, he reasoned, but Kilronan was their livelihood. They'd none of them survive if he took in every beggar that wandered in. "Why can't this Urika speak for herself?" he'd asked.

Caity had a ready answer for him as usual. "Urika doesn't speak English. Just Osage. But Mary and Gabe know Osage. Isn't that lucky?"

In the end he'd relented and let Urika stay. If the Indian girl had asked for wages, he couldn't have kept her on. His coin box was empty. Anything that they needed between now and the time he delivered his stock to Fort Independence in the spring, they'd have to do without.

Shane shook his head as he led Cherokee toward the nearest empty stall. Women. Once they put their heads together and started to scheme against him, a man didn't have the chance of an apple in a hog pen.

The barn was dark and shadowy with the windows and doors battened down, but it was a lot warmer than outside. Scents of drying hay, oiled leather, and horses filled Shane's head, and he let the day's worries slide off his shoulders.

He'd come a long way for an Irish boy with holes in the soles of his brogans. He had a willing wife in his bed, land of his own, and a son. And unless he'd guessed wrong, Caity had been stirring up some of her soda bread for the noon meal.

Then the faint sound of something scraping against the boards overhead broke through his reverie. As his head snapped up, a few stems of hay sifted through the cracks and drifted past his face.

Instantly wary, Shane tensed and released his horse's bridle. Cherokee trotted on, nosing up to a stablemate before shoving open the stall door with his head.

Shane listened intently, but he heard nothing except the scrape of his buckskin's tongue against a salt block.

"Gabe?"

When no one answered, Shane dropped his hand to rest on the worn handle of the Colt revolver at his hip.

"Who's there?" he called as he moved toward the ladder that led to the hay loft. "Justice, are you up there?"

A cloud of hay filtered down through the hatchway. Shane's fingers tightened on the grip of his pistol.

" 'Kenna!" Derry's small face appeared in the opening overhead.

"Derry?" He snatched his hand away from the gun. "What are you doin' up there?"

The child's bottom lip began to quiver. "Can't find kitty."

"Are you out here alone? Is Justice up there in the loft?" Shane crossed to the ladder and lifted his arms. "Come on down."

"C-can't." A fat tear rolled down her nose. "I climbed up an' can't get down."

"There are no cats in this barn. Come on, little one. I'll help you."

"Kitty," she repeated stubbornly.

"How the hell did you get out here without Mary or your mother seeing you?" It was freezing outside, and none too comfortable in here. "Where's your coat, nubbin?" Shane shuddered inwardly as he thought of how easily she could have crawled into one of the corrals where the horses were penned or even wandered away from the barn and become lost in the woods.

"Inna house. I for-got."

"Climb down from there," he ordered.

Derry shook her head so hard that her pigtails swung from side to side. Her dark hair was full of hay, and stems clung to her dress and pantalettes.

"Jump if you're afraid to come down the ladder backwards. I'll catch you."

She sniffed and stuffed a dirty thumb into her mouth; then her impish face vanished from the loft hatchway.

"Whoa there, button," he called. "Stay right where you are. I'm comin' up." He seized hold of a rung and swiftly climbed the ladder.

Derry was standing several yards away, backed against a pile of hay. She looked scared to death.

"Easy now," Shane soothed. He took a step in her direction, and she began to cry. "Shhh, don't do that." He didn't know much about little girls, but he did know about skittish foals.

He crouched down. "Don't be scared. I'll sit right here until you come to me."

For several minutes he waited and she cried. Then Derry peeked through her fingers at him.

"I chase . . . chase a kitty," she stammered.

"No kitties here. Mice, maybe rats, but no cats."

"Justice said," she flung back.

"Would you like to have a cat?"

Both small hands came away. "Kitty on a boat."

"Yes," he agreed. "There was a cat on the boat, but there aren't any on Kilronan."

Derry wiped her face, smearing dirt and hayseed down

one cheek. Shane could see that the child was shivering, and he wanted to snatch her up and wrap her in his coat, but instinct made him wait.

"I'm hot," she admitted.

"Cold?"

"Um-humm." She nodded and looked at him wistfully. "No kitties?"

Shane shook his head, then slowly removed his coat. "Mama will be looking for you, Derry. If we don't go in the house, who will eat her bread and wild plum jelly?"

"Justice."

"So what are we goin' to do about that?"

She took a small step toward him.

"I won't hurt you, nubbin."

Derry pointed to the ladder. " 'Kenna climb. I climb."

A small flake of hay must have lodged in his eye. Shane rubbed at the irritation. "If I go down, you'll follow?"

She nodded. "No kitty."

He shook his head. "Nope. No kitty, but McKenna will try to find you one come spring. Maybe in Fort Independence when I go to trade my livestock."

A cat. He hated cats, and here he was promising her one. "Damned, softheaded fool," he muttered as he climbed down the ladder.

Derry peered down. " 'Kenna?"

"What?"

"Want hay?"

She giggled as an armful of hay tumbled onto his head. "Derry!"

" 'Kenna catch!" she cried.

Half blinded by the hay, he threw up his arms, and the warm, laughing child fell into his grasp. Derry's tiny arms tightened around his neck, and he felt her damp kiss on his cheek. "I wove Papa."

Shane wrapped his thick sheepskin coat around her.

" 'Kenna?" she demanded from inside the thick folds.

"What?"

"You wove me?"

"Yes," he replied. "I love you."

Caity was standing on a chair in the great room trying to hang an Indian blanket over one of the front windows. She wore a white apron over her blue taffeta gown, and her hair was tucked up under a linen cap. She looked so adorable that Shane would have grabbed her around the waist and kissed her—if he hadn't been so furious with her over letting Derry slip out of the house.

"Oh, Shane." Caity smiled at him over her shoulder. "Give me a hand, would you? This blanket won't—" She broke off as she spied the child in his arms. Dropping the red-striped trade blanket, she hopped down off the chair and confronted him. "Whatever are you doing with Derry?"

"I found her in the barn."

"In the barn? In this weather?" Caity snatched the little girl away from him. "Have you lost your wits, man? You've no sense at all to take a baby outside without her hat and cloak. She's half frozen."

"Mama! I chase a bad kitty."

Derry began to spill the tale of her escape, but Caity paid no more attention to the colleen than she did to him. "Shame on you," she cried. "Suppose she takes a chill? What kind of father are you?"

"Not much of one, it seems," he said. "I only discovered the babe you should have been watchin'."

Caity's cheeks paled and a deep flush swept up her fair, freckled face. "I owe you an apology," she replied. "I'm sorry. I only saw her with you and thought—"

"She's your child, Caity. This isn't County Clare. Keep a closer guard over her or you'll lose her."

"The fault is mine. She is mine alone, and if she comes to tragedy, the responsibility will be mine."

Derry frowned and began to whimper.

"There, there, my sweet," Caity murmured to her. "It was wrong of you to go out of the house without an adult, but we won't worry about that now." Caity went to the doorway. "Mary! Would you ask Urika to give Derry a hot bath and put her in her nightgown?"

There was a flurry of activity as Caity told Mary what had happened, and the older woman hurried the child off to the kitchen hearth. Then Caity glanced back at him.

"It's only proper that you admonish me for not doing my duty by the children."

Shane felt the first twinges of regret that he'd spoken so harshly. Caity was a good mother, not just to her own daughter but to his son as well. She showed the patience of Job in dealing with the boy, and anyone could see that she was well on the way to civilizing him. "Maybe I was wrong, too."

When the silence between them made him shift his weight from one foot to the other, he glanced around the room. Caity had been busy in here, he could see. Pine boughs lined the mantel over the huge, stone hearth, and the wide floor planks had been scrubbed and polished until they shone. There wasn't much furniture, just two rough benches and a straight-backed chair, but the windows were clean and the walls gleamed with fresh whitewash. She'd hung two small paintings on the far wall, a portrait of a man wearing an old-fashioned military uniform and a sword, and another of a handsome woman in a hooded green cape.

"Uncle Jamie wouldn't know this house if he walked in the front door," Shane said. "You've done well with it."

"Have I?"

"No need to take on so," he answered. "I didn't mean to start a war. I just wanted you to know how much danger the child—"

Caitlin crushed the corner of her apron between her fingers. "Didn't you? Well, congratulations. You've done it without trying."

"Peace, woman," he said. "Are you in your flux that you're so peevish?"

Her eyes widened. "I'll thank you to keep a decent tongue in your head, sir," she said. "My . . . my personal . . . Such things are none of your affair."

He shrugged. "I'd think that would be a husband's affair, especially when his wife turns to a shrew every month."

"That's unfair!" She whirled around, clearly meaning to flee the room in a huff when she suddenly stopped short. "Who would not turn into a shrew when a husband calls out another woman's name in their bed?"

"You're still holdin' that against me?" He took a step toward her. "It was a dream, Caity, nothin' more."

"You still think about Cerise. Admit it."

"Once," he said. "Just once I mentioned her name in my sleep and—"

"More than that," Caity said angrily. "Three, four times—just last night you did it again. Do you compare us?" She caught her breath. "How do I match up with her?"

"What do you want me to say?" he demanded. The back of his head felt as though someone were driving a ten-penny nail through it. "What Cerise and I had was different than what I felt for you when I married you, but it was real."

Caitlin whitened. "And now? Do you love me now, or do you still love her?"

"Love can die, Caity. The love I felt for Cerise died that night she was murdered. She killed it when she asked for money to get rid of our child—when she told me that she'd never leave the life she had to scrub and cook for one man."

"If you don't love her, then why can't you let her go?"

"Because her blood is on my hands. Because I was crazy drunk and—" He broke off, unable to go on, unable to say that he'd been mad enough to want her dead, to admit to Caitlin that he'd grabbed Cerise's shoulders and shaken her as he'd seen his father do to his mother dozens of times.

"Did you kill her?" Caitlin asked.

"I've told you that I didn't. Isn't that enough?"

"Your word." Tears streamed down her cheeks. "You want me to take you on your word, yet you can't take me on mine. You can't accept the truth about Derry."

"Truth can be different dependin' on where you stand to look at it," he whispered hoarsely. "But I didn't stab Cerise to death, and if you can't believe that, then to hell with you."

"I want to believe someone else killed her, Shane," Caity cried. "I do believe it." She covered her face with her hands. "Do you think I'd be here with you if I thought you were a murderer?"

He went to her and folded his arms around her. "Don't cry," he said. "It tears me up when you cry." Damn but he hated fighting with Caity; he always came out thinking she held aces and he had nothing but a pair of deuces.

They'd kissed and pretended to mend the quarrel that night, but the hurt remained underneath like the seeds of winter wheat under a February snow.

And then the next evening after supper they found reason to disagree again.

"Christmas is coming," Caitlin said after the children

were abed and he was sharing a pot of tea with her. "We must do something about buying gifts for the children."

"They have warm clothes, plenty of food, and a roof over their heads. I can't afford fancy store-bought presents."

"Not even for Christmas?" Caity's stare told him more than her words. She thought he was a tightwad, too penny-pinching to provide for his kids.

"I told you, Caity," he answered. "Until I sell my stock at Independence—"

"You're too poor to keep Christmas."

Shame burned his neck and crept up his cheeks. His wife knew little of grinding poverty. How could she understand the helplessness he'd felt as a boy watching his baby sister cry for a gingerbread man in a shop window that Shane couldn't buy for her?

There had never been Christmas presents in Patrick McKenna's house, and few Christmas dinners either. Justice and Derry were rich compared to what his brothers and sisters had endured.

"Justice is too old for toys," he answered brusquely. "And the less Derry expects, the easier it will be for her."

"You're serious, aren't you?" Caity said.

"Bake them cookies or something. Kids like cookies."

"Naught but cookies on Christmas morn?"

"Some children would think themselves well off if they ate as ours do. Meat every day and cake on the Sabbath."

"But your children don't have to do without," she protested. "You have six hundred acres and a house and barns to your name! Horses and cattle and—"

"Damn it, woman! Can't you understand. I have Kilronan, but I have no money until I sell my livestock. It took all I had to send for you."

Her anger faded; puzzled, she stared at him. "You mean we're penniless?"

"Aye."

"Why didn't you tell me?"

He exhaled softly. "It's not a wife's place to worry over finances. A husband—"

"Poppycock! A wife should be a partner to her husband. I understand being without money. After my father died, Maureen and I struggled to buy food and fuel for the fires."

"My uncle left Kilronan in debt, Caity. I've fought to pay off what he owed. I'm cautious, but I'd not begrudge you or the children anything if I had coin to spare."

"I feel like such a fool," she answered. "I've wronged you without reason. Forgive me, Shane."

"No, the fault is mine. I should have told you before, but I'm a proud man. It was easier to have you name me a skinflint than to tell you that I'm what I've always been—a Paddy without a shilling in his pocket."

She shook her head. "Just this," she said, waving her hand to take in all of Kilronan. "Just half of Missouri. Don't hold me so cheap, Mr. McKenna. I can be a help to you instead of a hindrance. I could help you earn money."

"Could you, now? And how would that be? Could you help us break horses?"

"Don't make fun of me. I'm serious. I could teach school, or I could sell some of the things I've brought from Ireland."

He felt another wave of inadequacy run through him. "I'll not have my wife peddlin' her goods on a street corner. I'll take care of us. You go on the way you have, lookin' after the kids, makin' this house a real home. I'll tend to the rest."

He was already thinking, trying to figure a way to give

her what she'd asked for. And then he remembered the man in Saint Louis who'd made him an offer.

"I want to help, Shane. Really help."

"You are," he assured her. "And you'll have lots to do in the next two weeks. I'm goin' to Saint Louis."

"Why? You didn't say anything about it before. Can I go with you?"

"Business." He covered her hand with his. How soft it felt, he thought. He hoped he could keep it that way; he didn't want her hands to become lined and callused like Mary's were. "And you can't come. I mean to travel fast and be back by Christmas."

"But why?" she demanded. "Why now with winter weather coming on?"

"Trust me," he said. "I know what I'm doin'."

"But I don't want you to go."

He leaned over and kissed her. "And those words are music to a husband's ears, darlin'. It's what every man wants to hear."

Chapter 18

Caitlin opened the kitchen door and stared at the ominous gray sky. It was two days before Christmas, and Shane had been gone a week and a half. She hadn't looked for him to return from Saint Louis until yesterday, but now with the weather getting colder, she was beginning to worry about his safety.

Why had she argued with him about the children's Christmas presents? If only she'd known that Shane was short of money. He'd said as much, but she hadn't understood that in America land didn't mean money. She hoped that her mistake hadn't prompted him to go to Saint Louis to take out a loan on Kilronan or something equally as foolish.

Married eight years and they knew so little about each other. Had she and Shane been together from the time of their wedding, they would have smoothed out the wrinkles in their personalities by now—or at least they would have come to accept each other's eccentricities.

She wondered if they'd ever bridge the chasm of mistrust between them, or if Cerise's memory would fade. Shane had said that he had the woman's blood on his hands but that he hadn't killed her. Caitlin prayed that he and Justice were telling her the truth.

She'd missed Shane since he'd ridden off on Cherokee, but she was determined to go ahead with her plans for

Christmas. With or without bought gifts and store candy, the children must have a special holiday.

She and Mary had baked pies while Urika plucked and cleaned a wild turkey that Justice had shot. Gabe had cut and dragged in a huge Yule log for the great-room fireplace. And Caitlin had decorated the house with holly and pine and crowfoot. She'd even managed to weave a mistletoe ball from willow sprigs and mistletoe that Justice had climbed a tree to retrieve.

At home, before the potatoes had blackened and rotted—when Mama and Papa had both been alive—Christmas had been a magical time. Her mother had played the great Irish harp, and her father the harpsichord. She would pluck the strings of the small ebony-framed lyre that her great-grandfather had brought back from Greece, and Maureen sang. If she closed her eyes, it seemed to her that she could almost hear the strains of music echoing through the house and the village children singing carols in the courtyard.

Those times seemed far away, Caitlin mused. There would be no music for Christmas this year in Missouri. Somehow she could not picture Big Earl or Rachel Thompson joining in a round of Yuletide chorus. Caitlin knew the words and melodies, of course, but her voice was not as sweet and clear as Maureen's or Mama's, and she would never have the nerve to sing alone without accompaniment.

This morning Caitlin was determined to ride to the Thompsons' and invite them for Christmas dinner. It wasn't right that the only families for miles around should be at odds with each other. Regardless of what had happened in the past, she hoped that if Shane and Earl Thompson got to know each other better, they would find a way to end their differences.

Caitlin longed for another woman to talk to—other

than Mary and Urika. Mary was a good soul beneath her gruff exterior, but she was more aunt than confidant, and Urika rarely spoke at all. Caitlin missed her sister and her friends in County Clare. For all Rachel's odd ways, she was only a little younger than Caitlin, and Caitlin hoped that they could find some common ground.

Mary had been dead set against Caitlin's going to Earl Thompson's house. "Big Earl no like McKenna. You go there, make trouble."

"It isn't far to the Thompson home, is it?"

"Not far." Mary pointed to the lane that led out of the yard. "Big Earl live at end of road."

"Good." For all the unpleasantness that had occurred when the Thompsons had come to Kilronan, Caitlin was certain that she was in no personal danger from the neighbors.

She'd dressed warmly for her ride, and she'd packed a basket of jellies, sausage, and fresh-baked scones. Justice had gone to the barn to saddle her a horse. She'd decided to ride Ladybug. Despite Shane's faith in Bessie, Caitlin didn't want to show up at Rachel's door on a mule.

"McKenna not want you go," Mary insisted.

"Well, McKenna's not at home, is he? If Mr. McKenna isn't here to make the decisions, I must make them for him," Caitlin said with more authority than she felt.

Gabe was away from the house as well, keeping vigil on the fences and checking the livestock. If the wrangler had been there, Caitlin knew he'd have insisted on riding with her, and she wanted to do this alone.

Even Justice had wanted to come, but she'd turned him down as well. Caitlin didn't want the Thompsons to feel threatened, and a respectable woman extending a dinner invitation was certainly harmless.

Justice watched her mount Ladybug in silence.

"I'm counting on you to stay here and take care of Derry and the women," Caitlin instructed.

Justice frowned, but he stayed put when she rode away from the house.

Ladybug held her head high as she stepped along. The mare's mouth was dainty, and her gait was as soft as goose down. Caitlin had ridden for about ten minutes when she heard the sound of a running horse behind her.

Justice came over the ridge, riding flat out on his pinto. He galloped up to her and wheeled his pony around. Both boy and animal were damp with sweat. Justice's hat had fallen off and was hanging down his back.

"What's wrong?" she demanded.

Justice held out a heavy flintlock pistol. "Take this. If you need me, just shoot in the air and I'll come."

"I'll be all right." Justice's willingness to put his own life in jeopardy to protect her made her want to hug him. "But I'll take the gun, and I'll signal if I need you."

His gaze met hers, and in that instant she knew that the months of trying to reach this troubled child hadn't been in vain. Somehow, amid the frogs in her laundry basket and the salt in her sugar bowl, Justice McKenna had begun to raise the curtain to his heart.

"I'm proud of you, Justice," she said. "Your father would be, too. But you have to trust me in this. I'll come to no harm. All that western gallantry—"

"It didn't help my mother, did it?" Pain flashed in his fathomless obsidian eyes. "But she weren't no lady."

"No, I suppose you're right," Caitlin admitted. "She wasn't. But it's still all right for you to love her."

"I don't." He spat the words so low that she almost missed them.

"Cerise loved you, Justice. No matter what she was, she did love you. Her last thought was not for her soul, but that Shane take you as his son."

"The only person she ever loved was herself. She didn't care nothin' about McKenna neither."

Caitlin prayed for the right answer. If she gave the wrong one, she was afraid that Justice would slip out of her grasp, and she'd never reach him again. "Maybe some of us have a deeper well of love to give," she said. "How do you know she didn't care about Shane?"

" 'Cause he got her caught, and she didn't want it."

Caitlin shook her head. "I don't understand."

"You know . . . he got her in the family way."

"How did they know that he was the father? If . . ." Caitlin tried to put her question delicately. "If there were other men in her life . . ."

"Oh, you mean 'cause she was a whore." Justice blushed beneath his heavy tan. "Cerise only slept with one man at a time. There were lots of them, but just one at a time. She earned her keep at Fat Rose's by dancin' and cheatin' at cards."

"Oh." Caitlin averted her eyes.

"It was his baby growin' in her belly, all right. But she got rid of it."

Caitlin started to say that Cerise had asked Shane for money to abort the child, but the words lodged in her throat.

"I seen it," Justice continued. "I seen it, a little thing no bigger than a . . ." He kicked his pony closer. "You cryin'? Don't cry."

She wiped her eyes. "I'm sorry." She sucked in a ragged breath. "It's not an evil a child should—"

"I ain't no kid."

"No, you aren't, are you?" She forced a smile. "That was wrong of her . . . to do it, and to let you know."

"She just wrapped it in a scarf and told me to throw it in the river behind Fat Rose's."

"Oh, Justice." What kind of woman would involve her own son in such evil?

He shrugged. "I seen worse."

"I hope not."

He tugged his felt hat down over his forehead, and Caitlin noted that Justice had creased the hat to look like Shane's. "I didn't do what she said," he confessed. "I went down to the bank of the Missouri, but I couldn't throw it in like she wanted me to. I sprinkled some water on his head—I think it was a boy, but it was hard to tell. I knew you were supposed to have a name; the priest always says a name. So I said Gabriel."

"Gabriel is a good name." Caitlin longed to touch him, but she knew if she made a move in his direction, he would flee.

"Then I sneaked over to the churchyard in the middle of the night and buried it next to one of them big, stone angels. I thought it were fittin'."

"It was, Justice. It was very *fittin'*." Tears were coming again, and she couldn't stop them. "Does Shane know?"

"Not about what I did." The boy looked relieved and embarrassed at the same time. "Cerise said it wasn't a baby, just a thing. She asked McKenna for money to get rid of his baby, and he didn't want her to. He said she should have it, and he'd take care of us."

Caitlin bit her lower lip until she tasted the salt of her own blood.

"Cerise lied to him," Justice went on in a dry monotone. "The baby was already buried in the churchyard. She took poison. Fat Rose gave it to all the girls when they got caught."

"Did Shane and Cerise argue about the baby the night your mother died?"

Justice nodded. "It was a bad fight. They was both drunk as French whores. Cerise hit him with her fists and bloodied his nose, but he never punched her back. She cursed him something fierce, and she tried to cut him with the knife. He got real mad, and he shoved her back on the bed. But McKenna never kilt her. Lots of folks claim he murdered her, 'cause it was his knife, but he didn't do it."

Caitlin felt numb all over, but she clung to the mare's reins and tried to keep from trembling. "How do you know what happened, Justice? Were you there?"

He shrugged.

"Did you see who did kill your mother?"

"Maybe." Justice yanked back on the reins hard enough to make the pinto rise on his hind legs. "Do what I said," Justice ordered. "Fire that pistol if you need help." Then he slapped the pony's neck, and the animal bolted away, leaving Caitlin alone and shaken by the boy's revelations.

That Justice confirmed Shane's innocence in Cerise's death reassured her. She'd never believed her husband capable of killing a woman, but at times nothing could keep uneasy suspicions from creeping into her mind.

Shane believed that his baby died with Cerise, so he mourned not only the woman but the life of his own unborn child as well. And yet he had managed to set aside his own pain and take Cerise's fatherless boy to raise.

Caitlin looked at the pistol. She didn't want it, but she knew that Justice would never forgive her if she threw it away, so she jammed it into the sack amid her loaves of bread and jellies.

The mare looked at Caitlin quizzically, and Caitlin clicked softly to her. The animal broke into a trot.

So many questions . . .

The wind was cold on Caitlin's face. She thought of turning back.

If Shane hadn't murdered Cerise, then who had? The thought that it might be Justice was too awful to consider. Who? And why? And if Justice knew the truth, why had he kept silent?

And why had the boy picked Gabriel as a name for Shane's dead babe? Did Justice know Gabe before Shane brought the child to Kilronan? Or was there some stronger connection among Gabriel, Mary Red Jacket, and Shane's adopted son?

Ladybug stopped so sharply that Caitlin almost lost her balance. Caitlin looked up to see a gate just ahead. Mary had told her that the fence marked the property line between Kilronan and the Thompson place.

Caitlin led the mare through the opening and replaced the poles. Getting back into the saddle without a mounting block was a challenge. She led Ladybug close to the fence and used the bottom railing to reach the stirrup.

Secure in the saddle again, Caitlin guided the mare along the barely visible trail. Off to her left grazed a herd of cattle with long, curving horns. She watched them uneasily, but they paid her no mind and went on eating.

The path wound across a low spot and then through a grove of trees. As she rode out into the field beyond, Caitlin caught sight of a low log house and outbuildings ahead.

As she approached the first paddock, two hounds began to bark at her. "Hello!" she called. "Is anyone here?"

"What have we here?" A man wearing a blacksmith's apron stepped from the barn. He was one of Big Earl's employees who'd come to Kilronan with the others. Caitlin thought that he must be the cowboy who'd worked for Shane and been fired. She tried to remember his name.

"How do you do?" Caitlin said. "I've come to see Mr. Thompson or Miss Rachel Thompson."

"Miss Rachel, is it?" the man mocked. A pair of hoof nippers dangled from his left hand, a hammer from the other. He dropped the tools on the ground and came toward her.

Caitlin tried to urge the mare past him.

"Not so fast." Smirking, he grabbed her reins, revealing yellow teeth in his unshaven, soot-streaked face. "McKennas ain't welcome here."

"Release my horse," she said, more angry than frightened.

"Spunky, ain't ya? Ole Nate likes that in a woman." He put a filthy hand on her riding skirt.

Caitlin didn't hesitate. She snatched up the bag of foodstuffs and swung it over Ladybug's neck. The heavy sack slammed against the man's head with a satisfying thud. He let go of her horse and clutched his chin. Caitlin yanked back on the reins and her mare reared. Ladybug's front hoof struck the cowhand's chest, and he fell back onto the ground. Caitlin fought to stay in the saddle without dropping the bag containing the pistol.

"What the blue hell's goin' on?" Rachel Thompson ran toward them with a rifle in her hands.

Nate Bone scrambled up with blood running from his nose and lunged at Caitlin's horse. The mare threw up her head and shied away.

Rachel fired a shot into the air.

Nate stopped in his tracks.

Caitlin got her horse under control. Her hat had fallen off, her hair had come undone, but she was still in the saddle with the reins in her hands.

"What are you doin' here?" Rachel demanded.

Caitlin pointed at the cowboy. "This ruffian needs to be taught manners. He laid hands on my mare and on my person. I don't know what passes for decent behavior in Missouri, but in Ireland, he'd be horsewhipped."

Rachel whirled on Nate. "You son of a bitch. Get your sorry ass back to shoeing that horse. The next time you forget yourself, you're out of here."

"Your brother would have somethin' to say about that." Nate wiped his face, streaking blood and soot down his chin and onto his already stained vest.

"Swive Beau, and swive you, too." Rachel motioned with her rifle. "Get out of my sight."

Swearing, Nate did as he was told. When he disappeared into the barn, Rachel turned her attention to Caitlin. "Why in hell are you here?"

Caitlin grimaced. "I think it was a bad idea."

"Do you have many of these bad ideas?"

"I'm afraid so." Suddenly the two of them were laughing.

"Since you're here, you might as well step down." Rachel motioned toward the house. "Least I can do before Big Earl gets back is offer you a cup of what passes around here for coffee."

Caitlin extended the bag. "I brought you some bread and . . ."

"I kin smell it." Rachel grinned, and for a moment her plain face with its overlarge mouth and chin was almost attractive. "Course, it must be pretty hard bread, the way you wacked Nate's skull with it."

"Actually," Caitlin confessed, "there's a pistol in there, too."

"A pistol?" Rachel looked unconvinced. "Blue hell! McKenna's got hisself a live one after all." She began to laugh again. "Come on in and take a load off."

Offering a silent prayer, Caitlin dismounted and followed Rachel Thompson toward the house.

The single-story log structure consisted of many additions and various rooflines. Two sections were joined by a roofed dogtrot and at least four stone chimneys.

Windows seemed placed haphazardly; there weren't many of them, and they were small.

More dogs spilled out of the house. These animals added their whines and sniffing to the clamor of the first two hounds, which had never stopped barking. Rachel motioned to a hitching rail. Caitlin tied her mare and followed Rachel inside.

The interior was spotlessly clean but smelled of dogs. Rachel waved Caitlin to a chair at a long, plank table and retrieved a coffeepot from a cast-iron cookstove.

"I hope you like it black and strong," Rachel warned.

"Thank you." Caitlin didn't, but she had more sense than to admit it.

Over the cups of coffee, Caitlin explained the reason for her visit, and Rachel unwrapped the gifts of food and returned Caitlin's cloth bag and her weapon.

"Big old horse leg like that," Rachel said, pointing to the pistol, "knock you flat on your ass if you fired it." She chuckled at her own joke. "Make a hole big enough to run a calf through. Give a man cause to think before he messed with you again." She slathered a big slice of soda bread with jam. "Fine-tastin' stuff," she said. "My mother made such. She died before she could show me the hang of it. Wish I knowed how. I got me a sweet tooth, just like her."

"I'd be glad to teach you; it's easy."

"Easy for you maybe," Rachel replied. "Might take you up on that. Sweets do slide down good on a cold winter morning." Then she fixed Caitlin with a hard look. "You know our stud Natchez has come up missin', don't you?"

Caitlin shook her head. "No, I didn't."

"Gone, out of his pen without so much as a thank-you-ma'am. Two other good mares in there with him, and they're still there. Ain't natural. Most Injuns don't stop at stealin' one horse if there's three to be had. And a man hangs just as high for stealin' one as three."

"We've had no trouble for weeks," Caitlin answered. "Shane's away in Saint Louis, but—"

"Away, is he?" Rachel licked the jam from her fingers. "Gabe said McKenna was—" She flushed and broke off. "I meant to say . . . Blue hell, Mizz McKenna—"

"Caitlin, or Cait if you like. We're neighbors. I want us to be friends. Can't we just be Cait and Rachel?"

Rachel got up and poured herself another mug of coffee. She offered the pot to Caitlin, but she didn't think she could swallow another spoonful. The coffee was strong enough to take paint off a wagon wheel.

"Me and Gabe . . ." Rachel looked around and lowered her voice. "I like Gabe. He may be an Injun, but he's a good friend. If Big Earl knew, he'd likely lynch Gabe. To him, the only good Injun is . . ." She shrugged. "They killed Ma, see, and Big Earl holds a grudge. Anyway, Gabe said that McKenna wasn't to home. Bad for him if Big Earl finds out."

"How so?" Caitlin asked.

"He'll figure your Shane stole our stallion and sold him in Saint Louis. Big Earl and Beau are out lookin' for Natchez now. All the boys are out except worthless Nate. Big Earl left him here to keep the McKennas from over-running us." She grinned. "Guess it didn't work, huh?"

"Shane's not a thief. I don't know why he went to Saint Louis, but it wasn't to sell your horse."

"I know that. Hell, Big Earl would know that if he used his head. But Beau's all the time filling his mind with shit. 'Scuse my mouth. I ain't got much in the way of learnin', Cait. You have to take me as you see me or not at all."

"I think I like you fine," Caitlin replied honestly.

"Rough ways and all, and that invitation to Kilronan for Christmas still stands."

Rachel sniffed and reached for another slice of soda bread. "Might just surprise you and take you up on it," she said. "Stranger things have happened."

Chapter 19

December 24 dawned gray and bitter. Sleet knifed against the icy windowpanes, and blasts of wind rattled the house and howled down the chimneys. Caitlin eased from the feather bed, taking care not to disturb Derry. When the weather had turned ugly, Caitlin had feared that the child wouldn't be warm enough in Shane's old room, so she'd brought Derry in to sleep with her.

Caitlin refused to admit that having the tot beside her kept her from thinking too much about being alone in the bed. Knowing that Derry was safe helped to ease her fears.

The little girl slept soundly, her pink, rosebud mouth puckered and slightly open, one small hand flung over her head. Caitlin couldn't resist bending down and kissing Derry on the crown of her head. How sweet the babe smelled. Heaven's scents couldn't be any better, Caitlin decided.

She smiled as she gently tucked the quilts around Derry's chin and placed a pillow on either side of the child to make sure she didn't tumble out of bed. "Yes, darling," Caitlin murmured. "Whatever else happens, I've got you."

Caitlin's bare feet burned from the cold as she hurried to the hearth and added another log. The thick walls of Kilronan were built to withstand Missouri winters, but not even a constant fire could take the damp chill from the air or make the floorboards comfortable on a day like this.

Hastily Caitlin pulled on her wool stockings and her shoes and the warmest overshift she could find. She couldn't take the time to dress before going downstairs to see if Shane had gotten safely home in the night. Instead, she donned a silk dressing gown and swiftly brushed her hair and tucked it under a linen cap.

She'd done everything she could to make Kilronan ready for Christmas. The miniature she'd secretly painted of Justice for Shane was dry and wrapped in a bit of azure silk. She had her father's watch and a new shirt for Justice, a silver locket for Urika, and her mother's beautiful lace shawl for Mary.

What to give Gabriel had been a puzzle. Her chests and boxes were nearly empty except for old clothing of her mother's that might be used to make new garments. None of the material had been suitable or large enough to make the wrangler a shirt. And she wasn't sure that Gabe would like anything she had to give. In the end she'd settled on presenting him with her copy of *Robinson Crusoe*. He liked the story so much that she hoped he might value it, even though he couldn't read.

Caitlin had been making small gifts for Derry since summer: a cloth doll, bean bags, a necklace of pearls cut from an old pair of gloves. Caitlin's favorite was a collection of smooth, gray creek stones on which she'd painted the letters of the alphabet. She'd also sewn Derry a knee-length hooded cape of red silk with a royal blue velvet lining. And, on the chance that Rachel Thompson might come to Christmas dinner, Caitlin had dug through her silk scraps and cut and stitched a handful of multi-colored ribbons. She'd tied them into hair bows and wrapped them in a square of bright yellow satin.

Everything was ready for the Christmas celebration, but it would be hollow for Caitlin if Shane didn't get back in time to share the day's festivities. He'd promised he would be home in time, but time was running out.

What if Shane had been attacked by renegade Indians, fallen off his horse and broken his leg, or been swept away crossing a river? If he died in the wilderness between here and Saint Louis, she would never know what happened to him. Fear made Caitlin's stomach uneasy. She'd had little appetite the night before, but that she'd attributed to Rachel's coffee.

As she descended the staircase, she heard Gabriel's laughter drifting up from the kitchen. Maybe Shane had arrived, she thought hopefully. A shiver of anticipation ran through her as she hurried to the doorway.

A figure in a black hat and long coat stood in front of the fireplace with his back to Caitlin. Disappointment hit her hard. He wasn't tall or broad enough to be her husband.

The visitor turned and grinned.

"Rachel?" Caitlin had hoped she would come, but she hadn't expected her until Christmas Day. "Welcome," she said warmly.

"Cait." Rachel pushed back her hat, and Caitlin saw that she'd twisted her hair up into a bun on the back of her head and tied a bit of rawhide thong around it. "Hope you don't mind I come early. A heap of snow gonna fall between now and tomorrow."

Caitlin nodded to Mary and Urika. Justice and Gabe were sitting at the table eating corn cakes drowning in honey, but the cowboy's gaze was fixed on Rachel.

"Your father and brother?" Caitlin asked.

"Big Earl?" Rachel scoffed. "Not likely. He still thinks Shane stole his horse. He and Beau will sit there and get sock-eyed like they do every Christmas."

Mary pointed to the coffeepot.

"Obliged," Rachel said. "Cold as a witch's tit out there."

Caitlin took Rachel's coat. "Put your boots on the hearth to dry, and I'll find you some stockings to wear."

Rachel sipped the coffee and sighed with pleasure as Urika set another place at the table.

"I ate before I left home," Rachel said as she slid onto the bench across from Gabe. "But this weather makes a body hungry enough to eat a bear, hide and all. McKenna not back yet, huh?"

Justice watched her stonily. "No."

"Nasty weather," Rachel repeated, glancing at Gabe and then back to the plate in front of her.

"McKenna will find his way home." Gabe tore his gaze away from her. "Miss Rachel brought Justice a new saddle blanket, red and black striped."

Rachel colored. "Christmas gift," she muttered.

"Butter and milk, too," Mary added. "Milk froze."

"Milk?" Caitlin cried. "Real milk! That's wonderful. Derry hasn't had any in months. Do you have a cow?"

"Big Earl likes his butter," Rachel explained. "We always keep a few head." She dug into a vest pocket and came up with a tin whistle. "Reckon your button would like this?"

"Derry will love it," Caitlin answered. "Of course, I'm not sure how much Shane will appreciate the noise."

Rachel and Gabe laughed together.

"Didn't come empty-handed," Rachel said. "I brung a few chickens and some beefsteaks along with a jug of Big Earl's best drinkin' whiskey. We can fetch it from the barn."

"No need for you to worry," Gabe put in. "I'll get it. I need to feed up anyway."

"You already fed up," Justice said.

Gabe gave the boy a playful shove. "Best you mind your own business. You don't, I might give that new halter to Miss Rachel instead of you."

"Nothin' I'd like better than a good Osage braided halter," Rachel teased.

In the end Rachel and Gabe both bundled up and went to the barn. Mary glanced at Caitlin knowingly as they went out the door, and Urika giggled.

"There's trouble there," Mary warned.

Justice shrugged and poured himself another cup of coffee. "He likes her."

Mary frowned. "No more coffee. Boy drink too much."

"McKenna drinks coffee," Justice argued.

Mary said something to him in Osage.

When he started to reply in a sarcastic tone of voice, Caitlin interrupted. "Mind your grandmother."

Justice's eyes widened in surprise.

Caitlin turned to Mary. "He's your grandson, isn't he?"

Mary removed her pipe and tapped it against the stone hearth. The truth was written plainly across her weathered face. "You tell McKenna?"

"He'll send her away," Justice said. "Gabe worked for McKenna's uncle. When Cerise died, Gabe talked him into hiring Mary." Then he murmured the Osage word that he'd told Caitlin meant *grandmother*.

Mary folded her arms over her chest. For a moment she rocked back and forth in silent grief. "Mary's Cerise dead," she said finally. "Mary have three sons, two daughters. All dead but Gabriel. Gabriel here, Justice here on Kilronan. All here. Where else old woman go?"

"Gabriel is your son?" Caitlin asked. That part of the secret she hadn't guessed. "You're all related and Shane doesn't know it?"

Mary shook her head. "Now Missy-Wife say Mary go. Maybe McKenna send Gabriel away, too."

Caitlin went to Mary and embraced her. "But I do want you," she insisted. "I want you very much. Justice needs you. Derry and I need you."

Mary patted Caitlin's shoulder awkwardly and then pushed her away. The older woman's faded eyes glistened with moisture, and her voice came thick with emotion. "Mary not want cause trouble. McKenna have much anger."

Caitlin smiled. "For one who doesn't want trouble, you've given me enough."

"Mary have shame," the Indian woman admitted. "No want Missy-Wife come this place. Mary think Missy-Wife hate Cerise's boy. Get rid of boy."

"Do you still think that I want to be rid of Justice?" Caitlin asked softly.

Mary shook her head. "No. You make better mother than Cerise, Mary think."

"Justice is Shane's son, and I hope someday he will be my son as well," Caitlin said. "And there will be no more talk of you leaving Kilronan. You and Gabe are family. You have as much right—no, you have more right than I do to be here."

"Missy-Wife no tell McKenna?"

"It isn't my place to tell Shane. It's yours and Justice's."

"We tell him later," Mary replied.

"Much later," Justice agreed.

Caitlin wanted to say that McKenna would understand why they had to keep the relationships hidden, but she wasn't sure what he would do. He'd seemed so determined to keep Justice away from his mother's family when they discussed it.

"Uncle Gabe can tell him," Justice suggested. "McKenna needs him to break the horses."

"Next year," Mary said.

Justice grinned. "That's Indian time. It means sometime far off."

Caitlin looked suspiciously at Urika. "I suppose this is another relative?"

"Urika same clan," Mary answered. "Urika no can marry Gabriel."

Caitlin chuckled. "Well, we've got that much straight at least. I'd hardly think Urika is old enough to marry anybody."

Giggling, the girl covered her face with her hands.

"Urika wife of bad man," Mary explained. "Drink whiskey, beat woman. Bad man."

"And where is this bad man now?" Caitlin asked.

"Dead," Justice said. "Urika—"

"Don't tell me." Caitlin threw up her hands in defeat. "I don't want to know."

As the day passed, Caitlin grew more and more concerned for Shane's welfare. She kept busy all morning baking cookies and chasing after Derry. The child was so excited, she was practically bouncing off the walls.

"Father Christmas coming! Bringing me a dolly and a kitty."

"I hardly think Father Christmas can fit a kitten into his sack," Caitlin warned.

"Maybe a big kitty," Justice suggested. "A cougar."

"Wonderful," Caitlin said. "That's all we need."

After the noon dishes were cleared away, Caitlin stirred up a batch of molasses taffy, using some of Rachel's precious butter. Everyone took turns stretching the warm candy. When the batch was finished, more had gone into hungry mouths than into the box for Christmas day.

Snow continued to fall, and Caitlin found herself lingering at the windows, looking out for a lone rider. And for the first time, she confronted her worst fears. What if Shane didn't come back? What would she do with two children to support?

Her breath melted a small circle of frost on the window pane. Idly, Caitlin rubbed her finger against it. "What would I do?"

Her answer came from deep inside.

She'd stay, she thought. She'd stay on Kilronan and raise horses and mules and sell them, just as Shane had done. She'd learn what she had to, and she'd get as tough as she had to—or she'd die trying.

"This is home," she whispered.

"Mama! Mama!" Derry pulled on Caitlin's apron. "Popcorn! Gabe's making popcorn!"

For the children's sake, Caitlin brushed away her tears and blamed her reddened eyes on the chimney smoke. She hid her worry for Shane and joined in the merriment.

Nightfall came early amid the blowing snow, and Rachel, Gabriel, Mary, Urika, Caitlin, and the children gathered near the kitchen hearth and nibbled on Mary's sweet, persimmon corn cakes and drank steaming mugs of sassafras tea.

Caitlin read the story of the first Christmas from her father's Bible, and then Mary recited Osage *wi-gi-es*, or story poems, from her peoples' rich heritage. She told about the Tzi-Sho, the Sky People, and the Honga, the Earth People, and how those supernatural beings helped to create life on earth. Then she told a tale about Buffalo Bull and taught the children an ancient song to honor him.

When Mary's voice grew hoarse, Rachel whispered to Gabriel. He shook his head, but she would not take no for an answer. Finally he nodded, and Rachel glanced shyly at Caitlin.

"We could sing—if ya want," she offered. "It ain't a

Christmas song, but it's an old ballad from back home in the mountains. My grandma used to sing it to me."

"Please," Caitlin replied.

Gabe took pieces of firewood and clicked them softly together, and Rachel began to sing in a deep, clear voice.

> *Oh, give me yer hand, pretty Polly,*
> *Give me yer hand, says he,*
> *And I'll take ye home to yer father's house,*
> *And married shall we be.*
>
> *I won't sit down, said pretty Polly,*
> *I'll not sit on your knee,*
> *Six foolish maids have you drowned here,*
> *And the seventh I shall not be. . . .*

Rachel's song went on for verse after verse, and soon Gabe, Derry, Justice, and the rest of them were joining in on the chorus.

When she'd finished "Pretty Polly," Rachel and Gabe went on to sing "The Cuckoo" and "The Wild Moor" together. Derry fell asleep in the middle of "Gypsy Davy," but Caitlin held her in her arms for more than an hour longer. Then Rachel and Caitlin tucked the child into Caitlin's bed.

When they came downstairs, Mary had chased Justice off to bed, and Gabe was banking the kitchen fire. The adults talked for another hour or two; then Mary and Urika retired to Mary's cabin, and Gabe said good night as well.

Caitlin showed Rachel to Derry's room and changed into her own night clothes and dressing gown. Caitlin knew that she should try to sleep, but she was too restless. Instead, she took a lamp and went back downstairs to the kitchen. She pulled Mary's rocking chair closer to the fire and sat down and stared into the glowing embers.

"Shane McKenna, where are you?" she whispered. "Please come home . . . come home alive."

She found herself reciting prayers that she'd not offered for a long time. She'd fallen out of the habit after Mama had died. Caitlin had prayed so hard and long that her mother might live . . . that the potatoes wouldn't blacken . . . that Shane hadn't gone to America and forgotten her.

"Please, God," she murmured. "If you could just spare a small miracle on this holy night. The children need him. I need him."

How long Caitlin sat there she didn't know, but sometime in the darkest hours, she felt a bitter gust of wind and smelled the biting scent of snow. The flames crackled on the hearth, and the draft extinguished her oil lamp and sent a whirlwind of ashes and smoke howling up the chimney.

Shivering, only half awake, Caitlin scrambled to her feet. "Who's there?"

A bulky shape loomed up out of the shadows. Then something whined, an odd high-pitched sound that made the hair rise on the back of her neck.

"Who is it?" Caitlin demanded. She fumbled for the iron poker and raised it menacingly. "Don't take another step!" she warned. "I'm not afraid to use this."

"Caity girl, is this the welcome a man gets in his own home on Christmas Eve?"

With a cry of joy, Caitlin dropped her weapon and threw herself at Shane. His coat was crusted with snow, and her stockinged feet trod on his icy boots, but she didn't feel the cold. "Shane! Shane!" Suddenly she was laughing and crying and trying to kiss him at the same time.

"Easy, woman, you'll murder my—"

A loud, protesting meow rang out from the depths of his coat. "A cat? You've found Derry a cat?" Caitlin demanded.

"Aye, I have, if you can call it that. More clawed demon, I'd say." He dug into the wrap around his chest, and Caitlin saw a blur of red and white streak up over his shoulder and dash across the kitchen.

"You wonderful, wonderful man." She stroked his face and found his week's growth of beard ice encrusted, but she didn't care. She locked her arms around his neck and pulled his head down so that she could kiss him full on the mouth.

"That's more of the sort of welcome I'd planned on," he teased, shrugging off his greatcoat and peeling off layers of clothing between kisses.

"Where have you been? Why didn't you come back?" she murmured. "I was half out of my mind with worry."

"Let me near the fire. I'm froze as stiff as a corpse."

She half dragged, half pushed him into Mary's rocker and then dropped to her knees to pull off his boots. "Your feet are like ice," she fussed.

"Hush, woman," he interrupted, scooping her up and into his lap. "No need to take on. I'm here, and I've got all my fingers and toes." He tilted her chin up and kissed her.

Caitlin went all giddy as she tasted and smelled him. "Darling, darling," she murmured. "I've missed you so much."

"Maybe I should go away more often."

Shane's strong fingers kneaded her shoulders and caressed the nape of her neck. He was so cold, but she knew she could warm him.

Then he parted her dressing gown and lowered his head to kiss her throat. "I've missed you bad," he said.

Caitlin shivered as the tip of his tongue brushed her skin and all her defenses crumbled.

"Caity . . ."

She felt his excitement growing as he continued to kiss and fondle her and murmur her name.

"Oh, Shane," she whispered. "You mustn't . . ."

"Do you like that, darlin'?"

"Yes . . . but . . ."

"And that?"

Her pulse quickened.

"Oh, woman . . ."

"Shane . . . What if one of the children wakes and comes down? What if—"

Caitlin gasped as he cupped her breast through her night garments.

"Thinkin' of you kept me in the saddle these past hours." His raspy voice echoed with the sweet music of County Clare.

Shane pinched her nipple gently, and Caitlin felt it harden. Instant desire lanced through her and fanned a growing heat in the pit of her belly.

"I want you," she whispered.

He chuckled. "I was hopin' you'd say that."

"Not here."

He laughed again. "Give me a chance to warm up my tack, and I'll see what I can do to change your mind." He pushed her off his lap and got to his feet. "First, you've got to see what I brought you for Christmas."

"Me?" She didn't want a present. She wanted him to go on touching her. She wanted to keep touching him. "You didn't need to do that. It was only the children that I was thinking of."

"It came to me about three days' ride out of here that you've not asked for a single thing for yourself." He kissed the tip of her nose. "But it's a husband's duty to provide for his wife."

"Duty?" she murmured. What about love? She wanted

him to say he loved her—wanted it so badly—but she'd not ruin this night with another argument.

Shane picked up a large sack by the door. "I've boots for both of the kids, and a saddle for Justice. That's in the barn. And I bought store candy, like you wanted. But I wanted to give you your Christmas gift tonight."

"Oh, Shane, you shouldn't have spent your money on me."

He laid the odd-shaped bundle on the table. "Open it."

With trembling hands, Caitlin emptied the bag and unrolled the red wool blanket. Whatever was inside was about two and a half feet high and heavy. "I can't imagine—" She broke off with a small cry of astonishment.

"What do you think?"

Words wouldn't come. Caitlin stared speechless at the gleaming strings and worn wooden frame of an old and obviously much-loved lyre. With a trembling hand, she reached out and plucked one note and then another. Like water cascading from mossy rocks, the clear tones flowed out and filled the shadowy room with pure magic.

"Oh, Shane." Caitlin began to weep.

"Caity, Caity, stop. I didn't mean to make you unhappy!" He pulled her against his chest. "I thought you'd like it."

"I do. I do . . . like it," she sobbed. "I love it."

"You've a funny way of showing a man."

"Oh, Shane, how did you ever find a lyre out here in the wilderness?"

He held her tightly, trapped in the heat of his arms. She laid her head against his chest and closed her eyes. He must love me, she thought. He wouldn't do this if he didn't. But deep down inside, she knew that Shane still held back a part of himself, and that the words she wanted to hear wouldn't come.

"I told you I was going to Saint Louis. It's a civilized

town, a place where a man can get almost anything for a price, even a Greek lyre."

"It must have cost you . . ." She trailed off, not wanting the argument of money to come between them, not wanting to spoil the magic of this night.

"There was a man there, Zacky King. He made me a standing offer for Cherokee. He's been trying to buy him off me for years."

"Your horse? You sold your buckskin horse to buy me a lyre?" Caitlin pulled away from him. "Not Cherokee! You love him."

His kisses smothered her protests, and Shane pushed her back against the table, and they made slow, glorious love while the wind howled, and the snow drifted high around the house, and everyone else slept.

Chapter 20

Kilronan, Missouri
March 1848

Caitlin added the column of figures a third time and sighed aloud when she reached the same answer. "You're right," she said to Shane. "We need to get a good price for your livestock in Fort Independence or we'll be hard pressed to pay the taxes, let alone buy supplies for the coming year."

Shane removed his hand from her shoulder and leaned over to skim down the columns with a lean finger. "I should have let you do the figurin' from the first, Caity. You've a head for it."

"Yes, you should have," she agreed, pushing back from the dining room table.

Caitlin still felt guilty for believing him to be a tight-fisted man in the months when she'd first arrived at Kilronan. Shane hadn't explained to her that her passage from County Clare had cost him the equivalent of two years' work.

Since Shane had returned from Saint Louis at Christmas, Caitlin had watched her marriage flower. They were more than joyful bedmates; they were friends.

She was all too aware of her husband's human frailties. Shane McKenna was quick to anger, proud, stubborn, and rarely expressed his feelings except in their bedroom. And although he never laid a hand on her or the children that wasn't gentle, he was quick to settle disagreements with men with his fists.

It was Shane's lack of trust that caused Caitlin the most unhappiness, that and his inability to tell her that he loved her. Nothing she could say or do would convince Shane that she hadn't given birth to Derry. He was perfectly willing to forgive her for committing adultery, but he could not believe her word. They had long since given up arguing the subject. They simply avoided it, as they avoided talking about why it had taken seven years for Shane's letters to reach her.

She smiled up at her rugged husband. In spite of those differences, she loved him with all her heart. However, that didn't mean she wasn't tempted at times to pound some sense into his head.

Yes, Caitlin mused as she closed the Kilronan account book, her marriage had blossomed, and the full fruit of that ripening would surprise her husband soon.

Caitlin was certain that she was with child, but she hadn't told him yet. By her reckoning, she could be three months along. Since her cycles had always been irregular, she couldn't be sure. The thought that she might give Shane another son or daughter brought her overwhelming joy, but also a secret terror.

She carried as Mama had, not showing her pregnancy in the early months. But her mother had miscarried four babes before anyone knew she was with child, and Caitlin was afraid that it might be the same for her. And so she had kept her own council, ignoring Mary's knowing looks and unspoken questions.

Besides, she reasoned, Shane had enough to worry about now. He didn't need to concern himself with her health and the coming responsibility of another child.

He'd promised to take care of her if she became pregnant, but she wanted more than a sense of duty from him. If he was unhappy about the baby, she didn't know how she would stand it.

Shane assured her that the winter, which had seemed harsh to her, had been a mild one. There had been periods of thaw when they could pasture the livestock, and they'd made it through the blizzards with only a few oxen and one mule lost.

"As soon as the weather breaks, I'll drive the animals we want to sell north and west to Fort Independence," he'd explained. "Choosing the right time to set out is vital. If I wait too long, other herds will arrive before mine. The first come get the best prices. Big Earl has been trying to beat me there for the past two seasons."

"But you don't want to go so long as there's a chance of a late snowstorm," she reminded him. Gabriel had chilled her with tales of one herd that had been caught in a March storm and died along with the four men driving them.

"It doesn't pay to get there ahead of the folks headin' west on the Oregon Trail," Shane continued. "Some of them bring their own animals cross-country from Saint Louis, but a lot of them come up the Missouri by boat all the way to the jumpin'-off spot to Independence. Oxen and mules would be my choice if I was goin' west—which I'm not. But a lot of men are dead set on ridin' good horses, which is where I make most of my hard cash."

Shane's plan was for the three women and Derry to remain at Kilronan while he, Gabe, and Justice made the drive.

"It's two hundred miles as the crow flies. It's all rugged country, no trails or settlements. It's times like this when I wish I had Big Earl's crew."

"Wouldn't it be safer for both of you if you combined your herds?" Caitlin asked.

Shane scoffed. "The only word I've had from Thompson this winter was when I saw Beau ridin' his side of my fence line. He accused me of stealin' his father's prime stallion and sellin' it in Saint Louis."

"You should have shot him," Gabe said, coming into the dining room from the kitchen.

"I probably would have, if I'd caught him tearin' down a fence, but he was just lookin'. You can't hang a man for that."

"Beau Thompson is worthless. Sooner or later, somebody will do him in," Gabe insisted. "It may as well be sooner."

"God knows I felt like shootin' the ba—" Shane glanced at Derry sitting at his feet putting a bonnet on her cat and broke off. "Good for nothin'," he finished.

"Killing never settled anything," Caitlin said. "A fence isn't worth a man's life."

"If it is Beau, I doubt Big Earl knows about it," Shane observed.

"Or Rachel." Gabe pushed his hands into his pockets.

None of them had seen Rachel since the day after Christmas. She'd ridden off through the deep snow with a jar of blackberry jam in her saddlebag and a red ribbon in her hair.

"No," Caitlin agreed. "I'm sure Rachel wouldn't do anything to harm us."

"Beau doesn't have the brains or the ambition to carry on a feud this long," Shane said. "Rachel does, but she's not the guilty one. I'd stake my right arm on it."

Caitlin touched Shane's shoulder. "You don't believe Beau could do this alone?"

"No, I don't," he replied.

"Who else is there?" she asked.

"Nate Bone, maybe some of the other Thompson hands."

"If you catch Beau breaking our fence or killing our cattle, why shoot him?" Caitlin asked. "Have him arrested. If you saw him, wouldn't that stand up in a court of law?"

"McKenna's word against Thompson's," Gabe said. "And Big Earl will back his boy all the way."

"If you could try to talk to Earl Thompson, maybe—"

Shane cut her off with a shake of his head. "Useless. If I meet up with Big Earl on the trail or in Independence, I'll tell him what I know. At least he'll be forewarned."

"I think you're wrong," Caitlin said. "Why would Beau conspire to steal his own horse or kill his own cattle? It must be outlaws."

Shane frowned. "We've only Rachel's word that they've had losses."

"She wouldn't lie," Gabe said. "Besides, Natchez wasn't Beau's horse; it was Big Earl's. There's more hate under that roof than love, at least between father and son."

"Whoever the culprit is, they've done nothing to us since early autumn," Caitlin said. "Maybe it's over."

Shane shrugged. "I hope you're right, woman. I'd feel a lot easier about leavin' you on Kilronan while I make the drive if I knew it was."

A week later Caitlin leaned against the rails of the corral fence and watched as Shane and Gabriel divided up horses and mules for the drive to Fort Independence. Derry was napping under Mary's watchful eyes, and Justice stood by the gate, letting animals in and out at Shane's orders.

Shane had planned on setting out by the first of April. He'd told Caitlin that he expected to take about two weeks to reach the fort, spend two or three days there, and then arrive back at Kilronan in another five or six days.

"I hate leavin' you alone," he'd said for the tenth time, "but since the Thompsons will be on the trail, you should be safe enough."

She'd decided to tell him about the baby when he got back. Once he'd sold the livestock and had the money he needed for another year, she would feel free to give him the news.

"That's it for this lot," Shane shouted to Justice. "Fifteen horses and four mules."

"I saw two oxen and another three horses grazing near the low spot," the boy said. "Want me to ride out and round them up? One of them is that paint gelding you wanted to sell."

"No," Shane said as he coiled the lariat he'd been using and dropped it over his saddlehorn. "I'll do it myself." He looked at Caitlin. "Want to ride out with me?"

"Watch out for Goliath," Justice warned. "That's where I saw him last. He hasn't gotten any tamer over the winter."

"He doesn't have to be pleasant. He just needs to breed the cows I'm intending on bringing back." Shane grinned at her. "I'll try and find you a milking cow and calf, but I don't want to drive it from Independence. I expect I can find one to suit me at Kane's Crossroads."

"And I suppose you'll expect me to learn how to milk it," she teased. She knew that dairying was considered women's work out here. She'd never tried to get milk from a cow's teats, but if Rachel Thompson could do it, so could she.

"Let Caity take your Red," Shane said to Gabe. "He's already saddled."

Gabe nodded and rode around the outside of the corral to Caitlin and dismounted. He cupped his hands to give her a boost up on the big chestnut gelding. Caitlin felt comfortable on the animal even though he was a half hand taller than Ladybug. Gabe's horses were well mannered and quick to heed any command.

Caitlin gathered the braided leather reins and urged Red into an easy trot. She'd gradually become accustomed to riding astride and found she actually preferred it to riding sidesaddle. At home, in County Clare, she would have caused a scandal with her pantalette-clad legs exposed beneath her riding skirt, but out here there was no one but family to see and none to protest.

Shane waited for her, then touched his roan with his heels. The two animals trotted side by side out of the yard. Caitlin felt Shane's eyes on her, but she kept her attention on her mount.

"You've got good hands," he said approvingly. "I think we'll make a vaquero out of you yet."

"I've got a long way to go to catch up with Justice."

"He's a natural."

"Like his father?" Caitlin suggested.

Shane's eyes narrowed. "We don't know who the boy's father was. Likely Cerise didn't even know."

"I know," she replied. "Shane McKenna's his father. And I think Justice looks more like him every day."

"I waded into that one, didn't I?"

She chuckled. "You did."

"He's a good boy, Caity. But if he turns out to be a decent man, you'll have a lot to do with it."

"He's really smart. He knows all the words in his first primer already, and he's halfway through the second."

"He's gettin' ahead of me."

She laughed. "You'll have to study harder."

"It's not the readin' that's so bad, it's the writin'. Those letters all run together like chicken tracks."

They stopped long enough for Shane to unhook a gate and hold it open for her to ride through. Then he backed the roan alongside the fence and dropped the bar to lock it shut. Shane's gelding was dependable, but he didn't have Cherokee's fire. Caitlin knew Shane missed the buckskin, even though he never spoke of him.

Caitlin felt a twinge of guilt whenever she looked at the lyre, but she'd never let on to Shane. She wouldn't ruin his sacrifice by regretting what couldn't be changed.

And the music did lift her heart. When she ran her fingers over the strings and the first sweet sounds resounded through the room, she could smell the peat smoke and hear the familiar voices of County Clare.

He doesn't need to say that he loves me, she thought as she and Shane cantered their horses across the rolling meadow. The lyre says it for him. Why can't I be satisfied with what I have?

They rode until they reached the slope that led to the willow grove. Then they reined their mounts to a walk, taking care to avoid loose rocks that might injure their horses' legs.

A low, muddy spot at the bottom of the incline was churned with cattle and horse tracks. Shane dismounted and inspected the sign, pointing out to Caitlin a large imprint that he was certain belonged to the bull.

"I'm going to ride in there and take a look-see," he said, pointing to the thicket. "You wait here. Don't come in after me, and if you see Goliath, don't run from him. He's got no reason to chase you. You're on horseback. If he catches wind of you, he won't pay you any mind."

Caitlin waited as Shane rode into the tangle of intergrown saplings. She watched the willow coppice, jumping at each crack and rustle of branches.

A loud, angry bellow erupted from the woods. Caitlin raised up in her stirrups and stared into the trees.

Two doves flew from the grass, darting upward in a

wild flurry of gray feathers. Caitlin's chestnut flicked his ears but didn't panic.

Flies buzzed around Caitlin's face, and she swatted at them. The waiting was excruciating. What if Shane were hurt? What if the bull gored his horse?

Then she heard a loud crashing and gasped in surprise as two dun mules burst from the underbrush and galloped past.

"Haaa! Get on!" Shane shouted. His voice was muffled by the distance and the trees, but still clear enough to understand.

Caitlin let out a small gasp of relief.

A minute later Shane came into full view, whirling his rope overhead and driving two horses ahead of him. "You see any mules go by?"

"Yes! They went that way!" She pointed.

He threw a loop over a bay mare's neck and tied the rope to a tree. "I'm going back in for another horse."

"Did you see the bull?" Caitlin noticed a long bloody scratch along his jawline and another cut over his right eye, but she knew better than to fuss over him.

"Saw Goliath and whacked him on the butt when he wouldn't get out of my way. I told you, out here, he's little danger to anyone. He just wants to eat, swat flies, and chase the ladies."

"Sounds just like a man to me."

Again she waited while Shane hunted for his stray. When he rode out driving it ahead of him, he untied the line that held the pinto and handed it to her. "Just wrap the end around your saddle horn," he told her. "There's a brace of oxen I need to find before we head back."

"Oh, look," Caitlin said. A gray fox loped boldly across the pasture, his plumed tail waving behind him.

"Let's hope he stays away from the house." Shane

chuckled. "If Mary thinks he's a danger to her precious duck, she'll make a fox rug out of him."

Caitlin couldn't remember a more beautiful spring day. The air was full of birdsong, and green grass was springing up everywhere, growing—it seemed—almost before Caitlin's eyes. So many shades of green, she thought, like home.

Shane located his oxen and circled around to drive the long-horned animals back toward the barn paddock. One ox went the way Shane wanted it to, but the second splashed into the main creek and stood there bawling.

Shane leaned from the saddle and plucked several purple-blue violets. He grinned. "Don't ever say that I never brought you flowers."

Caitlin heard what sounded like a dull *pop.* Startled, she glanced up and saw a flash of metal on the hillside across the stream. Before she could point it out to Shane, something whizzed past her ear.

"Caity!"

Why was his voice so odd? "Shane!"

The violets fell from his hand. Caitlin watched them drift—almost in slow motion—toward the ground. Shane jerked in the saddle, as though he'd been punched by an invisible fist.

"Shane!" she screamed again.

"Ride, Caity!" he yelled as he dragged his rifle from the saddle scabbard. "Get the hell out of here!"

Shane raised and cocked his weapon, but his movements were strangely wooden.

Caitlin slapped his horse across the rump with the trailing leather reins and headed toward him.

Shane fired his rifle. Dirt sprayed up on the hillside. Then Caitlin saw a man stand free of the trees. He was holding something in his arms.

"Get down!" Shane shouted. This time Caitlin heard a

faint *crack* on the wind as Shane's body recoiled from the force of the bullet.

Instantly a crimson stain spread across the front of Shane's vest. He slumped forward over his horse's neck and tumbled forward to sprawl face first onto the ground.

Caitlin yanked hard on Red's bridle. He skidded to a stop as she scrambled from the saddle and ran toward Shane.

He was on his hands and knees reaching for his fallen rifle. "My gun," he rasped.

She snatched it up just as a third bullet smashed into Shane's thigh. He groaned and went limp.

"Damn your black soul!" Caitlin screamed at the shooter and threw herself across Shane's motionless body. "Damn you to hell, you coward! Damn you!"

Chapter 21

Another bullet thudded into the grass beside Caitlin's right knee. She closed her eyes and clung to Shane.

He was dead.

She knew he was dead. Frantically she held her fingers over his mouth, trying to feel some sign of breath. "Please, God," she whispered.

There were no tears for her pain. The faceless scum who'd haunted Kilronan had come back to destroy their world. One second she and Shane had been laughing, and in the next heartbeat . . .

It was impossible. He couldn't be dead. She wouldn't let him be dead.

But without drawing breath . . .

Strangely, she was beyond fear. The worst had happened. Her own death could be no more bitter than the loss of this man whose flesh and blood had become dearer to her than her own.

Then the image of a fair-haired babe formed in her mind's eye, and she heard the bubbling echo of an infant's laughter. *Shane's child.*

The words seared through her.

She carried Shane's baby, and it was her duty to protect that innocent life—at any cost.

Caitlin opened her eyes as a slug tore through the toe of Shane's boot. She ignored the danger and concentrated on the one item that might save her unborn son or daughter—Shane's rifle.

Where was it?

Once she located the weapon, she lay motionless, waiting for the killer to reload and fire again. She counted out the seconds. Any instant now . . .

Zing.

The bullet dug a furrow along the surface of the ground just beyond them.

Now! She lunged toward the rifle, seized it, and rolled onto her stomach. She couldn't feel her hands, but her fingers moved just the same. She eased the hammer back, aimed, and pulled the trigger.

Nothing happened.

She stared at the rifle in astonishment.

And then the air cracked with the sound of gunshots— not from the hill but behind her. She twisted around to see Gabriel riding toward her at a hard gallop. The cowboy clung low on the pinto's left side, firing his rifle over his mount's neck at the assassin.

Caitlin crawled back to Shane, fully expecting to feel the force of the killer's bullets, but the hillside was quiet. "Coward!" she shouted. "You'll run now, won't you, you son of a bitch!"

Gabe flung himself off the piebald's back and knelt beside Shane.

"He's dead," Caitlin said dully. Each breath she drew filled her head with the scent of Shane's blood. There was so much of it, staining his clothes, running down to puddle on the flattened spring grass, soaking into the brown earth.

Gabe shook his head. "No, he's not."

"He isn't breathing," she argued.

Gabriel rolled Shane over onto his back, and Caitlin's

stomach clenched as she saw the holes in her husband's body.

"See," she insisted. She was suddenly cold, her teeth chattering.

The wrangler pressed his ear against Shane's gore-soaked chest. Then he leaped up and grabbed Caitlin around the waist. "Get Mary!" he shouted, swinging her up onto his saddleless horse.

"But there's no use," she protested, grabbing hold of the gelding's mane. She felt numb, too shocked by what had happened to break free of the trance that held her. "No use," she whispered.

"He's still got a heartbeat," Gabe said. "Do as I tell you!" He thrust the reins into her hands and slapped the pony's rump. The animal leaped forward, and it was all Caitlin could do to hang on.

He's alive, she thought as the horse galloped toward the house. Shane was alive. But how long could they keep him that way?

They carried Shane back to the house in a wagon and laid him on the plank table in the kitchen. Still dry-eyed, Caitlin washed his wounds with strong soap and water . . . while Mary stood at her back muttering in Osage.

Shane groaned, but his eyes remained shut. His breathing was so faint that Caitlin had to put a mirror over his mouth to be certain that he was still alive.

Mary's lined face was grim as she waved a tiny clay bowl of burning herbs over him. "Lose much blood," she said. "Bad."

"We must send Gabe for the doctor," Caitlin said.

Mary shrugged. "You learn slow, Missy-Wife. We fix, or McKenna die. White-man doctor fool."

Caitlin nodded. "Do what you can, Mary."

She grunted. "No whiskey left. Must . . ." The Indian

woman's face twisted in an effort to come up with the right English words to convey her meaning. "Burn clean." She put her bowl on the mantle over the hearth and donned a clean apron before washing her hands and arms thoroughly with the yellow lye soap.

Caitlin looked at the children. Derry's face was tear streaked, and one braid had come undone. She was clutching her red-and-white cat so tightly that Caitlin wondered how the animal could breathe.

Justice showed no emotion at all. His handsome features were expressionless, his black eyes as flat as volcanic glass.

But Caitlin had seen the depths of joy in the boy's gaze when Shane had rested a hand on his shoulder or ruffled his hair. And she knew that this child would suffer more than any of them if Shane died.

"Justice. Take Derry upstairs."

For once, the boy didn't argue. "Come on, little sister," he said. "Mary will make McKenna better. Bring Mittens and . . ." He grimaced. "We'll dress her in baby clothes."

Derry glanced hesitantly at Caitlin.

"It's all right, darling," Caitlin soothed. "Go and play."

"But . . . Da . . ."

"Your . . ." Caitlin's voice cracked. "Your daddy is hurt very badly. We are going to try to make him better."

Derry nodded vigorously. "I don't want 'Kenna to go to heaven."

Caitlin swallowed, unable to speak as Urika hustled Justice and Derry out of the room. Just as he rounded the corner, the boy glanced back and met Caitlin's eyes, and she read the unspoken pleading there.

"He will be all right," Caitlin insisted.

Gabe scoffed. "Easy to say, but McKenna is hurt bad. One bullet went completely through his upper thigh but missed the bone. It might give us trouble from infection.

Another passed through his side. That one bled plenty, but if we can clean it out good, it won't kill him. It's the bullet in the shoulder that's bad."

"It has to come out, doesn't it?" Caitlin asked.

Mary muttered in Osage, and Gabe nodded. "We'll need rope to bind him," he said to Caitlin before he hurried out of the kitchen.

Mary lifted a kettle of boiling water away from the hearth and poured some into a basin. Urika slid two knives into the pan without looking into Caitlin's face and began to chant softly in Osage under her breath.

Mary motioned for Caitlin to fill a tin mug with the boiling water. Then she stirred a handful of salt into the hot liquid. Using a clean cloth, she soaked up the brine and dripped it into the bullet hole in Shane's thigh and side. As she tended the terrible wounds, she echoed the song that Urika sang.

Caitlin didn't understand the words of the heathen prayers, but the cadence filled the air and helped to soothe the aching inside her.

Shane moaned and tossed his head from side to side as Mary worked over him, but he didn't open his eyes. Using two more cups of salt water, the Indian woman repeated the process. Then she spoke to Urika in the Indian tongue, and the serving girl brought a pot of honey to the table.

"Honey?" Caitlin asked.

Mary nodded. "Today, honey. 'Nother day, McKenna live, use . . ." She sighed impatiently. "Web of spider. Make strong medicine."

"Honey and spiderwebs," Caitlin murmured. God help us, she thought, but she made no protest. Whatever Mary knew or didn't know about nursing, it was more than her own knowledge.

Gabe came back with a length of rope and proceeded

to tie Shane to the table. Then Mary took the sharpest knife, held it over the glowing coals until the steel took on a rosy hue, and returned to stand by Shane.

"Mary open hole. Missy-Wife take out bullet," she ordered.

"Me?" Caitlin felt light-headed.

"Small fingers," Mary said. "You do."

Somehow Caitlin managed to remain upright and keep her wits about her as they dug the lead from Shane's shoulder and tried to staunch the fresh flow of blood. She flinched, but she didn't faint when Gabe brought a red-hot poker from the fireplace and seared the open wound to keep Shane from bleeding to death.

And only after the gore was cleaned away and Shane's wounds were bandaged did she walk calmly out of the house to the necessary in the garden and allow herself to be violently sick.

When she came back into the kitchen, Urika was waiting with a fresh washcloth and towel. Then Mary pushed a cup of strong tea into her hands. "Strong woman," Mary said. "Make good Osage."

Caitlin sipped the black tea and sank into the rocking chair next to Shane. Now there was nothing to do but wait and pray.

Caitlin couldn't be sure how much time passed. Shadows danced around the circle of yellow light from the flickering lantern. The wood snapped and crackled on the hearth, and heavy odors of wild cherry and tobacco settled over the room.

Caitlin was terribly sleepy. She didn't want to drift off; she knew she needed to stay awake for Shane. She wouldn't give in to her own weakness. She'd be strong. She could do that, but she was so weary, and her eyelids were so very heavy.

Mary laid a strong hand on the nape of Caitlin's neck.

"Sleep," she said as she massaged Caitlin's cramped muscles. "Mary watch."

"No, I'll watch him," Caitlin replied, but even as she said the words, her eyes drifted shut. She forced them open, and then lost the battle.

It was daylight when Caitlin woke to find Shane running a fever but semiconscious. And it was another two days before he came to his senses, and Mary pronounced that he would live.

"Not ride soon," the Indian woman said. "But McKenna live. Strong, like warrior."

"I don't . . . feel much like a warrior," he whispered hoarsely as he clung to Caitlin's hand. "I . . . feel . . . like a fool. I've let . . . let you down. I let myself get . . . get shot."

"If you are, then I love a fool," Caitlin said as she leaned close and murmured in his ear. "Do you have any idea how much you mean to me?"

"No." He forced a painful grin. "But I'm willin' to have you try to tell me."

Caitlin promised that she would, but she knew that his recovery would be slow. Shane was still too weak to rise from his bed, and he didn't have the strength to lift a spoon of broth into his mouth. He could barely sip the willow bark tea and the doses of painted trillium root that Mary poured down him every hour around the clock.

The ugly burn from the hot poker was slow to heal and would leave a scar that Shane would carry to his grave, but it did not fester. And Caitlin realized that no matter how horrible the cure, the fire had purified the bullet wound that otherwise would have mortified.

"Fetch Gabe for me," Shane whispered.

And when she did as he bade her, Shane ordered the

wrangler to turn the livestock out of the paddocks to graze. "There won't be a drive this year," Shane said.

Caitlin looked away, unable to bear the anguish in Shane's gaze. If they couldn't sell the livestock in Independence, there would be no money to live on for the coming year and no money for taxes.

She slipped from the room and waited for Gabe in the kitchen. "Couldn't you and Justice take some of the horses?" she asked him. "Just a few, so that—"

He shook his head. "We could drive them up to Fort Independence, but when we got there I couldn't sell them."

"Gabriel hang for steal horse," Mary said.

"She's right," he agreed. "You know I'd cut off my right arm for McKenna or Justice, but my face is the wrong color. An Indian showin' up with Kilronan stock wouldn't last long."

Mary spread her gnarled hands in a gesture of finality. "No horses go Independence," she said. "My Gabriel, my Justice, not go to hang."

Caitlin drew in a long, slow breath. "What if they didn't go alone?" she ventured. "Can a white woman sell livestock?"

Gabe fixed her with an intense stare. "You?"

Caitlin nodded. "Shane said my riding was coming along. We can do it, Gabe. I know we can. You, me, and Justice. We'll take McKenna's livestock to Fort Independence, and we'll get it there ahead of the other herds."

"You know what you're lettin' yerself in for?" Gabe asked.

"McKenna no like," Mary said.

"McKenna won't know, until it's too late to stop us," Caitlin answered.

"It will be dangerous," Gabriel warned.

"You mean you think whoever tried to kill Shane will

try to kill us?" she asked. She hadn't thought of that. She'd been so worried about Shane that it hadn't occurred to her that someone might want to kill her as well. "If we leave him, do you think they'll come after him again?"

"No," Mary said.

Caitlin looked at her. "Why not?"

Mary's eyes narrowed to slits. "Gabriel tell Rachel that McKenna is dead."

Caitlin glanced at Gabe. "You lied to Rachel? Why?"

Mary scoffed. "Nobody kill dead man."

"So what about us?" Caitlin asked Gabriel. "If we drive these horses, will we be a target for the killer?"

He shrugged.

"But if we stay here at Kilronan," Caitlin continued, "Shane loses everything he's worked for. And what's to say they won't come after us anyway?"

The wrangler nodded slowly.

"You keep those animals penned up," Caitlin said with more authority than she felt. "We'll leave at daybreak tomorrow."

Gabe nodded again. "All right. We'll try it, but if we don't succeed, we won't have to worry about bein' broke or about being ambushed by Beau Thompson. McKenna will murder us all."

Six hours from Kilronan and halfway across the first river, Caitlin realized that she'd made a big mistake. Going on a horse drive when some of the animals were barely broken to saddle was ludicrous—ridiculous. Not only was she going to lose Shane's entire herd, but she was going to kill herself and his unborn child in the attempt.

Justice had already reached the far side of the river with the lead horse, called the bell mare, a big rangy bay with streaks of gray around her eyes and a spiky black mane and tail. The bell mare's name was Nancy, and a small copper bell hung from her halter and tinkled when she moved. The familiar sound told the other animals where she was at all times and comforted them, according to Justice.

"Horses are flighty," the boy had explained. "Knowing that Nancy is up ahead and in charge keeps them calm."

Caitlin watched as two paint horses scrambled up the rocky bank on the far side. The bulk of the herd was still in the water, swimming the deep part of the river. Gabriel was downstream keeping the stock away from the swiftest area of current, and she was clinging to a mule upstream, about a third of the way across.

The water was icy cold and fast running, and Caitlin was already soaked to the waist. Her teeth were chattering, and she was concentrating on staying in the saddle when Gabe yelled at her and waved his hand frantically.

She looked over her shoulder to see two mules and a gray gelding turning back toward the southern side.

"Go get them!" Gabe shouted.

"Me?" Caitlin replied in astonishment.

The cowboy's answer was lost in the sound of the river, which Caitlin thought was probably for the best, considering the expression on his face.

So what if they lost those three? she argued with herself. Gabe had already made the decision to leave the oxen behind at Kilronan because they were so slow. The powerful but gentle beasts were greatly in demand by settlers taking wagon trains west, but Gabe had insisted there was more profit in the horses and mules.

"We're already late," he'd said on the morning they'd departed Kilronan. "The Thompson herd started two days ago. If we want to get to Independence in time to get a good price for the livestock, then we go without the oxen."

Caitlin looked back at the wayward horse and the two mules, and then at Gabriel. The cowboy obviously had his plate full in dealing with the main herd. Either she retraced her steps and rounded up the runaways, or they'd be lost.

Then she glanced ahead at Justice. It was clear from the way the boy was shouting at her that he expected her to bring the animals back. She and Shane's son were just beginning to understand each other. If she let him down, would he ever forgive her?

"Damn mules," she muttered under her breath as she reined her animal around the way she'd come. A branch banged against her leg and scraped against her mount's hindquarters, and she kicked it away.

Bessie laid back her ears and fought the bit as the last of the horses swimming the other way passed her. "Get up!" Caitlin urged. When the animal balked, Caitlin slapped her neck with the reins.

The mule found her footing on a sandbank and lunged forward, throwing Caitlin sideways in the saddle. Caitlin regained her balance and dug her heels into Bessie's sides.

A few more yards, and they regained solid ground. One of the mules that Caitlin had come back to catch brayed a greeting, and Bessie nickered in return. "Get on," Caitlin yelled. "Get!"

She urged Bessie in a circle around the stragglers and tried to drive them back toward the river. By the time she got the horse to the water's edge, one of the stray mules had gone left, the other one right. Both were eating grass and showed no sign that they felt like going for another swim. And as soon as she left the horse to chase a mule, the horse wandered away from the riverbank.

Gabe had the rest of the herd on the far side. He and Justice were bunching them up to drive them north. Would they leave her alone on the wrong side of the river?

Gabriel had sent her back to get three runaway animals, and she barely had control of the one she was riding. She was freezing to death, and her bottom and legs were so cold that she could hardly feel whether or not she was in the saddle.

"Stupid, senseless beasts!" she cried. "Stay here. Get eaten by wolves. See if I care!" She urged Bessie up alongside the horse and smacked it on the rump with the ends of Bessie's reins.

The horse leaped off the bank into the river, and Caitlin's mule plunged after. The water hadn't gotten any warmer.

Bessie slipped and fell sideways, then struggled up and began swimming. The gelding kept pace with the mule until they reached the middle, where the current was the most dangerous.

Caitlin held the reins in a death grip. Her fingers were laced into the mule's stiff mane, and her knees gripped the animal's sides with all her strength. She was a good swimmer, but if she fell off, the weight of her riding skirt, petticoat, and Gabe's breeches that she wore underneath her own garments would pull her down.

Desperately, Caitlin started praying for Bessie's safety.

After what seemed hours, the water grew shallower, and the gray swam ahead and waded ashore. Bessie was two lengths behind him when the carcass of a dead deer came tumbling down the river. The mule took one look, laid back her ears, and began to buck.

Caitlin never felt herself leave the saddle. The next thing she knew, the river was closing over her head. She touched something cold and stiff and furry, screamed, and swallowed a mouthful of water. Then she surfaced and screamed again as the stench of dead buck engulfed her.

"Help me!" she cried.

Bessie's rump and hindquarters flew up over the river-bank. The other two mules that she'd thought she'd left behind splashed past, nearly scaring Caitlin to death and knocking her under again. "Help!" she shouted. "I'm drowning!"

And then she touched bottom. When she stood up, the water barely came to her chest. Weeping tears of anger and frustration, saying words no lady should ever admit knowing, she clawed her way up the bank. "Gabriel!" she shouted, shivering so hard that she could barely speak. "Get me a rifle! I'm going to shoot that mule!"

Justice trotted over on his pinto pony. "Good work," he said. "I didn't think you'd get them mules."

"Get off that pony and build a fire," she ordered.

"But we've got three more hours of daylight," he protested.

"I'm wet."

He grinned, looking amazingly like his father. "You are wet."

"Justice."

The smile faded. Justice hadn't survived as long as he had without knowing real danger when he saw it.

"A fire."

Reluctantly the boy swung down off his pony. "All right, if you say so. But we're never gonna get to Fort Independence if you're goin' to act like a girl."

"Not another word." She dropped onto the deep grass and began to tug at a wet boot.

"Well, you did get the stock," Justice admitted. "That's something."

Gabe rode up. He studied her from head to toe, but he made no mention of her soaked condition, and he never cracked a smile. "I take it we're campin' here for the night?"

"Yes, we are," Caitlin said with as much dignity as she could muster. "And as soon as I shoot Bessie, and Justice builds a fire, you can grill us some delicious mule steaks for supper while I'm drying off."

Chapter 22

All that first day Mary had kept Shane drugged with a medicated tea, so it wasn't until the following morning that he realized that Caitlin was gone. "Where is she?" he'd roared. "And where's Gabe? And Justice?"

"Take horses to fort," Mary answered. She held out another cup of her special brew. "Sell stock," she added, as if Shane couldn't figure the rest out for himself.

"The hell they have!"

"No danger," Mary said. "Gabriel tell Thompson woman you dead."

"No danger?" Shane repeated. "Two hundred miles of open country. Renegades, crazy mountain men, army deserters, and horse thieves. One wrangler, an Irish lady, and a boy? Just how do you figure they're in no danger?"

Derry hid behind Mary's skirt and peeked out with big eyes. " 'Kenna mad at Mama?" she asked.

"No, darlin'," he managed between clenched teeth. He fixed Mary with a cold stare. "Why did you go along with this? You've got more sense than the three of them put together."

Mary shrugged. "This place Justice home. He keep, he need fight, maybe."

"Saddle me a horse, if they've left me one."

Mary stuck her pipe between her teeth. "McKenna too

sick ride," she mumbled. "McKenna sleep. Eat. Ride tomorrow."

He sat up and immediately sank back onto the pillow. His shoulder was as stiff as a block of wood, and it burned as if it were on fire. His gorge rose, and he was afraid he'd disgrace himself by vomiting all over the bedcovers.

"Bring me my clothes," he said.

"Too sick—"

"Now, Mary!" He pushed himself to a sitting position and stayed up by sheer willpower. The room was spinning, and his stomach was trying to turn itself inside out.

"Pants!" he insisted. "And get that baby out of here. I'm stark naked under this sheet."

Mary shoved some clothing at him and shooed Derry from the room. Sweat broke out on Shane's forehead as he set about dressing himself. He thought he'd been in pain when the bull had stomped him, but that was nothing compared to this. "Pack food and make a bedroll for me!" he shouted through the closed door. "I'm goin' after them."

Mary didn't answer.

Gabe drove the herd hard all the next day and harder still the day after that. Caitlin's back ached, and her face and hands were sunburned. Every bone and muscle in her body felt as if it had been pounded with a blacksmith's hammer and then stretched like Christmas taffy.

They ate on horseback during the daylight hours, and supper was whatever Gabe or Justice shot during the day. The third night out, Caitlin ate rattlesnake roasted over an open fire and was too hungry to even protest.

"If we'd brought the wagon with us, we could have had coffee and corn cakes and beans," Justice said. "But the wagon and team would slow us down. The Thompsons travel with two wagons. We can go over the rough spots that would snap a wagon wheel like tinder."

No wagon also meant no extra blankets and few changes of clothing. A single blanket roll and two saddlebags contained all Caitlin's belongings for the trip. As she left the house, she'd snatched Shane's hat off a peg for a good-luck charm, and she thanked God for it. Her fair skin blistered and peeled in the warm Missouri sunshine, but the hat kept down the glare and shielded part of her face. The broad brim also helped to keep some of the rain out of her eyes.

They crossed streams and rocky valleys and threaded through thick forests that had grown there for thousands of years. They rode through foggy mornings and bright afternoons. Gabe started the horse herd moving when the last stars were just vanishing in the eastern sky and kept them walking at a fast pace until twilight faded into dusk.

Caitlin saw deer and bear, foxes and coyotes. She watched eagles wheel across the sky and great vees of ducks and geese winging overhead. Her head was filled with images of bright-colored birds, wild creatures, ancient trees, and swirling sunsets. But ever constant were the horses and mules that made up the Kilronan herd.

Gabe and Justice knew every animal by name and personality. And many of them Caitlin came to recognize as well. Nancy, the bell mare, was short-tempered and would kick if you came up on her left side, but nothing startled her. The black mule named Trot hated water and had to be driven across any creek, and Babe, a stocky gelding, would wander off if someone didn't keep him in the center of the herd.

Caitlin was riding Jack, a big-headed paint, on the left flank of the herd when they reached a dead end of a narrow valley. On two sides the ground rose sharply in a tangle of rocks and scrub trees. The remaining route, westerly, seemed scarcely better. The steep incline was stepped upward in sections scattered with loose gravel.

"We've got to turn around and go back," Caitlin called to Gabe. The bell mare, Nancy, had already circled inside of the natural corral and was headed out.

Gabe pointed. "Nope, we're headin' up there."

Caitlin was sure that her expression must have revealed her doubt, because the cowboy grinned. "These animals can do it. We'll take half a day off our trip by cutting over this ridge."

"Trust your horse," Justice said. "It's not as bad as it looks."

She trusted the pinto. It was her riding that she worried about. What if she fell off and rolled back? Caitlin gritted her teeth and pushed the image of her crushed and broken body out of her mind.

Gabe was always right where the horses were concerned, wasn't he? Caitlin shuddered. "Have you come this way before?"

He shouted an answer, but it was lost in the clatter of hooves and his whoop as he whirled a rope over his head and drove Nancy and two other animals up over the first ledge. Bessie plunged after them, followed by a black mare.

Caitlin's heart fluttered like a trapped bird in a chimney as she closed her eyes and dug her heels into Jack's sides. The horse leaped up the hill, seemingly oblivious to loose rocks and jostling animals. Caitlin ignored Shane's riding lessons and held on tightly to the saddle horn.

To her left, a bay stumbled and went down on his knees. A dun crashed into him and whinnied in pain. Then both animals scrambled to their feet and climbed on. Caitlin looked back over her shoulder to see Justice on his pinto pony gamely driving the last of the mules up the rugged slope.

Caitlin held her breath as Jack's powerful legs drove them on. Once he slipped and came close to coming down on his right knee, but then he found solid rock and continued up. Caitlin didn't look back again until they had reached the crest of the hill. To her surprise, there were no injured horses or mules lying helplessly on the valley floor. Even Justice's pony had made the climb successfully.

The descent down the far side was rough but nothing like the rocky slope. And at the bottom of the hill was a grove of trees and a fast-running stream.

"I want to see the Thompsons get their wagons over that," Caitlin said triumphantly.

Justice laughed. "Me, too."

"I told you the herd could do it," Gabe said.

The boy caught Caitlin's horse and held it so that she could dismount. "Wait until McKenna hears about this," he said.

"Doesn't Shane come this way with his herd every year?" she asked.

Gabe laughed. "Hell, no—" He broke off and flushed red under his tan. "McKenna never thought we could make it up that hill with the herd."

"You . . . you . . ." Caitlin opened her mouth to call him the worst name she could think of, but all that came out was laughter. "We did it, didn't we?" she said when she could speak again. "We really did it."

"Yep," Justice agreed. "And Gabe thinks we'll pass the Thompson herd sometime tomorrow."

It was Caitlin's turn to build the fire. Justice hobbled the horses while Gabe walked off to hunt some game for dinner. No other herds had passed this way, and there was wood lying along the creek.

The three of them worked well together. Caitlin was surprised at how different Gabriel acted toward her than he had at home on Kilronan. He'd always been polite, but here on the trail, he laughed and joked with her, including her in conversations he had with Justice.

Caitlin could see why Shane valued Gabe so highly. He had a magical way with horses; he always seemed to know exactly where he was going without landmarks or roads. Gabe's patience—even toward her and her ignorance about camp life—seemed unending.

That night, after they devoured the grouse and grilled trout over the open fire, Caitlin, Justice, and Gabe sat up for a long time, staring into the fire and talking.

Justice had so many questions about Ireland and her sea voyage to America. He wanted to know if she'd seen whales or pirates, and he asked about the ocean waves and fish that flew through the air.

"How does the captain drive the boat? Did you see—"

"One question at a time," she said. But Justice's excitement was contagious, and it thrilled her to see how eager he was to learn about the world. "Someday you'll see it all," she promised. "You could go to college in Dublin or Edinburgh."

"Don't fill his head with such," Gabriel warned. "Indians don't go to school in Missouri, at least not to regular schools with white folks."

"Justice is only part Indian. He's French and—"

"And what?" the boy asked wryly.

"Irish," she replied without a moment's hesitation. "And it makes no difference in my homeland. They've never seen an Osage there. He's little darker than Derry. A McKenna he is, the son of Caitlin and Shane McKenna, and a McKenna with the coin to pay the fee would be welcome in any college in Europe."

Gabe chuckled. "You're a devious woman."

"Thank you."

They all laughed at that.

Caitlin sighed and stretched and gazed up at the glorious night sky arching overhead. It looked like a bottomless fairy pool filled with diamonds. The burnished copper moon—as large as a dinner plate—hung so low that she was certain Gabe could throw a rope around it. And the air . . . she'd never smelled anything that made her feel so alive. The scents of the animals mingled with that of the cherry wood embers, the new grass, and the leather saddle she lay against.

Justice's eyes grew heavy, and he began to listen more than talk. And after a few minutes, his head slumped sideways onto Caitlin's shoulder.

She slipped an arm around him, and immediately he stiffened and sat bolt upright. "I'm sorry," she said. "I know you don't like to be touched."

The boy averted his eyes. "I don't care. Not so long as it's you."

"He's a little skittish because his mother beat him," Gabe said as he tossed another log on the fire.

Justice frowned. "Only when she was liquored up. Whiskey made her crazy mean."

"Irish and Indians," Caitlin murmured. "I guess they're more alike than I'd guessed." Her gaze met Gabe's across the campfire. "Shane doesn't drink anymore, does he?"

"No," the wrangler replied. "He used to, but no more. Not a drop since Cerise's death."

"He blames himself," Caitlin said. Here in this lonely place with the endless night sky stretching over them, a sense of comradeship linked the three of them. Caitlin felt comfortable talking of what she couldn't at Kilronan.

"I told you," Justice put in. "McKenna didn't kill her. He ain't the one who stabbed her."

Caitlin covered Justice's hand with hers. "Who did?" She gave him a squeeze. "You know, don't you?"

The boy's eyes widened in the firelight. "You think I kilt her."

"He's innocent," Gabe said. "Tell her, Justice. Tell her what really happened that night."

Caitlin tensed.

"No!" Justice jumped to his feet. "I'll never tell! I swore I wouldn't."

"And you keep your promises, don't you, boy." Gabe crouched beside the fire and stared into the glowing coals. "He was there, hidin' under his mother's bed. McKenna didn't know it, and I didn't know it either."

"You?" Gooseflesh rose on Caitlin's arms. "You were there, Gabriel?"

The wrangler nodded. "I killed her. She was my sister, and I killed her."

"That ain't so," Justice protested from the far side of the fire. "It was an accident. She kilt herself."

"How?" Caitlin asked.

"She and McKenna fought over the baby, like I told you before," Justice said angrily. "Cerise was drunked up out of her head. She always wanted to cut somebody when she got that way. McKenna struggled with her, but he was as drunk as she was. He hit his head on the table and passed out."

"I'd come to town with McKenna that night, and I was outside on the balcony," Gabe said. "I wasn't spyin' on them. I'd come to see my sister."

"Indians aren't welcome in Fat Rose's—at least not as customers," Justice explained. "Gabe always had to climb over the roof and in the window. Cerise never told nobody that Gabe was her brother—least of all McKenna. She was ashamed of him because he looked Osage."

"We argued," Gabriel continued. "We always argued. I

wanted her to stop the drinkin'—to go with McKenna or some other decent man and stop sellin' her body. And when I heard her tell McKenna she wanted money to get rid of the baby, it made me furious."

"Gabe never meant to hurt her," Justice said.

"She shamed me and she shamed our people. But she was still my sister, and I loved her."

"Cerise swung at him with the knife," the boy explained. "Gabe tried to take the knife away from her, but she slipped and fell on it."

"I ran away," the cowboy finished. "I let McKenna take the blame because I knew an Indian couldn't get a fair trial. Nobody would have listened to me tell what happened. A dead whore, a dead Indian."

"But you can't tell either," Justice said. "Mary doesn't know. Nobody knows but us."

Gabe covered his face with his hands. "I didn't have the courage to tell my mother that I killed my sister. I still don't."

Caitlin ached for them both . . . and for Shane. Her eyes stung with unshed tears. "But you told me."

"You'll keep our secret," Justice said.

"Can you be sure?" she asked him.

The child nodded. "I guess I know who I can trust and who I can't."

She looked at Gabe. "But Shane should know. He's carried a terrible burden of guilt for her death. If it was all her own fault . . ."

"Someday," Justice promised. "Someday I'll tell him, but not yet. And if you tell—"

"I won't," she said softly. "But I think you need to. He'll understand. I know he will." I hope he will, she thought.

"But what if he doesn't?" Gabe asked. "He's my friend, and I betrayed him."

"Did you believe he'd hang for killing your sister?" she replied.

"A white man? A landowner? If they'd found him guilty, he'd have been let off with a fine. Twenty dollars, tops for killin' an Indian whore."

Caitlin went to Justice and hugged him. "Have faith in Shane," she said as she ruffled his thick hair. "Your uncle is his friend, and you're his son. He may have loved Cerise, but he loves the two of you as well. He'll see why you thought you had to do what you did."

For a minute Justice returned her embrace, and then he pulled back, embarrassed. "You don't have to get mushy on me. I'm too old for that stuff."

"Not from a mother," Gabe suggested.

"She ain't . . ." Justice looked at Caitlin, and then back at his uncle and shrugged. "Well, I suppose, since she ain't got a boy of her own . . ."

"We could . . . sort of pretend," Caitlin offered. "Since Cerise isn't here, maybe she wouldn't mind if I did the mothering in her place."

"I guess it would be all right," Justice agreed with a great show of reluctance. "So long as you don't act stupid in front of other people."

"Deal." She offered her hand. "Shake on it?"

Justice laughed. His small, callused fingers grasped hers. "Deal, Ma."

"Mama," she corrected.

He shook his head. "Quit while you're winnin'."

"Ma, it is," she conceded gracefully. "Your Irish grandmother, my mother—rest her soul—is probably turning over in her grave at that."

Caitlin stirred and felt around with her hand, uncertain where she was. She touched grass at the same time she opened her eyes. The stars still winked faintly in a misty sky, but the moon was nowhere in sight.

She listened, hearing nothing more than the chirp of crickets, the *ribit, ribit* of a frog, and the restless shuffling of horses' feet. She sighed and turned over, noting the outline of Justice sleeping only an arm's distance away from the fire. Gabe's blanket was there, but she knew he dozed upright in the saddle, catching what rest he could as he rode guard on the herd each night.

From far off Caitlin heard the rumble of thunder. A thin needle of lightning shimmered on the far horizon. "Please, God," she whispered sleepily. "No rain." It would be dawn soon, and she'd be back on a horse. She'd do what she had to when the time came, but for now all she wanted to do was catch another hour's sleep.

She snuggled down and pulled the blanket over her head. The ground beneath her was not as hard as it would have been if Justice hadn't crafted her a mattress of evergreen boughs.

"They keep away bugs," he'd told her when he dragged the branches to the campfire.

"So long as they keep away snakes," she'd replied.

Snakes. Ugh. She shivered. Why did she have to think about snakes now? She rolled over onto her left side and curled into a ball.

A horse's whinny brought her half awake, heart thumping. Nancy's bell jingled, and another animal on the outside of the herd snorted.

"Justice?" Caitlin whispered. "Do you—"

A man's hand clamped over her mouth. Instinctively Caitlin slammed upward with a fist and bit down on dirty fingers at the same time. Her assailant jerked away his hand and delivered a stunning blow to the side of her jaw.

Pinwheels of light exploded inside Caitlin's head. She

rolled and screamed Gabe's name, then began to crawl away as gunfire erupted from the far side of the herd.

A mule leaped over the fire and galloped past, nearly crushing Caitlin's skull with an iron-shod hoof. She tried to scramble to her feet, but someone wrestled her face down in the grass and seized a handful of her hair. "No!" she spat out dirt and screamed as he yanked her head back at an impossible angle.

"Let go of her!" Justice shouted.

From the corner of her eye, Caitlin caught sight of the boy, fists flying, hurling himself onto the man.

"Get away from me, you little red bastard!"

Caitlin struggled to free herself from her attacker as he fought off Justice. The man's vile curses rang in her ears. I know that voice, she thought frantically. It's Thompson! Beau Thompson! She got up onto her knees, turned, and butted him in the stomach. The three of them went down in a tangle of arms and legs.

Beau cursed and knocked Justice away. He let go of Caitlin's hair and grabbed his arm, and Caitlin saw blood welling up through his torn shirtsleeve.

"You bastard," Beau swore, and fumbled for his pistol with his bad arm.

"No!" Caitlin cried.

Still clutching his knife, Justice sprang up defiantly to face him. "Run, Ma!"

Caitlin knew that Beau meant to kill the boy, and she knew just as surely that she couldn't face Shane if she let that happen.

Lunging forward, she grabbed Beau's bleeding arm and forced the muzzle of the weapon toward the ground. "Run, Justice! Run!"

The thunder of hooves drowned her screams.

Horses and mules stampeded through the camp, scattering the fire and engulfing Caitlin, Beau, and Justice in

clouds of smoke and dust. Beau heaved Caitlin aside and
cocked his weapon, but he could no longer see the boy in
the river of churning horseflesh.

Caitlin grappled with Beau, beating him with her fists,
trying to knock the gun from his hand. But he was too
strong for her. He clamped an arm around her throat and
began to drag her away.

Choking, unable to draw breath, Caitlin clawed at his
arm and kicked his legs. Then, as her strength failed and
she feared she was losing consciousness, a man on horseback appeared beside them.

"Give her to me!" he shouted.

"The hell with her!" Beau yelled back. He shoved
Caitlin aside.

She would have fallen if she hadn't slammed into the
rider's horse. Gasping, she sucked in ragged gulps of air
and tried to keep from tumbling beneath the feet of the
passing animals.

Beau seized the cowboy's saddle horn. "Get me out of
here, Nate!"

Nate's horse leaped forward, and Caitlin staggered
sideways. Another animal dashed toward her, and she
grabbed the trailing reins amid the tangle of hooves. Her
fingers closed around the leathers, and when she saw
Gabe's saddle, she realized that this was the paint the
wrangler had been riding.

For a second, she thought she could hold on to the
reins, but the pony's terror made him uncontrollable. Her
heart sank as the leather tore out of her grasp.

"Catch that horse!" Nate shouted at Beau. Then his
hand closed on Caitlin's shoulder, and he dragged her up
across the front of his saddle.

She screamed and tried to shield her head as Nate
drove his horse into the melee. Then the animal beneath
her was galloping with the rest. Caitlin groaned in pain as

Nate's saddle horn pounded against her ribs, and the dust rose in choking clouds.

She was going to die, Caitlin realized. She was going to die there without ever seeing Shane again. That was the last lucid thought she had before blackness closed over her.

Chapter 23

It was midmorning the following day when Shane McKenna came upon Rachel kneeling in the ashes of Gabe's campfire and holding her brother's dying body.

"Where's Caity," McKenna demanded.

Rachel flinched under his gaze. She'd looked into the eyes of killers before; she'd even watched one hang in Saint Louis. But she'd never felt the chill she did now as she faced Shane McKenna's merciless stare. Gabe had told her that McKenna was dead, and from the looks of him, he might well have ridden back from hell's gate.

"No sign of her or Gabe." Rachel lowered Beau's head onto her lap. Her brother was past knowing whether she talked to him or not. He was past everything but meeting his final judgment.

McKenna couldn't miss seeing Beau beside her, and Rachel knew he didn't need to be told that Big Earl's only son had been trampled beyond redemption. The animal tracks and the ruin of Beau's body were plain to see.

"My boy?" McKenna asked.

McKenna's skin was the color of old tallow, and he was hurting bad. Rachel noted the stained bandage around his waist and the blood seeping down his trouser leg. But he sat there in the saddle as proud and straight as a Comanche chief outlined against a clear blue sky.

She shook her head. "I tracked Beau, Long Neck Jack, and that useless piece of dog shit, Nate Bone, back here from our herd. When they cut out, I guessed they were up to no good."

McKenna waited, his Black Irish features as hard and cold as the gray steel of his rifle barrel. His cheeks were sunken in, his lips dry. She wondered if he'd eaten or slept since he'd ridden off Kilronan.

"Beau could still talk when I found him," Rachel said. Funny how a body could say the words as easy as if they were talking about frying up a chicken for supper. Maybe Big Earl was right, and she wasn't a natural female. Or maybe, as a kid, she'd shed too many tears when she'd had to wash her dead mother's ravaged body to make it decent for the coffin. Could it be that God only gave her one bucket of tears to last a lifetime and that her pail was empty?

Most folks thought her hard and mannish, but it was difficult to act like a woman when she'd had none to teach her how. And it was harder still to mourn a brother she'd had to fight away from her bed ever since she'd sprouted breasts.

Beau jerked and stiffened in her arms. He gasped once and sighed a hollow, whistling sound. When Rachel looked down at his eyes, she saw that the light had gone out of them like an extinguished candle.

For a minute she went numb, and then she realized that her tears were dripping onto Beau's forehead. "Rot your greedy bowels." She sniffed, ashamed of her own weakness. "You never were a brother, and you never were worth the powder to blow you away."

Rachel closed his eyes. He almost looked asleep, if you didn't notice what he looked like below the neck. "You're s'posed to put pennies on their eyes to keep them shut," she said. She dug in a pocket and came up empty, then glanced at McKenna. "You got any coin on you?"

He tossed two quarters into the dirt.

"Obliged." Rachel wiped them on her pant leg and laid them on her brother's eyelids. "I know he wasn't no good," she said. "But he was blood kin."

McKenna nodded, but his fierce look didn't soften. "Did Beau tell you what they meant to do?"

She took a breath and then let it all spill out. "They meant to steal your herd, I reckon. The same way they stole Big Earl's Natchez. Beau told me, not an hour ago. Him and Nate Bone sold that horse to a Frenchman headed for New Orleans. The slimy little worm stole his father's prize stud, stared him right in the face, and blamed it on you and Gabe."

"What did I ever do to your brother to make him hate me?"

"Nate hates you, sure enough, but it was pure greed drivin' Beau. Nate told him that he'd inherit Kilronan once you and Big Earl were dead."

"Ahead of my wife and son?"

Rachel shrugged. She'd never been frightened of McKenna, not even when she was fifteen and lied to Big Earl about McKenna trying to force himself on her. She'd always thought McKenna was too decent of a man to hurt a woman.

Today was different. McKenna was different, and the icy sensation running down her spine was fear.

"Sorry's too small a word to use, McKenna. But it wasn't me done this wrong, and it wasn't Big Earl. My father's pigheaded, but he's no horse thief, and he sure ain't no murderer." She went to her horse and took a canteen off the saddle. "You look like you could use a drink of water."

He took the container and uncorked the neck. He drank

long and deeply, and when he was finished, he wiped the stray drops off his mouth. "Thanks. Mary's maybe a half day behind me in a wagon. She's got Derry with her. If you want to wait, I know Mary will help you dig a grave."

McKenna didn't offer to help her himself, but Rachel didn't need to ask why. A man in his shape could ride, but he couldn't dismount and then get back into the saddle again.

"I wasn't plannin' on takin' the time to bury him," she answered. "There's a tree yonder, and I've got a rope. I thought to pull him up high enough to keep the coyotes away from him and ride on to look for Gabe."

"If he's alive, he'll be trackin' the herd."

"Beau said Nate was supposed to shoot Gabe while he grabbed Cait. I looked for blood, but if there was any, the horse sign covered it." She let her breath out slowly. "I didn't find no bodies. Only Beau's. Maybe Nate's got Justice and Cait."

McKenna's gray eyes narrowed. "You and Gabe?"

She nodded. "Injun or not, he loves me and I love him."

"Big Earl won't—"

"To hell with my father. I would have helped Beau if I could, but he's dead and Gabe's alive. I'm goin' after my man." She took the rope off her saddle. "I've got to finish here, but if I can catch up, would you mind if I rode along with you?"

McKenna removed his hat and wiped the sweat away from his forehead. "It's a free country."

"I can shoot straight, you know the truth of that," she said. "You might need another rifle."

"I might," he admitted, "but if my family's come to harm, I mean to take Nate Bone apart Osage fashion, one inch at a time."

* * *

Caitlin vomited until she was reduced to dry heaves. She crouched on her hands and knees at the edge of a clearing in the woods. Nearby were the thirty horses and four mules that still remained of Shane's herd. The others had been lost in the wild chase over rocky ridges and moor that had lasted until midafternoon.

Some of the animals had bolted away from the herd; others had simply vanished. One mule had broken a leg; Nate had left the animal braying in pain beside a ground-squirrel burrow, and Long Neck Jack had doubled back to shoot it.

Sometime around dawn, Nate had dropped a loop over Gabe's pony and put Caitlin on it. He'd tied her ankles to a rope that ran under the paint's belly and her wrists to the saddle horn. The hemp had cut into her flesh so tightly that her hands were streaked with blood.

Once during the day Nate and Long Neck Jack had driven the herd across a river. Water had risen up to Caitlin's knees, but she'd been unable to drink. It was thirst that tortured her now.

Nate had water. She'd watched him drink from a leather flask, but he hadn't given her any, and she'd been too proud to beg.

A shot rang out in the distance, and Nate gave a grunt of approval. "Reckon Long Neck has got us some supper." He pulled a hunting knife from a waist sheath, strode over to Caitlin, and leaned down. In one quick motion he slashed through the ropes that bound her wrists. "Get on yer feet, bitch, and build a cook fire."

She stood up and rubbed her lacerated wrists. Her back ached, and her head was splitting. She knew she needed water soon, or she'd be too weak to fight him.

"Why?" she asked. "What did I ever do to you?"

In answer, Nate seized the high neckline of her russet

wool riding habit and ripped it, exposing the rise of her breasts above her camisole. "Nice tits," he said.

Face flaming, she turned away and tried to cover herself, but a blow to the side of her head made her ears ring.

"I told you to build a fire," he reminded her.

Caitlin bit back a retort and decided that staying alive was her best option. As a child she'd heard stories of her great-great-grandmother, who'd saved herself from ravishment by killing an English soldier with a knitting needle.

If she could be so courageous, so could Caitlin. She was Irish, and the Irish were survivors.

She would do whatever she had to. She carried Shane's child under her heart, and so long as she bore that precious burden, she would put self-preservation before any other consideration. She would get the best of Nate Bone, and she would live to go home to her husband and children.

And when I get the chance, Caitlin thought, I'll kill the bastard.

Gabe caught the big pinto gelding easily. He saw the horse nibbling grass in a gully and whistled. Babe nickered in reply and came trotting up to him. The wrangler fashioned an Indian bridle of wild grape vine and mounted despite the bullet wound in his arm.

He turned the horse's head in the direction Nate Bone and the herd had gone, and kicked Babe into a gallop. He hadn't gone an hour before he heard a shout, and Justice slid down out of a tree almost under the horse's front hooves.

"Gabe! You ain't dead!" the boy shouted. "I thought you was dead."

Gabriel's chest lost some of its tightness as he looked at the child he loved as much as he would a son of his own blood. Justice's left eye was swollen almost shut, his lip was split, and his jaw was black-and-blue, but he didn't seem to have any injuries that wouldn't heal as right as rain.

He motioned for the boy to leap up behind him on the paint. "What did you think you were doin'?" Gabe asked once Justice was mounted and his arms were locked around his uncle's waist.

"Trailin' the herd," Justice answered. "McKenna would expect me to get them horses back . . ." His voice cracked and the man faded, leaving only a frightened child. ". . . get her back," he finished. "Beau Thompson was with them, but he's done for."

"Nate Bone's got Caity."

Justice swore. "Devil take'm."

Each jolt of the horse made Gabe's arm hurt something fierce, but the bullet had gone in one side and out the other. He knew he was lucky. "You tracked them this far on foot?"

"Course I did," Justice said. "What took you so long?"

"I took a slug through my upper arm. It knocked me off my pony just before they stampeded the herd. And then, when things quieted down, I had a talk with Beau."

"He talked to you?" Justice asked.

Gabe didn't explain. Better the boy didn't know what he'd done to get Beau to tell what he knew. "He said Nate wanted McKenna dead because that rustler McKenna hung was Frank Bone—Nate's brother. After McKenna threw Nate off Kilronan, Nate and Frank took up thieving. The one that escaped the noose that night was Nate."

"You were right," Justice said. "McKenna should have shot them both last summer."

Gabe nodded. "Shot them, buried the bodies, and driven the horses over the graves to hide the fresh dirt."

They rode in silence for a while, and then Justice tightened his arms around his uncle. "I'm glad you ain't dead, Gabe."

"Me, too."

Gabe smiled as the boy laid his head against his back and slept.

Caitlin looked at the bloody strips of venison with disgust. "You can't expect me to cook this with all this dirt and hair on it," she said to Nate.

The other man, the one Nate called Long Neck, pointed to an opening in the trees. "There's a spring back there," he said. "Wash the meat off."

"And wash your face while you're at it," Nate taunted. "You're filthy as a pig, and I like to see what I'm forkin'."

Ignoring the threat, Caitlin straightened her shoulders and walked away with as much dignity as she could.

"And don't think you can run away. There ain't no place to run!" Nate shouted after her.

Her steps quickened as she smelled water and heard the gurgle of the spring. She dropped the piece of deer meat and ran to plunge her head and arms into the small clear pool below a rocky outcrop.

As much as she wanted to, she didn't drink from the water hole. She shook the water out of her hair and waded through the natural sink to the place where the icy flow trickled out of a crack in the rocks. Then she pressed her lips against the stone and let the life-giving liquid fill her parched mouth.

She swallowed only a small amount, then went back to rinse her arms and face again. Her hair was a tangle of dust and knots, and she washed and braided it into a single plait before returning to drink from the spring.

"What's takin' you so long?" Nate yelled.

"I'm coming," she answered. Reluctantly she went back for the meat and began cleaning it.

She needed a plan. If she could get to a horse, maybe she could outride them. But that was unlikely. Her ribs ached with each breath, and her legs were raw where they'd rubbed against the stirrup leathers.

"Do I have to come and get you?" Nate demanded.

"Coming." She bent to pick up the venison and felt a faint fluttering sensation in her womb. "Oh." She gasped. And then she felt the same movement again.

Her baby. Her baby was alive and kicking.

Instinctively Caitlin placed both palms over her belly. "I love you," she whispered, "and I'll protect you. I promise."

The snap of a twig brought her instantly alert. She grabbed the venison and started back toward the campfire. Although it was the early part of April, the underbrush was thick with green leaves and growing vines. So green and lovely a place, she thought. Nothing terrible should happen in so beautiful a spot.

Nate's gaze made her skin crawl as she entered the clearing. "Makin' yourself all pretty for me, huh?"

"For us," Long Neck Jack added with a chuckle. "I ain't riskin' my life for the money we get for these broncs. We're partners, and I expect my share of everything."

She could kill him as well as Nate, Caitlin thought. But she kept her face expressionless as she went to the fire and threw the meat down on a flat stone. "I need a knife to cut up the venison," she said. "Unless you plan on waiting until tomorrow night to eat, I've got to—"

"I'll do the only cuttin' around here," Nate said. She heard the hiss of steel against leather as he drew his knife. "You'd love to get your hands on this, wouldn't you? Cut my throat, wouldn't you?" He laughed. "Maybe not. Thinkin' about killin' is a lot easier than actually doin' it, ain't that so, Long Neck?"

He sliced through the meat with sharp, quick slashes. "Now, me, I don't mind getting blood on my hands," he continued. "I put a bullet through that man of yours, and I did for that dirty Injun cowboy." He lifted the gore-stained knife and held it to Caitlin's throat.

She jerked back away from him and put the fire between them. "Barbarian," she muttered.

Nate spat a wad of tobacco into the fire and laughed. "Wonderin' if I'll do for you, too, ain't ya? Maybe I will, and maybe I won't. It jest depends on how sweet you are to me."

Caitlin knotted her fingers into fists and didn't answer. She wanted to scratch out his eyes and push him into the flames of the campfire. But what Nate said was true—killing a man was hard. She might have only one chance, and she didn't intend to risk it by acting hastily.

By the time the venison was done, Nate and Long Neck were half drunk on whiskey and rolling dice to see which one would have her first. Caitlin told herself that she had to eat to keep up her strength. She put the grilled meat into her mouth and chewed, but she couldn't force down a single bite.

The men cut hunks off the venison with their knives. They chewed noisily, wiping the fat off their mouths onto their shirtsleeves, and then washed the food down with more whiskey.

A golden dusk was settling around them. The sun had dropped below the trees, and the air was already turning cooler. It would be dark soon, and Caitlin knew that if she was going to act to save herself, it must be now.

"Please," she said, coming close. "I need . . . I need to relieve myself."

"Piss where we can see you," Long Neck replied. "I'm winnin', and I don't want to lose sight of my prize."

She felt a hot flush spread up her throat and face. "I need to . . . the other."

"Go on, then," Nate said as he threw the dice again. "But you try to run and I'll carve your face so Long Neck will throw a saddle blanket over your head before he jumps ya."

Caitlin entered the woods near the spring. Hastily she took another drink and then ran through the trees as fast as she could. She came up on the far side of the herd, near the hobbled bell mare, and tried to think straight.

Gabe might ride a horse without a saddle or bridle, even Shane or Justice might, but she couldn't. Nate had ordered Long Neck to unsaddle the mounts they'd ridden into the camp, and he'd taken the bridles off so that the horses could graze.

Unsure what to do, Caitlin crept closer to Nancy, whispering to the mare in soft, soothing murmurs.

"Where are you, you bitch?" Nate shouted.

Nancy shied and her bell jingled. A small black mare with a white blaze pushed between Caitlin and Nancy. Caitlin seized hold of the black's mane and flung herself belly down across the animal's withers. The horse snorted and took a few steps as Caitlin struggled to get her right leg up over the animal's back. In spite of her skirt and petticoats, she'd almost succeeded when she heard Long Neck Jack's voice behind her.

"Goin' somewhere?" The rustler's hand closed on her thick braid, and he yanked her back off the horse. She hit the ground hard, and he knelt with one knee on either side of her. "You don't want to go before the funnin'," he said as he fondled her breast roughly.

He brought his face down to kiss her, and she

screamed and drove the palm of her hand up into his nose. Blood sprayed. Long Neck let out a yelp and jumped back.

Caitlin scrambled up and ran, dodging through the milling horses. Cursing, he raced after her. A mule kicked out at Caitlin, and she tripped and nearly fell before steadying herself against a bay and then darting between two more animals.

Her spirits soared. A few more yards and she'd be in the trees, her flight hidden by the restless herd. She ducked under a gelding's belly and dashed straight into the arms of Nate Bone.

"Goin' somewhere?" He grabbed her by the arm and twisted it behind her back. "Not yet, you're not."

Caitlin screamed in fury and fought him with every ounce of her will. Her blows seemed useless as he dragged her away from the horses.

"Fight!" he taunted her. "I like it when my women are feisty." As soon as he reached a clear spot in the trees, he threw her down in the grass.

"No!" she cried.

"This is as good a spot as any," he said, fumbling with his trousers. "Once you see what I got here, you'll scream a different tune." He unbuckled his belt with its fringed knife sheath and holstered pistol and let it fall to the grass.

"No! You son of a bitch! I'll kill you first!" she flung at him.

Nate laughed. "I told ya, you're gonna love it." He dropped his pants around his knees.

Caitlin rolled and made a grab for Nate's gun, but he seized the belt and tossed it away. He kicked off his pants and lunged for her.

She screamed and struck out at him with her fists. She

knew she was weakening fast, but she didn't care anymore. She'd rather die than let him put his filthy hands on her.

Nate slapped her face and flung her back against a tree.

Caitlin's head was ringing so that she didn't hear the pounding of hooves until Shane was almost upon them. His lathered horse burst through the trees, scattering the herd. Shouting her name, he wheeled the exhausted gelding in a tight circle. "Caity!"

"Here!" she screamed. "I'm here!"

Shane spurred his horse at Nate and sighted down his rifle barrel at the outlaw. Nate dodged out of the path of Shane's horse, but at the last second Shane took his finger off the trigger and smashed the rifle barrel against the cutthroat's head.

"There's another man!" she screamed. "There!" She pointed to where she'd last seen Long Neck Jack.

A shot rang out, and the horses panicked and began to scatter. Shane rose in his stirrups and fired his rifle. Another shot ricocheted through the clearing.

"Caity! Get down!" Shane shouted. He drew his pistol and tried to find his target through the trees.

Then a movement on the ground caught Caitlin's eye. In spite of the blood running down his face from Shane's blow, Nate had dragged himself into a half-sitting position. From a hidden holster strapped to his right calf, he pulled a small brass-plated derringer.

As Caitlin watched in horror, Nate raised the weapon, cocked it, and took aim at the center of Shane's back. "Shane! Behind you!" she shouted as she scrambled for Nate's discarded belt.

Shane heard her warning cry and glanced back. At the same instant Long Neck Jack appeared in the midst of the horses. His rifle spat smoke and lead, and Shane twisted in the saddle and returned fire with his pistol.

Long Neck's bullet missed; Shane's didn't. The outlaw went down.

"Look at me, McKenna!" Nate Bone shouted.

Shane turned to face him.

"Your pistol's empty," Nate said. "You've done for Long Neck, but I'll swive your woman over your dead body."

Sweat ran down Caitlin's throat, and her heart hammered against her chest so loudly that she feared Nate would hear it. She crouched within arm's length of Nate's back, her fingers outstretched, desperately reaching for the ivory grip of Nate's still holstered pistol.

"You thought you were smart, didn't ya, McKenna?" Nate boasted. "But you never knew that I was the one stealin' your stock, and you never knew it was my brother you hung."

Caitlin felt Shane's eyes on her, trusting her, adding his strength of will to her own. One final effort and she grasped the weapon. It slid from the worn, leather holster without making a sound.

Chapter 24

"You never should've taken that Indian's side against mine, McKenna!" Nate said. "Have you got anything else to say before I blow ya to hell?"

Caitlin saw the muscles along Nate's neck twitch and knew that Shane was a heartbeat away from dying. She didn't hesitate.

She fired.

Nate slumped sideways, and the derringer fell from his lifeless fingers. Caitlin kicked the weapon away as she ran toward Shane.

When she reached his side, she was crying too hard to speak. She clung to his leg and dampened his dusty trousers with her tears.

"No need to take on so, woman," he said, caressing the crown of her head awkwardly. When she stopped crying enough to look up at him, he traced the line of her eyebrow and trailed down her cheek with rough fingertips. "Shhh, shhh, don't cry, Caity. Don't cry. You rip my guts out when you cry."

She held her arms up to him, and he shook his head. "I can't get off," he admitted.

"You what?" The absurdity of his statement broke through her near hysteria. "You can't get off your horse?"

Shane drew his knife and handed it to her, hilt first.

"I'm tied into the saddle." He tried to grin, but the pain in his eyes was impossible to miss. "It was Rachel's idea. She said I was too weak to ride unless we made sure I couldn't fall off."

"Rachel? How did Rachel . . ." Her question died uncompleted as she realized how hurt he really was. "Your wounds," she cried. "You've started them bleeding again." With trembling hands she began to saw through the leather bonds that held his booted feet tightly in the stirrups.

"No, wait." Shane took several deep breaths and gathered his strength. "Is there a creek? Water?"

"Yes."

"Take me to the water. Once I get off this damned horse, it will be hell getting me back on."

"You should have stayed at Kilronan," she began and then broke off as she realized how foolish her words were. "No," she corrected herself. "I needed you, Shane. I needed you more than I've ever needed anyone in my life, and you came for me."

He wound a lock of her hair around his finger. "Did you think I wouldn't come for you?"

She smiled up at him with all the love in her heart. "I knew you would," she whispered. "We knew you would."

If Shane noticed the *we*, he made no mention of the fact. He gritted his teeth and reloaded his rifle and pistol. Her assurances that the outlaws were dead and couldn't hurt them didn't matter.

"I don't intend to be caught with an empty gun next time."

"There won't be a next time," she promised as she led his horse toward the spring. "It's over. Nate was the one who wanted to kill you. Nate—"

"Are you all right?" Shane leaned down and grasped her shoulder. "He hurt you."

She touched the swollen bruise on her cheekbone. "I'm battered, but not broken," she answered. "You came in time to keep him from—"

"It doesn't matter. Whatever happened to you," Shane said fiercely, "it doesn't matter—only that you're alive and—"

"You thick-pated Irishman. What have I been telling you? My virtue—your honor—is safe enough. He would have had his way with me if you'd been a quarter-hour later, but—"

"Nothing could ever tarnish your virtue, Caity," he managed thickly. "You've got more honor in one finger than any man I've ever met."

"I'm all right, husband." Husband. Nothing could dim the thrill of that word . . . so right, so perfect for what Shane was to her. "My bruises will heal. It's yours I'm worried about. And . . ." She glanced into his bloodshot eyes. "I think we lost some of your horses."

"To hell with the horses. I've got what I want."

They reached the spring, and Shane's weary gelding lowered his head to drink. Caitlin let the horse have only a little water before tying him to a tree. "We'd best get you down," she said to Shane, "so that I can see what you've done to those bullet wounds."

"Nothing that a week's sleep and you in my arms won't fix."

She cut the last of the ties and helped to ease him out of the saddle. His knees buckled, and she slipped an arm around him.

Shane cursed softly under his breath, but he put one foot in front of the other and walked to the edge of the rock bowl. Then he lowered himself painfully to the ground.

"Don't drink that," Caitlin warned. She went to the

trickle of water, rinsed her hands, and cupped them to catch the precious liquid. She carried the water to him and held it to his lips.

Shane drank from her hands and then met her gaze steadily. "You are like this to my soul, Caity," he said. "Springwater to a thirsty man."

She went into his arms and kissed his cracked lips. "Shane," she murmured. "I love you so much."

He held her so tightly against his chest that she could feel the thump of his heart. "And I love you, too. I wouldn't want to live a day without you."

"You never said the words," she whispered. "I've waited and waited for you to tell me so."

"I should have," he said. "Maybe I was afraid to admit how much I loved you . . . even to myself . . . for fear of losing you."

"You'll never lose me."

And then she remembered Justice, and a chill settled over her joy. Pushing away, she got to her feet. "Justice," she said. "I don't know what happened to him. We were separated and—"

"He's fine," Shane assured her. "An hour's ride behind me with Gabe and Rachel Thompson. Gabe took a bullet in his arm, but he'll survive it. They're gathering up the loose stock that got left behind."

"Justice is safe?" How could she have forgotten him? Or Gabriel? "Justice fought Beau to save me," she said. "If anything happened to him—"

"He was trackin' the herd when Gabe found him. Like you, the boy's got a few bruises, but nothin' serious."

"Why did you come alone?" she demanded as she brought him more water in her clasped hands.

He waited until after he'd drank to answer. "Gabe lost a lot of blood. I knew if he came with me, there'd be no way to keep Justice out of trouble. I asked Gabe to watch out for our son." He exhaled slowly. "I figured there were only two rustlers, and I should have been able to take them." His mouth tightened. "I was wrong."

"You weren't wrong," she answered. "You did . . ." She trailed off, suddenly at a loss for words. Killing Nate seemed unreal. She'd done it because she had to, and she supposed she should feel some sense of horror at committing such a violent act. But instead she just felt numb. It was Shane or Nate. Nate never had a chance.

"He was a predator, Caity," Shane said. "Put him out of your mind."

"But the church teaches us that killing is wrong. Does what I did make me as evil as Nate?"

"I'm a poor one to ask about religion, Caity. But you saved two lives by takin' his."

She nodded. "He can't hurt us or anyone else again, can he?"

"No more, darlin'. Not anymore."

Caitlin sat beside him on the grass and laid her head against his shoulder. "Where's Derry? Did you leave her with Mary? Will she be safe at Kilronan?"

"Yes . . . and no." He cleared his throat. "It's a long story, Caity, and I haven't eaten in days. If I tell you, do you think you could find me something—"

"Not a bite until you tell me where my daughter is."

"Just like a woman," he teased. "You take advantage of a man when he's too weak to fight back."

"Where is Derry?"

"Mary is bringing her in the wagon. Mary didn't think I could ride. I proved her wrong—didn't I?" He managed a crooked grin.

"I think we both proved her wrong," Caitlin replied. "But now what do we do?"

"Gather the troops and press on to Independence," he said. "We've come too far to turn back. And the way you and Gabe and Justice moved that herd, we might just get to the fort in time to get a decent price for our stock."

Fort Independence, Missouri

A week later, Caitlin came out of a dry-goods store in Independence with her arms full of fabric, thread, a dozen pairs of stockings in various sizes, and two pairs of leather boots. Shane had promised that he would take her to Saint Louis to stock up on supplies in a few months, but she couldn't pass up the first opportunity she'd had to shop since coming to Missouri.

Shane got stiffly down from the wagon seat and helped her to load the purchases into the back, while Derry bounced up and down in excitement. Shane had insisted on buying her candy earlier, and the child had managed to smear peppermint all over her face and onto her bonnet strings.

"Look at you," Caitlin scolded mildly as she pulled Derry into her lap. "Don't touch me. Don't touch anything until we wash those hands."

"Is that it?" Shane asked as he climbed back into the wagon and gathered the reins. His wounds were healing slowly, and Caitlin worried about him, but he'd refused to see a doctor and insisted time would make him right.

"I'm done," she replied.

Shane nodded and urged the team back into the main flow of traffic down the dusty street.

Caitlin still couldn't believe how many people were

traveling west on the Oregon Trail this spring. She'd long since given up counting the farm wagons, two-wheeled carts, and even pushcarts that she'd seen since arriving at Fort Independence.

The dust and the noise were frightful. Cowboys, pale-faced easterners, Mormons, mountain men, Tennessee farmers, Indians, and Mexicans flowed through the streets, laughing, arguing, bargaining, and commenting on the weather. Dogs barked and scrapped; chickens, packed into small crates and tied to the backs of wagons, cackled, and pigs squealed.

Riders and barefoot children herded horses, mules, oxen, and cows amid the tangle of wagons. Babies wailed and men cursed. Caitlin longed for the peace and quiet of Kilronan.

"You wanted civilization," Shane reminded her as they barely missed colliding with a freight wagon loaded with barrels of flour. Caitlin clung to Derry with one hand and the wagon seat with the other.

"This isn't what I had in mind," she replied, coughing.

He laughed. "We'll head for home tomorrow. Our business here is finished until next year."

"I don't understand why all these people want to go to Oregon instead of staying in Missouri or settling in Kansas or—"

"Indians in Kansas. And there's no free land left in Missouri. They want free, not cheap."

Caitlin looked at the rickety farm wagon ahead of them pulled by two slat-ribbed mules. A heavily bearded man in a shiny black suit two sizes too small limped beside the team. Caitlin counted eight skinny children of various ages and at least three dogs hanging out the back of the wagon. A hugely pregnant woman with stringy blond hair walked behind carrying a runny-nosed infant.

"I can't believe that family will ever make it to the mountains," Caitlin said, "let alone over them to Oregon."

"Some won't," Shane admitted. "But this is America. They don't hang you for tryin'."

She and Shane had remained at the camp near the spring for several days while Shane regained his strength. Gabe, Justice, and Rachel had joined them the day after Caitlin had killed Nate. Since Shane was running a fever, he'd decided that he and Caitlin would wait for Mary while the other three drove the herd on to Independence.

"Damned if I won't get top price for your stock!" Rachel had boasted. "And we might just get them there ahead of Big Earl, too. I know which trail he's takin'. Gabe and me can take the shortcut."

Caitlin had tended Shane's injuries and prayed for Derry and the Indian woman's safety. And eventually they'd arrived.

"Mary not go fast like lightning," Mary had clarified for Caitlin. "Slow like oak tree. Live long time."

Derry's nose was sunburned, and she wore moccasins on her feet instead of shoes. But the child's cheeks were rosy, and she was as talkative as always.

"We saw wolfs!" she proclaimed. "A mama wolf and a baby wolf. And a buff-a-fant."

"A buff-a-fant?" Caitlin had asked with a glance at Mary.

"Buffalo," Mary supplied.

Derry had nodded. "That's right. I see a buff-a-go."

Their arrival in Independence would have been exciting for Caitlin, but the past weeks had been so overwhelming that she was ready to accept almost anything as normal. Gabe, Justice, and Rachel had met them near an old trading post just west of the fort, as planned.

"I told you I'd get prime money for them broomtails,"

Rachel had said proudly. "Sold every head of them in two hours, most to the army."

Nancy the bell mare, Bessie, and a few of the herd remained. Shane hadn't intended to sell them. They would need extra mounts for the trip home, and Nancy would lead next year's drive. "That ole mare knows the trail so well that Gabe and me don't have to ride herd on them," Justice said. "We can just set her on her way and meet her here."

"Ought to be some way to teach Nancy how to bargain with the dealers," Rachel teased.

"I'm plannin' on teachin' her that," Gabe insisted, "as soon as she learns to talk."

Rachel grinned and then glanced at Shane. "Gabe wants to speak to you, McKenna. It's important."

Gabe pulled off his hat and crumpled the brim in his hand. "It's best told in private."

"All right. But Caity is my wife. I want no more secrets from her."

"Derry, would you like to have a ride on my horse?" Rachel asked the child. Derry nodded, and Rachel led her away. Mary followed them.

"I got to stay," Justice said.

Gabe exhaled slowly. "First off, you should know that Justice is my nephew. Cerise was my sister."

"Mary told me that," Shane answered quietly. "Just before I left Kilronan. She said she was Justice's grandmother."

"You never said a word to me," Caitlin said. "Why—"

"You knew, didn't you?"

Caitlin nodded. "Were we wrong to hide it? Mary was afraid you'd send her away. Would you have?"

"If I'd known who she was when she first came, I probably would have," Shane admitted.

"When you brought Justice home, I thought he needed

a grandmother's hand," Gabe said. "Isn't that what happened with Moses in the Bible? Somebody got the boy's mother to act as—"

"I don't need any preaching this morning," Shane said. "You all pulled one over on me, and I was fool enough to fall for it."

Gabe grinned. "Well, one Indian looks pretty much like another, don't they?"

"But there's more," Justice put in, grinding the sole of his boot into the dirt. "I was hidin' under the bed the night my mother died. I saw what happened, or most of it."

Shane's face paled. "Then you knew I didn't kill her."

"It was an accident," Justice continued. "There was another man in that room besides you, but he didn't stab her either. She fell on her own knife."

"I was that man," Gabe admitted.

"You?" Shane stared at him.

Gabe nodded. "I was angry with her for the way she was living. We argued, and she tried to cut me with the knife. I tried to take it away from her, but . . ." He trailed off. "I should have told you, McKenna. I was afraid— afraid to tell my mother and afraid that they'd hang me for killing her." He met Shane's gaze. "I loved her, too. And I've got to live with knowing that I was partly to blame."

"Cerise was the only one to blame," Justice said. "I loved her . . . I love her, but she died by her own hand. Drink killed her, and maybe unhappiness." He looked up into Shane's face. "But it wasn't Gabe, and it wasn't you."

"I'll understand if you want me and my mother off Kilronan," Gabe said.

Caitlin shook her head. "No! You—"

"It's all past and done with," Shane said. "Best we get on with livin' and let Cerise stop tearin' us apart."

Later that morning, Gabe and Rachel had vanished without saying where they were going, and Shane had driven Caitlin to do her shopping.

Justice and his grandmother stayed to set up camp beside the trading post. Sleeping rooms were impossible to find in the town, so every year Shane rented the same open-sided shed from an Omaha Indian woman.

Shane turned the team onto another street, past several buildings in various stages of construction, and circled around a tent city of peddlers, laundresses, and snake-oil salesmen.

"They'll sell these settlers anything," Shane said, pointing out a man in a frock coat displaying a folding table to a young couple. "Guns that won't shoot, elixirs that won't cure warts, and worthless gewgaws to trade to the Indians. Not that any self-respecting Indian would buy such trash, but the settlers won't find that out until it's too late."

Caitlin knew that Shane had been shaken by what Gabe and Justice had told him about Cerise's death, but she felt it was best to wait until he wanted to talk about it.

"Gabe said that there was one wagon train forming up on the north side of the fort that was all Irish immigrants," Caitlin said. "Maybe we could ride over there this afternoon and see if any of them are from County Clare. I mailed a letter to my sister yesterday, but it will take months to get news from home. Someone might know if the potatoes failed again last fall or—"

"I'll take you if you want to go, Caity," he replied, "but don't count on seeing anyone you know. Thousands of Irish are headin' west."

Derry wiggled on Caitlin's lap. "Can I have more candy?" she begged.

"No more peppermint," Caitlin said. "You'll get a bellyache. If you eat it all now, you—" She broke off as she caught sight of Justice galloping toward the wagon on his pinto pony.

"McKenna! McKenna! Come quick!" the boy shouted. "Big Earl's gonna shoot Gabe!"

"Hold on tight," Shane ordered and slapped the reins over the team's back. The wagon lurched forward and bounced over the rutted trail.

When Shane got close enough to see the shelter and the horsemen gathered near it, he yanked back on the reins. "Whoa! Justice! Stay here and watch out for the women!" He jumped down, grabbed his rifle, and ran toward Big Earl.

Caitlin scrambled from the wagon seat, lifted Derry down, and turned to Justice. "Give me your pony."

"But McKenna said—"

"Now, Justice!"

He dismounted, and Caitlin swung up into the saddle. She gathered the reins in hand and glanced back at the children. "Justice, you watch Derry here. Keep her safe. I'm counting on you." Then she pulled the pony's head around and kicked him into a gallop toward the confrontation.

Caitlin didn't stop until she'd reached Shane's side. He stood facing Earl Thompson, three of his hired hands, and a dark-haired man who looked vaguely familiar to Caitlin. But Big Earl wasn't paying any attention to Shane; he was yelling at his daughter.

Rachel and Gabe were on foot, and Gabriel had an arm around Rachel's shoulders. Both of them looked very pleased with themselves, considering Big Earl's temper and the torrent of abuse he was heaping on them.

"Injun scum," Big Earl continued. "Blow him to . . ."

Caitlin stared at Thompson's face. His eyes were so red that if she didn't know better, she'd have sworn Big Earl had been crying.

"It's not legal in Missouri!" Big Earl shouted. "I'll have him hung."

"You'll do no such thing," Rachel yelled back. "Beau's dead, and so are Nate and Long Neck Jack. Surely that's enough bodies to suit you. They were rustlers and would-be murderers, and if the good Lord hadn't seen fit to do away with them, someone would have had to hang them."

"I'm your father!" Big Earl bellowed back.

Thompson's tirade was not as loud as it had been. Caitlin glanced down at Shane. His features were stern and he gripped his rifle tightly in his big hands, but he didn't look like a man who thought he'd have to shoot his neighbor any time soon.

"No daughter of mine will ever marry a red Injun," Big Earl grated.

"Not will. *Has!*" Rachel waved a paper at her father. "Signed, sealed, and blessed by a shaved-head Jesuit priest. Rachel Thompson and Gabriel Larocque. Married this mornin' with a church full of witnesses."

Big Earl pulled off his hat and flung it to the ground in frustration. "You can't marry an Injun in Missouri."

"You prove he's an Injun, Big Earl. Prove it. Gabe's got a birth certificate what says he's the son of a French national named Larocque and one Marie Rouge."

"He ain't no Frenchman. He's an Injun," Big Earl argued. "Anybody can see that."

Rachel scoffed. "That fella ridin' with you has got hair as black as Gabe's. And his skin's ever' bit as dark! My husband is a Frenchy, Pa, and you or nobody else can prove otherwise."

"I don't need to prove nothin'," Big Earl answered. "I can blow him away where he stands."

"You're not shootin' anybody, Thompson." Shane raised his rifle. "Just calm down. Rachel's of age. I suppose she can marry any man she chooses."

"Any white man," Big Earl flung back.

"Gabe's a long sight whiter than your son was," Rachel said, "and he'll get whiter the longer you look at him."

"I'll not look at his red face. I'll disown you."

"Do it, you old fool!" Rachel shouted. "And who will you leave your land to? Your horse? I'm all you've got, and I've picked myself a good man. If you can't see it that way, then sit there alone and rot."

"Rachel, girl," Big Earl argued. "You can't do this to me."

"Done it," she said. "And if I was you, I'd offer McKenna a big apology. It was Beau and Nate Bone doin' all the wickedness against Kilronan these last two years. And it's partly your fault."

Big Earl turned his head and glanced back at Shane.

Caitlin was certain Earl Thompson was crying. His cheeks were wet with tears.

"Is it true, what she said about my boy? About Nate Bone, and how they died?"

Shane nodded. "You have my word on it, Thompson."

Big Earl's shoulders sagged, and Caitlin noticed how gray his hair was and how lined his face. For all his bluster and his authority, Earl Thompson was no longer in his prime. He was an aging man who'd just lost his son. He'd become estranged from his daughter and seen her wed to a bridegroom he couldn't accept. Caitlin couldn't help but feel sorry for him.

"You can't bring him home with you," Big Earl threatened Rachel. "You can marry him, but you can't expect me to keep him."

"I've got a job," Gabe said quietly. "I can support my wife." He looked at Shane. "Unless me and Rachel are a problem. If we are, we can go west to Oregon with—"

"You've got a place on Kilronan as long as you want it," Shane said.

Big Earl cleared his throat and wiped a gnarled hand over his face. "I guess it's all said, then. Ain't nothin' more—"

"No, Pa, ain't nothin' more," Rachel said. "Except, I still love ya. And if you want, me and my man will take you back to where Beau is and help give him a burial."

"I'll find him myself," Big Earl answered hoarsely. "You stay where you're wanted." He reined his horse around and motioned to his men.

Then the dark-haired rider moved close to Big Earl and said something Caitlin couldn't hear. Earl Thompson pointed at Shane. "That's McKenna, there," he said.

"Shane McKenna?" the stranger asked. "Of County Clare?"

"Aye," Shane answered. "What of it?"

Caitlin stared at the newcomer.

"I'm Liam Shaughnessy, late of County Clare myself, and I'm married to my brother's widow, Maureen."

"You're married to Maureen?" Caitlin cried. "But that's not allowed. You can't marry your sister-in-law."

Liam grinned. "I can in America, and I have. English law doesn't rule here."

"My sister's here?"

"Oh, my Maureen's here, right enough," Liam Shaughnessy said. "I've come about her girl, Derry. You've got the child, so I'm told."

"Derry?" Caitlin felt a chill run through her.

"Derry Shaughnessy. That's her. She's the babe of my dead brother Thomas and my Maureen. And 'tis fortune indeed. Maureen had given up hope of locating her sister. We mean to settle up with you before we head west for Oregon country."

Chapter 25

"Can you ever forgive me, Caity?" Shane took hold of Caitlin's shoulders and stared into her tear-stained face. God help him, he loved his wife more than his hope of salvation, and he'd believed her a liar and an adulteress.

How could he have misjudged her so? And why had he been too stubborn to see what a pure and good woman she was? He'd made her life hell, when he'd been the only one to break their marriage vows.

"You're the one person in my life who never betrayed me, and I couldn't believe you were telling me the truth about Derry," he said.

She laid her head on his chest, hiding her tears. "I kept telling you she was Maureen's child."

He rocked her against him and swore softly. "Yell at me, woman. Call me names. Tell me what a block-headed fool I've been."

She sniffed. "You're doing pretty good on your own."

He kissed the crown of her head. "I'm sorry, Caitlin. I wronged you. I'll make it up to you, I promise."

"Oh, Shane." She began to weep again. "Derry . . ."

"They can't have her."

"But my sister loves Derry, too. How can we keep her from Maureen?"

"Your sister gave birth to her, but she lost her rights to Derry when she sent her to America with you. You can't trade kids back and forth like used saddles. She's ours now."

"But Maureen gave her to me to keep her from starving."

"We haven't discussed Derry with them yet. This Liam seems a reasonable man," Shane said, trying to calm Caitlin. "Maybe they'd be content to settle here in Missouri if I gave them a hundred acres."

"You'd trade part of Kilronan for Derry?"

"Gladly," he answered, "but let's hope it doesn't come to that."

Shaughnessy had said he meant to take his family over the plains and mountains to Oregon. Anything could happen to a three-year-old child on the journey. Images of cholera and Indian attack rose like specters in Shane's mind.

What if Derry wandered off on the prairie? Would Liam Shaughnessy have enough sense to track down a lost child, or would he abandon her to keep up with the wagon train?

"Damn it, Caity, I'm her father," Shane said before he realized that he was speaking his feelings aloud. "I love the both of you, and I'm not about to give either of you to someone else."

Caitlin wiped her eyes. "We can't think of ourselves, Shane. We have to do what's best for Derry. Maybe we're being selfish."

"We're best for Derry."

"I can't break Maureen's heart." Caitlin's restless hands moved over her patched skirt.

Mary had washed and mended the rips in Caity's once elegant riding habit. The garment was fit for a decent woman to wear in public, but it would never pass for a fine lady's dress again. And his Caity, who he'd thought was too delicate for life in Missouri, had proved far tougher than her clothing.

"You said she was expecting another child when you left County Clare," Shane reasoned. "If the baby lived, then this Liam already has one stepchild to feed. He may not want another." He reached for a saddlebag and a bedroll. "To hell with them. We'll take our kids and ride for Kilronan."

"No." Caity's pain was so evident that he wanted to smash his fist into a log wall to stop his own hurting. "We can't do that. It would be dishonest," she cried.

He flung the saddlebag and blanket to the rough plank floor. "I thought you wanted to keep Derry."

"I do, but not that way. How could I face the child, knowing that I'd stolen her from the woman who bore her?" She touched his cheek. "Shane, there's something that I haven't told you."

Her fingers felt soft against his face. God, but he wanted to protect this woman. Trouble was he didn't know how. All his life he'd used his fists to fight his way out of trouble. Now, it seemed if he did the right thing, he'd lose the child they both loved. And if he took Derry by force, Caity might never forgive him.

"Shane, listen."

"I am listenin'."

"What I'm trying to tell you might make a difference in the way you feel about keeping Derry."

"Nothin' could make me stop lovin' that child."

Caity looked so vulnerable that he ached for her. And then his world tilted.

"I'm having your baby."

"You are?" He stared at her. "When? How?" He took a breath and then another until his head felt giddy. Caity was having his child. He had another chance at what he thought he'd lost forever when Cerise died on the floor of Fat Rose's whorehouse.

He closed his eyes for a second, and when he opened them, golden sunlight flooded the rough shelter. Caity's hair had never looked so coppery red or her eyes so beautiful. "When? How?" He grinned at her.

She smiled. "In autumn, November, I think. I'm not really sure," she answered. "But as to how . . ." She chuckled. "In the usual way, I'd think."

"That's great. Great news. A brother for Justice."

"Or a sister."

"Girl or boy, it doesn't matter to me, so long as you're all right and the baby's healthy." He straightened his shoulders and nodded. "A sister for our Derry would be fine. So long as you don't object to my teachin' her to shoot."

Caity's joy faded. "But we won't have our Derry, will we?"

"You think another child would make me change how I feel about our nubbin?"

"I hoped it wouldn't."

"God knows I've given you reason enough to doubt me. I've let you down, Caity, but I'll not fail you again, I swear it."

"You're happy about the baby?"

"Of course I'm happy. Nothin' means more to me than you and our kids. If we have a dozen, I'll—"

"Don't set your heart on a dozen."

He embraced her and kissed her tenderly. "How long have you known?" he asked when they parted.

"Long enough to be certain."

He tilted her chin up. "You knew, yet you risked your life and our babe's by helpin' Gabe drive the herd." The thought of what he could have lost to Nate Bone made his gut clench.

She nodded. "It seemed the right thing to do."

"And do you still think that? After all that happened on the trail? After Nate Bone and—"

"We got the horses here, didn't we?" Then the pride in her eyes dimmed. "Only . . . if I hadn't come, Liam Shaughnessy wouldn't have found us. He and Maureen would have gone on to Oregon, and we'd—"

"McKenna!" Rachel shouted as she reined in her horse so tightly at the entrance to the shelter that the animal reared. "McKenna!"

Shane shook his head. "Not now, Rachel. We've trouble—"

"Hell's bells, McKenna! This is important. Gabe's found—"

Caitlin cut her off. "Rachel. My sister—Derry's mother—is here in Independence."

"Blue hellfire, Cait. I saw that Irish fella talkin' to McKenna, but I had no idea he was kin to you."

"My sister's new husband, Liam Shaughnessy," Caitlin explained. "They're on their way west, and they've come to claim Derry."

Rachel's face blanched. "Damn. Double damn and shoe the coyote! Gabe said you was tellin' the truth about that mite bein' your sister's. They come to take her back?"

"They're not gettin' her," Shane said.

Rachel turned her attention to him. "Gabe wants you right away."

"I can't come now. Caity and I have to go meet with her sister and Shaughnessy."

Rachel shook her head. "This can't wait, McKenna. Come now, or forget about gettin' Cherokee back."

"What?" Caitlin's eyes dilated in surprise. "Shane's horse?"

"It's what I come to tell you," Rachel said impatiently. "Gabe spotted Cherokee in a corral with a herd from Saint Louis. Your buckskin pony's about to be auctioned off. You can buy him back if you move fast."

"Are you sure it's Shane's buckskin?" Caitlin asked.

Rachel guffawed. "Gabe don't make mistakes where horses are concerned."

"It makes no sense," Shane protested. "The man I sold him to wanted him for his son."

"Hell's ashes, McKenna," Rachel exclaimed. "Are you gonna stand there jawin'? You ought to have enough money to top any bid, considerin' how much I got for the rest of your herd."

He glanced at Caity.

"Go ahead," she urged. "I'll wait here for you. I want to wash Derry and fix her hair. I don't want Maureen to see her looking like a wharf rat."

"Take my horse." Rachel dismounted and tossed Shane the reins. "Just don't let anybody auction him off by mistake."

Caitlin was near panic an hour later when she saw Shane coming on Cherokee. Derry sat proudly on Shane's lap holding on to the saddle horn, and Justice rode behind the saddle with his arms around Shane's waist.

"Where have you been?" she demanded of the children.

Derry looked as though she'd been swimming in a hog wallow. One pigtail was undone, her calico bonnet was missing a string and trailing down her back, and her shoes were caked in brown, gooey mud.

Justice appeared little better. He sported a fresh cut on his lip, and he glared at her with an expression that would have scorched cowhide.

"I've looked everywhere," Caitlin scolded.

"Gabe caught the two of them in a fight with some town boys. There was a circle of screamin' kids around them, or he might never have realized they'd slipped away from us."

"Where were you going?" Caitlin demanded. "I was worried sick. You know I would never let Derry off by herself with all these people around. She could have been run over by a wagon or—"

"She wasn't alone," Justice said as he slid off the rump of Shane's horse. "She was with me."

"And good care you've taken of her," Caitlin replied angrily. "Didn't you know I'd be hunting for you both?"

"What for?" The boy's dark eyes were full of venom. "So you could give her away?"

"Justice!" Shane admonished. "Don't talk to—"

"I heard ya!" Justice answered. "Derry is my sister. She stays with me on Kilronan."

Derry's bottom lip quivered. "I never be a bad boy no more."

"Any more," Caitlin corrected. "And you're a girl, darling, not a boy." Caitlin took the child from Shane. "Look at you," she fussed. "You look a sight. I'll have to wash your hair again and give you—"

"No!" Derry wailed. "Don't give me away!"

Caitlin cradled the little girl against her. "It's not like that," she soothed. "I would never—"

"Yes, you would," Justice said. "You don't care nothin' about either of us."

Shane dismounted and reached for the boy, but Mary appeared around the corner of the shelter and he fled into her arms.

"Mary, speak to him," Shane said. "Make him understand—"

"Justice understand good," Mary replied. "He don't like what you say. He not want you give Derry to Irishman."

Shane stiffened. "I'm not goin' to."

Caitlin caught sight of a tall man and a woman and children walking toward the lean-to. "Shane, look." She took a few hesitant steps toward the approaching group.

"Caitlin?" the woman called.

"Maureen?" Caitlin gave Derry to Shane and ran to throw her arms around her sister. "Maureen! Is it really you?"

"Caitlin, Caitlin!"

After hugs and kisses and a frenzy of greetings, Caitlin stepped back to study her sister. Maureen's clothing was not as expensive as it had been before the famine, but it was stylish. Her waist, which had always been small, even after Derry's birth, was definitely thicker. "Oh, Maury," Caitlin said. "Are you . . ."

Maureen laughed. "Yes, I am." She caught hold of Liam Shaughnessy's arm. "Liam and I are expecting our first child. You remember Liam, don't you? He's Thomas's older brother. He used to live in Limerick with his wife's family."

"My Hilde died of fever," Liam explained. "I brought the little ones home for my mother to care for."

Caitlin glanced at the half-grown children standing behind Liam and staring at her. "Can that be Brigid?"

"Yes," Maureen answered. "She's twelve and a great

help, I can tell you." Maureen squeezed her husband's arm. "And that's Brett." She pointed to a fair-haired boy a half head taller than Brigid. "Alma," she continued, pointing to a fair-haired girl about ten who was dandling a baby boy on her hip. "And Albert, Alma's twin. You should remember the twins. We went to their christening."

"Brigid, Brett, Alma, Albert," Caitlin murmured. "And the baby?"

"Baird, but we all call him Bay-Bay for short." Maureen let go of her husband to take the black-haired baby. "He's usually such a lamb," she said, "but he's been teething for weeks."

Caitlin noticed how much little Baird looked like Derry. "Yes," she replied. "Teething can be a trial. On the ship, Derry was . . ." She broke off, unable to continue.

Maureen never noticed. "Baird is Thomas's, but we never mention that. Do we, Liam? It couldn't have worked out better for us—considering. When we fell in love, we wanted to come to America so that we could marry. But we hadn't the money." She took a breath and went on. "Liam's first wife's brother John was a solicitor, and John suggested that we appeal to Father's old employer, Lord Carlston."

"Your father worked for him for thirty-odd years," Liam said. "It was only fair that Lord Carlston do something for his faithful manager's orphaned daughters."

Caitlin felt confused. "Lord Carlston gave you money?"

"Only a little," Liam replied. "Enough to buy passage for us."

"I'm afraid I spent your share as well, sister," Maureen explained. "America is so expensive. Liam had the oxen to buy, and a wagon and plow. Supplies are dear, very dear, indeed. And with seven children to—"

"Seven?" Caitlin added again. Even with Derry, she counted only six.

Maureen laughed. "Donald and Doyle are five-year-old twins and such a handful. I left them with Mrs. O'Leary. She's our neighbor in the next wagon."

"Salt of the earth, the O'Learys," Liam added.

"You must let me introduce you to my family," Caitlin said. "Our camp is a little rough, but Independence is so crowded that it's impossible to find a decent place to stay for only a few—"

"Don't say another word." Maureen cut her off with a patronizing smile. "Mr. McKenna, I remember well. How do you do." She nodded coolly. "I believe you and dear Liam have already met."

Caitlin felt a flush of anger warm her cheeks. Maureen had always thought Shane was low class, and it was plain by her expression that she'd seen nothing to change her mind.

"And here is Derry," Caitlin said awkwardly. "Hasn't she grown?"

Shane held the child tightly.

Caitlin struggled for control of her emotions. "This is our son, Justice, and his grandmother, Mrs. Red Jacket."

"Derry!" Maureen reached for her daughter, but the child clung to Shane's neck like a mussel to a rock. "Give Mama a kiss," Maureen pleaded.

"She's wonderful," Caitlin said. "You can be very proud of her."

"No!" Derry screamed. "No! No! No!" Then she turned her head and stuck her tongue out at Maureen. "I hate you!"

"A precious child," Liam mumbled.

Alma whispered to Brigid. Brett snickered.

Maureen leaned close to kiss Derry's cheek, but Derry struck at her with her fist and buried her face in Shane's neck. All Maureen got was a soggy braid.

Justice moved to his father's side and folded his arms over his chest. "She's ours," Justice insisted.

"Mind your manners," Caitlin said to him. "Please, Maureen, Mr. Shaughnessy, you must come in and have some coffee."

"No," Liam answered. "We can't. I know this is abrupt, but our wagon train leaves at dawn tomorrow. There are many things that must be done before that. I wish I could give you more time with your sister, but—"

"We must settle our business," Maureen said. "I know that you will find this hard to understand but . . ."

Her husband pulled a small bag from his pocket and held it out to Shane. "Here's some money, not much but—"

"Keep your damned money, Shaughnessy," Shane said gruffly. "We want no money for Derry."

"It's only fair," Liam argued.

Maureen laid a hand on her husband's. "Now, Liam, dear, if they don't want the money, don't force it on them." She turned to Caitlin with a stiff smile. "It's just that we have seven children already and another on the way. Dear Liam has been so understanding about Baird, but . . . Frankly, Caitlin, you can see how he'd be reluctant to take on the responsibility of another girl."

"You don't want Derry?" Caitlin grabbed Shane's arm to steady herself. "You don't—"

"Baird will be of use on the new farm," Liam explained, "but Derry—"

"Derry's fine where she is," Shane grated.

"You're sure?" Caitlin asked her sister. "I can keep her?"

"Well, she does seem . . . robust," Maureen said. "And a year is so long. What with the new baby and dear Liam's motherless babes . . ."

"Good decision," Mary said. "Better we keep Derry, you go Oregon."

"Exactly," Liam agreed.

Caitlin could only nod her head and wrap her arms around Shane and Derry and Justice.

"Unless you'd like to consider joining our group and traveling on to Oregon," Liam suggested hesitantly. "If you have the money for an outfit, I'm sure you could better yourself by going west."

"No," Shane said quietly. "We've got all we need, right here in Missouri."

"Well, that's it, then," Maureen said. "I take it your address will remain the same? Kilronan, general delivery, Kane's Crossroads?"

Caitlin nodded again. "It will."

"Then there's just one thing more. Brigid?" She glanced at her daughter. "I want to give you this, sister. By rights, Papa's Bible should be mine, but space is limited in the wagon."

"Thank you," Caitlin whispered.

It was Maureen's turn to blush. "There are some letters in there, letters that were addressed to you." Brigid handed her mother a leather-bound Bible, and Maureen passed it on to Caitlin.

"To me?" Caitlin asked.

"Yes." Maureen sighed. "From Mr. McKenna. They came for you after he left Ireland. Papa hid them. He didn't want you to go to America and leave us."

Caitlin's hands trembled so that she could hardly turn the pages. There, pressed into the center of the Bible, were several faded letters.

"Those are mine," Shane said. "Uncle Jamie wrote them for me. I'm not . . . not too handy with writin'."

"No, I imagine not," Maureen said. "Dear Liam writes a beautiful hand."

Shane ignored her comment. "What about the money I sent for Caity's passage? It was nearly two years' wages."

"All gone," Maureen replied. "Papa was no thief. You must realize that. But times were very hard, and so many homeless people came begging to our door."

"He spent my money," Shane said.

"I'm afraid so. But it went for a good cause. I hope you can forgive him. He simply couldn't bear to lose his daughter to a McKenna."

Caitlin looked up into Shane's face. "You did send for me."

"You won't hold this against Papa, will you, Caitlin?" Maureen asked. "It was the distance as much as your marriage to an uneducated Catholic boy."

"I can forgive Papa if my husband can forgive my doubting him all these years," Caitlin said, never taking her gaze from Shane. "Can you?"

"I can," he answered, pulling her even closer against him, "considerin' my own doubts."

"Now what?" Justice demanded.

"Now we go home," Caitlin said. "Home to Kilronan."

"Me, too?" Derry demanded, wiping a teary eye.

Shane leaned down and kissed Caitlin tenderly. "All of us," he said huskily.

"Can I have a baby wolf?" Derry asked.

But Caitlin couldn't answer. She was too full of happi-

ness for words and too busy kissing Shane McKenna—
her husband—and the finest broth of a man it had ever
been her good fortune to meet.

Epilogue

Summer 1855

Seven years later, on a hot Friday afternoon, Caitlin stood on the porch at Kilronan and watched as Shane, Justice, and six-year-old Rory rode in from the City of Jefferson. They'd been gone a week, and Caitlin and Derry couldn't wait to tell them the news.

"Caity!" Shane rose in the stirrups and waved to her.

"Mama! Mama!" Rory cried. "Papa bought me a puppy!"

"Where is it?" Derry, almost eleven, forgot her new-found dignity and ran, skirts flying, from the porch to greet her father and brothers.

"We don't have it yet," Rory shouted. "It's too little to leave its mother. Mr. Steele will bring it next week."

Derry bubbled over with questions. "What color is the puppy? Did you name it? Did you bring me anything, Papa?"

Shane swung down from the saddle and swept his daughter up in his arms. "Were you good? You get nothin' if you were bad while I was gone."

"Oh, Papa, I'm always good," she replied saucily. "And you'll never guess—Rachel had two babies at one time! Twins, a boy and a girl."

Caitlin left the rose-covered porch and met Shane

halfway down the walk. "Welcome home, husband." She raised her face for a kiss.

"Are you all right?" he demanded, enfolding her in his powerful arms. "The baby is—"

She nodded. "I'm fine, and the baby's fine. Kicking like a yearling colt." She'd suffered an early miscarriage when Rory was four and hadn't become pregnant again until this past winter. Now, at five months along, she was certain she'd passed the most dangerous time, but she still hadn't wanted to risk the trip to Jeff City.

Shane grinned and kissed her tenderly. "Missed you somethin' fierce."

"And we missed you—all three of you." She looked at him suspiciously. "Did you remember my trunk?"

"Trunk? What trunk?" His brow furrowed. "I don't—"

"It's on the packhorse, Ma," Justice said, coming up behind Shane and giving Caitlin a quick hug. "The last of the stuff you brought from Ireland."

She sniffed. "And eight long years it took him to get them all here. I can't even remember what's in this one."

Justice shrugged. "See, Ma, how bad could you have needed all that stuff in the first place?"

"Go ahead, take up for your father," she said. "You always do."

"But I love you best," he teased.

At eighteen, Justice was nearly a man. He'd never be as tall as Shane, but he was lean, tough as a rawhide whip, and as darkly handsome as Caitlin had suspected he would be. He was a son to be proud of, she thought. No one would recognize him as the same sullen-faced boy she'd met when she first came to Missouri.

Shane had just finished a three-year contract to supply mounts for the U.S. Cavalry. This trip to the City of

Jefferson had been necessary to receive his final payment from the government.

"Is supper ready?" Rory hurled himself through the gate and wiggled between his mother and father.

"What, no kisses?" Caitlin asked.

"Aw, Mama." Rory hugged Caitlin with all his might. "I'm too big for kissing."

"We're starvin'," Shane said. "We ate a cold breakfast on the trail and rode straight through."

"You got the money?" Caitlin asked.

"Paid in full," he assured her, "with the bonus on every head."

"Glory," she said. "We're rich. Did you wire the money to Philadelphia? When Gabe rode over to tell us about the twins, he said that there had been another bank robbery."

Missouri was growing by leaps and bounds, but lately there had been a lot of ill feelings between slave and anti-slave factions in the state. Lawless gangs of men robbed and burned outlying farms and drove off livestock. Kilronan and the larger spreads had been spared attack, but Shane made it a practice to wire their profits to the Bank of Philadelphia.

"You did put our money in the bank, didn't you?" Caitlin asked. When Shane didn't answer, she glanced from him to Justice. "Well? Out with it. What have the pair of you done?"

Shane looked hurt. "You might let a man have his bath and dinner before you plague him with questions."

"I know, I know," Rory said, hopping from one foot to the other in a burst of excitement. "Papa—"

"Rory, hold your tongue," Shane admonished. "Take your sister outside and show her the palomino mare I've got hidden behind the barn for her."

"Papa!" Derry screamed. "Thank you, Papa!" Both children tore off in the direction of the barn.

"McKenna, Justice." Urika came out onto the porch in her starched white apron and multicolored wool turban, which she wore over her hair both summer and winter. "Welcome home." Urika had recently married Toby, an English immigrant who'd come to take over the kitchen at Kilronan, and her apron barely hid her advanced pregnancy.

"Where's Mary?" Justice asked.

"Helping with the new babies," Caitlin said. "She went over as soon as Rachel went into labor. You know Gabe isn't much help with newborns."

Rachel had inherited Big Earl's land when her father passed away, and Gabe had his hands full learning the cattle business. Their marriage had prospered, despite the prejudice some people felt about Gabe's Osage blood.

"I hope there's plenty of hot water," Shane said as he followed Caitlin into the house.

"Oh, now you appreciate my bathroom," she teased. When Rory had been born, she'd insisted that Shane build a special room at the back of the house, complete with a huge tile tub and holding tank with its own stove for heating water.

"A good wife would come and scrub my back."

"And a good husband wouldn't keep his wife waiting to tell her what mischief he's gotten into," she replied tartly. "Urika, could you find Shane some fresh towels?"

Shane winked at Caitlin. "I'll be waiting for you in the tub."

"I'll bathe in the creek," Justice said.

Caitlin walked to the bottom of the staircase with him. "Well, what has your father gotten himself into this time? He's entirely too cheerful to be innocent."

Justice grinned.

"Out with it," Caitlin urged. "Tell me the worst."

"It's better if he tells you."

"Great," she replied. "I suppose he's lost all our money in a card game at Fat Rose's. Or—"

"Talk to him, Ma. He wants to tell you."

"I'm sure."

Urika came through the parlor door with an armload of towels. "Clean, Missy-Wife. Just off line."

"Thank you," Caitlin answered. "And tell Toby that we want to eat as soon as possible."

As she opened the bathroom door, Shane had already scrubbed off the worst of the grime and was just stepping into the tub.

"Howdy ma'am," he said. "I was wonderin' if you meant to leave me all alone."

"Hush," Caitlin replied. She stacked the towels on a shelf, took down a bottle of scent, and dumped the contents into the water.

"Hell, woman," Shane protested. "I'll smell like a French whore."

"I'll do worse if you don't tell me what you're up to. What did you do in Jeff City that you don't want me to know about?" She locked the bathroom door and dragged the stool close to the tub.

"Now, Caity . . ."

"Caity, nothing."

Shane lay back and let his head sink under the rising water. "Damn but that feels fine," he said when he came up for air. He grabbed a bar of soap and began rubbing his chest.

"I'm waiting," she reminded him.

"Stop yappin' at me. Can't you see I'm relaxin'? I'll tell you my news when I'm good and ready."

"Will you?" Taking a pitcher of cold water off the table, Caitlin dumped it over his head.

"Lord, woman!" Shane sputtered. "You fight dirty."

"I can fight dirtier than that," she said mischievously. Moving closer to the tub, she undid the top button of her dress.

He chuckled. "Come into the tub with me, Caity."

"In the middle of the day?" Another button came free.

"I dare you."

Caitlin slowly loosened a third button.

"Woman . . ." He groaned. "You're torturin' me."

When she tossed her blouse aside and unhooked her skirt, he stood up in the tub and reached for her.

"We'll not hurt the baby, will we?" he asked.

"No." She moistened her bottom lip with the tip of her tongue. "We'll not harm her."

Shane helped Caitlin into the tub, then sat down so that she straddled him. The water came to her nipples as she sank onto his lap. "Mmmm," he said. "Nice, very nice."

"I did miss you, darling," she whispered.

"It was a long week without you curled beside me at night." Then he kissed her, a long, heated kiss that made her tingle all the way to her toes.

"I'm waiting," she said.

He teased her left nipple until it hardened to a dark pink nub. "Beautiful Caity," he said. "You're more beautiful now than the day I married you."

"Shane."

"All right." He cupped her breast in his big hand. "I bought us land, Caity. In California."

"You what? How could—"

He silenced her with another kiss. And when he finally let her up for air, he explained. "I didn't plan it, Caity. I just got a chance, the opportunity of a lifetime. Three thousand acres of rolling hills, grassland, and good water. The owner died without heirs, and the Bank of Philadelphia foreclosed on the property. I met one of the bank officers in Jeff City, a man named Edward Shepherd. He was on his way home from California, and he'd just inspected the estate."

Numb, she stared at him. "Three thousand acres? You couldn't have bought so much land with what we got for the sale of the horses."

"All I had to pay were back taxes and the balance of the loan. The bank was anxious to get rid of the property, since it was so far from the gold fields. And Shepherd was pleased to do business with one of the bank's old customers. The money from the horses made a healthy down payment."

"But California . . . Why, Shane? You never wanted to go into debt before."

"Kilronan will bring a top price. Steele said he knew of investors in Philadelphia that would buy it, sight unseen. We could own the California land free and clear."

"Sell Kilronan?" She stared at him in astonishment. "I know you said that Missouri's getting crowded, but I thought that you—"

He began to remove the pins from her hair, one at a time. "It's not just that, darlin'," he said. "More and more slave owners are movin' into the state. Blood will flow here soon, rivers of it. I don't want you and the children in the middle when it happens."

"Kilronan was supposed to be Justice's. What about—"

Shane grinned. "He's all for it. He says Kilronan's fenced and tamed. He wants to see new country, bigger country. And in a few years, he'll be too old to remain under a father's thumb."

"You should have talked to me first."

He exhaled through clenched teeth. "I saw a chance and took it. If you're dead set against California, I could—"

"Admit it, Shane, you want to go farther west. You can't blame this on Justice."

He kissed her bare shoulder and wound his fingers in a length of her hair. "Caity, girl . . . if I don't have a challenge, I'll sit on the porch and grow old."

She clasped his shoulders tightly. "Do you still love me, Shane?" she asked him. "After all these years?"

"Do I still love you? What kind of damned fool question is that, Caity McKenna? I've loved you since I was twelve years old."

"Good." Her heart was racing so that she felt light-headed. "I just like to hear you say it once in a while."

He raised an eyebrow. "Shall I climb up on the barn roof and shout it at the top of my lungs?"

She chuckled. "I wouldn't mind."

"I'll do it right now," he offered. But when he started to stand up, she pulled him back.

"Without a stitch on?"

"Why not?" He grinned lazily. "Well, maybe with the kids out there, I should pull on my pants first."

"I think I'd rather have you right where you are for now."

"I guess I'll stay." And then he grinned and shouted. "There's only one woman for Shane McKenna!"

"Hush, hush." She clapped her hand over his mouth and giggled. "Shane, the children."

"They know it, don't they?" he teased. "They should know it." And then he kissed her, a slow, sensual caress that made her go all shivery inside. "You're my wife and the mother of those children," he said. "You mean more to me than heaven and hell."

"Yes," she whispered.

"Yes, what?"

"I'll go to California with you, Shane. I'll go anywhere,

so long as you promise to build me a house when we get there."

He laughed. "Oh, there's a house there already, a huge house with gardens and grape vines and fruit trees. There's an enclosed courtyard with old mission bells and a fountain. You'll love it, Caity, I promise. I'll go out in the spring and get everything ready. Then I'll come back to Missouri to fetch you and—"

"You most certainly will not." She tilted his chin up and stared stubbornly into his eyes. "I go with you, every step of the way."

"But I want—"

"Close your mouth, Shane McKenna; you'll catch flies. I waited seven long years for you the last time you went ahead to make things ready for me. And I'll not give you the chance to do it a second time."

"But Caity, darlin' . . ."

"Together, my love." She took his soapy hand and placed it over her swelling belly. "We go together, all of us." And then she kissed him and kept kissing him until his arguments were lost in the heat of their rising desire.

One thing led naturally to the next.

And Caitlin reasoned that no matter where they lived, such sweet passion would surely last them throughout this life and on to the green fields of heaven.

On sale now!

From *New York Times* bestselling author
Elaine Coffman
comes another tale of spellbinding romance
to enthrall you.

IF MY LOVE
COULD HOLD YOU

Charlotte Butterworth had sworn she'd never let a man touch her. And she kept her word until the day she interrupted a hanging party in her own front yard. Suddenly a bold stranger was in her custody, taking charge of her farm and challenging her at every turn. Walter Reed intended to pay his debt to the red-haired beauty of Two Trees, Texas, and then disappear. But he did not count on the passion that flared between them, a passion that threatened to engulf them both in the flames of everlasting love.

Published by Fawcett Books.
Available wherever books are sold.

Love Letters

Ballantine romances are on the Web!

Read about your favorite Ballantine authors and upcoming books on our Web site, LOVE LETTERS, at **www.randomhouse.com/BB/loveletters**, including:

♥What's new in the stores
♥Previews of upcoming books
♥In-depth interviews with romance authors and
  publishing insiders
♥Sample chapters from new romances
♥And more . . .

Want to keep in touch? To subscribe to Love Notes, the monthly what's-new update for the Love Letters Web site, send an e-mail message to
loveletters@cruises.randomhouse.com
with "subscribe" as the subject of the message. You will receive a monthly announcement of the latest news and features on our site.

So follow your heart and visit us at
www.randomhouse.com/BB/loveletters!